The Midnight Court

HOUSE OF ARKHANGEL'SK

BOOK TWO

JANE KINDRED

Entangled Publishing, LLC
2614 South Timberline Road
Suite 109
Fort Collins, CO 80525
Visit our website at www.entangledpublishing.com.

Edited by Stacy Abrams

Print ISBN   978-1-62061-107-4
eBook ISBN   978-1-62061-108-1

Manufactured in the United States of America

First Edition   August 2012

For Elena Volfovna.

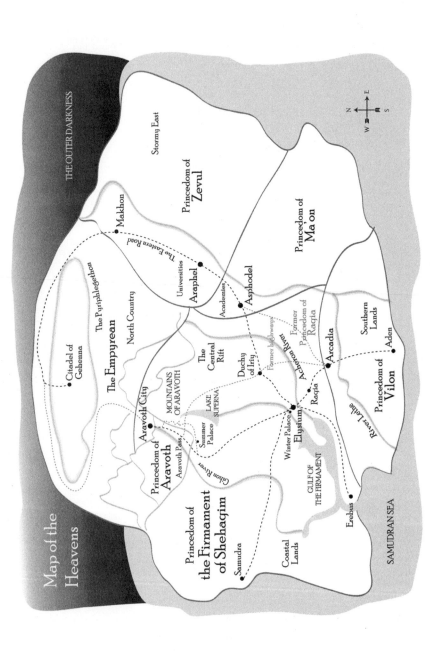

Map of the Heavens

THE OUTER DARKNESS

Stormy East

Princedom of Zevul

Princedom of Ma'on

Makhon

The Eastern Road

The Pyriphlegethon

Citadel of Gehenna

Universities

Araphel

Academies

Asphodel

North Country

The Empyrean

Aravoth City

MOUNTAINS OF ARAVOTH

The Central Rift

Former highways

Former Princedom of Raqia

Southern Lands

Arcadia

Aden

Princedom of Aravoth

Aravoth Pass

Summer Palace

LAKE SUPERNA

Duchy of Iriq

Acheron River

Raqia

Princedom of Vilon

Gihon River

Winter Palace

Elysium

River Lethe

Princedom of the Firmament of Shehaqim

Samudra

Coastal Lands

GULF OF THE FIRMAMENT

Erebus

SAMUDRAN SEA

N
E
S
W

HIERARCHY OF THE SPHERES

THE FIRST SPHERE
The Heavens ("Heaven")

First Heaven: The Empyrean
Capital: Gehenna
once populated by the the Host of the First Choir, now abandoned

Second Heaven: Aravoth
Capital: Aravoth City
populated by the Order of Virtues

Third Heaven: Shehaqim ("The Firmament")
Capital: Elysium
populated by the Host of the Fourth Choir

Fourth Heaven: Ma'on
Capital: Asphodel
populated by the Order of Powers and Fourth Choir military recruits

Fifth Heaven: Zevul
Capital: Araphel
populated by the Order of Dominions and Fourth Choir scholars

Raqia
(formerly the Sixth Heaven, now annexed as a district of Elysium)
Capital: None (formerly Arcadia)
currently populated by the Fallen

Seventh Heaven: Vilon
Capital: Arcadia (formerly Aden)
populated by the Host of the Fourth Choir

THE HOST (ANGELS)

First Choir: Spirits of Air
Orders: Tafsarim ("the Aeons"), Elim ("the Ardors"),
Erelim ("the Splendors")
mysterious beings none living have seen

Second Choir: Spirits of Fire
Orders: Seraphim, Cherubim, Ophanim
*elemental beings of fire who are able to manifest wings in
Heaven—bodyguards, brute squads, and palace guards of the
reigning principalities*

Third Choir: Spirits of Earth
Orders: Dominions, Virtues, Powers
*philosophers and administrators; scientists & investigators;
military officers*

Fourth Choir: Spirits of Water
Orders: Principalities, Archangels, Angels
nobility, merchants, and commoners

Supernal House of Arkhangel'sk: *Heaven's imperial family, it takes its
name from an earthly city named for the monastery of the Archangel
Mikhail, founding principality of the House*

Malakim: *Messengers to the world of Man from the
Order of Archangels*

Elohim: *An elite sect and ruling body of princes (sars) of the
Order of Virtues (Aravoth is the only princedom ruled by a governing
body rather than a principality)*

Hashmallim: *Elite warriors of the Supernal Army from
the Order of Powers*

THE FALLEN (DEMONS)

Common demons: *angels of mixed blood—
the serfs, demimondes, and outlaws of Heaven*

THE SECOND SPHERE
The World of Man

Terrestrial Fallen: *demons who permanently reside
in the world of Man*
Grigori: *Watchers from the Order of Powers sent to
observe the world of Man; the first Fallen*
Nephilim: *hybrid offspring of Grigori and Man*
The race of Man: *humans*
Night Travelers: *a secret society of gypsies who act as liaisons
between the world of Man, the celestial* militsiya, *and terrestrial Fallen*

THE THIRD SPHERE
Nezrimyi Mir (The Unseen World)
*the realm of the Unseen, located in the Russian
forest in the world of Man*

THE UNSEEN

Syla: bereginyi: *spring syla;* mavki: *summer syla;*
samodivi: *autumn syla*; snegurochki: *winter syla
female nature spirits*
Leshi: *male nature spirits*
Rusalki: *female water spirits*

THE FOURTH SPHERE
Irkalla and the Realm of the Dead ("Hell")

Nehemoth: *servants and gatekeepers of Irkalla*
The dead: *formerly living souls of the First and Second Spheres, now
permanent residents of the Realm of the Dead*

***Pervoe:* Summer Fires**

from the memoirs of the Grand Duchess Anazakia
Helisonovna of the House of Arkhangel'sk

She is the daughter of a demon, this child of mine. Her birthright as
the last scion of the House of Arkhangel'sk ought to be the throne of
Heaven, but we are Fallen now and live as demons in the world of Man.
In this ice-bound Russian port, this land of sullen winters of perpetual
dusk to balance months of midnight sun, we have found a home with
the demons who once sought ransom for my life.

I was a fool to think it could last forever.

On the eve of Ivan Kupala, the tranquility of our dacha at
Arkhangel'sk began to crumble like brittle autumn leaves. Amid the
bonfires of midsummer, a more malicious blaze was kindling. I took
it at first for the glint of wishing candles winking in the brief twilight
between one northern summer day and the next. It was on such a night
I had first met the creatures who called themselves syla, the dainty
wood spirits who came to me when I thought I might die of misery
after my family fell to my cousin's sword. The company of my demon
protectors was little comfort to me then.

Despite the occasional flickering glow that danced like fireflies in
the trees beyond, the garden this evening remained still and empty. I
pressed my lips to my daughter's sun-kissed head. The syla were not to
grace us tonight.

As I lifted Ola, heavy with sleep, something flitted on the periphery of my vision. The flat, silvery leaves of the birches moved like the scales of a serpent in a wave across the yard. It wasn't the nature of the syla I had seen before, yet there was no wind that could have caused it.

Straining to see, I stepped toward the rippling leaves. The wave flowed onward past the gate, moving swiftly and now touched with flame. Ola remained asleep against my shoulder while I ran barefoot along the path of crushed flowers. Outside the gate, a figure poised for a moment, spun away from me, and was gone.

I called out for her to wait. The lone syla winked into the waning light for an instant and once more vanished, but not before I saw her look of anguish. A wind-devil picked up the leaves at my feet. I ran after it as quickly as I could, and followed the fluttering leaves into a bower of thicket. Branches scored my calves beneath the short pants Belphagor called *pedal pushers*—so much more suitable for mischief than the corsets and gowns I'd worn as a grand duchess in Heaven—as I climbed through into the little hollow among the trees. I paused to catch my breath while the leaves settled to the ground.

The wind wailed through the trees around us like a woman in pain. Then I saw as clearly as Ola in my arms a naked woman with dark hair whipping about her face as if lifted by heated air. She burned from the center of her body outward until all of her had been engulfed in flames. I watched in horror as the vision disintegrated into bits of red-rimmed ash that blew away on the wind like remnants of burning paper.

Another woman's face appeared within the trees, half formed of leaves and burned away on one side. *"The flower."* She gasped out the words. "The queen shall take—" And then she, too, disintegrated.

I held Ola to me and reached out with one hand, as if I could stop whatever terrible thing was happening. Another voice whispered on the wind. I couldn't make it out, until I heard one word clearly: *Seraphim.* I turned in a swift circle, afraid the Seraphim who'd pursued me when I'd first fled Heaven had found us once more. But there was no radiating heat or burning, white-hot light.

Ola woke and began to cry. The wind had stilled and there were no more rustling leaves, no half-heard voices. I tried to soothe her, bouncing her on my hip as I climbed back out of the bower. Under the pale blue light that marked summer's darkest hour, we made our way through the thicket until I stumbled over something on the path near the gate. A pile of leaves seemed to cover a charred tree limb. When I set Ola down beside me, I saw the limb move.

Afraid it was a snake, I snatched Ola up again, but a moan from within the leaves gave me pause. I brushed them aside. Beneath lay one of the syla, pieces of her red tatting dress burned away across her torso, and below that—I pulled Ola's head into my bosom so she wouldn't see.

The syla was barely alive. Her shallow breaths seemed little more than the random sounds of the forest, but she opened her eyes and reached for me.

I took her hand, tears obstructing my vision. "What's happened?"

"The queen." Her voice was tight with pain. "She knows."

The words sent a chill up my spine, along with a spark of anger. So Aeval had survived. She called herself the queen of Heaven, but the woman who'd turned my cousin's head and put him in her thrall was the former queen of the Unseen World. I'd wounded her in my escape from Elysium, and while it may have been naïve to hope the wound was fatal, in a year, we'd heard nothing from Heaven. With each passing day of celestial silence, I'd let myself believe we were safe.

"She knows what? What has she done to you?"

"The flower. The Seraphim punish…" Her breath caught and she twisted in the leaves.

"She knows I had it," I said.

The syla had enraged their former queen by withholding the coveted flower of the fern—and its attendant power—for more than a century before giving it to me.

"The fiery ones want secret but we do not tell." She clutched my hand against a wave of pain etched on her delicate features. "They take us one by one. Each syla feels others."

Shocked tears spilled over my cheeks as I realized what she meant. In the earthly realm, the touch of the Seraphim burned away flesh. From the pattern of her burns, and from the way the others had disintegrated, it was clear where the Seraphim had touched.

"I'm sorry," I whispered. It was foolishly inadequate.

She shook her head. "Syla fail Fallen Queen."

"No." I was adamant. "You haven't failed me; I've failed you. This is my fault. If I hadn't lost the flower—"

"This the syla do not tell. We tell only what we see." She closed her eyes and was quiet a moment, and I was afraid she was gone before she took another labored breath. "We see Little Queen. Little Queen shall take the flower of the fern." It was their name for Ola, and they'd seen that she'd take the flower back someday.

The syla's eyes opened once more, focused on me with sorrow and shame. "We tell what we see." Her hand slipped from mine and she stared sightlessly into the cerulean light.

Ola fussed, unhappy with how tightly I was holding her. I tried to cover the syla's body once more, but each leaf that touched her seemed to consume her form, and soon I could no longer see its shape.

When I lifted Ola and straightened, I wasn't alone. Inside the gate, with chestnut eyes wide and her mouth half open, stood Ola's young nanny, the gypsy who called herself Love.

Love didn't believe in the unseen. We had engaged her as both a nanny and an agent of intelligence, for despite her skepticism, she had her finger on the pulse of the gypsies' underground network in a way no demon could ever hope to. Love used the technology of the world of Man to monitor communications from faraway ports I couldn't even pronounce, aware almost instantly when credible talk of celestials surfaced. How she managed to sift the credible from the profoundly absurd so abundant in what I'd seen on the glass of her devices, I couldn't guess—particularly since she thought it all an elaborate game.

"You saw the syla?"

"The what?" Love shook her head as if she thought she might be dreaming. "Why are you outside with the baby at this hour?" She came through the gate and took Ola brusquely from my arms as if I were a naughty child, though Love and I were close in age and she was not yet twenty. Ola wrapped her sleepy arms around Love's neck. "What were you doing with the leaves?"

"Burying the syla. You saw her." I turned back, but there was nothing left where the body had been.

"Burying the force?" She translated the Russian word into angelic. Though she didn't believe in Heaven, she'd humored us in the year she'd spent with us by learning what she called our "code language."

"No, the syla." I reached in vain within my knowledge of the language. My grasp of the local tongue would never be quite as good as that of my companions Belphagor and Vasily, who had many more years' practice in its usage; I could understand it far better than I could speak it.

"Spirit," I said. It was the closest angelic word I could come up with, but it was inadequate. Though *spirit* in angelic did mean *force* in some sense, neither term did the syla justice. I tried the Russian word for the spirit-creatures of the stories in my little brother Azel's favorite books. *"Feya."*

Love regarded me doubtfully. "You buried a fairy."

It was close enough. "She died. You must have seen her."

Love turned toward the dacha with a yawning Ola. "The night sun can make you see strange things, Nazkia. You should get some sleep."

I was tempted to show her some strange things, to release my wings and display the radiance of my cardinal element—towering pennons of water that moved like living crystal. It was, as Belphagor had referred to it once, the terrestrial magic for which the Fallen fell, unavailable to us in the rarefied air of Heaven.

Instead, I made a face at her back like a child.

As we headed in, there was no further sign of the syla. They seemed to materialize from the trees, but I had never known where their true realm lay. Wherever the Seraphim had waylaid them, it wasn't here. The brilliance of seraphic radiance couldn't be missed.

Though it was barely an hour past midnight, dawn was already creeping toward the horizon. I paused in the kitchen for a cup of tea while Love took Ola up to bed, the ruby highlights in my daughter's hair touched off by the unearthly light as they climbed the stairs. She had the honeyed curls of the House of Arkhangel'sk, kissed with the color of fire from her father, with his intense eyes. Fire or water—we had yet to see whose element she would favor. I had never known anyone who had mixed them, though of course the Fallen must do it all the time.

That the dominant element of a demon might be from any one of the four celestial choirs was a testament to the mixing of blood that marked their peasant origins. As an airspirit, Belphagor must have had a First Choir angel—a Splendor, perhaps, or an Ardor, or even an Aeon—far back in his ancestral line. It seemed nearly as inconceivable to me as the Second Choir ancestor who must have once mixed Vasily's firespirit blood. I shuddered at the thought of being touched intimately by a being of pure, elemental fire. Within the air of Heaven, the Seraphim's fire was merely an intensely radiating heat, but even standing close to one could be uncomfortable.

Generations removed from those origins, Vasily could temper the heat of his body in ways I'd never imagined. I had certainly never imagined I would relinquish my angelic virtue to a demon of fire, though no one had been more surprised than he when I'd climbed into his bed. Though our opposing elements came together in an unexpected spark of potent radiance, the most astonishing effect of that union had been Ola.

The wooden stairs creaked. I looked up to see Vasily descending, dressed in the white ribbed undershirt and boxers he slept in no matter the time of year. He yawned and rubbed the bridge of his nose beneath the black wire frames of his spectacles, a gesture very like his daughter's when she was awakened after a few hours' sleep. I smiled as I turned away from the samovar and stirred sugar into my tea.

With the build and demeanor of a Cossack warrior, he did his best to look fierce. Long, tangled locks in the color of burning embers made him even more imposing—as did the rows of sharp metal bars decorating the flesh on both sides of his neck. But beneath his rough exterior, he had a tender heart, and as Ola grew, I saw more of her in him than I saw of him in her.

"I just heard Love putting the baby to bed." His rough voice always sounded as if he'd smoked one cigarette too many. He padded down the stairs, his footsteps muffled by the ever-present *tapochki*, the slippers we wore indoors. "Were you out in the garden at this hour?"

I lowered my head over my cup, wondering what I should tell him. The syla were my secret. But they were in danger, and it was I who'd put them there. "It's Tvorila Night. Ivan Kupala tomorrow."

"Ah, your midnight tradition." He poured himself a cup of tea. "But where's your garland crown? Didn't you make one this year?"

I set my cup aside and considered the answer. I had guarded my secret jealously, as if telling it might take this special thing away, and I had lost much. But this was no longer my confidence to keep. "I don't make them, Vasily."

"What do you mean?"

"They're given to me."

He scratched at the rusty sideburns that lined his jaw. "Given to you? By whom?"

I braced myself for ridicule or disapproval. "By…spirits."

Vasily stopped with his cup raised halfway to his mouth.

"When I ran off into the woods in Novgorod that first Ivan Kupala, I didn't just get lost. I lied to you."

His hazel eyes grew shadowed, but he waited for me to go on.

"The spirits—the syla—they led me to their grove."

"The syla?"

"They said they belonged to the Unseen World." I hesitated. The rest would sound absurd. "They bowed to me and said I was the Fallen Queen they'd been waiting for, and I must take the flower of the fern."

"The flower of the fern." Vasily reached behind me to spoon more sugar into his tea, his face guarded, as if he thought the blow I'd suffered from a falling branch that night two years ago had damaged my brain. "And why would these Unseen spirits want you to have a mythical flower?"

"You don't believe me."

He lowered his eyes as he sipped his tea. "I'm trying to believe you, Nazkia. I can't imagine why you'd make this up."

"I am *not* making it up. I met them first at the Winter Palace. The one in St. Petersburg, I mean, not the one in Elysium. But they were invisible there. When I found them in Novgorod, they told me they'd manipulated things to bring us to where I could see them."

Vasily set down his tea and leaned back against the counter. "Wait. When were you at the Winter Palace?"

"When I got lost—*actually* lost, that time in St. Petersburg after we first fell." I bit my lip when I remembered where he'd been while I was wandering through the empty museum so like the home in which I'd spent my celestial childhood. "The day the Seraphim caught you."

Vasily pushed his spectacles up the bridge of his nose in an unconscious gesture. His poor eyesight, the only thing the unexpected blending of our elements had been unable to fully heal, was a reminder of the pain he'd suffered at the hands of the Seraphim to keep me safe.

"All right, so let's say I believe these syla brought us to Novgorod to give you this flower. Why did they want you to have it?"

"They said it would protect me when I returned to Heaven. They'd hidden it from the queen who abandoned them, and she was looking for me." I paused. "They'd hidden it from Aeval."

He quivered with tightly controlled fury at the mere mention of her name, the shadows in his eyes now red with his element, like a furnace burning deep within. "*Aeval*? You're telling me the queen of Heaven isn't even a celestial?"

I cringed at his tone, though I knew his anger wasn't really at me. "Apparently she lied, too."

"Why didn't you tell us this before? Why didn't you tell Belphagor?"

"I wanted to protect the syla." Though having something that was mine alone was closer to the truth. I choked on the next words. "And I failed."

The flame of his fury went out in an instant. He pushed away from the counter and took me in his arms. "What is it? What's wrong?"

As always, an involuntary shiver of need went through me at his touch. I whispered against his chest. "The Seraphim—they attacked them. The syla were burning and I couldn't do anything to stop it."

He knew better than I did what it was to be touched by a Seraph within the earthly plane. He'd survived their attack only because of the peculiar spark of our combined elements. Some of it danced over our skin even now, a miniature aurora of pale violet.

"She survived," I said. "Aeval's alive, and she knows I took the flower. She's sent the Seraphim to punish them."

"Seraphim?" Belphagor's voice, sharp with tension, came from the stairway.

Jumping at the sound as if he'd touched a live wire, Vasily let go of me.

Belphagor ran a hand through his dark hair as he came downstairs, the tattooed bands and crosses on his fingers blending with the spiked tips. "You saw them?"

I put my hands in my pockets, self-conscious in the face of Vasily's discomfort. "No, but I saw what they'd done. It must have happened somewhere else."

Belphagor raised an eyebrow, the steel bar that decorated it glinting in the early-morning light. "I suppose that answers the question of whether Aeval's still queen."

Vasily kept his head down, concentrating on his tea. "Was it really in doubt? Surely we'd have heard something if power had changed hands in Heaven."

"I would have thought we'd hear something—*anything*—even if it hadn't. The quiet is a little unnerving." Belphagor descended the last few steps, his stature changing the physical dynamic between the two demons, but not the emotional.

Vasily's ruddy complexion turned ruddier as Belphagor wrapped a hand around the taller demon's neck and pulled his head down for a kiss.

Though I'd borne Vasily's child, he had been Belphagor's paramour since long before we met. After the initial surprise at learning his lover had fathered a child in his absence, Belphagor had given Vasily his blessing to maintain a physical relationship with me. Despite his assurances, however, it had been months since Vasily had touched me. He was riddled with guilt—while Vasily had kept me warm through a subarctic winter, Belphagor had been a slave to the queen's basest whims, and in the end, her whim had been to let my cousin Kae beat him almost to death.

But Vasily had come to save his love—and he hadn't come alone. A small army of Fallen had assembled for Belphagor's aid. It was the Code of Thieves. The *vory v zakone* of the terrestrial demon community looked out for their own.

Belphagor held Vasily's gaze for a moment, hand gripped tightly around his neck, before letting him pull away. Though Vasily surpassed him in height and sheer bulk, there was no question who dominated their relationship—and that Vasily liked it that way. The look that passed between them as they parted spoke of all they seemed unable to say. As far as I knew, Belphagor had never told him what he'd done in service to Aeval, though Vasily, I think, had guessed at its nature.

When the three of us sat at the table with our tea, Vasily made a point of keeping space between himself and me. Though I'd never made any claim on his affections, he seemed as reticent to be demonstrative with Belphagor in my presence as he was to be seen touching me in Belphagor's. I worried about what effect this conflict in his head was having on their relationship. I'd neither seen nor heard any signs of their intimate relations since Belphagor's recovery, and they were not the sort to do things discreetly, no matter how much they imagined themselves to be.

Love's arrival dispelled the awkward silence. "I guess *everybody*'s up." Her soft voice was almost scolding. She grabbed some of Ola's teething biscuits from the counter and nibbled on them as she joined us at the table. "It took me forever to get Ola calmed down enough to sleep." Now she was definitely scolding. "And you're drinking tea, Anazakia. It's no wonder the baby can't get to sleep."

"She's barely nursing anymore," I said defensively, but I set down my cup with a twinge of guilt. Love came from a large family, and she knew far more than I'd ever imagined there was to know about the care of infants. She even insisted "the boys" give up smoking their cigars and cigarettes, though I occasionally found all three of them by the garden shed sharing a smoke as though it were an illicit drug.

Opening the portable computer she kept plugged in at the kitchen table, Love began clicking away in a manner that mystified the three of us. Belphagor was somewhat familiar with the device, but he said the "web" Love navigated effortlessly had been little more than a glimmer in someone's eye the last time he'd fallen.

"Might as well check the chatter," she said. "As long as everyone's *up*."

The three of us shared a round of guilty looks; the sitting room beside the kitchen was where Love slept.

"Chatter" was what she called the odd bits of information that came to her from various sources, often buried in what she called "clutter" — random messages on discussion forums and in virtual communities that seemed meant to mask the real communications of the underground. Sometimes she even found chatter in games.

"Wait," said Love, as she always did when she found something of interest, as if the rest of us were on the verge of taking the computer from her to skip past whatever she'd found. As if we could. "There's something from our old friend 'possessed85.'" She glanced up at me. "He's the Romani contact who helped us locate you and Bel." *Roma* was the name she used for her people, though she spoke of the "gypsy underground," just as Belphagor and Vasily did. "He's sent me a PDF." She ignored our blank looks. "Looks like a newspaper clipping or a pamphlet. The beginning is cut off. But I think it's about you, Nazkia."

"About me?"

"I recognize your name in here, but it's in that 'angelic' script you're all so fond of, so I can't really make out much."

Belphagor stood behind her and read from the screen: "'Construction on the new wing of the palace—replacing the former Celestial Glory burned to the ground by the Grand Duchess Anazakia Helisonovna of the House of Arkhangel'sk in her fit of madness—to be completed in time for Her Supernal Majesty's Grand Equinox Gala.'" He gave me an apologetic look. "She really took to that story I made up for her."

I shrugged, though it was still a sore spot. There was nothing to be done about it now, and he'd meant well. By suggesting I was mad, Belphagor had given Aeval an excuse to let me live. Of course, when fortune had placed me within her grasp, the queen had ordered my execution all the same.

"'This tragic conflagration,'" he continued, "'as Host and Fallen alike will sadly recall, took the lives of every worker who came to petition Her Supernal Majesty in the Palace Square that infamous morning. Her Supernal Highness the Grand Duchess Anazakia Helisonovna managed to poison her chambermaid—'"

"I did not!"

"'—and escape from the comfortable seclusion in which Her Supernal Majesty had restrained her after her first fit of madness cost the Firmament its former principality and nearly every member of the supernal House of Arkhangel'sk.'"

While I seethed silently at this lie, Belphagor swallowed and went on.

"'On that early summer morning, nearly a year to the day from her first attack, Her Supernal Highness summoned the strength only the mad possess and struck down every agent of the Palace Guard who did not perish in the fire. Her Supernal Majesty the queen narrowly escaped murder at the hand of the grand duchess now dubbed "Bloody Anazakia" by the citizens of the Firmament.'"

"Bloody Anazakia!" My face reddened with embarrassment and outrage. "And now I'm not only the murderer of my family, I'm responsible for the fire her own Seraphim started!"

"There's more." Belphagor's expression was almost meek. "'Her Supernal Majesty has set aside an official Day of Observance to commemorate the tragic events of the Solstice Conflagration, and to pay homage to the last legitimate heir of the House of Arkhangel'sk…'" He paused and reread this part. "'The last legitimate heir of the House of Arkhangel'sk, His Supernal Majesty the Principality…Kae Lebesovich, who also perished in the fire.'"

It struck me like a physical blow, much harder than I'd expected. The Kae I knew had died on a winter's day in the mountains of Aravoth when he'd fallen under Aeval's enchantment, though no one had known it yet. He'd died to me for certain the night he put his sword through the bellies of my family, including the pregnant belly of his own wife, Ola's namesake. But now he was forever lost.

Though I hadn't wanted to acknowledge it, I'd been harboring a secret hope that somehow I could free him from the queen, that someday he'd return to himself, the beloved cousin of my youth. That hope had been consumed by fire a year ago, and though I'd feared it was likely, we'd heard nothing, and I'd allowed myself to hold on to a fantasy. To hear the truth with certainty was devastating.

I tried to keep the tears from falling. I had no right to mourn him. He had no right to be mourned. I rose and used the pretext of rinsing my teacup in the sink to hide my face.

Pushing back his chair with a jerk, Vasily growled low in his throat. "Tell me you're not crying for that son of a succubus. You saw what he did to Bel. You were there."

"Vasya," Belphagor said gently. "Let it alone."

"No, I will not let it alone!"

I squeezed my eyes shut and gripped the edge of the sink. A muffled *thud* followed, as if Vasily had shoved Belphagor away.

"He would have taken you from me. Another day—if I'd wasted one more day—you'd not have survived that filthy hole!"

"*Moi malchik.*" Belphagor whispered the private name he used for Vasily: *my boy.* I'd never heard him say it, had only read it once in a note I wasn't meant to see. Love and pain and desire were captured in that single breath.

"Don't you dare." Vasily's voice was huskier than normal. "You had no right to leave me. Not for her. Not for the odds, not for anything. You had no right to put yourself in that hole and nearly leave me forever."

There was a moment of pregnant silence before Vasily went to the entryway, kicked off his *tapochki* as he grabbed his outdoor boots, and departed with a slam of the door that rattled the dacha. Upstairs, Ola began to cry, and Love jumped up out of habit.

"*I'm* her mother." The protest came out more harshly than I'd intended.

She sat back down, chagrined, and I hurried up the stairs, glad not to have to look Belphagor in the eye. I took Ola to bed with me and nursed her back to sleep, more for my solace than her own, while I cried silently against the sunset gold of her Arkhangel'sk curls.

The cousin who'd killed everyone I loved had once been my best friend, so close that my sister Omeliea, to whom he'd been betrothed since childhood, had sometimes viewed our friendship with suspicion. But she'd never had anything to worry about. Kae had worshipped the ground she walked on—until the day he'd killed her.

In the morning, I picked up a book from the nightstand and sat watching Ola over the tops of the pages I wasn't seeing, watching her breath rise and fall. In the early days of her unexpected life, I'd sometimes woken her just to make sure she was still breathing, just to be sure she was real.

There was a soft knock on the door, and Belphagor opened it

without waiting for my answer. Reflected in the mirror beside him, my eyes were red and puffy. I tried to hide them by letting my curls swing over my face, but Belphagor sat on the bed beside me and tucked my hair behind my ear.

I met his eyes reluctantly. "I'm sorry."

"Nazkia. You have nothing to be sorry about. You told me once you still loved your cousin, and I told you there was nothing wrong with that. And I meant it. He was still your family. He was still taken from you by the tragedy that took the rest. You have every right to mourn him."

"But Vasily's right. He would have killed you."

"Vasily's hurt. I frightened him. Heaven knows, I frightened myself." Belphagor grimaced. "I had no business trying to make that deal with Aeval. He's right about that. I should never have gone back to Heaven on my own. But you mustn't feel guilty about your affection for your cousin. Vasily may not understand, but I do." He sighed. "There were times when I actually liked the fellow myself. Not so much near the end, of course."

Belphagor never spoke of the assault he'd suffered under my cousin's *knut*, a wicked tool of punishment once used on wayward peasants in the world of Man. Kae had also flayed the soles of the demon's feet to ribbons. Those injuries had eventually healed, but the mangled wreck of Belphagor's back had taken far longer. It had given him fever for a time as some of the older, deeper trenches cut into his flesh became infected, and it had left him with permanent scars that were painful to look at.

He smiled ruefully. "At any rate, that's not what I came here to talk about. I didn't hear everything you were telling Vasily last night, but I caught enough. The Seraphim attacked these—what did you call them? Sylphs?"

"The syla."

"Because they gave you something of Aeval's."

I nodded glumly and explained to him about the flower of the fern.

Belphagor eyed me with a careful lack of expression. He would have called it his "wingcasting face," the trick that made him a master of the card game. He didn't believe me any more than Vasily had. "The flower—this '*tsvetok paporotnika*'—where is it now?"

"I lost it." My voice was sharp with anger at myself. "I'd kept it in the locket you pinched from my nurse. When Helga saw me wearing the locket, she took it, and I couldn't get it back."

In the aftermath of my family's murders, my childhood nurse had changed toward me. Years of hiding her Fallen identity while serving the House of Arkhangel'sk had made her bitter, and she blamed me for surviving while my brother Azel had not. But I couldn't be angry with her. She was the reason I'd survived. It was Helga who'd hired Belphagor and Vasily to hide me in the world of Man.

Belphagor looked baffled. "When on earth did Helga see it?"

"Not on earth," I said pointedly. "In Heaven. She used the charm you gave her, thinking to bring you to her. She heard you were at the palace and she was furious, wondering what you'd done with me. But I had the callstone in my pocket, and it called me from the dacha instead."

He groaned. "*Bozhe moi.* The callstone. I'd forgotten it." The wingcasting face was gone as he narrowed his eyes. "I thought you said you returned to Heaven on your own, to spite me."

"I meant to. I just didn't have the nerve."

Belphagor laughed out loud, startling Ola awake. Her tousled curls popped up from the blankets beside me and she grinned at Belphagor and reached out for him with her little fingers, saying *"Beli"* with nearly supernal insistence. Much to Belphagor's chagrin, Ola had managed to pick up Vasily's pet name for him, even before she'd first said "Papa."

He lifted her and tossed her lightly in the air, catching her as she giggled. It was her favorite game. Despite the shock of discovering his Vasily had fathered a child, Belphagor was devoted to her.

"Nazkia." He shook his head as he grinned and tickled Ola. "You don't know how close I came to striking you when you told me you'd shown up there on purpose." He was still smiling at Ola, but his words were deadly earnest. "That was a very dark moment, finding you there after what I'd traded Aeval to keep her off your trail."

"I know," I said unhappily.

Belphagor sighed. "It takes off a bit of the sting to know you didn't come willingly. At any rate, if you're right about these syla, if Aeval's sent the Seraphim to find that flower, I don't think we can stay here any longer. Even with the protective charm the Grigori placed around the dacha, our presence in Arkhangel'sk Oblast can't be much of a secret. Vasily's rescue party last summer wasn't exactly discreet."

Though I'd known it was coming, I'd been dreading the day he would say this. I loved our dacha, and I mustered a halfhearted protest. "But if anyone knew we were here, surely they'd have made a move by now."

Belphagor passed Ola off to me, to her visible disapproval. "Love found more communications after you went to bed. I don't know why Aeval's been quiet this long, but apparently she's suddenly in the mood for proclamations. There's an official bounty on your head. Anyone can collect the reward. All they have to do is return you to Heaven—dead or alive."

Vtoroe: **Cause and Effect**

Whether Anazakia had really encountered her invisible friends, Belphagor declined to venture a guess, but it seemed unlikely she'd actually possessed the flower of the fern. The Russian folktale stood in for a fertility rite sublimated by the Orthodox Church's feast day for St. John the Baptist. Perhaps Love had told her about the tradition: young maidens traipsing into the woods with their suitors on midsummer's eve to look for the fiery blossom. Legend said it bloomed only for an instant at midnight on this single night of the year, and if a lad were quick enough to grab it, he'd have good luck. But ferns didn't flower. It was a euphemism for getting laid.

That stupid rumor he'd begun about her madness had no basis in truth, but Anazakia had been through more than one event traumatic enough to prompt a bit of fantastic imagination. In a very real sense, she'd been murdered along with her family. With the help of a demon elixir that had allowed her to be in two places at once, one of her had been losing to Belphagor at cards in the Demon District of Elysium, while the other had been at the palace. When the shade of her murdered double reunited with her, she would have died a second time had Vasily's firespirit radiance not healed the wound the shade brought with it.

Belphagor sometimes wondered if that intimate moment in the washroom of a train car in the middle of Siberia had been the start of Vasily's and Anazakia's attraction to each other. Certainly the literal spark between them had begun when the angel returned the favor and healed Vasily after the Seraphim nearly killed him. But one thing was certain: if Belphagor hadn't left Vasily alone to go on his fool mission to the queen, his *malchik* would never have taken the angel to his bed.

If, if, if. Belphagor nipped that line of thinking in the bud with a growl of irritation at himself. It was foolish to dwell on things that started with "if." *If* Vasily had never taken the angel to his bed, there would not be Ola. Any amount of jealousy he felt over Vasily desiring someone else was insignificant next to the joy the child's existence brought him. Her little flame was the light of his life.

And it was almost certain *she* was the fiery blossom Aeval sought, not some mythical fern.

He knew damned well they should never have stayed here this long, but he'd been sick for months after their escape from Heaven, and by the time he'd gotten back on his feet, it seemed too much like home to let it go. And home was something he'd never had before. Playing house with Vasily and Anazakia was too appealing—he'd let himself be lulled into complacency. It was well past time to move on. But moving on would be difficult with Vasily pulling one of his famous disappearing acts; he hadn't come back last night.

It was the way the gruff firespirit always dealt with emotion he couldn't reconcile. In the early days of their relationship, the younger demon had returned to the streets where Belphagor had found him whenever conflict arose. The conflict then was of Belphagor's own making, trying to reconcile Vasily's obvious devotion and desire for him with his equally obvious youth and inexperience. Invariably, Belphagor would wind up dragging the boy away from whatever trouble he'd gotten himself into and back to the rented room at The Brimstone for a sound thrashing—which only led to more conflict. It had been worse than torture to deny himself what Vasily was so eager to give. And in the end, utterly futile. Vasily had worn him down.

Where Vasily might have disappeared into the northern Russian burg of Arkhangel'sk, however, Belphagor couldn't imagine. A six-foot-five demon with flame-red locks and neck piercings wasn't exactly inconspicuous. Belphagor knew he sometimes spent time at the banya in town when he was gone for less than a day. It wasn't a surprising choice, given the steamy heat and the birch branch flogging that typified the Russian baths. Vasily also knew Belphagor wouldn't pursue him there; stripping down to display his scars and prison tattoos for a bunch of provincial strangers wasn't Belphagor's idea of a good time.

There wasn't much point in worrying about Vasily's safety. The firespirit could take care of himself. All Belphagor could do was wait for him to return.

In the meantime, he had to get in touch with his old friend Dmitri, chieftain of the Grigori. Once Heaven's "Watchers," they were the most powerful clan of Fallen in the world of Man, direct descendants of angels from the Order of Powers who'd fallen when the world was new. News from Heaven had been nearly impossible to get since the assault Dmitri had staged with Vasily on the celestial Winter Palace to get Anazakia and Belphagor out. The Fallen residing in Raqia didn't trust the ancient clan of purebloods, and demons who fell and remained in the world of Man were leery of those who'd allied themselves with a grand duchess of the supernal House of Arkhangel'sk, deposed or not.

The result was a near total blackout of news that had once flowed freely between the spheres. They still had the gypsy underground, the information conduit of the Roma who called themselves Night Travelers—a secret society that believed in the unseen world, they served as liaisons between the celestial Host and the disparate clans of terrestrial Fallen. Of course, there was little to liaise on when no one was speaking to anyone else, but the Night Travelers were the best source for reaching Dmitri. He moved frequently and kept his location private. Officially, the Grigori—and their Nephilim kin descended from human interbreeding—didn't exist. Unofficially, they were Heaven's Exiles, and fair game for any Seraph who might be sent to the world of Man in pursuit of celestial fugitives.

With the breakdown in communication, there'd been no contact with Dmitri in nearly a year. Belphagor had convinced himself that in this case, no news was good news, but it was bad strategy at the wingcasting table to assume your opponent was weak simply because he was silent. Success at the game relied on quiet planning and careful watching.

And Aeval was clearly still in the game. Blackout or no blackout, Belphagor needed to determine precisely what was going on in the celestial sphere.

• • •

Heaven's renovations were coming along nicely. It had been a stroke of genius, Aeval had to admit, to turn the workers' strike to her advantage. Blaming the deaths on that insipid grand duchess had turned burgeoning hatred and mistrust into sympathy and civic pride. Aeval was suddenly just as much a victim as they were, and the villain of the piece was the House of Arkhangel'sk.

The people forgot that Aeval's policies had not only continued the oppression of demonkind, but had made the proscriptions against them stricter. She could frame the relocation camps that had begun to empty the squalid streets of Raqia—with its illicit and immoral business her predecessors had overlooked—as a program of common welfare. The red pentacles the Fallen were forced to wear on their collars and sleeves when they went out became a badge of pride, not a mark of Cain; the curfew, a measure for their protection against the hooligan angelic youth who were prone to harass them.

Aeval promised freedom, holding out the unsigned Liberation Decree as a lure to ensure demonic cooperation. She'd been on the verge of signing it, she told her people, when Bloody Anazakia had wreaked such havoc in Elysium that it had to be postponed until order was restored and the proposed document could be given the attention it deserved. Well-bred angels, freshly home from the universities at Zevul, took up the cause in an effort to view themselves as enlightened men, and Aeval became their champion of celestial equality.

Regrettably, it had been necessary to sacrifice Kae to achieve these aims. As principality, he'd been a surety for her claim to the throne in the beginning, but he'd become a liability as her power grew. To be sure, he'd made a most elegant scapegoat, achieving near-martyrdom. Even the Fallen had mourned his demise.

Smiling to herself, Aeval recalled the brilliance of her gambit. She'd controlled the angel so thoroughly that when his impertinent cousin had managed to wound Aeval and sap her strength, he'd given her his own vitality in the same way he was controlled: with a kiss. Her kiss bound him to her, and the blood in his veins answered her call. But it also left him docile and compliant, and with the peasants in revolt, she'd needed him enraged. She'd sparked Kae's passion by spilling his blood, and with his blood on her kiss, licked from the blade, she'd riled him to madness.

He'd killed for her yet again, incensed by the sight of the vital fluid he was spilling. With his own nearly dormant beneath the strength of her will, he seemed enamored of the heat and vigor of the blood of others. He littered the floors of the Winter Palace at Elysium with the corpses of the ungrateful demons who defied her, saving her the bother of draining them of elemental power one by one.

When the greater threat of the palace fire had closed in on them, Aeval had called forth Kae's radiance, normally visible only in the terrestrial sphere. At her insistence, the elemental water that dominated his blood as a Third Choir angel of the Order of Principalities rose from within him like wings of silvered glass, and at the touch of her lips to his, every drop of it turned to ice. Like an exquisite sculpture kneeling before her, her angel had taken the brunt of the flame, and his element had repelled it. The shattering of his radiance was something she hadn't anticipated.

But Kae had served his purpose. With the captive power of his element, Aeval had propelled the flames into the square and cleansed it of rabble in a tidal wave of destruction. There was nothing left of the workers' rebellion and none who could report on what had become of the last principality of the House of Arkhangel'sk.

Aeval stretched her arms across the balustrade of her Summer Palace veranda and sighed with satisfaction as she surveyed her domain. Across the wave of deep green beyond the estate was the northern boundary of the Arkhangel'sk empire: the shining peaks of Aravoth. Even in summer, the ice caps rose from the darker earth like giant diamonds piercing its soil. Reachable only by careful passage through the rugged mountains was the small princedom of Aravoth itself. This was the Second Heaven, and beyond Aravoth lay the First, the frozen and uninhabitable Empyrean. But Aeval had always had trouble with boundaries.

These invisible lines in the world and the Heavens merely represented to Aeval things Not Hers. She hadn't been bound by the mystical separation of Heaven and Earth, and she would not be bound by celestial law. All the Heavens would belong to her, and everything below them. And not simply because she deserved it, but because Heaven and Earth *needed* to be brought to heel. Men and angels needed to be put in their places. Both had overrun their natural habitats, and neither had any respect for balance. Millennia of mismanagement had thrown the spheres out of alignment. If Aeval had to sow chaos for a brief interlude in order to achieve harmony, the concord she brought would be all the sweeter. And if it fulfilled her personal desire—what a happy coincidence.

What stood between Aeval and her desire until now had been the wickedness of the syla. She had presided over them for more than a thousand years, providing for their every need, but like the simple folk of the world of Man who petitioned her Midnight Court, they'd turned against her.

She had asked them nicely for the flower of the fern.

At the close of the nineteenth century, few believed in the Unseen World, and her power had become nearly irrelevant. Women who once sought the justice of her court from every woodland village across the land ceased to come to her. It was certainly not for lack of need. Across every age, there were men guilty of the neglect and abuse of women. It was a universal truth that men feared the power of the genitive sex and sought to suppress it. The Slavic peasants of the northern lands were no exception, and in previous centuries, they'd possessed the perfect combination of coarse brutality and superstition—and bountiful, untouched woodlands.

But as the twentieth century neared, this perfect triumvirate began to wane even there. Men began to be educated, if not exactly enlightened, and woodlands were in increasingly scarce supply—a circumstance that personally offended her as a force of nature. There was also an increasing lack of respect for the natural world and its innate power, orchestrated by none other than celestial messengers. Though the pagan traditions driven into near extinction in the green isles of the West had continued to thrive for several more centuries where Aeval had established her new court, "progress" eventually whittled the sphere of her influence until she was forced to adapt.

If petitioners would no longer come to Aeval, she would create a new order in the world of Man. She was a master at manipulating men, but this would require influencing large numbers of them at once, and for that, she needed the power of the *tsvetok paporotnika*—the flower of the fern.

The syla had guarded it for eons, offering a tantalizing opportunity at every midsummer for any mortal to possess it, but always playing tricks on those who came close, confounding their direction and inflaming their desires. Most seekers were effectively distracted from their purpose before midnight marked the end of the hunt for another year, finding a tangible opportunity for carnal pleasure more satisfying than the fleeting one of a mythical bloom.

Aeval, however, was the syla's queen, and when she asked for it, they should simply have given it. She had no need to justify herself to them. Instead they spoke nonsense about the queen of Heaven. It was to the first queen of Heaven this bloom had belonged, and only a queen of Heaven, they insisted, would have it. Aeval had boiled with outrage, unable to force their hands. But when at last someone sought the justice of her court, Aeval found the perfect opportunity to gain power in the world of Man.

The Polish ballerina desired the love of a tsar, and so Aeval had given it to her. The petulant dancer was a woman Aeval could easily control—and through her, Aeval could control an empire. She gave Mathilde Kschessinska the prestige she wanted on the Russian stage, besotting not only the Grand Dukes Sergei Mikhailovich and Andrei Vladimirovich, cousin and nephew to the reigning tsar, but the young Tsarevich Nikolai himself. Nikolai dallied with the ballerina for three years, lavishing her with gifts and purchasing an apartment for her in St. Petersburg where he visited her as often as he liked, and then summarily informed her he would marry a German princess and Mathilde must step aside.

The prima ballerina came to Aeval again, scorned and humiliated, and begged Aeval to make her Niki pay. Just beyond the palace of the tsar himself in the village of Tsarskoe Selo, the Midnight Court convened—unseen by all human eyes but the petitioner's. Aeval heard Mathilde's impassioned pleas and granted the petite dancer her revenge. What Niki dreaded most was his future, and so Aeval thrust it upon him, sickening his father, Tsar Alexander, a strong and healthy mountain of a man whom she felled with a simple flu. The ill-prepared Tsar Nikolai and his equally ill-prepared bride entered marriage and his reign surrounded by bad omens. Yet despite the unfortunate incidents and setbacks that marred their public life, the couple was blessed with a deep love for each other, and with four beautiful daughters.

The syla were responsible for this overflowing cup. They had spun the cords of queens since time immemorial, and they had given this domestic bounty to a man whom Aeval desired to punish. Tsaritsa Aleksandra, however, had prayed for an heir, and since prayers to the god of Man were lost in the empty sky, Aeval grabbed this one and fulfilled it. The son Aleksandra bore Nikolai was even more beautiful than the daughters, but Aeval made certain he was also fatally flawed.

And then those silly, wicked syla had sent the Russian tsaritsa a Holy Fool.

The monk kept the boy alive, when his death should have driven the tsar into a state of crushing despair. Further, he protected the four grand duchesses from harm of any kind, making it impossible to curse Nikolai with personal calamity, the only thing that might break his bond with Aleksandra.

Aeval had tried other methods. Used to dealing with the faithless and the neglectful, she'd erred with Nikolai in presenting herself to him in her usual form. When she failed to tempt him to unfaithfulness, she tried planting doubt, spreading rumors among St. Petersburg society that the monk had not only had improper relations with Aleksandra, but with her daughters as well. Yet the tsar remained steadfast in his belief in his beloved Sunny, and he would listen to no one who attempted to sway his mind. Worse still, the Holy Fool had become more than just a barrier to her means of weakening the tsar; he had begun to have his own undue and ultimately disastrous influence upon the tsar's decisions through his closeness to the family.

The Fool needed to die, but it had proven to be more difficult to achieve this than it ought. There were members of his considerable social circle who were more than willing to do the job at Aeval's prompting, but the monk had proven unnaturally resilient. She was convinced her betraying syla had charmed him. Ultimately, it required poisoning, shooting, stabbing, beating, and then drowning him under the ice of the Neva to rid the imperial family of their protector.

By then, however, the monk's innocent intimacy with the family—and his not-so-innocent intimacy with half the women in St. Petersburg—had done irreparable damage to the tsar's reputation. Even if Aeval were to succeed in swaying Nikolai toward her control, there was no chance of redeeming him in the eyes of his people, so she whispered in the ears of willing revolutionaries that the time was ripe to topple the House of Romanov. Yet no matter what indignities were heaped upon Nikolai and his little family as the dynasty began to crumble and revolution swept the land, they maintained their joy in one another. Aeval had no choice but to destroy them utterly.

And then once more, the foolish syla took their revenge on Aeval's machinations, spinning queensdaughters in the celestial plane who might one day reign as queen of Heaven—a queen worthy of the flower of the fern. The intent had been to put their precious flower permanently out of her reach, but it had opened doors of possibility to Aeval that had never occurred to her before their meddling. Why seek to rule on Earth, when one could be a queen in Heaven?

She'd taken delicious pleasure in disturbing the waters of supernal seed, completing the family picture the syla had begun with the birth of fragile Azel. Such flaws were uncommon among angels, but even angelic royalty carried recessive genes that could cause trouble, and Aeval had called these genes forth as the principality and his queen copulated.

Out of a penchant for the theatrical, she waited until the children reached the ages of the slaughtered Romanovs before making her move. Now she no longer needed the flower the syla had kept from her. She held the Heavens in her hand. Kae had proven most valuable, though he'd gone above and beyond what she expected of him in cutting his own child from his beloved Ola's womb. It had shocked even Aeval's sensibilities. She feared she might have thoroughly destroyed his mind, making him useless to her, but he eventually recovered.

She played the merciful angel to him for the benefit of the Firmament, nursing him back to health after slitting his throat herself and leaving him for dead. Only one thing eluded her, though she managed to pull every other memory from his head: she had never been able to get him to tell her how he'd disposed of the tiny corpse.

With his blood in her command, he was nearly as empty as the bodies rotting in the Arkhangel'sk vault. Aeval molded him into a vessel, filling his empty carcass with whatever struck her fancy, though her efforts were particularly successful when she allowed him his volatile emotions. The jealousy and hatred he felt for her demon pet sparked a delightful streak of sadism in him, and she had happily turned the demon over to him to see how far he would go.

Before the damned earthly Fallen had violated their exile and pierced the Heavenly barrier to rescue Belphagor, her puppet principality had come close to calling the blood of the demon himself through sheer brutality. It was a shame she'd never had the opportunity to see her slave create his own demonic version of himself. But Kae had beaten something out of the demon before his escape that intrigued her. Belphagor was not the father of the angel's child as he'd claimed. His lover, the firespirit Vasily, had impregnated the girl.

Aeval had known the infant couldn't belong to Belphagor from the moment the child displayed her elemental radiance in Heaven. She had some natural immunity to the Seraphim that invoked it, as well as an immunity to Aeval's ability to call the elements to do her bidding. Like the blue celestine stone worn by the angels of the supernal family to ensure the higher-order angels couldn't harm them, the child protected her mother as well.

No minor airspirit mutt like Belphagor could have produced such an intriguing mutation. Air and water blended to make nothing but vapor. But fire and water, which usually made no more than steam, could be a potent combination in just the right amounts. The diamonds she used as an object of focus to command the cardinal elements were one example of the elemental perfection known as ice and fire; the *tsvetok paporotnika*, the flower of the fern, was another. And the child, it seemed, was an embodiment of this perfection. Aeval had been a fool to let the little demon-spawn get away.

Now that she'd achieved her objectives in Elysium, it was time to do something about it.

Tritya: Safe as Houses
from the memoirs of the Grand Duchess Anazakia
Helisonovna of the House of Arkhangel'sk

Following the news of the price on my head, Dmitri assigned a pair of Nephilim to stay with us in Arkhangel'sk. The product of Grigori unions with the humans they'd been sent to watch, the race of Nephilim were endowed with the celestial strength of their progenitors. Vashti, who'd helped storm Aeval's palace to break me out, arrived from the earthly city of London with a Nephil I hadn't met before.

Zeus was as pale and blond as Vashti was richly ebony. Both were tall by any standards, but Zeus towered over even Vasily—or he would have, had Vasily not made himself scarce. It worried me that he hadn't returned to the dacha since our disagreement, but Belphagor assured me he just needed time to himself. I hoped that was all there was to it, but Belphagor's look was guarded, and I couldn't be sure.

Vashti was her usual aloof self—I had the feeling she didn't approve of my pure angelic blood—but she seemed reluctantly charmed by Ola, who was awed by her difference. In particular, Ola seemed captivated by Vashti's unfamiliar London accent, listening with rapt attention whenever the Nephil spoke.

Among the Fallen dwelling in the world of Man, the human-descended Nephilim were the best equipped to provide us protection. Where angels of the Third and Fourth Choirs and their mixed-blood demon descendants could be easily overpowered by elementals such as the Seraphim, humans were invulnerable to their fiery touch. The Nephilim, half Host, were not completely immune to it, but they could withstand far more of a Seraph's touch than a full-blooded celestial could without sustaining permanent injury.

But it wasn't the Seraphim we should have worried about.

With our new protection in place, we procrastinated at Arkhangel'sk. I doubt any of us wanted to leave. The little dacha, though not big enough for six adults, had become a haven in our secluded plot in the Arkhangel'sk countryside. Love moved upstairs to share a bedroom with me and Ola, while Zeus and Vashti flipped coins for the couch and floor downstairs.

There were also practical reasons the move couldn't be rushed. The communications Love had been intercepting lately didn't bode well for me. We heard nothing more from Heaven, but angelic messengers known as the Malakim had been sowing seeds of discord among the community of Travelers since Aeval's rise to power, and it had apparently begun to yield its crop. The lie that I was the murderer of my own family, of countless numbers of the Ophanim Palace Guard, and of hundreds of demon peasants, had spread not only through the gypsy underground but had made its way among the small communities of the Fallen who relied on this network for communication.

The larger enclaves of Nephilim and Grigori tried to counter the misinformation with the truth of what had happened on that infamous morning, but the trouble was that none of us had remained in Heaven long enough to see what had become of the demon uprising. There was no other likelihood than that Aeval had killed them all herself, but there were no witnesses; there was only Aeval's word.

The Malakim she sent to do her work in the world of Man had gained a significant following among the Travelers, even before the storming of the celestial Winter Palace. What came of that early morning's work in Heaven merely served to strengthen the influence of the Malakim. As a result, communicating with the Fallen who were still on our side was becoming increasingly difficult.

At least we had Love. For all her lack of belief, or perhaps because of it, she was stubbornly loyal to us, and members of her extended family who attempted to persuade her otherwise only infuriated her and hardened her resolve. To Love, these Roma were hopelessly deluded, being used by the slick-talking, charismatic outsiders who were the Malakim. She hadn't made up her mind about *who* we actually were, but *what* we were, she firmly believed, was a group of ordinary humans with intentions Love viewed as noble in its most basic sense.

That Ola and I had escaped imprisonment, she had no reason to doubt, and that Belphagor had been beaten by someone within an inch of his life she had seen with her own eyes. I believe she thought of me as an heiress who'd strayed from a powerful earthly family who threatened my life. It was as close to truth as anything. For her steadfast heart, and because she had been brought to us by our dear friend Knud—who died defending me against Aeval—I trusted her completely.

Because Belphagor and Vasily were known to be companions of the now-infamous "Bloody Anazakia," finding a new safe house for us had become a challenge. Vashti had a brother in London who offered to put us up, but it would only be temporary, and from the sound of it, the space was small and not meant to accommodate a toddling child. Belphagor wanted to keep looking until we found something permanent, insisting stability was important for Ola, and I had no objection. I was content to remain at Arkhangel'sk as long as possible.

Though the syla's plight still nagged at me, I'd seen nothing more of them and there had been no reports of Seraphim sightings in the world of Man. Whatever had happened, it seemed to be over.

Night began to return to the north, and I spent as much time outdoors with Ola as I could while the sun still graced us. Though we had little more than two hours of full dark now, in two months' time, we would have more than twelve. The temperature was already dropping a little each day and we could no longer go about in bare sleeves; soon it would be time to put away our warm-weather things. Winter came early to Arkhangel'sk, with barely four hours of daylight at the deepest of it, and lingered long. The ice on the River Dvina had lasted this year into early May.

If we were to leave Arkhangel'sk, the long winter would be one thing I wouldn't miss, though it almost broke my heart to think of the beauty of the Northern Lights over the rime-frosted trees. And if there were no ice or snow where we ended up, would the *snegurochki* syla come to us at Winter Solstice? I couldn't be sure. Though I would be glad of a warmer climate, I'd discovered the starkness of northern winter could be exquisite. As Vasily might have said, there was ecstasy in suffering I had never imagined in my sheltered, celestial life.

Vasily, however, had me deeply worried. He stayed away for nearly a week after the news of Kae's death put a strain between us. Belphagor remained unconcerned—it was Vasily's way, he said—but I couldn't imagine where Vasily could go in Arkhangel'sk without courting trouble. Though I rarely went into town, the rest of our household was looked on with some suspicion when they did, and had been accused a number of times of being gypsies. Love warned that if anything went missing while they were in town or any illness struck someone nearby, they'd be blamed for it. She was used to such discrimination; it seemed gypsies in the world of Man had much the same status as the Fallen in Heaven.

When Vasily did return, it was with a hangover that made even the Nephilim stay out of his way, and a conspicuous black eye. The smoldering glower in his pupils from within the purpling bruise was a clear challenge to Belphagor. The two demons retreated behind closed doors for the confrontation I knew Vasily had been aching for. As mystifying as it was to me, Belphagor's anger was like air to Vasily, and he'd taken nothing but shallow breaths since Belphagor's return from Elysium.

The rest of us took refuge in the sitting room and kitchen while Vasily rattled the ceiling above us with his furious pacing and shouting, and even Ola, seated on my lap, stayed unusually quiet, with a wide-eyed solemnity. Belphagor's voice was barely raised. I knew before he returned downstairs that Vasily hadn't gotten the precious drink of air he so desperately needed—the string of obscenities that followed in Belphagor's wake before the door slammed shut again was merely a formality.

After his return, Vasily barely spoke to me. I couldn't reach him, and his coldness was as painful as an Arkhangel'sk frost. The sting was doubly so for its echo of the change in Kae before his madness. My cousin had been my dearest friend until Aeval's enchantment had chilled his blood. It was like dull steel in my breast to feel such a similar intemperateness from Vasily, who was the embodiment of heat.

It was clear there was an even greater strain in Vasily's relationship with Belphagor, and I hated that I was the cause. If Belphagor would only rebuke me for my grief over the death of my cousin, I was certain the impasse between them would end. But he had not, and would not, and I could see it eating away at Vasily, pushing them further apart like a wedge being gradually driven between them.

Before the end of August, Belphagor decided to take Ola on a short cruise to see the white beluga whales off the coast of the nearby Solovetsky Islands. It would be an opportunity, he said, for me to have a break from mothering. I hadn't spent a single night apart from Ola since I'd brought her home, but I had no desire for a break. I was anxious at the idea of her being away from me, but Belphagor said the whaling cruise was a once in a lifetime experience. I argued that she was too young to remember it, but he was insistent, and I guessed that the real reason he'd planned this was to give me time alone with Vasily.

They would take a bus to the small airport in Arkhangel'sk on Monday and be back Wednesday afternoon. I was nervous about Ola traveling in an airplane, but Belphagor assured me it was safer than an automobile—not that I considered those particularly safe. Vashti and Zeus would go along to make sure Ola was protected and I insisted Love accompany them; with her along, Ola would be less likely to be anxious at my absence. Despite the threat, there had been no signs yet of anyone attempting to collect on Aeval's bounty, and with half a dozen Nephilim just a telephone call away on Dmitri's "Arkhangel'sk detail," I felt safe enough with Vasily at the dacha. If only Vasily were speaking to me.

He kept to his room, so I went out to work in the garden while there was still time for things to grow. My little vegetable garden had yielded several small cucumbers and tomatoes this year, and I was learning how to preserve them so we could enjoy them into the winter months. Absorbed in the pleasure of working the earth, I stayed out until it was late enough that the sun was heading toward its brief dip below the horizon. I was on my hands and knees in the dirt, patting down a new plot I'd sown, when the door to the dacha slammed and I heard Vasily coming with determined strides around the path.

He stopped under the arched trees that covered my secluded garden, his arms folded over his chest, and stared furiously at me. "Well?"

I sat back on my heels and squinted at him, baffled, holding one hand up against the low-lying sun. "Well, what?"

"Well? Are you ever going to speak to me again?"

"Am *I*? I thought you weren't speaking to *me*."

He came closer, towering above me like the statue of Vladimir Lenin in Petrovsky Park, and growled between his teeth. "You ought to have rejoiced at the news that the *sukin syn* had died."

I stood slowly, wiping the dirt on my trousers. "Vasily, Kae was a brother to me. I grew up with him. He was my sister's husband. The man who killed my family, the man who tortured Belphagor—that was a stranger, a madman. It's not *his* death I mourn. I don't even know who that was."

"I don't care who he was! He nearly took him from me." Vasily grabbed my wrist in his large hand and the violet radiance shocked me lightly as if he'd brushed the soles of his shoes across a carpeted floor. His face was white with rage—though as I studied it more closely, I thought it might be fear.

"But he didn't," I said softly. "You saved him."

He was motionless, staring at me as if I were speaking another tongue.

"It's not me you're angry with." I understood the look on his face at last. "You're angry with Belphagor."

"Of course I'm angry with Belphagor!" He grabbed my other wrist and pulled me up close. "The fucking son of a bitch." His habitually hoarse voice was nearly a whisper, and his eyes were dark with pain. "He hasn't come back to me, Nazkia. He's still there. Still in that hole. He has nightmares, and if I touch him to try to wake him, he shrinks from me as if he thinks I'm going to hit him. Sometimes he even speaks to him in his sleep. 'I am His Supernal Majesty's eternal slave.' He says it over and over."

I gasped at this. The last words my cousin had said to me had been almost the same, only he'd said it of Aeval: *I am Her Supernal Majesty's eternal slave*. It was a conditioned response; he had seemed barely conscious of saying it. Aeval told me she'd called his blood, that she controlled him in every way. Yet Kae had apparently demanded the same obeisance of Belphagor.

"He's not touched me since he's come home. Not really." Vasily looked down at his hands and softened his grip on my wrists when he realized how he was holding me. Our radiance flickered and he slid his palms up my arms and watched it follow his fingers before pulling me close. I lifted my face to him when he released me, and he lowered his head and kissed me as he hadn't done in months, the spark of our elements playing like a tiny static charge against our tongues. He pulled back and looked into my eyes as if for permission, the deep flames of his element dancing in his.

"I need someone to touch me." His voice was low with desire.

More than my eyes were giving him permission as I nearly melted under the heat of his gaze. He scooped me up in his arms and carried me into the dacha, leaving the door thrown open as he took me up the stairs and tossed me into the center of the bed he shared with Belphagor. I fell against the pillows, breathing in sharply at the reminder that he could toss me with such ease. I watched as he pulled his white T-shirt over the thick ropes of his flame-colored hair and yanked the buttons from his jeans, his muscles as hard as all of him was. I had always loved to watch him undress, seeing each part revealed as I waited to be possessed by him.

As he pulled off the jeans, Vasily slipped his hand into his pocket and produced a small, square packet. "Protection." He blushed slightly. "Knud gave them to me." Knud had chastised him for our carelessness after Vasily had reacted badly to the news of my unplanned pregnancy. There was no birth control in Heaven, and though I hadn't heard of this earthly innovation when Vasily first took me to his bed, he'd spent enough time in the world of Man to know better.

He held the packet between his teeth as he crawled over me and undressed me, and I shivered beneath his touch and the dance of the violet light. It was like breathing pure oxygen after having been deprived of fresh air for months. I'd missed it so much, it almost made me weep.

I closed my eyes, arching up to meet his hand as he pulled down my trousers, and then he stopped suddenly. I looked up and saw the packet fall from his teeth onto the carpet as he turned his head to the door. Behind him, Belphagor stood gripping the doorframe. Blood was running down the side of his face.

"Vasya." He stumbled and Vasily leapt up and caught him before he hit the floor.

Jerking my trousers back on, I scrambled in the bedclothes for my bra and shirt. I held them awkwardly to my chest as Vasily led Belphagor to the bed.

"What's happened?" Vasily touched the blood on Belphagor's face, completely oblivious to his own nakedness.

"Where's Ola?" I clutched my shirt. "Is she all right?" Terror gripped me when Belphagor looked up at me but didn't answer.

I jumped from the bed and ran downstairs, pulling my shirt on and buttoning it as I went. There was no one below, and the door still stood open on an empty twilight. Calling Ola's name, I went out along the garden path, pushing past the overgrown branches of tea roses I'd meant to trim, to the little white gate on the walk. Before I opened the gate and hurried down the drive toward the road beyond, I stood and stared at the empty stones as if Ola and Love must surely be there and I was simply failing to see them. Vashti and Zeus would appear in a moment, with Love holding a sleepy Ola between them. They had to. There was no other acceptable possibility.

When they didn't come, I ran along the country road that led to the dacha, shouting for them frantically, ignoring the carpet of pine needles that pressed sharp and damp against my bare feet. I went as far as the end of the road where it met the paved highway, but fear wrapped around my heart and tightened like a garrote when I could see the open road. As always, there was no one for miles, just the empty, late summer dusk settling among the peaceful birch and poplar.

It was all I could do not to fall screaming to my knees. I returned to the dacha, my feet slowing, as though delaying the moment Belphagor confirmed it could stop what I already knew.

I let the gate swing loose behind me and hugged my elbows in the evening chill. Just this morning, Ola had picked a bouquet of awkward wildflower stems and weeds from this path as I'd walked it with her, holding her hand while she practiced her steps, not quite confident yet to walk on her own. Inside the dacha, the bouquet was still sitting on the table in a canning jar. Her building blocks were scattered on the floor in the sitting room, her little blue summer jacket just on the chair where she'd left it. Everything was where it should be. Everything but Ola.

Upstairs, Vasily had closed the bedroom door. As I approached the landing, I could hear him speaking in low, earnest tones, but I couldn't make out the words.

And then I heard Belphagor's voice quite clearly. "It's my fault. It's all my fault." There was a long silence crackling with tension, and then something spoken low and plaintively, followed by the sound of a fist hitting flesh.

Chetvertoe: **The Room in the Elephant**

Belphagor would have given anything not to have to answer that desperate plea. Vasily and Anazakia had been in bed together—or almost in bed together. It was what he'd expected to happen. It was what he'd hoped would happen, even though it stung just a bit to see that it had. Vasily had been denying himself any pleasure out of guilt, and Belphagor…he couldn't seem to move past the shame to be what Vasily needed him to be. Vasily had seen him beaten, broken—pathetic. For a time, he'd been as dependent on Vasily as a child. Whenever he did make an effort, Vasily pulled away from him, as if he could sense Belphagor's self-loathing.

And Anazakia tiptoed around him as if he were something delicate she was afraid to disturb, all the while secretly looking at Vasily with a naked longing she thought Belphagor didn't notice. As Vasily always smelled to him of firewood and the comfort of a hearth, whenever Anazakia and Vasily touched, they seemed to give off a scent of the electrified air after a thunderstorm, making it impossible to ignore the powerful connection between them. Right now, the scent of that elemental fusion was heavy in this room. The sheets beneath his cheek were charged with it.

These had all seemed very great worries until this afternoon.

They had stopped for a picnic lunch along the coast after the short flight to the Solovki Airport, and Love and Zeus had gone to find driftwood for a fire. Vashti had unpacked the food they'd brought with them while Belphagor entertained Ola, and when Vashti handed him a bottle of soda, he downed it quickly, his mouth parched from the salty air. As the Nephil smiled at him and reached to take Ola from his lap, he realized something was wrong. His extremities were going numb and his vision was blurring, and his throat felt tight.

"Don't worry," Vashti told him. "You'll only sleep for an hour or two. Long enough for us to reach Kem."

Belphagor had tried to speak, but his mouth refused to cooperate, and he could only slur unintelligibly. Vashti slipped Ola's diaper bag from his shoulder and put her hand behind his head, easing him to the ground. He watched, paralyzed, as she hoisted Ola and stood.

"Say *poka* to Beli, Ola," he'd heard her say as she held out Ola's arm toward him. "Wave to Beli." And then he could only hear the crunch of Vashti's boots and the surge of the frigid waves of the White Sea against the rocky shore of the island as she walked away toward the dock and a boat to Kem.

He'd tried to move, and for a moment, there was still some feeling in his upper arms, but he'd only managed to flop sideways and bash his head against the rocks. After that, he could only remember waking as the sun was moving low on the horizon. He was alone on the beach. Zeus and Love had never returned.

Anazakia was waiting for an answer.

"They took her." His voice was barely a whisper. "The Nephilim and Love." He didn't try to sit up, still dizzy from whatever Vashti had given him and from the desperate flight he'd made on his own after dark, trying to stay out of view as he coasted on his wings to keep from falling into the sea.

Vasily was pacing naked by the window as if trying to control the urge to beat the hell out of him. He deserved it. Belphagor had failed him utterly, had failed them both.

"Why?" Tears poured down Anazakia's cheeks. "Why would they do that? Where did they take her?"

"I don't know." He examined the blood on his hand from his lip, trying to make sense of anything.

"How could you let it happen?" Vasily whirled from the window and yanked him from the bed. Holding Belphagor by the collar with his feet nearly off the floor, Vasily roared his rebuke. "Did you suspect nothing? Did you do nothing? You just let Vashti walk away with my child?"

"I told you. She put something in my drink." Belphagor looked up at him hopelessly. "We'll find her. We'll bring her back."

Vasily flung him onto the bed. "We? She's not your child, Belphagor. She's mine. I'll damn well find her. This no longer has anything to do with you." He grabbed the jeans he must have stripped out of and tossed to the floor some minutes before Belphagor's unwelcome arrival, and pulled them on with angry jerks. The words stung worse than anything he'd yet said.

"You know I love Ola as if she were my own."

"Really?" Vasily's eyes were cold instead of burning with celestial fire. "Well, I would have died before I'd let them take her from me, Belphagor. And you're not dead, are you?" He buttoned his jeans almost violently. "Get out. Just get the fuck out."

"Don't." Anazakia's voice broke in a sob. She put her hand on Vasily's arm as Belphagor climbed from the bed and stumbled toward the door. "Please don't. I can't stand this."

Vasily jerked his arm away. "Then go with him."

Anazakia stepped out into the hallway after Belphagor and pulled the door shut, her white, drawn face streaked with tears. Inside, he could hear heavy things being thrown about the room, as if Vasily had picked up the furniture itself and hurled it. Belphagor turned unsteadily to the stairs, unable to face the misery in the angel's eyes, but she grabbed him by the arm.

"You're hurt. What happened? Tell me everything."

Her kindness was unbearable. Belphagor preferred the bilious rage of Vasily. She helped him downstairs and made him tea, washing the blood from his face and tending the cut he'd gotten from the rocks as he told her how Vashti had left him and how he'd woken to the terrible certainty that Ola was gone.

"How did you get back so quickly?"

He winced at her ministrations. "I flew. Not by airplane, I mean. I took wing."

The hand holding the damp, bloody cloth dropped to her side. "You displayed your radiance? In plain view?"

"My radiance isn't much. Not like yours or Vasily's."

Vasily's fiery wings were a brilliant vermillion, and though Anazakia's were like a clear fountain of water surging up from her shoulder blades, she could spark a blue flash so pale and pure it was almost white and light up the sky. Belphagor's element merely produced a broad expanse of darkness, air that glittered if the light hit his wings right, like a black slick of oil on the surface of a lake, swirling with a spectrum of dark color.

"I couldn't just stay there and wait for the flight on Wednesday. And there was no one to see me anyway. Or hardly anyone, just the monks at the monastery. But it was dark. No one was about, and I kept to the ocean most of the way. I'd circled the islands and the coastland for a sign of Love or the Nephilim—a boat, anything—but it was too late by then. They were taking the ferry to Kem. If they had a car waiting there, they could be anywhere." He cupped the warm drink between his hands and forced himself to meet her eyes. "I'm so sorry, Nazkia. You haven't said it, but this is my fault. I shouldn't have taken Ola out. I'm to blame."

"And I'm to blame for taking my cousin riding on the day Aeval poisoned his blood. But we don't talk about such things in polite conversation." She went to the sink to rinse out the cloth. "Don't tell me to be unkind to you, Belphagor. You don't know what you're asking. If I speak what I feel, I'll say terrible things. Things I'll regret. Vasily will regret it when his anger's passed." She turned off the water but remained where she stood, holding the dripping cloth. "Just find a way to get Ola back. Use your skill at the game."

The game. It was the only thing he was good at. The wingcasting table was the one place he excelled. But neither bluffing and card counting, nor sleight of hand, could possibly be of any use in this, whatever it was. He wasn't even sure if the Nephilim had taken Ola for a reward from Heaven, or for ransom, or for some other purpose. He didn't know the rules of this game.

"Love," he said suddenly. "What's her part in this?" He set down his tea and grabbed the computer Love kept on the table, a small phone plugged into its side connecting it to the vast resources of a network of information far greater than the gypsy underground.

He found her mail open and fumbled awkwardly with the navigation toggle on the keypad to see the last few messages she'd read.

"The gypsy underground has been contacting her." He scanned the contents in surprise. "There's talk of the Malakim…talk of breaking the alliance with the Fallen in favor of a new alliance with Heaven." He shook his head. "Those sons of bitches."

The Fallen and the Travelers had lived side by side for thousands of years, with the Night Travelers keeping the secrets of the Fallen and the Fallen keeping the secrets of the Night Travelers. Though as humans, the Roma had immunity from the powers of the Seraphim who pursued criminal elements of the Fallen community, there were other celestials to contend with. The Malakim took it upon themselves to whisper in the ears of Men and foster false hopes while simultaneously encouraging the prejudice that kept such marginal groups oppressed. It kept the world of Man from looking for the world of Heaven, but ever longing for it. And people like the Travelers who lived on the fringes were always the first to suffer under the mighty *knut* of manmade gods.

"What is it?" Anazakia had seen him wince.

"Nothing. Just an unpleasant memory." He focused once more on the message in front of him and swore as he read it. "The Parliament of Night Travelers instructed her to turn Ola over to the Malakim for her own safety." He looked up at Anazakia. "This was days ago. It looks like she finally took their advice."

"*Why*? Why would she? She doesn't believe in the Malakim, or Heaven, or even Aeval!"

"Maybe she believes in the Parliament of Night Travelers. What I don't understand is why the Nephilim would help her. They stand to lose if the Travelers ally themselves with the Host." A search of the mailbox revealed nothing relating to Nephilim.

Belphagor closed the laptop. "This is good news, Nazkia. I know it doesn't seem like it. But if the Malakim are behind this, all we need is some muscle. We'll get Ola back before they have a chance to take her to Aeval. They can't just will themselves to Heaven like the Seraphim; they'll be taking the train to the celestial portals at Irkutsk. We'll put the Grigori on every stop of the Trans-Siberian rail. We'll have them before they get to Yekaterinburg. We'll find her."

Doubt and hope played across the angel's features.

"And when I find Love," Belphagor added darkly, "I'll whip her ass until she believes in the devil."

• • •

Love moaned, meeting resistance when she tried to reach up to find out why the back of her head hurt so badly. She discovered her hands were bound behind her to the frame of a wooden chair, and some kind of hood had been pulled over her head. A musky-sweet scent surrounded her, a smell of ancient confinement and the dampness of the earth beneath it. Wherever she was, it was cold.

"Awake now, Lyubov?" It was the Englishman, Zeus.

"What are you doing? What's going on?"

"I want to talk to you." His breath was warm at her ear. "Vashti and I need your help with a little project. We didn't expect Belphagor to bring you along, but since you're here, I think I can make use of you."

Love jumped at the stroke of his hand against her bare arm. "What do you mean? Take this off me so I can see you."

"Not just yet, Lyubov."

She yanked against the rope in irritation. "Why do you keep calling me that? My name is Love."

"You're not English." He turned her covered head about by the chin, as if he were examining her face. "*Love* is an English word. You're a Russian girl. A gypsy girl, *humani*."

"What is that? Umani? I'm *Ro*mani."

"*Humani*." He nearly spat the word at her. "It's ancient angelic. It means human."

Love sighed. "Is that the game we're playing? The angel game? Fine. You're an angel. You've got big wings. Now take this off!" She yelped in surprise as Zeus cuffed her through the hood.

"I'm not an *angel*." He said the word with disdain. "I'm Nephili. The superior seed of human and celestial. I'm evolution." He dragged another chair across the wooden floor in front of her. "Vashti told me you didn't believe in the unseen world. She didn't tell me just how ignorant you were, but no matter. I figured I'd have to show you one way or the other to get your cooperation. Now. I'll take off the hood" — she felt his hands on the bottom of the cloth — "if you'll stop being such a little bitch. Are we clear?"

"Yes," said Love, subdued.

Zeus pulled the hood over her head, and she blinked in the glare of a bare bulb behind him hanging from the curved, whitewashed ceiling. Only a single wooden door, its ornate iron fixtures rusted with age, broke the monotony within the windowless stone walls of the small room. When Love looked back at Zeus, his eyes were a gleaming, solid black. There were no whites.

He smiled at her reaction. "Just one of the unseen things."

"Black contact lenses," she scoffed. "You can get those anywhere."

"You are really quite determined to live in the boring world of the *humani*." He pushed back his chair and stood, and with a graceful shrug, a pair of bat-like, netted wings rolled out from behind his shoulders. The tips curled into multiple points terminating in protrusions that looked like glossy black claws as they unfurled. The wings spanned at least eight feet.

Love looked up at the tall, pale giant of a man, his dark eyes unblinking and his sinewy wings moving slowly with the rhythm of his breath. "You must have drugged me. Made me hallucinate."

"Lyubov. You're trying my patience. Vashti and I need someone who can be relied upon to do as we say without questions. I can't even rely upon you to believe your own eyes." He circled her slowly, strong muscles visible at the base of the wings at his shoulder blades where they forced his shirt down beneath them. Whatever he'd given her, whatever prosthetics he was using, the illusion was very realistic. "What have you been hearing on your little underground network? What do the gypsies say is happening in the unseen world?"

"Right now? A group called the Malakim wants Anazakia's daughter."

"And why do the Malakim want her?"

"Because they think she's some kind of angelic royalty. The last heir of a celestial dynasty." Love tried to shrug, and winced as her muscles strained against the ropes. Her hands were growing numb.

"The Nephilim clan I belong to believes Ola is a threat."

Her stomach knotted. "You haven't done something to Ola?"

"Ola is fine. For the moment." He stopped in front of her, so close she had to tilt her head back to meet his gaze. "Some of us would prefer the House of Arkhangel'sk—the celestial Arkhangel'sk—leave the stage for good. But Vashti is softhearted. She convinced me to have Ola put away, out of reach of idiots like the Malakim."

"Belphagor was finding a safe house. I was about to make contact with someone in Provence."

Zeus waved his hand dismissively. "Belphagor is a small-time grifter. Easily duped. Easily caught out when he thinks he's being clever and subtle. Might as well put a big red X on top of any safe house he sets up." Zeus shook his head, the wings flapping back as if in irritation at the very idea. "No, this is too important to leave to an ex-con and his fire demon boy-toy. Vashti and I have found the perfect 'safe house' here at the monastery."

So this cold cell was in the Solovetsky monastery. Love could vaguely recall Zeus carrying her down a flight of stairs after dazing her with a blow to the head, but she couldn't remember how they'd gotten inside this fortress. The bruised lump and the throbbing headache, however, were starting to bring back the stunned moment on the beach in painful detail. Zeus had swung at her with something that felt like a heavy log while she bent to pick up a piece of driftwood.

"We have an inside man among the brothers. He can keep the contents of these cells sealed tighter than a virgin's ass." Zeus smirked at Love's expression of disgust. "The remaining problem now is you." He straddled her over the chair and gripped her face. The wings flapped up around them, making her shiver as they stirred the air. "Can we count on you to do as you're told?"

She made an effort to nod, though his fingers were digging into her flesh.

"That's good." With his free hand, he reached under her shirt, and Love squirmed as he grabbed her breast. "You won't make much of a wet nurse. But I'm sure Ola won't mind the bottle." Laughing as her cheeks burned, he pinched her roughly beneath the shirt before letting go. He patted her cheek a bit too hard. "You'll do just fine, Lyubov. Welcome to *slon*."

As he climbed off, the wings retracted and disappeared behind him with a flourish, and with a quick wink, his eyes returned to their normal cold blue. She blinked at Zeus as he went out through the low wooden door, stooping to keep from hitting his head. The iron latch clattered with finality from the outside.

The phrase "Welcome to the elephant" confused her for a moment until she remembered Belphagor talking about the monastery on the short flight from Arkhangel'sk. *Slon*, the Russian word for elephant, was also the acronym for the *Solovetsky Lager Osobogo Naznachenia*—the Camp of Special Designation. The first and worst camp of the Soviet Gulag had been established here. Belphagor had described the place as if he had intimate knowledge of it, the way he often spoke of Russian history.

The latch lifted and a young, bearded monk entered, his eyes on the floor, the soft step of his sandals beneath the black *podryasnik* and *ryasa* robes almost soundless. He crossed to the chair and loosened the ropes.

She tried to rub the feeling back into her wrists. "*Spasibo.*"

The monk shook his head at her. "No Russian. Only angel tongue. You speak only when I speak you." The halting words were in the language the others at the dacha called angelic. It was clear he knew even less of it than Love did.

From under his vest, he produced a rolled-up set of garments like his own, with a pair of sandals tucked inside them. "You will put. Leave you clothings here. Knock when you have put."

She didn't like the idea of wearing a dress, and especially didn't like leaving her good boots behind, but when he'd closed the door, she did as she was told, hoping cooperation would get her out of this as soon as possible. Her leather belt, however, she fastened around her waist before she put the heavy garments on; it was expensive, and it might come in handy later. There was an extra piece of cloth when she'd finished getting dressed—a nun's head covering: the *apostolnik*. With a sigh, she put it over her head and shoulders.

When she knocked, the monk let her out and directed her through a series of corridors and stairways to another cell, more intimate than the first, containing a cot and a small window—too small to climb through, but she might be able to see outside if she stood on her toes. The monk turned to the door, a dark blond ponytail visible beneath the *skufia* pulled down around his ears.

"What do I call you?" She was careful to ask in angelic.

Startled, he looked up at her, revealing wide eyes of aquamarine beneath long lashes. Without the beard, he might be handsome. "I am called Brother Kirill." He stroked the thin length of beard awkwardly. "But you must not speak, Sister Lyubov. I tell brothers you have take vow of silence." With that, he went out and bolted the door.

Love sat on the cot with frustration. She was thirsty and she hadn't had a chance to ask him for water, and now her stomach was starting to growl. Fortunately, she didn't have long to wait. A key turned the bolt in the door some minutes later and Brother Kirill opened it to admit Vashti, with Ola in her arms.

"Ola!" Love jumped up, relieved. "Thank God she's okay. I think your friend Zeus has gone mad—"

"Shut up," Vashti interrupted. "Someone will hear you. You're supposed to be silent." Ola squirmed in her arms, reaching for Love, and Vashti handed the baby over.

"Lub." Ola tugged on the *apostolnik* as if she wanted Love to take it off and look like her usual self.

Love lowered her voice. "What's going on?"

"What's going on," said Vashti as she handed her the diaper bag, "is that you're the nanny. So just…*nanny*, and stop asking questions."

"Are you going to keep us here? In this little room?"

"Those sound like questions to me, nanny." Vashti swung her long braids behind her and folded her arms. "Zeus said he'd explained everything to you."

"Not exactly. How long are we supposed to stay here? Where's Belphagor?"

Vashti shrugged. "He was taking a nap last time I saw him. I think he was relieved to have Ola out of his hair."

Love bounced Ola on her hip. "What about Anazakia and Vasily? Do they know about this? Are they coming here?"

"No, they are not coming here. Just do your job and take care of the baby. I'm not answering any more questions—and if you open your mouth again, *humani*, I may just slap it shut."

Love scowled. There was that word again, *humani*. She had a feeling it wasn't just one of their made-up words, but an insult of some kind. Though it was one she'd never heard before today, it had an air of antiziganism to it. She'd met enough Roma-haters to recognize the disdain with which the word was said.

Vashti seemed satisfied by her begrudging compliance. "There are several cans of baby food, along with powdered formula and fresh water in the bag. And enough diapers to last a couple of days. It's too late for you to get anything to eat tonight, but Kirill will bring you breakfast in the morning."

"And what if I need to go to the bathroom?"

"Then you wait until Kirill comes to take you, don't you." Vashti gave her a dark look of warning and Love closed her mouth on any more questions. "You're not to speak to anyone, understand? Kirill will bring you everything you need. If he doesn't bring it, you don't need it."

Love nodded sullenly.

"Just keep the baby fed and quiet. That's your job."

• • •

Finally alone with Zeus later at the little cabin they'd rented on the island, Vashti tossed her brown lambskin coat onto the spare bed and peeled out of her matching pants while Zeus watched her, hands clasped behind his head against the carved wooden headboard, his broad chest bare. The place was charmingly appointed, with two little twin beds covered with red and white bedspreads in traditional Russian embroidery. They were barely big enough to hold one of them, but Vashti wasn't about to sleep alone.

Pulling her ribbed ivory tank top over her head, Vashti climbed onto Zeus's lap and yanked the belt free, unbuttoning his fly until she had what she wanted.

He grinned as she straddled him. "Long day."

"God, that was a bloody fortunate fuck-up, him bringing that girl along." She moaned appreciatively as he grasped her hips and pulled her down hard while he thrust himself into her. "Now I won't have to play nursemaid after all." Her braids swung over her shoulders like a curtain cocooning them as she looked down at eyes as blue as Onega Bay. There was nothing like Nephil cock. She was convinced their race had gotten the best of the sorry genes on both sides. She'd been called an abomination by both demon and human, but if this hard, beautiful god beneath her was an abomination, she'd take one any day over the "pure."

The Nephilim chose their names at adulthood, and Zeus had chosen well. Her brother Nebo considered him arrogant, the name a fitting tribute to his ego, but Nebo had never had Zeus's cock up his ass—*Thank Heaven*, she thought with a laugh.

Zeus pulled her down and cupped her breast as he brought it to his mouth. "You can play nursemaid to me instead."

• • •

As promised, Kirill showed up bright and early with a tray of breakfast. When Love sat up, he nearly dropped the tray, whirling away from her, his ponytail swinging behind him as if it, too, were shocked.

"You must put clothings!"

"They're too warm." Love picked up the robe and shimmied into it over her bra and panties. "I can't sleep in them."

"No Russian. Angel tongue only." When he faced her once more, Kirill's cheeks were such a painful red that Love felt guilty. "Clothings not too warm in winter." He set the tray on a hand-whittled pine stand in the corner. "You keep them put."

"Winter?" Love gaped at him in dismay. "Will I be here in winter?"

He gave her a noncommittal shrug. "If baby stay, you stay."

"How long?"

Kirill shook his head as he brought the tray stand to the side of the cot.

Love stared at the single bowl of kasha with jam, a serving of toast, and a pot of tea. "No food for Ola? For baby?"

"Baby eats…" He paused for a moment and then gave up and said, "*Moloko*."

"She doesn't just drink milk. She eats food also. She's fourteen months old." Love set the bowl of kasha aside. "I'll share."

"*Nyet*." Kirill sighed, clearly frustrated by his unusual duties. "I bring more. What more baby need?"

"Juice, bread, anything I eat. She likes biscuits. And milk—*moloko*."
She gave up on the angelic, seeing he was struggling to understand her
elementary vocabulary. "She doesn't like the formula and she doesn't
really need it anymore. We just brought that along because it doesn't
spoil. And if you're going to keep us in prison indefinitely, she's going to
need a lot more diapers and wipes. And more clothes. And some toys."

"Is not prison." Kirill looked offended. "No more speak. I bring
paper. You write list for baby."

"Her name is Ola."

Kirill put his finger to his lips with a frown and went out.

When he returned with the pencil and paper, Love scribbled down
everything she could think of, not knowing how long these supplies
would have to last. The prospect of trying to keep Ola occupied and
confined wasn't a pleasant one. What could that fucking Zeus have
been thinking? She couldn't imagine how they'd expected their plan
to work without dragging Love into it. Had they thought Ola would
just sit quietly on a cot by herself, waiting patiently to be fed or have
her diaper changed? It was as if they knew nothing at all about babies.

Kirill clearly didn't. His mouth dropped at the size of the list. "This
all for one baby?"

"A few things for me," she conceded.

When the monk reached the bottom of the list, his face went red
again, this time to the tips of his ears. She'd requested tampons.

"Don't abduct fertile young women if you're not prepared for it,"
she snapped in Russian.

Kirill put the list in his pocket and turned on his heel.

The monk brought almost everything Love asked for, but he would
say nothing more to her in the days to come, ignoring her or shushing
her sternly whenever she tried to engage him in conversation. Ola was
frustrated by the locked door but was soon engaged enough by the

array of toys Kirill delivered that Love was able to keep her crying to a minimum. When the door opened for mealtimes, Ola would look up hopefully, asking in no particular order, "Mama?" "Beli?" "Papa?" But she asked for them less and less with each passing day.

She took her first unaided steps without Anazakia or Vasily there to see it, and her vocabulary was growing in little words every day as Love read to her from the children's books Kirill had given them. As for Love herself, she thought she'd go mad from boredom until Kirill at last brought her some grown-up books and magazines, but she went through them quickly, with nothing more to do but play with Ola. The routine of waking, eating, and sleeping began to blur into an endless repetition and Love lost count of the days. The only indication of the passage of time was that the hours of daylight were growing shorter, and through their small window, the light had begun to change.

"I need to get out of here," she told Kirill one morning as he brought breakfast. "I need to go outside. *Ola* needs to go outside. You can't expect us to stay cooped up in here."

As he often did when she pestered him with unwanted conversation, Kirill moved his hand to the knotted prayer rope in his pocket, as if it were a talisman against her. "I will ask Mr. Zey-us." He looked alarmed as soon as the words were out.

"They're still here on Solovetsky!" Love exclaimed. "Zeus and Vashti?"

He shook his head, flustered, fingering the knots of the *chotki*. "I have orders. There is…communication." He would say nothing more when she pressed him.

The following day, he directed Love into the hallway before him. She and Ola had been allowed baths once or twice a week in a large bathroom upstairs, and she thought perhaps this was where they were headed, but instead, he steered her down the stairs, stopping at the room where she'd first found herself with Zeus.

"You will wait." Kirill picked up Ola and left Love alone.

Love paced angrily, not liking the idea of not knowing what was happening to Ola.

After several minutes, Zeus entered, smiling. "And how are we doing?"

"*We* are going stir crazy," snapped Love. "Why are you keeping us here? If you and Vashti are still on Solovetsky, why doesn't Ola stay with you? Why are we in a damn prison?"

Zeus took off his coat and hung it over the back of one of the chairs. "Sit."

"Go fuck yourself." Love regarded him hotly. "I want some answers."

Zeus moved her chair as if to hold it out for her, and then without warning, he slammed her in the gut and shoved her into it. "Kirill tells me you're making things difficult for him." He sat before her as if nothing unusual had happened, while Love groaned and hugged her stomach, trying not to be sick. "He's told his brothers you've taken a vow of silence and come here in penitence to give your child born in sin to the house of God. Yet you continue to speak to him when he asks you not to. You make demands like you're staying at Club Med."

Love glared up at him, her voice tight. "Asking for tampons is hardly Club Med."

Zeus smiled. "Yes, he told me something about that. Something about how fertile you are? Did you really discuss that with a monk?" When she didn't answer, he yanked her chair toward him. "Is that why you're going stir crazy, Lyubov? Cooped up like a nun not the thing for you?" He played with the buttons on the robe between her thighs, and Love slapped him away, only to have him belt her across the side of her face.

Love recoiled with a cry, her hand to her cheek. "What is *wrong* with you? I thought you people were Belphagor's friends!"

"You people?" He pulled her from the seat with a fist in her bangs. "Who the fuck do you think you are, you little pikey cunt?"

Love clawed at him, but with frightening strength, Zeus captured her wrists in one hand, swung her over the back of the chair, and bashed the side of her head into the wooden seat until she was stunned into compliance. She tried to fight him once more as he unbuttoned his fly, but he was resting his weight on her so that any struggling was ineffectual.

"Please don't," she begged. "I won't ask him for anything else. I'll be quiet!"

"Make as much noise as you like." He kicked her legs apart. "I like it when a girl shows a little appreciation. And no one can hear you down here anyway."

***Pyataya:* Tsarskoe Selo**
from the memoirs of the Grand Duchess Anazakia
Helisonovna of the House of Arkhangel'sk

Love's betrayal stung me far worse than that of Vashti or Zeus. Though
Vashti had helped me escape from Heaven, she'd never warmed to
me, and Zeus I knew nothing of. But Love had been a member of
our unconventional little family. With her, I'd felt a small fraction of
the closeness I would never have again with my sisters. I'd often found
myself feeling shy around her easy and unapologetic manner—she was
not afraid to speak her mind—but never for one moment had I felt I
couldn't trust her.

Belphagor had used her contacts to get a message to Dmitri. The
Grigori chieftain, outraged at the betrayal, convened a meeting of
every Grigori and Nephilim clan leader on the continent. Only Zeus's
clan didn't show. Though Vashti officially belonged to the *Karibskii*
Nephilim, she'd lived in London since her early teens and was under
the protection of the *Angliski* clan. When she was found, Dmitri said—
and he promised grimly that she would be found—Vashti would face a
twofold punishment: one for her crime, and another for her deviation
from the will of the Grigori. I cared nothing for their ancient laws. I
wanted only the return of my child.

Despite the mobilization of the Grigori, there had been no sign of
Ola. Surveillance of the Trans-Siberian Railway and the old Circum-
Baikal line from which the portal of Heaven could be reached turned

up no indication of movement among the Malakim. Dmitri was certain Belphagor had moved fast enough after the abduction that the Malakim couldn't have eluded them if they were intent on Heaven. There was no time. Even if they or the Nephilim had flown, it would have been known to the Grigori.

As for the Roma, they'd become stubbornly mum, refusing to say whether they knew Love's whereabouts and refusing to claim responsibility for Ola's abduction or deny involvement. Fallen relations with the gypsy underground had immediately ceased. One thing was certain; if the Malakim hadn't been in on the abduction from the first, they were well aware of it now.

It was maddening not to be able to question anyone who might be able to shed light, to have no demand for ransom nor any sign of Heaven's involvement. Zeus's clan had declared mutiny against the authority of the Grigori. The only motive we could discern from their declarations was that they believed the Grigori had broken their covenant first in aiding one of the Host. Dishearteningly, the celestial-born Fallen who now lived in the terrestrial plane had sided with the *Angliski* Nephilim. Belphagor and Vasily were pariahs to them. Thanks to Aeval's proclamation, we were now infamous.

As weeks wore on with no leads as to Ola's whereabouts, life in the dacha became strained. Dmitri had convened the Grigori Duma, a governing body that was rarely assembled and whose inner workings were for Grigori eyes only. We were strongly counseled against leaving the dacha in search of Ola, the Duma's consensus being that she had been taken to draw us out. He and his network would follow any leads and police all possible routes to Heaven to be certain Ola was not smuggled out of the world of Man. This sat hard with all of us. There was little concrete action we might have taken, but leaving it to the Grigori was like being bound hand and foot, with everything beyond our control.

To enforce the Duma's "recommendation" in a manner that seemed to me like barring the stable door after the horse had bolted, Dmitri set a rotating detail of Nephilim to guard the perimeter of the dacha property, leaving us feeling like prisoners in our own home. Though it was for our own protection, I could not help thinking of the family mine had resembled in its tragedy—the last of the House of Romanov. At the start of the Bolsheviks' October Revolution, they had been placed under house arrest in their palace at Tsarskoe Selo, the pastoral town outside the metropolitan center of St. Petersburg where the tsars had once retreated from the bustle of the city.

I had read accounts of the indignities they suffered as their house arrest turned to confinement in a commandeered home in Yekaterinburg, where they would end their days in a cellar, shot down like dogs. The Nephilim treated us with no obvious disrespect, but it was clear in their demeanor when one of us crossed their paths that the Exiles were not all of one mind. They obeyed Dmitri because of their dependent relationship with the Grigori—none of them wanted to end up with the uncertain fate of the *Angliski*—but privately, they displayed an icy civility that did nothing to reassure me of their loyalty.

And it was privately that the strain was greatest. Despite Belphagor's tireless efforts to learn all he could of Love's former connections, tracking leads on her computer and liaising with the Grigori to make certain no stone was unturned, Vasily hadn't apologized to him for his cutting words as I'd expected. Instead, he became more distant with the waning summer sun, refusing to confide even in me.

Again it brought to mind the gradual loss of Kae's confidence, like a cancer spreading through him, and the sorrow I still felt over my cousin's death compounded my guilt at the rifts between each of us. Was I to lose everyone? I could not think of Ola's absence as permanent or something inside me might break. In the delicate chrysalis of hope and worry in which I had enveloped myself, Vasily's withdrawal hit me even harder. As a consequence, I turned increasingly to Belphagor for solace.

From the contemptuous glowers Vasily bestowed on both of us, it was clear he looked on this as a betrayal.

With the tension among us, the house seemed doubly quiet. We had all become used to the whims of Ola's infant temperament. The absence of her mercurial tears at frustrations and disappointments, and of her sudden squeals of pure delight when she discovered something new—or something recognized, like Belphagor playing peek-a-boo behind a chair—left a ghastly emptiness between the walls. We could not fill the silence with words, knowing what words might come forth, and so it swelled until it deafened.

I woke often in the night believing I heard Ola crying, and on one occasion it seemed so real that I slipped on my *tapochki* and ran down the stairs calling for her. Belphagor, on the couch, stumbled out of sleep and caught me as I ran into the garden. Autumn was falling fast, and I stood shivering beneath the half-bare trees. Belphagor held me and let me cry as I realized I'd only been dreaming. Above us, Vasily's window slammed shut.

Something rustled within the dead leaves on the ground. I breathed in sharply and stepped back, reminded of the terrible images of the syla I'd put out of my head the moment my own loss had overshadowed them. *"The flower of the fern."*

Belphagor looked down at the leaves as if expecting to see the flower there. "What about it?"

"The syla—the Seraphim forced them to tell what they knew, what they saw in the future. And they saw Ola taking the flower. I think that's why Aeval sent the Malakim after her."

Belphagor's wingcasting face wavered on his features before he sighed and looked up at the stars. "Nazkia, I doubt the queen cares a whit about some *Russkie* fairy tale. If she wants Ola, it's not because of unseen spirits and magic flowers. It's because of her element."

He hadn't truly believed anything I'd told him about that night in Novgorod, or what I'd seen on this last midsummer's eve. "You actually think I'm mad."

Belphagor frowned. "Of course I don't. But you've been through a great deal. It's only natural you might be prone to…" He paused, as if realizing he'd said more than he meant to.

"Prone to what?" When he didn't answer, I folded my arms and stared him down. "Prone to *what*?"

"To…flights of fancy."

"Flights of fancy?" Tears of anger sprang to my eyes. "So I'm just imagining things, just imagined the syla were killed in front me."

His eyes were unbearably kind. "Sweetheart, you saw your entire family killed in front of you."

"Don't you dare patronize me."

"I'm not patronizing you; I'm suggesting there may be other factors to consider regarding your perception. And it doesn't matter whether I believe you or not. What matters is that we find Ola, whether the queen wants her because of some flower or because of Vasily's fire and your — ice."

I sucked in a breath of frosty air. "What did you just say?"

Belphagor licked his lips. "I didn't mean that the way it sounded. It's just something the Fallen call the Fourth Choir Host, ice instead of water. It came out automatically."

I ignored his apology; I wasn't interested in the slur. "*Ice and fire* — that's what the syla called the flower of the fern. And it's what Aeval said she used as an object of focus to call the elements." I shook my head slowly. "But she doesn't know Vasily is Ola's father. I never told her. She couldn't know Ola might have both."

Belphagor put his hands in his pockets, looking down at the ground as he rocked back on his heels. "I told her. Or rather, I told *him*. Kae must have passed it along to her." He raised his eyes with the look I'd seen in them so often lately: guilt and a longing to be absolved of it.

"Why? Why in Heaven's name would you do that?"

He shook his head. "It didn't seem to matter anymore. I didn't think it could matter. I was tired."

"You were *tired*?" I had the urge to strike him as Vasily had done. "What have you *not* said to the queen of Heaven?" I tried to hold the words in, but they were swarming to get out. "With every syllable from your mouth, you have done me nothing but harm. If you hadn't gone to make your deal with her, if you hadn't taken her my ring in your misguided attempt at 'protecting' Vasily and me, none of this would have happened."

I had finally said it. He'd suffered at Aeval's hand and at Kae's because of his own mistake in judgment. As well-intentioned as his actions had been, a small, mean part of me had felt he deserved it.

"Ola wouldn't have happened," he said quietly.

"Yes, and I wouldn't feel this hole in my heart!" I hated him at that moment for making me say it, for making me acknowledge the thought I'd tried to ignore even before her disappearance: how much easier things would be if Ola had never been born.

What kind of mother could think such a thing? I loved her dearly, but there had been times already in her short life when the weight of being responsible for another person, of being always at her beck and call, instinctive and innocent though it was, made me wish for a moment—or a night, when she cried all through one for no reason I could discern—that she didn't exist. Perhaps the fates had answered my selfish wish, and I deserved this. I deserved it especially for wishing she hadn't been born merely to spare myself the misery of losing her. Staring at Belphagor, mute with his eyes full of guilt, I hated us both.

Before I could say anything more, before I could take anything back, the leaves rustled again, the autumn wind lifting them into a tiny whirlwind that almost took a solid shape, as if a syla were trying to reach our world, but couldn't quite.

I forgot my anger. "Did you see that?"

Belphagor lifted his shoulders with effort. "It was just the wind."

The funnel rose up once more, and something fluttered at its center, a filmy auburn silk whipping like a flag wrapped about a pole.

"There!" I cried as the leaves dropped back to the ground. "She was there! You must have seen it."

Belphagor regarded me as if I might have snapped under the strain of grief. "It's much too cold out here, Nazkia. Come on. Let's go inside."

I had seen them before only on the two opposing poles of the year, the summer and winter solstices. Perhaps he was right, and I simply wanted to see what wasn't there. I turned with him on the stone path leading into the dacha, but from the corner of my eye, I saw the outline of a form once more in the half-denuded branches of a birch tree. I gripped Belphagor's arm as the bark of the trunk took on the silky, rippling texture I'd seen before. The wind whispered *Tsarskoe Selo*, and the image vanished. Belphagor was still staring blankly.

"But you heard her, didn't you?" I asked incredulously. "Tsarskoe Selo?"

The lines of worry deepened on his brow as he shook his head.

When he took my arm to lead me inside, I pulled away from him. "I'm not imagining them. They come to me. Ola has seen them; we've worn their garlands. They showed me the flower—the stupid, useless flower that has caused all this!"

Belphagor gripped my arms to steady me and looked me in the eyes. "I believe you. I believe you've seen them. But perhaps this once, you're simply overtired…worn down with worry."

I searched his face to see if he meant to be spiteful, pretending not to have perceived the syla out of hurt at my blaming him, but he seemed truly baffled by my insistence that something had been there.

He let me go, and I went past him toward the dacha. A cold nod from the Nephil at the end of the footpath seemed to punctuate the disconnect between the solid and tangible and what I was certain I had seen.

I paused at the stairway as Belphagor followed me in and closed the door. "You really didn't see? You didn't hear anything?"

He shrugged. "I'm sorry, Nazkia. I didn't."

Staring at the ceiling after I'd gone back to bed, I remembered Love's face when she'd followed me out of the garden to the bower where the syla lay dying. Love had denied seeing anything as well, but her face had told a different story. And Ola, young as she was, had clearly interacted with them when they came. It couldn't be my imagination. The syla spun the cords of queens, they'd told me. Did they mean women? Could only women see them?

Love had seen. I was certain of it now. She'd heard everything the syla told me. There was no other way the Malakim could have learned that Ola's element and the *tsvetok paporotnika* were one and the same.

When I finally fell into a fitful sleep, I dreamt of the syla repeating like an Orthodox prayer the words I'd heard in the garden: *Tsarskoe Selo.* The syla had spoken them for a reason, and I meant to find out what it was.

I rose early and sat at Love's computer while I drank my tea, careful not to wake Belphagor on the couch. I had gained a rudimentary understanding of the machine from Love before she left, and I could use it for a simple search.

Tsarskoe Selo, I discovered, was the St. Petersburg suburb now called Pushkin. I scribbled a crude map on a piece of notepaper and put it in my pocket. I would not sit here impotently for another minute not knowing what Love and the Nephilim had done with my child. If the syla who'd escaped Aeval's wrath wanted me to go to Tsarskoe Selo, I would go there. They were the only hope I had.

Shestoe: **The Prayer of the Heart**

Zeus had buttoned up when he'd finished with the gypsy and given her a firm smack on the ass as he let the robe fall back down to cover her.

"Come on, now. Pull yourself together." He walked to the door as she stumbled against the chair. "Feeling sorry for yourself, Lyubov?" He winked at her when she raised her head. "Consider it a lesson in penitence."

At the end of the hall, the monk had waited with the infant, giving her cookies to keep her quiet. Zeus didn't consider it a wise course of action to keep the abomination alive, but it wasn't for Vashti that he'd hesitated to do what ought to be done. The clan leader feared retaliation. They'd already gone against the Grigori, which meant expulsion for the entire clan. Not that the Grigori had ever done anything for the Nephilim as far as Zeus could see. But it would mean all-out war if they were to kill someone under the Grigori's protection, and the leader of the *Angliski* clan was not yet prepared for war.

Zeus held out his hand. "Brother Kirill." He nodded as Kirill clasped it. "I think you'll find we've come to an understanding with Sister Lyubov. She was unclear on the seriousness of her vow—or of yours. But I've explained it to her."

Kirill eyed the scratches on his hand.

"Ah, she's a wildcat, that one." Zeus laughed and nudged the monk with his elbow. "She was so excited to see me I nearly had to fight her off to have our talk first. But *ce que femme veut, Dieu le veut.* What woman wants, God wants, eh?"

. . .

When Zeus had gone, Love gripped her stomach, bruised and sore from being pressed under his weight against the chair. She'd been determined not to give him the satisfaction of crying, but a wave of tears threatened and she blinked them back angrily. She had to compose herself for Ola. She pulled the *apostolnik* into place over her head, trying to cover any marks from where he'd struck her, and straightened her robe as well as she could.

Kirill arrived a moment later with Ola in tow, and he gave her a look of tight-lipped disdain.

Ola held up a chocolate wafer in her fist. "Vaf," she said proudly.

"Oh, I see." Love stifled a gasp as she lifted her. "You've got *vafli*."

Remaining silent behind her as she climbed the stairs to her cell, Kirill slammed the door on her once she was inside.

Love tried to entertain Ola for the rest of the morning without behaving strangely, biting back cries of pain when Ola climbed or bounced on her. Ola was tantrumy, perhaps sensing something anyway, and wouldn't go down for her midday nap. When dinnertime came and went and Kirill hadn't come, Love tried reading to her. Usually, Ola was eager to point out any picture of her favorite animals, a *kot* or *sobaka*, but tonight she would have none of it. Eventually, she cried herself angrily to sleep after a particularly exhausting fit of kicking and rolling about on the floor.

Love carried her to the bed and pulled the covers over her before taking a look in the toy mirror on Ola's doll case. She pulled off her *apostolnik* and examined the swelling on the left side of her face. The right side of her head where Zeus had slammed her into the chair was actually caked with blood beneath her hair. She tried dabbing at it with a baby wipe, but it was too sticky and matted for the wipe to do anything more than hurt. With another wipe she cleaned between her legs, even inside herself as much as she could, though it stung like hell.

She wanted a shower, and she wanted these damned clothes off, but the bruising would be too alarming if Ola were to see her undressed. At last, she lay down next to Ola and curled around her, holding her little sleep-warmed hand for comfort.

Kirill was absent again in the morning, finally showing up close to lunchtime with the breakfast tray.

"Thank you." Love spoke to him curtly in angelic while Ola reached eagerly for her bowl of kasha. "Ola was getting very hungry." She gave Ola a spoon and sat her before the tray. "I need to ask you for something." Kirill followed reluctantly when she stepped over to the other side of the room. Love swallowed her pride, speaking in Russian to be clear. "I need…do you know what Postinor is?" She glanced up at him, but Kirill shook his head. "It's a pill for women. To prevent pregnancy…after."

Kirill's eyes bored into her as if he'd seen the Whore of Babylon. "Is mortal sin. I will not do such thing."

She hadn't really expected any other answer. Love returned his disdain in equal measure. "Then if I could have a hot shower and some clean clothes, I won't bother you further."

His brow furrowed with annoyance. "Why you need clean clothings? Is wash every week."

She studied his perplexed expression. "You really have no idea." Love pulled back the *apostolnik* and showed him the caked-in blood and the lump like a broad skipping stone beneath the deep cut on her scalp.

The monk's face blanched and he forgot about the angelic tongue completely as he touched his fingers to her head. "How did this happen?"

"How do you think?"

He shook his head, his eyes troubled. "Mr. Zey-us? But he is God's messenger. Why would he harm you?" Kirill's troubled expression changed to one of dread as Love fixed him with her stare, uncompromising. "No. He wouldn't. He couldn't have. Besides, I thought you...he told me..."

"If he told you anything happened between us with my consent, he's a liar."

A look of horror seized Kirill and she thought he might actually collapse under the weight of his dawning understanding. He pulled the woolen *skufia* from his head and held it to his chest, his hands twisting the fabric. "I sent you to him. I waited while he—" Kirill crossed himself and lowered his beryl blue eyes with shame. "I beg your forgiveness, Sister Lyubov." His voice fell to a whisper. "I should not have let this happen in God's house."

Love wondered whether God would be less offended if she'd been assaulted somewhere else, but she kept her mouth shut.

Kirill pulled on his beard, clearly agitated by the cognitive dissonance of his predicament. "I will bring you a clean *podryasnik* and *apostolnik* when I can get the washroom free. Your...other g-garments—" He stammered and blushed. "I can't get."

Love nodded and studied his woven sandals beneath the hem of his robe.

"I beg your forgiveness." His voice went even quieter. "I thought he only meant to talk to you. And then when he told me you—" Kirill swallowed as if he couldn't complete the thought. "I judged you. The Lord would not have done such a thing. And I punished the little one for a sin I had ascribed to you. *Pomilui mya greshnago.*" *Have mercy on me, a sinner.* Love didn't know whether he was speaking to her or to God. "I will come again when is possible." He had returned to the angelic tongue. "I pray for you, Sister Lyubov."

Love sighed as he left her. He could pray all he liked. Unless God came to him in a vision and told him to let her go, it was of little use to her.

The monk surprised her with a hot bath when he took her to the large washroom later. The eremites bathed in the frigid water of the islands to be closer to God, and her last few baths had been quick dunks, scrubbing as fast as she could, while she gave Ola only sponge baths to keep her from catching cold. But Kirill had apparently boiled and hauled water from the kitchen to fill the tub for her. Love asked him to take Ola with him so she wouldn't see the bruises, and Kirill complied with a grave expression.

He left clean clothes on a stool inside the washroom and told her to leave what she was wearing on the floor. "I will burn it," he said vehemently.

When Love undressed, she left her underwear folded in the pile.

Afterward, instead of taking them back to the cell, Kirill announced they were going for a walk. He led her out onto the grounds and Love shivered in surprise at the sharpness of the autumn wind as they strolled past the ancient stone buildings within the walled kremlin.

"How long have I been here?" she asked Kirill in angelic under her breath.

"Yesterday was the Feast of the Nativity of Mary."

Love remembered the feast from her school days and counted back. *Six weeks.* She looked up at the sky she'd only seen from the narrow hole in her cell wall for more than a month. It was a stunning blue, as if the world had been turned upside down and she was looking at the ocean. They'd just passed the equinox. The days would be getting swiftly shorter now.

"Are you letting us go?"

Kirill's eyes reflected profound conflict, searching hers as if she could tell him the answer. "I…I must trust in God's will."

"You can't believe any of this is God's will."

Ola struggled to get down, but Love was afraid she might trip in the tall grass and hurt herself on the ancient brick and stone of the venerable buildings.

"No, sweetheart," she murmured. "You can't get down."

Ola pointed insistently toward the glimpse of sea over the wall. "Mama." She hadn't asked for Anazakia in weeks. She was adamant now, patting Love's shoulder and pointing as if Love didn't understand this simple request. "La go Mama." It was the first sentence she'd put together spontaneously with herself as the subject.

"No, Ola. We can't go to Mama right now."

Ola began to cry, reaching with both arms toward where she believed her mother to be, as if she recognized the sea over which they'd come and remembered Anazakia was on the other side of it. "La go Mama," she wailed, squirming miserably in Love's arms. Love felt like a monster for refusing her.

"We must go in." The monk was apologetic but firm.

Love looked toward the stone path leading out of the walled enclosure, wondering if she could make a run for it, or if any tourists were still outside the fortress who might hear her if she screamed.

Kirill gave her a look of warning. "You will only frighten the child." He took her by the arm and steered her swiftly through a nearby door. The short walk in the fresh air was over.

Ola was inconsolable. Back in their room, she cried for hours, and nothing Love did to try to distract her had any effect. She kept repeating her new sentence as she sobbed against Love's neck, until Love herself thought she might cry. Outside their small window, the first storms of autumn were rolling across the island in heavy sheets of rain.

Sedmaya: **Hall of Echoes**
*from the memoirs of the Grand Duchess Anazakia
Helisonovna of the House of Arkhangel'sk*

On the morning after I'd seen the syla, I left Arkhangel'sk without saying good-bye. I knew Belphagor would attempt to dissuade me, and I couldn't bear the thought that Vasily would not.

I left a note saying only that I was going to St. Petersburg in search of Ola. There was no point explaining where I was bound. I would only be reinforcing Belphagor's suspicion that I was losing my mind.

I borrowed one of Love's telephones and I left its number, promising to contact them if I found any sign of Ola or the three who'd taken her. I wasn't quite sure how to use the little box, but I could find someone to show me if the need arose. I took the lighter coat I hadn't worn since we were last in St. Petersburg and left the heavy winter clothes of Arkhangel'sk behind. Because I couldn't make my way about by confounding the unwary or using sleight of hand as Belphagor did, I also took the stash of ruble bills he kept in a tin in the kitchen.

It was easy enough to slip past the Nephilim before daylight. As oppressive as their presence was, they were watching for anyone trying to get in, not one of us trying to get out.

In case they thought to pursue me, I'd decided to take a route they wouldn't expect, and I found one using Love's computer. Besides the train that had brought us here, there was really only one other possibility for travel out of Arkhangel'sk—I would have to fly by airplane. On such a flight, Ola had disappeared into the unknown, and I felt compelled to take the same journey to be near her in spirit. No one would be looking for me on a flight to the Solovetsky Islands. From there, I could take the ferry to the town of Kem, as Love and the Nephilim had, and board a different train altogether to St. Petersburg and Tsarskoe Selo. It was a roundabout way to get where I was going, but it would do.

The flight by airplane was nothing like soaring by wing.

With a handful of hours to wait between arrival on Bolshoi Solovetsky and the departure of the ferry, I wandered the island, touched by its haunting beauty. The walls of the kremlin surrounding the great monastery had been built with the massive stones found at hand, and they rose above the grassy hills as if from the center of a giant emerald within the sea. Above them, the silvery wooden tiles of its cupolas pointed the way toward Heaven. There were still late-summer visitors here, clustering in tour groups and boating along the canals connecting the island's lakes, but it wouldn't be long before these waterways would be frozen over, as would the sea itself.

From one of these tour groups, I heard a child crying, and it sounded so like Ola that my heart leapt. I ran to the sound, unable to control the irrational swell of hope and maternal anxiety, and found myself inside the kremlin walls. Black-clad monks crossed paths here with tourists in large, organized groups, while others wandered on their own, as I did, but there was no sign of the crying child.

I was being foolish. It was impossible that the acolytes of the god of Men could be harboring a stolen infant within these walls. The Malakim, in any case, wouldn't have hidden her away. It was Aeval who wanted Ola, and they would be mad to delay so long in this part of the world, even if the Grigori were preventing them from getting her to Heaven. Still, as improbable as it was, I was not quite able to shake the idea that Ola could be here somewhere.

Telling myself I was only curious about the place, I circled the grounds along the cobbled walks, scanning the ancient walls. The whitewashed chapels and living quarters nestling against the backdrop of the stone towers of the fortress and the azure blue of the sky possessed a serenity that was inexplicably heartbreaking. Throughout the enclosure, along grassy paths worn smooth by the soft soles of their sandals, the monks went about their business with silent reverence, and yet from time to time I could swear I still heard a crying child.

On the far side of the complex, the place seemed deserted. I studied the small, high windows of the monastic cells as the chilly wind streamed my hair across my face. Under the eaves of one of these dormitories, a wall cobbled together of ancient brick masonry and the massive stones of the island held a low, recessed arch. Within it, an iron door stood unguarded.

My heart began to pound. The door seemed to compel me, and I approached it. With a tentative grip, I turned the latch, and it opened with effort. A cloistered, musty smell with a hint of incense met me as I stepped inside and waited for my eyes to adjust to the darkness. At my feet, a narrow stone staircase descended below the ground. I no longer heard the crying, but then the thick walls had a muting effect.

"*Devushka.*" The soft voice behind me nearly made me topple down the steps. An elderly monk put a gentle hand on my shoulder to steady me as I turned. "This is not allowed, *devushka*. You must find your group. The monastery is closing to visitors now."

I blushed and gave him a respectful bob of my head. "*Izvinite.* I must have gotten turned around." I hesitated. "It's just that I thought I heard—"

An indignant wail interrupted me, and in the arch of the passage across from us, a young, toddling boy stomped his feet in the grip of a tantrum as his mother smacked his bottom. It was then I recognized that the crying I'd heard had been that of an older child and not an infant, and here was the most likely source. The realization hurt my heart and I hurried away to keep from dissolving into tears of my own, my wild, preposterous hope dashed to pieces against the stones.

While there was still time before I had to catch the ferry, I wanted to stand on the spot where Ola had last been seen—the spot where Belphagor had watched her disappearing into the distance in Vashti's arms. I took the dusty road through the village near the monastery toward the western shore of the island, passing through a quiet birch wood shrouded in mist and dotted with late season wildflowers, until I came to the deserted stretch of beach Belphagor had described south of the harbor.

I stood on the rocky shore, the wind whipping at my summer coat, and tried to imagine where Love and the Nephilim had been bound after Kem. The train might have taken them anywhere—but why? Why take her if they didn't mean to deliver her to Heaven or demand a ransom? Not knowing where she'd gone was killing me, but not knowing why…it was the question that haunted my dreams.

The deep jewel of the ocean was empty and still as glass, offering no answers. While I waited, storm clouds rolled in over the arctic waters, turning the sky the color of steel.

By the time I left Solovetsky on the ferry, rain was coming down in sheets. It drove us swiftly toward the shores of Kem, and with the cold, wet wind at our backs, we reached the small seafaring town in less than three hours. I waited nearly as long for a tram to take me to the train station, wishing now I'd brought the winter coat instead. At the station, only *platzcart* tickets were available to St. Petersburg. I found myself at length in a crowded car where there were no private compartments, only rows of open sleeping berths for the long ride through the stormy Russian night.

The rule of the *platzcart* seemed to be that sleeping was optional, and in fact might be considered rude. Travelers shared bottles of vodka, having apparently started on them some time ago, sitting together in loud groups of spontaneous parties among the bunks, with little regard to whose bunk the party moved to. To be polite, I drank a bit of vodka when it was offered to me, but I was feeling chilled from the rain, and I didn't want to let down my guard with so many strangers around me. I'd learned my lesson upon my first experience with the favored spirits of this world.

I rolled over in my bunk after a few hours and pretended to sleep to avoid further socializing, but it seemed as if the motion of the train were still the motion of the choppy arctic sea.

By morning, I was shivering and feverish, and by the time we arrived in St. Petersburg that afternoon, the *provodnitsa* nearly had to carry me from the train. Though I had no idea what I meant to do once I got there, I had to reach Tsarskoe Selo. The metro line that would take me to the *elektrichka* into the suburban parks of Tsarskoe Selo was adjacent to the train station, and I somehow managed to stumble onto the right car and exit at the right station in order to make the five o'clock train. It was standing room only, and I clung to a post near the door as commuters pushed past me, grumbling.

"*Suka*," someone muttered as I stumbled against the other standing passengers when the train lurched forward. My grip slipped from the post, and the words coming from the angry faces around me dissolved into a meaningless lake of sound.

"Open up, now, *devushka*. Just a little swallow." A sharp-tasting liquid was poured into my mouth, burning as it went down, and I coughed and choked. "There she is, now. She's coming around." Anxious faces peered down at me. They were faces I didn't know.

"Where's Helga?" I pushed away the spoon being held to my mouth. "I want my nurse."

"Maybe we should take her to the hospital after all."

"The note says to keep her here. No authorities."

My head felt heavy and I was burning up beneath a smothering layer of covers. I tried to push them off and sit up, but soft hands urged me down and covered me again.

"Lie still, *devushka*. You need to rest." An ice-cold cloth was laid against my forehead, and I tried to pull it off.

"Leave me alone, Maia!" Two years younger than Maia, I'd shared a room with her since infancy, and she was forever playing tricks on me.

"Stop fussing." Maia placed the cloth on my forehead again and held my hand away as I tried to remove it. "You're very ill."

I opened my eyes and tried to focus, though my lids felt as though they were on fire. It wasn't Maia's clover honey curls but my sister Ola's darker ones, like rich amber, that hovered over me. I closed my eyes again as her face began to blur.

"Ola," I murmured. "I've been looking everywhere for you. I had a terrible dream."

· · ·

The four of us tumbled in the snow at the foot of our mountain at Aravoth, laughing as our skirts tangled together. The silver trays we'd stolen from the kitchen of the hunting lodge had slipped from beneath us as we slid down the embankment; only Tatia had managed to hold onto hers, but she was sliding on her stomach behind it as it carried her down. Maia threw a snowball at Tatia, who was resting against Ola's stomach, and it struck her square in the face. With a shriek, Tatia scrambled over Ola to put snow down Maia's coat into her bodice.

"It wasn't me!" Maia laughed as she squirmed away. "Nazkia did it!"

Tatia's carefully pinned hair, clumped with snow, hung over her face beneath her fur cap as she scrambled back up the hill to me. I tried to climb away, my fur muff hanging from one hand, but Ola pinned me down and held me while Tatia filled my bodice with icy snow and I shrieked at the cold. Maia was laughing in delight at a safe distance below us.

"You'd better not sleep tonight, Maianka!" I squealed from beneath my grinning tormentors.

Ola's cap had fallen off and tumbled toward Maia, and Maia grabbed it and filled it with snow, clambering up the hill to pull it down over Ola's ears.

"You devil!" Ola shrieked and let go of me, and I took advantage of the opportunity to pull her down into the bank of snow by the knees, with my arms about her skirts. Tatia happily switched to tormenting Ola, and the three of us packed her bodice while she struggled, laughing too hard to put up a good fight. "Stop!" she gasped. "I'm a married woman. Show some respect!" She squealed helplessly as Tatia began to tickle her.

Tatia was merciless. "I'm sure Kae will warm you up back at the lodge, little missus!"

"No doubt." Laughing, Ola tried to scramble away while Maia and I grabbed for her feet. "You'd have to bury him in the snow to cool his blood."

"Virginal ears!" I cried in mock dismay, hands to the sides of my head.

"Poor little Nazkia!" Maia abandoned Ola to pounce on me. "You mustn't speak of hot blood in front of the baby, Ola! She's never been kissed!"

"Quick, cool her down!" cried Tatia. "Before she has a fit!" They fell on me once more, and I struggled in vain while my older sisters covered me in a pyramid of snowballs, drenching me to the core as the flakes began to fall on us once more.

• • •

"Fever's breaking." A cool hand brushed the damp hair from my face. I was shivering uncontrollably.

"She'll be all right. Let's get her back to bed, poor thing."

A man's strong arms lifted me out of the icy cold, and I put my own around his neck, resting my head on his shoulder as he carried me to a soft bed.

"I missed you, Kae," I murmured.

He patted my hand as the covers were drawn up about me. "Hush now, Anazakia. You're all right."

Warm and dry at last, I let my head sink into the pillow. I was so terribly tired.

The smell of *blinchiki* frying woke me and I opened my eyes, suddenly aware that I was famished. I was in a brightly colored bedroom with blue-and-silver-papered walls, the narrow wooden bed in which I lay draped with layers of cotton brocade and thick wool. I sat up and drew my knees to my chest beneath the covers, wondering how I'd gotten here.

"Ah, there she is!" A round-faced woman with short, auburn curls and bright, smiling blue eyes brought in a tray filled with *blinchiki*, tart *smetana*, and jam, along with a steaming cup of tea. "We thought we might have lost you for a bit there." She set the tray on my lap.

"Where is this? I don't remember…"

"I'm not surprised, dear. You were delirious when they brought you." She nodded at the tray. "Go ahead and eat. You need your strength." She pulled up a chair and sat next to the bed while I dove into the plate of little pancakes. "I'm Yulya Volfovna." The name seemed vaguely familiar, but I couldn't place it. "Your friend Belyi sent you here."

"Belyi?" She could only mean Belphagor, but I was surprised he'd have given his name that way. It was so close to Beli, Vasily's private pet name for him. Both of them had been somewhat mortified when Ola picked it up. "I don't remember him sending me."

"You collapsed at the train station. A couple of boys searched your pockets for identification and found this." She took a folded piece of paper from her apron and handed it to me. Belphagor had given me the note more than two years ago when we first came to St. Petersburg, escaping Heaven. About to face certain death at the hands of the Seraphim, he'd written down the address of the only person he could trust—an address in Tsarskoe Selo. I must have missed it when I'd transferred Belphagor's callstone to my winter coat.

"He was a boarder of mine a few years ago," said Yulya. "Down on his luck, poor dear. I grew very fond of him." She nodded at the note. "It says to keep you from the *militsiya*. I gather you're in a bit of trouble, as he was then. You can count on my discretion."

"Thank you."

"Drink your tea, dear. You need to get some fluids into you. It was all we could do to get you to swallow a few ice chips while you were in the fever."

I took her advice and drank the sweet, black tea. "How long was I ill?"

"The boys brought you nearly a week ago. I was afraid your fever had gone too high at one point. We put you into a bathtub packed with ice. Perhaps we should have taken you to the hospital, but the note… well, thankfully, you managed to pull through."

Yulya was insistent that I properly convalesce. When I told her my daughter had been taken by her nanny and I had to find her, she expressed dismay and sympathy, but asked how I meant to go about this. I had to admit I had no idea, other than the vague answer that something had driven me to Tsarskoe Selo. She insisted I'd be better equipped to begin my search once I'd gotten my strength up, and I had to agree. I could barely walk to the washroom that first day after my fever broke.

She sat with me to try to retrace Love's steps and work through where she might have gone. I didn't bother to tell her of the Nephilim, as I would have had to leave out much. Instead, I told her Love had taken Ola to a restroom on a trip to Solovki and never returned. When I said we were living in Arkhangel'sk, Yulya looked at me with such stark perplexity, saying, "*Pochimu*?" that I had to laugh. Why, indeed? Fate seemed the only answer.

She brought me books of photography to look at while I rested, and one was a souvenir book of the imperial parks at Tsarskoe Selo. This picturesque setting among the trees seemed a likely spot to begin my search for the syla. When I was feeling strong enough, I asked Yulya how to get there.

She smiled and told me we were three blocks away. Insistent that

I was still too weak to go alone, Yulya walked with me to the grounds of the palaces. Like the Winter Palace in St. Petersburg, these, too, were eerily familiar. The Alexander Palace bore a striking resemblance to our Summer Palace at the foot of the mountains of Aravoth, and the Yekaterina was a stunning copy of the Camaeline, where Kae and Ola had spent the brief days of their marriage.

I humored Yulya by touring the blue confection of the Yekaterina Palace, feeling every interminable moment of the passing time but uncertain how to separate myself from my well-meaning host. Wandering the grounds among the burnished filigree of the dying trees, Yulya led me over a bridge above a mossy canal and into a more wooded area. It was the perfect setting for the syla, and I considered how to politely ask Yulya to leave me here alone. I doubted they would come if someone else was with me—if they'd come at all, since it wasn't the time of year in which I customarily saw them. But the words "Tsarskoe Selo" had been quite clear, and I could feel something in the air, something that said I'd come to the right place.

"Have you ever seen a fairy ring?" Yulya asked the question abruptly as we stared down at the algaed green of the canal. Her eyes twinkled when my head sprang up. "You look as though you're searching for something you can't see. Perhaps the thing you're looking for isn't in this world at all."

Wordlessly, I followed her along a narrowing trail departing from the structured gravel paths of the park proper. I wondered if she'd spoken euphemistically or if she indeed knew of the Unseen World, but I didn't dare ask. The woods closed in around us, and the sky was becoming dark with clouds when we entered a small circle of trees where the branches bent overhead to keep the clearing secluded. A small grassy meadow opened within it like a hidden grotto. In its center rose a perfect ring of mushroom clusters like the one that marked the place I'd first met the syla in Novgorod.

I jumped as an announcement rang out over a loudspeaker that the park was closing for the day, but Yulya took my hand and led me forward to stand inside the ring. The trees around us began to move in the wind, the colored leaves fluttering from the branches over our heads like giant flakes of burnished metal as the late afternoon sun set them alight. With the breeze came a quiet, rhythmic whisper: *Padshaya Koroleva*. It was what the syla had called me before: the Fallen Queen.

The trees shimmered, vague shapes dancing in the light between the leaves as if they were superimposed over something else. I looked to Yulya to see if she was aware of what I saw, and she smiled back at me. The landscape shimmered once more before disappearing completely.

We were no longer standing in the wooded parks of Tsarskoe Selo, but in a vast, empty hall with walls tiled in brilliant, golden amber and a ceiling vaulted with sweeps and curls of gold. It was the inspiration for the opulent Amber Room I'd just seen in the palace, but on so much grander a scale that I could scarcely comprehend it.

I clung to Yulya's hand, dizzy and disoriented, though she seemed perfectly at ease. As I took in more of our surroundings, a cluster of graceful beings at the far end of the hall became visible. With hair of amber gold and shimmering bronze skin, they were dressed in garments so similar in color that at first I'd thought them part of the room itself. They curtsied deeply in my direction.

"Go on, *devushka*." Yulya released my hand. "They've been waiting for you."

I approached them, walking over a floor that was also tiled in amber. A dozen of the shimmering syla stood under the arched entrance, all genuflecting.

Such reverence always made me uncomfortable. "Please. Don't bow to me."

They rose and spoke as one. "You are Queen."

One of them stepped forward to speak for the rest. "The syla are grateful Queen has come. We lose many sisters to fire angels, but Hall of Echoes they cannot enter, so we ask Queen to come to syla when we cannot come to Queen."

"I saw your sisters," I said sorrowfully. "I couldn't help."

"The Queen will help. That is why you come."

"But I came because…I thought…" My face prickled with heat as I realized how selfish my assumption had been. I'd imagined they'd called me here to tell me where to find Ola, expecting them to help me while their sisters were being slaughtered. "Of course," I amended. "I'm not sure how, but I'll try to help in any way I can."

The syla's eyes softened with compassion at my fumbling. "You look for Little Queen. The syla have seen Little Queen."

My heart leapt. "You've seen her? Where is she?"

"We see Little Queen surrounded by a sea of white. Little Queen shall take the flower of the fern."

My hopes fell. They'd seen this before. It was what they told me after Ola was born. "That's why they've taken her. Your sisters told the Seraphim what they'd seen." It sounded as if I were blaming them, and I stopped, flustered.

"Come." The syla took my hand. "Walk with syla in *Polnochnoi Sud*." *The Midnight Court.* It was a term I hadn't heard before.

"Yulya…" I turned back, but she'd disappeared.

"*Tyotyushka* has seen many times."

I gaped at them. "Yulya is your aunt?"

The other syla laughed, the sound bubbling like a pebbled brook throughout the Hall of Echoes.

"She is mother to Little Brother. The syla call her auntie."

I was baffled by this but followed them to their *Polnochnoi Sud*.

A series of arches opened into a hall even more immense than the first. The opulence was nearly incomprehensible. The court was lined with columns covered in bands of sapphire, emerald, and peridot, rising from a floor that seemed to be made of black onyx, like a calm, deep ocean at our feet. The hall had no ceiling but was open to a sky that could not be the one above the Alexander Park, for this one was vast and dark, and full of stars.

Unfamiliar constellations winked in the night sky, and on the horizon in all directions, showers of stars fell to earth between the open columns. Against these streaks of intermittent light, the darkness showed nothing of the forest surroundings that ought to be there, only what seemed to be a velvety greensward—endless, rolling, and empty.

Between the two largest columns at the far end of the hall, a high-backed chaise covered in creamy velvet dominated the daïs instead of a throne, and twelve ornate silver chairs were arranged in a semicircle around it. My guide led me forward along the narrow runner that spanned the length of the room—like Aeval's decorative touches in Elysium's Winter Palace, it was in the same pale cream—and stopped before the platform.

"Is where Queen presides. Midnight Court of Man's transgressions. Our brothers build for Aeval when Man begins to spread seed over lands of syla and leshi."

"Leshi?"

"Brothers of syla. They tend the trees. Aeval says build a court of trees, and leshi build."

I turned about in astonishment. "This is built of trees?"

"Outside is trees. Inside is Unseen. Fallen Queen steps through trees. Now she sees. Just as only Queen sees when syla walk in world of Man, but all can see syla in *Nezrimyi Mir.*"

I shook my head, not really understanding. "But what is it exactly—the Midnight Court of Man's transgressions?"

"Women seek justice of Midnight Court when they do not find in world of Man. Aeval answers. But no more. *Polnochnoi Sud* stands empty one hundred summers. When syla will not give the *tsvetok paporotnika*, Queen Aeval no more comes."

"And now she wants my child to get the flower back."

The syla didn't disagree.

"But Ola doesn't have the flower of the fern."

"Little Queen will have. Little Queen will take."

I couldn't imagine how Ola was supposed to take the locket from Helga. She was only an infant. How could she take something Helga guarded so jealously? How would she even know to take it? If Aeval had known Helga possessed it, she would have simply taken it herself.

"I don't see how that's possible."

The syla smiled as if I were a child and couldn't comprehend. "Syla do not see how, only will." Leading me onto the daïs where her sisters now sat upon the silver chairs, she took the empty seat. "Just as syla do not see how *Padshaya Koroleva* will stop fire angels from consuming syla."

"You want *me* to stop the Seraphim? But they're of a higher order than my kind. I have no power over them." This wasn't entirely true. I'd vanquished them once from the world of Man, but there had been only three of them, and it hadn't been my element alone that commanded them. And even if it had, vanquishing couldn't stop them forever.

"Heaven sees order where is no order. Power comes from heart, and *Koroleva* will not be alone. The syla see Fallen Queen within the circle of ice and fire."

Ice and fire. There it was again. "What does that mean? What circle?"

"Syla do not know the meaning of all things we see. We see only *pryazha* on spindle of queensdaughters. In the circle of ice and fire, the Fallen Queen shall spill the blood of fallen angel. Then fire angels stop."

My own blood ran cold. "I won't. I won't take the blood of a fallen angel."

She shrugged, as if my objections were immaterial. "The syla do not tell Fallen Queen what she must do, only that she will."

I shook my head, horrified. Whom was I meant to kill? The only Fallen I knew were Vasily and Belphagor, unless it was one of the Grigori or Nephilim she meant.

The syla seemed to guess what I was I thinking. "Fallen angel is one close to *Koroleva*'s heart."

Vosmaya: **The Things We Do for Love**

Beside Vasily in the guest bed of Dmitri's St. Petersburg flat, Belphagor was sleeping soundly. Vasily hated him for it—a hatred added to the long list of hatreds that filled him of late, nailed into place like planks on the windows of a wintering dacha over the jagged hole in his heart. How could Belphagor sleep? How could he go about his days as if the world hadn't turned upside down and shaken him out into a blackened, burned-out sky? How could anyone do anything? Vasily could no longer remember how he'd once functioned or cared about anything at all.

Both Belphagor and Anazakia had gone on breathing, eating, and sleeping as though these motions were not like walking barefoot over shards of glass. Vasily wanted to scream at them—to beat at them. Taking a swing at Belphagor on that terrible night was the only moment he'd felt something other than despair.

Lying with his back to Belphagor in the borrowed bed, Vasily flexed his knuckles. He could still remember how Belphagor's jaw had felt against them. He'd never done it before; Belphagor was the one who expressed his feelings with the strength of his hands. Belphagor had administered the sweet pain of correction that kept Vasily grounded, had let him know he was alive, and that Belphagor's passions were aroused at the sight of him. He hadn't touched Vasily that way in nearly two years.

The last thing Belphagor had done before leaving on his fool's errand to Heaven was to measure the strength of his desire upon Vasily's flesh with a freshly cut birch switch. That night had been a reconciliation after years apart over a foolish argument and stubbornness on both their parts. Vasily had gone to sleep in his arms feeling whole again after such a long time of incompleteness, and had woken to find Belphagor gone. He hadn't returned until Vasily stormed Heaven to get him back nearly ten months later—ten months during which Vasily had taken comfort in the arms of an angel and she'd given him a daughter.

Everything came back to Ola. Never in his life had he considered having a child. He couldn't have been less interested in them; they weren't part of his world. He was angry at first when Anazakia told him, acting like a fool. And then he'd held Ola in his arms, regarding him with wide, lapis eyes like an alabaster doll. She'd stolen his heart. And Belphagor had let them take her away.

Vasily knew this wasn't fair. Rationally, he knew it. But there was a part of him that suspected Belphagor was jealous, a petty voice in his head that said Belphagor had wanted her gone. How would he have felt if it had been Bel who'd slept with Nazkia, if Bel and Nazkia'd had a child? He didn't like to think of the answer. He knew he was judging Belphagor by the worst of himself, which he also didn't like to think of. But none of that mattered now. All that mattered was Ola.

He'd come with Belphagor to St. Petersburg when Dmitri had acquiesced in the face of Anazakia's disappearance because it was at least some kind of forward motion. Sitting and waiting in the crypt-like silence of their unhappy dacha for word of Ola to come from others had been driving him mad. Anazakia had seen something on Love's computer that sent her here. Something Belphagor had missed.

That she'd gone without him only added to Vasily's bitterness. He'd often felt superfluous when it came to parenting Ola. The natural bond between mother and daughter was something to which he could only be a spectator. Never having experienced a mother's love himself, it mystified him, and he felt inadequate in comparison. Ola seemed to prefer even Belphagor's attentions to his own, always quieter around

Vasily, always staring up at him with that serious face, where Belphagor made her laugh.

Vasily sighed, tossing fitfully. He looked over his shoulder. Belphagor was peacefully sleeping. *Sleeping, the bastard.*

• • •

"This is getting us nowhere, just like before."

Belphagor buttered his toast while Dmitri's boyfriend, Lev, poured him a cup of tea. Vasily was speaking to him at least. It was something.

"We've talked to every gypsy who'll talk to us, Vasya. We've interrogated every damned Nephil in Russia and beyond."

Lev joined them at the table. "Has she answered her phone yet?"

"Ola?" Vasily asked incredulously.

"Anazakia." Belphagor had to bite back a smile. It wasn't funny, really. Vasily was so sick with worry that he was never more than half there at any given time. But the tension of the past weeks was threatening to come out of Belphagor in inappropriate ways. He answered Lev when Vasily said nothing. "No, she hasn't."

"Does she know to turn it on?"

Belphagor shrugged as he bit into his toast. "Maybe not." He spoke with his mouth full, knowing it drove Vasily mad. "Who would she have ever called?"

"So it could be as simple as that. Maybe she just doesn't know you're trying to reach her."

Vasily stared at his uneaten breakfast. "She had no business going off on her own."

"We don't know what she saw on Love's computer."

"That's my fucking point, Belphagor!" He snatched a pack of cigarettes from the table and went out onto the fire escape, slamming the wooden shutters behind him.

Belphagor cringed at the sound and almost dropped his teacup as he set it down on the saucer. "I've never seen him like this."

"I've never seen *you* like this." Lev put his hand over Belphagor's around the teacup. "Are you all right?"

Belphagor clutched Lev's hand. Even this touch was more than he'd had from Vasily in months. "No. Not really. I'm responsible for all this. I lost his little girl."

"Don't do that. It could have been any one of you that bitch Vashti drugged."

"But it wasn't any one of us, Lev. It was me. I insisted on taking Ola on that stupid cruise."

"It wasn't stupid." Lev squeezed his hand. "You had a nanny and two Nephilim with you who were supposed to keep the child safe."

Belphagor tried to pull away, but Lev wouldn't let him.

"I know how you are, Bel. That child may not be your own blood, but I can see in your eyes you're as broken to pieces over this as Vasily is. You love her."

"How could I not?" Belphagor whispered. "She's like a little drop of him. A beautiful little drop. You wouldn't believe how beautiful she is."

"I wish I'd been there to see her with Dmitri. I wanted to come, but he thought it might complicate things."

"I know." Belphagor's voice was rough as he composed himself. "I know you did, Lyova." He looked up and realized Vasily had come back inside. Belphagor snatched his hand away from Lev's with a guilty start, and Vasily gave him a cool look, devoid of any feeling.

The doorbell buzzed, dispelling the tense moment, and Dmitri came out of the front bedroom to answer it. With an intercom that worked as well as it had in Soviet times, there was no way to ascertain from their third-floor flat who was at the door, so Dmitri ran down the four flights, as one of them usually did.

When he came back, a face Belphagor hadn't seen in nearly as long as it had been since he'd seen Lev—and had never expected to see again—appeared behind Dmitri in the doorway. The lanky blond, still wearing his hair in a rather un-Russian ponytail, grinned at Belphagor.

"Mikhail Lesovich." Dmitri announced him somewhat dubiously.

"He says he knows you?"

The visitor stepped inside without an invitation as Belphagor rose to greet him. "I heard you were in town," he said.

"It's all right," Belphagor reassured Dmitri, whose hand hovered at the pocket where he kept his knife. "Misha." He greeted him, baffled at the young man's presence, as Misha clasped his hand warmly. "How is your mother?"

"Same as always. Trying to fix me up with a nice girl."

Belphagor laughed and then cut it short as Vasily shot him a look of disbelief. This was truly bad timing. He'd never told Vasily about Misha.

"Actually, she's the one who sent me." Misha's moss-green eyes were curious as he watched the silent exchange between them.

"Yulya Volfovna sent you?" Belphagor couldn't imagine why his former landlady would be seeking him out.

"She said to give you this." Misha handed him a folded note.

Belphagor opened it and stared in amazement. It was a note of introduction he'd written himself, intending to send Anazakia to Yulya if anything happened to him. He'd written it before Anazakia had even learned a word of Russian, repeating the address on the back in angelic script.

"Where did she get this?"

"From the girl you gave it to, I expect. Although it says 'take care of the boy.' That was a bit confusing. Maybe she took it from someone else? She says her name is Anazakia."

Belphagor shook his head, smiling with relief. "No. No, I gave it to her." There was no point in explaining to Misha that Anazakia had been disguised as a boy to hide her from the firehounds of Heaven. "So she's there? Anazakia's with your mother?"

Misha nodded. "She fell ill on the train from Murmansk and someone found the note in her pocket and brought her to Mother's. She was delirious with fever for a couple of days, but she's all right now."

"Murmansk?" Belphagor shook his head, baffled. "Well, thank Heaven she's all right. We were worried. She hasn't answered her phone."

"She told Mother about your nanny taking off with your kid. I hope you find her soon." His eyes were curious. "I have to say, I was a little surprised to hear you're a father."

"No—" Belphagor began, but Vasily interrupted him.

"She's mine." His eyes were stony, as if Misha had challenged him. "It's my daughter we're looking for."

"Oh. Well, that makes more sense. You must be Kae."

Vasily looked as if he might lunge at Misha, the red heat in his eyes dangerously close to the surface, enough that it might fall within the visible range of a human. "What did you say?"

Misha stepped back in alarm and threw a look at Belphagor.

"This is Vasily." Belphagor put a hand on Vasily's arm and was violently shaken off.

Misha's eyes registered understanding. It was after Vasily left him that Belphagor had fallen to the world of Man and ended up sleeping off an ugly night of drinking in an alleyway beside Yulya's Pushkin flat. He'd told Misha about Vasily when they'd first slept together, able to think of nothing else.

"Sorry. I just thought… She was repeating that name in her fever."

Fists clenched white at his sides, Vasily left the room.

Misha shrugged apologetically. "I'm sorry. I don't know what I said."

"Don't worry about it. Kae's her cousin, and Vasily doesn't like him much." Belphagor realized they were all still standing awkwardly in the foyer. "Why don't you come in and have some tea?"

Misha slipped his feet out of his shoes and into a pair of guest *tapochki*, then followed them back into the kitchen, where Lev heated the electric teapot. When Belphagor introduced Misha, Lev gave Belphagor a knowing look. He was well acquainted with Belphagor's taste.

Vasily confronted him later as they were packing up in the guestroom to head for Pushkin. "Just who on Earth *haven't* you slept with?"

Belphagor took comfort in the fact that Vasily still cared enough to be jealous. "I've fallen many times." He was aware of the unintentional double-entendre. "You know that. It was a long time ago."

Vasily tossed a duffel bag at him, hitting Belphagor in the chest. "Can't have been that long, Belphagor. He's barely got hair on his lip. How old was he, twelve?"

Belphagor set the bag down on the bed. "Don't be crude. He's older than he looks. He was older than you were when I met you."

Vasily scowled. "You really are an old letch. I had no idea just how old until Dmitri mentioned something about the Stalin era."

Belphagor's face flushed with embarrassment and anger. "You never asked how old I was when you got down on your knees."

It was Vasily's turn to blaze red, which he did to his pupils, the flames of his element a warning behind his glare.

"Do you really want to know, Vasya? I'll tell you how old I am. As near as I can remember, I'm one hundred and ten."

The fire went out of Vasily's eyes as if Belphagor had thrown water on them. "One hundred and ten?"

"One hundred and ten. The Bolsheviks had just taken power the first time I fell." Belphagor folded his arms, meeting Vasily's dumbstruck look with a challenge, daring him to show his revulsion. "So you'll pardon me if there are a few men in my past. If I wasn't exactly an angelic virgin when you came to me."

Vasily began packing the bag with deliberate movements, back to avoiding his eyes. "Not all of them came before me, Bel. Certainly not that...*Misha*."

"Since I met you, there've been fewer than you think. Misha was after you left. He reminded me of you."

"That doesn't make me feel any better." The gravelly murmur said he was done being angry.

"As it turns out, it didn't make me feel any better, either." Belphagor reached to touch the row of spiked piercings at Vasily's neck, but he ducked away. "You don't know how sorry I am. If I could take back that day, that stupid trip to Solovetsky—"

"Don't." Vasily's voice was a brusque warning that Belphagor wouldn't like his response if he continued.

Before they left for the train to Pushkin, Dmitri pulled Belphagor aside in the kitchen. "You're sure about this Misha? I'm getting a weird vibe from him."

"I'm sure. He's just weird because of Vasily. I trust him."

Dmitri looked toward the foyer. "I didn't want to say anything in front of Vasily and get his hopes up, but we may have a lead on Ola." He held up his hand at Belphagor's expression. "Don't get excited. I don't know anything yet. But I just might have a defector from Zeus's clan. He says he's willing to meet with me if I'll guarantee him asylum. Which I haven't done yet."

Belphagor answered without a moment's hesitation. "Do it."

"He might be someone who collaborated in the kidnapping. We won't be able to punish him if he's given asylum."

"I don't care. I want her back. Whatever it takes."

Dmitri nodded and squeezed his shoulder. "Call us when you get to Pushkin and let us know what Anazakia's found. I won't make a final determination until I hear from you." He let his hand linger for a moment. "I can't tell you how awful I feel about sending Vashti and Zeus. If I'd had any idea—"

"Of course you didn't." Belphagor covered his hand.

"I didn't know much about Zeus," Dmitri admitted. "But Vashti vouched for him and I would have trusted her with my life. It's just crazy. I've known her forever. If you hadn't told me she'd drugged you and taken the baby herself, I never would have believed she was part of it. I just can't understand how she could have gone along with this."

"They were sleeping together." Belphagor had an eye for that sort of thing.

"Oh." Dmitri grimaced. "Well. Shit."

The train ride to Pushkin took less than an hour, but between Vasily's stony silence and Misha's self-conscious chatter, it seemed interminable. Yulya greeted Belphagor warmly when they arrived at her flat, teary-eyed and hugging him as if he were her own flesh and blood. She plied him with *vafli* and tea, insisting he and Vasily sit and eat before they could get a word in edgewise. Anazakia, she said, had gone to the park.

"She wanted to see the palaces." Yulya pulled out more boxes of wafers in different flavors. "You boys have your tea, and then we'll walk over and meet her there."

"The park?" Vasily frowned, though even he couldn't resist Yulya's insistence and was eating his wafers obediently. "Why is she at a park? She didn't come to Tsarskoe Selo for sightseeing. She's supposed to be looking for Ola."

"She's been very ill. She's made herself sick with worry. I told her she needed the air, and I think a little time at the park will do her good, give her a fresh perspective. It will do you all some good." She pushed a box of cookies at Belphagor. "Eat them. I'll get fat."

"So you want *me* to get fat."

Yulya gave him a reproachful slap on his upper abs. "As if you could. Skinny as a rail."

When they'd satisfied her by making a serious dent in the sweets and finishing their tea, they headed out. Yulya took Belphagor's arm as they walked along the leaf-strewn sidewalks in the crisp autumn air, and Vasily followed, visibly unhappy to be paired with Misha.

"You've been very naughty not to visit." She gave Belphagor's arm a squeeze.

"I've been out of town."

"Yes, your Anyushka mentioned. Whatever were you thinking, living in Arkhangel'sk?"

Belphagor shrugged. "It's a long story."

"Misha's missed your company."

Belphagor thought he detected a note of disapproval, and he glanced at her, worried. He'd be mortified if she knew about the relationship; she was certain to view it as a betrayal of her trust—or something worse.

Yulya was smiling her sweet, motherly smile. "But you've been busy with your new baby."

"Oh, not me," he said quickly. "Vasily's the father. I'm just the... uncle."

Yulya raised an eyebrow but said nothing more.

Crossing under a stone arch beneath the golden spires of the tsars' chapel, they arrived at the grounds of the palace parks. Yulya led them past statues posed like Greek nymphs in the classical gardens, and then into a grove of fiery-painted trees, the orange and gold fallen leaves forming a thick carpet at their feet. The trail, off the beaten path, ended in a small glade where branches stretched overhead across the steely autumn sky.

"Where is she?" Vasily glanced around. "What are we doing here?"

Yulya let go of Belphagor's arm with a smile and stepped back from the center of the glade where she'd led them. Belphagor looked down at his feet and realized they were surrounded by a profusion of mushrooms that made a circular mound in the heart of the clearing. Misha grabbed his hand, and then grabbed Vasily's before the other demon could protest, murmuring something in a language Belphagor didn't recognize. The trees around them shimmered with light as though the sun had broken through the clouds. He felt suddenly faint, and stumbled onto one knee with his free hand to the ground. He pulled his other hand from Misha's and looked up to rebuke him, only to see they weren't in the glade at all. They were surrounded by sparkling walls of amber.

Vasily jerked away from Misha and stared at the glittering golden hall. "What the hell is going on? Where are we?"

Misha's eyes were fairly glowing with merriment. In fact, they *were* glowing, a fluorescent, brilliant green. His blond hair now had a greenish cast to it as well, twining down his back in a ponytail of vine-like ropes that gave him an even greater resemblance to Vasily. Though it was hard to be certain in the golden light of the luminescent amber, his skin appeared to have a tinge of greenish blue like a piece of pale, striated jade.

"Welcome to the Unseen World. But then, you're familiar with your own unseen world, aren't you?"

Belphagor straightened. "You knew."

"And you didn't." Misha shook his head. "I thought you might have guessed."

"What are you?" Vasily demanded.

"Leshi."

Belphagor stared at him, astonished. "You're a wood spirit?"

"Half, rather," Misha amended. "Mother's human."

Vasily was scowling at them both. "Why did you bring us here?"

Misha gave him a dismissive glance that suggested he was much more comfortable in his own element than he'd been in the world of Man. "You wanted to be taken to Anazakia. This is where she is." He turned and walked toward the arcade along the far wall, his lithe body sensual and relaxed. Belphagor and Vasily had no choice but to follow.

• • •

Vasily was startled by Anazakia's appearance when Misha brought them to her. The leshi had led them through countless halls, each more opulent and empty than the last. The hall in which they found Anazakia seemed to be in the open air, except the sky above was the pale, watery blue of a spring morning. Its arcade columns were the trunks of living trees decorated with moss and vines, and its floor a carpet of grass of the deepest velvet green. A mass of wild roses grew in a carefully directed chaos about a sapphire pool, and Anazakia was reclining on the ground beside it, staring into the water.

Draped in a long, silk dress in the color of flame against the honey gold of the soft curls about her shoulders, she seemed thinner and paler than she'd been a week ago. She didn't look up until they were standing over her, and when she lifted her eyes, they reflected the deep blue of the water beside her.

"Vasily?" She blinked at him as if in the grip of a dream.

His knees went weak like a schoolboy's and he forgot why he'd come here. He dropped to the grass beside her and took her hand, hardly aware that Misha had kept walking and Belphagor had followed him. "Nazkia."

"What are you doing here?"

"I came looking for you. I was worried about you."

"You were?" Her eyes glistened with tears as if this were the last thing she'd expected him to say. "I thought you were angry with me."

Vasily pulled her close and breathed in the sun-warmed scent of her. "Why would I be angry with you?"

"I don't remember. I lost something…"

An anxious feeling tugged at the back of Vasily's mind. There was something he needed to find, too, but the scent of flowers was making his head thick and he couldn't recall what ought to be bothering him. It felt so good just to let go. He sank onto the grass and pulled Anazakia down with him, and she rested her head against his chest as he put one arm behind his head for a pillow.

"Never mind." He twirled one of her curls about his finger. "Whatever it was, we'll think of it later."

• • •

Belphagor walked beside Misha through a hall of mirrors that reflected the leshi's unnaturally green eyes from all sides. Misha smiled and held out his hand, and Belphagor took it. He wanted to touch more of him and couldn't think why he hadn't already.

"You seem tired, Belyi." Misha rubbed his thumb along the bones of Belphagor's hand.

"Tired? I suppose I am. I feel as if I haven't relaxed in ages."

"I can see that." Misha's eyes were sad for a moment. "Come. I know just the thing for you." He opened a door in one of the mirrored panels of the corridor onto a cool, moonlit terrace overlooking a calm Mediterranean shore. It was furnished with a reclining couch, piled with pillows, and draped with silk and velvet in soothing colors of soft greens and steel blues.

"Take off your clothes," Misha murmured in his ear.

Belphagor slipped out of his leather jacket, letting it fall onto the tiles of the terrace, and sat down on the couch to pull off his boots. He stripped down to his skin without hesitation.

Misha stroked his arm. "Lie down. On your stomach."

Belphagor obeyed, and Misha made a soft sound of surprise as he straddled Belphagor's thighs.

"Who did this to you, Belyi?" He stroked the deep scars that raked Belphagor's back.

"An angel," murmured Belphagor, relaxing under his touch.

"Figures." Misha spread his hands over Belphagor's skin, the coolness of them easing every tension, and whispered in his ear. "Let me take care of you. You just lie still." The vine-like hair dangled over Belphagor's shoulders. Misha began to kiss his back, moving slowly down his spine, and Belphagor sighed. "You're mine now, Belyi, and you don't need to worry about anything," he said against his skin. "You belong to me."

· · ·

Zeus's latest visit caught Love off guard. He'd let himself into her cell while she was sleeping, waking her with a hand against her mouth.

"Be quiet," he whispered in her ear. "You don't want to wake the baby."

She was lying on her side and he'd climbed onto the cot behind her. Love tried to shove him away, but Ola stirred, and Zeus pulled up her robe, unconcerned with what Ola might witness. Love lay still, terrified that Ola would wake, and let him do as he pleased, one hand against the wall to keep the cot from rocking.

"Good girl," he murmured when he was done. "I like that you've stopped wearing underwear. Did you do that just for me?" He buttoned up and leaned down once more to whisper to her, his breath hot against her ear. "The really great thing is, Nephilim are only fertile with other Nephilim. We can have as much fun together as we like."

When he was gone, Love pulled down her robe and stared at the ceiling, her hand to her mouth to keep from crying aloud. She lay awake until Kirill came with breakfast.

As he set up the tray, he paused and observed her. "Something is wrong?"

Love glanced at Ola, who was yawning sleepily, only half awake. "Do you believe in demons?"

He answered in Russian. "The Lord allows us to be tempted by evil spirits. If we walk in Christ's light, we will not fear them."

"What if they come into one's room in the middle of the night? What does the Lord expect us to do then?"

"I don't understand."

"Zeus was here."

"Here? He came here?"

"While I was sleeping."

Kirill's face turned white and he nearly dropped the tray on the floor. "He is not to do this!" he exclaimed in angelic. "I tell him not to do this!"

"Apparently, he does what he wants." Love lowered her voice to a whisper. "You have to let us out of here, Kirill. You know this isn't right. God cannot want this."

Kirill pulled at his beard, his face twisted in an agony of conflict. "I will pray."

"You do that," Love said bitterly.

She hadn't expected him to do anything more, but the next morning when he came with the tray, Kirill placed a small white pill on her palm.

Love picked it up. "What's this?"

"I have pray. I pray all night." There were dark hollows under his bloodshot eyes that suggested this wasn't hyperbole. "God does not answer." He looked down at her hand and closed her fingers over the pill. "I bring what you ask for."

He'd brought her the morning-after pill.

"This is wrong." Kirill was shaking. "But what God allows of His messenger is more wrong."

Love didn't bother to try to convince him Zeus wasn't God's messenger. "Thank you."

"Do not thank me. I have condemned you. I have condemned us both."

Love stared at the pill after he'd gone. Zeus's delusion about their reproductive compatibility notwithstanding, she was grateful to have it. She wondered if she should just ask Kirill for the box of Postinor to avoid having this uncomfortable scene every time she needed it. When she realized what she was thinking, that she'd accepted in her head that being raped by Zeus had become a part of her life, it was all she could do not to kick the breakfast tray into the wall.

Ola was smiling up at her, eating her piece of toast.

She held the toast up to Love. "Lub eat."

Love took a bite to amuse her and Ola giggled. She couldn't let this happen any longer. She could not allow Zeus to touch her again in front of Ola.

• • •

Zeus had smelled of another woman. From the narrow bed they shared, Vashti watched him through the open door to the tiny bathroom while he showered. He seemed pleased with himself. He'd come back late from a meeting with the monk, he said. But he didn't smell of monk. He smelled of pussy. He'd fucked Vashti enthusiastically as always, perhaps more enthusiastically, but the scent was undeniable, and it was not her own.

She confronted him when he came out of the shower. "Are you fucking that gypsy?"

He stood before her, naked and dripping onto the thick carpets they'd laid down on the wood floors to cut the cold as winter came on like a bracing knife.

"Why the hell would I fuck a gypsy when I can fuck you?"

"I don't know." Vashti flashed a gold spark of radiance at him in anger. "Why the hell would you?"

"You're being paranoid." Zeus picked up his towel and came toward her as he dried off. He climbed over her on the bed and kissed her, holding her down when she tried to pull her mouth away from him. "It's going to be a long winter, Vash. Don't go all hormonal on me."

Vashti pushed him off. "And what about that? I thought we only had to stay until the freeze. Now you say we're going to be stuck here in this primitive village through a goddamned arctic winter?"

"Brother Kirill is having trouble controlling the girl." Zeus looked unconcerned, almost smug, as he dressed. "I think the Party is reconsidering the wisdom of keeping the child alive, but until the leader comes around to the sensible solution, we're to make certain she's secure. And since the monk doesn't have the balls to ensure that, we're stuck here." Zeus pulled on his boots and bundled up to go out. "Since you're obviously having your period, I'm going to the tavern for a pint."

Vashti grabbed a glass from the nightstand and hurled it at his head as he went out, and the glass shattered against the door. It was barely noon and he was drinking already. She swung her legs over the side of the bed and went to warm up in the shower. She might not be able to keep Zeus from fucking around, but she could damned well put a stop to him doing it with that gypsy bitch.

· · ·

Love was sitting on the floor with Ola building a castle out of blocks when the door to the cell was flung open. Bundled in a heavy coat laden with snow, Vashti stared down at her in a rage.

"That's right, sweetheart," Love murmured to Ola. "You keep making it taller while Love talks to Vashti." She stood up as the other woman slammed the door.

"You need to keep your little toy box shut around my man," she snapped when Love approached.

Love crossed her arms and stared up at her silently.

"Have you nothing to say, you little slag?"

"I thought I was supposed to be under a vow of silence."

"Don't be flippant with me. Right now you're going to talk. Have you been fucking him or not?"

"Watch your mouth around Ola."

Vashti grabbed her arm, her voice a harsh whisper. "You don't answer me and I'm going to beat the devil out of you. I want to hear you say it."

"No. I have not."

"Then why did I smell you on him when he came home last night?"

Love met her enraged eyes with fury of her own and replied under her breath, "Because he raped me. And not for the first time."

Vashti slapped her so hard she stumbled against the wall. "Liar!"

Ola began to cry.

Love went to her and picked her up, soothing her. "It's okay, sweetie. We just had an argument. I'm okay."

The tall woman stared at the two of them, her skin clammy with perspiration despite the bitter cold that seeped in through the ancient monastery walls. Ola hid her face and Vashti turned without a word and left them.

• • •

She had to talk to Nebo. Her brother was the only one she could trust, the only one who understood her. He was her twin, and though they hadn't always agreed on things, Nebo would die for her, as she would for him.

Vashti trudged along the snowy path with her head down against the wind. Her cell phone sometimes worked outside the village near the shore and so she kept it charged and in her pocket. She found a signal and pressed Nebo's speed dial, careful not to move from the spot.

He picked up before the first ring had finished. "Ti." Even without caller ID, he would have known it was her. It was just something they did. "Where the hell are you?"

"I love you, too."

He ignored her sarcasm. "Do you realize what's been happening? Do you know how much trouble you're in?"

"I'm beginning to. Nebo, I think I've made a terrible mistake."

"You think?" She could hear the expression on his face, the one that said he was no longer on her side, not in this. She'd disappointed him. "I think the Grigori are going to kill you, Ti. I don't know how I can get you out of this one."

Vashti gripped the phone as if she were grabbing his collar. "Listen to me, Nebo. This isn't about me. I don't care what happens to me. Zeus is…" Her breath caught in her throat as she realized what she was about to say. She couldn't do it. It couldn't be true.

Nebo's voice was low and threatening. "Is he hurting you?"

She shook her head, though he couldn't see her. "Not me. There's…" She was silent for a moment, and Nebo swore at her.

"Oh, my God, Ti. Has he hurt that baby? What have you done?"

"The baby's fine." Vashti took a breath. "She's safe. We just want to keep her away from the Malakim." Tears were freezing on her cheeks. "If Heaven gets that much power, the Nephilim will be the first to suffer for it."

"Now you're just quoting him," said Nebo with disgust.

"There's a girl," she said quickly. "A nanny. He took her to watch the baby." The phone shook in her hand and she almost dropped it.

There was silence for a moment on the other end. "Ti. What did he do?"

Vashti bit her lip hard to keep from bursting into tears like a child. "Oh, Jesus, Nebo. I am so, so stupid." The frozen tears were piling up on top of one another, impossible to stop. "I thought I knew him. I never thought he could—God, I thought he *loved* me. I loved him." She gripped her stomach, afraid she was going to be sick. "Fuck." Vashti held the phone away for a moment, cursing while she got herself together. "I guess none of that matters now, does it? I'm going to get her off the island. But I need your help."

. . .

Everything was frozen outside. Love could no longer see anything through the little window—though there would have been scarcely anything to see if she could. The sun now began to set not long after one o'clock in the afternoon, up less than four hours. Kirill had given her a thick black sweater to wear over the *podryasnik* to keep warm, and she was finally glad of the woolen knee socks, even wishing they were full-length stockings.

Ola had grown out of everything she had come to the monastery with. If Love's count since the autumn equinox was correct, she was nearly eighteen months old now, and she was no longer an infant. Kirill brought winter clothes that had been donated for the poor to bundle her in, and Love managed to keep her warm.

She watched Ola play for hours at putting construction bricks together, quieter than a child ought to be at such a young age. She was worried about how Ola's development might be suffering from this confinement, and she was saddened by how much her parents were missing. How much more would they miss? How much longer could this go on? Kirill had taken to not speaking to her for a day or two if she needled him about how long they meant to keep them here or tried to persuade him of the wisdom of letting them go. At least he seemed to be keeping Zeus away.

Just when she'd begun to relax enough to sleep without keeping one eye open, however, she woke once more in the early hours of the morning to the sound of the bolt sliding back on the cell door. But this time she was ready for him.

She kept the leather belt she wore under her robe wrapped in her fists at night, and when Zeus slipped his hand beneath her robe, she turned swiftly and threw the belt around his neck, sliding out of the bed behind him and pulling it tight. The element of surprise gave her an advantage her size did not, and he struggled ineffectively for a moment, strangling beneath her grip. It had all happened in silence, and if she could just hang on, he might pass out before Ola's sleep was disturbed.

But Zeus recovered from the surprise. He swung back with his elbow and struck her in the chest hard enough to knock the breath from her. As her grip slackened on the belt, he yanked it from her hands and from his neck.

"So this is how you want to play it." He backhanded her with the belt folded in his hand and thrust her face into the pillow so she could barely breathe as he pulled up her robe. She hadn't expected him to be so bold in front of Ola. Instead of his body, however, the flat of the belt met her bare skin as he swung it viciously against her thighs.

Struggling for air, she could hear Ola crying in her corner of the cot, and she cursed herself for underestimating Zeus's sadism. It wasn't an idle threat the first time he'd slipped into her room. He would do as he liked whether Ola was asleep beside her or awake to witness it. Love tore at his hand against the back of her head, but he was impossibly strong, and the belt was raining down blows on her with a brutal force.

The room was going black when Zeus's arm suddenly paused and his grip loosened on her hair. Love turned her head, gasping for air as she pushed away from the pillow, and Zeus dropped to the floor. Kirill stood over him. From Zeus's back, the handle of a heavy blade protruded, surrounded by a widening pool of blood.

The monk stared blankly at the red stain. "He cannot do this in God's house."

Love swung Ola into her arms, turning her away from the sight as Ola's crying reached a pitch of hysteria.

Kirill dropped to his knees, crossing himself and bowing toward the floor. "*Gospodi Iisuse Khriste, Syne Bozhii, pomilui mya greshnago.*"

He repeated the words like a charm as he made the gestures.

Love couldn't sway him from his vigil. She had to keep Ola from seeing. She curled up with Ola in her arms, rocking her back to sleep.

"Kirill." She prodded him periodically, but he was beyond hearing her. Love rocked with Ola, wondering how long it would be before someone discovered what he'd done.

When Ola was finally asleep, Love tucked the blankets around her and slipped from the cot to kneel down beside the monk.

She put her hand on his shoulder. "You were only defending me. I think he meant to kill me."

Kirill rocked forward, repeating his prayer.

"We have to do something, Kirill. We can't just leave the body lying there." Though it was cold enough, she thought as she shivered, that it would probably keep.

Before she could persuade him to take action, however, the door opened.

Vashti stared at the scene in horror, but instead of calling for help, she stepped inside and shut the door. "What happened?" She stopped in the midst of peeling out of her mittens, looking down at the belt still gripped in Zeus's lifeless hand. Her dark eyes were ashamed when she looked at Love. "In front of the baby?" When Love nodded, Vashti looked away. "Oh, God. Fuck. Fuck you, Zeus, you son of a bitch."

Kirill paused in his rocking to flinch at her language.

She crouched down and touched her fingers to Zeus's throat, and Love jumped in shock as he stirred slightly at the touch. Vashti looked up at them sharply and then back at Zeus. With a careful, deliberate motion, she covered Zeus's nose and mouth with her hand and held it firmly in place, pressing down as his body convulsed briefly beneath her and then was still.

***Devatoe:* The Unseen World**
from the memoirs of the Grand Duchess Anazakia
Helisonovna of the House of Arkhangel'sk

The heady smell of roses woke me. We were covered in them, as if the climbing vines of the wild bushes surrounding the pool had grown over us. I lifted one to my nose from the vine winding around Vasily's forearm and breathed in its warm perfume, the pale pink petals like silk against my fingers. Vasily drew his arms tighter around me, his beard tickling the back of my neck.

He murmured against my skin. "You smell like roses."

I laughed softly. "It isn't me. They're everywhere."

"So they are." He kissed my shoulder. "Where did they come from?"

I shrugged and closed my eyes. I was nearly asleep again when something cool touched my cheek. I brushed at it in irritation, and then felt more falling on my skin. I looked up into a light but steady snow. Though it didn't seem cold here, the pool beside us was frozen over. But the grass was still green, the roses seemingly unaffected by this precipitation.

On the other side of the pool, someone stood watching us. I sat up against Vasily's protests as he tried to pull me back. A naked woman with skin of palest blue was standing in a flurry of snow. When she saw I'd noticed her, she bowed her head and turned toward the passage beyond the colonnade, taking the swirl of falling snow with her.

"Snegurochka."

"*Sneg*-what?" Vasily grasped for my hand as I stood and disentangled myself from the twining roses.

"A snow maiden. One of the winter syla." I glanced around at the summery glade with its walls of living wood and moss. "I don't understand. They only come at my birthday, at the solstice."

"Lie down with me, Nazkia." Vasily pulled on my hand, but I stumbled back.

"How long have we been here?" I tried to remember what had brought me, tried to remember when. There was something about the roses that made it difficult to think. "When did you come? I was looking for…" It hit me like a terrible, leaden weight as the enchantment of the garden hall dissolved. *"Ola,"* I gasped, and ran after the syla.

There were twelve of them, always twelve, no matter the season. The *snegurochka* sat in a silver chair beside her sisters in the *Polnochnoi Sud* when I caught up with her.

The chaise on the daïs sat empty and I avoided it. "Where are the autumn syla?"

"Autumn is no more," she said. "Tonight is Longest Night."

It was impossible. I'd been here only a day, or so it seemed. If she told the truth, this was my twentieth birthday, but I couldn't have dallied so long, not while Ola was missing.

"But it can't be. I've only just come here."

"A day is as a thousand years. A thousand years is as a day."

"How can you have kept me here?" I demanded. "I need to find my daughter."

"The syla see Little Queen. She is surrounded by a sea of white."

"And she takes the flower of the fern," I snapped. "Yes, I know."

The syla shook her head. "She takes ship in sky over sea of white."

My mouth dropped open and I stared at the syla smiling placidly at me. The meaningless words they'd repeated like obscure prophetic ciphers were suddenly ordinary words, as if they'd simply been describing what they saw in literal terms all along. It wasn't possible.

"You can't mean the *Beloe More*?" I cried. "The White Sea? She can't have been on Solovetsky!"

The syla nodded. "Surrounded by a sea of white. But now she leaves."

"No." I covered my mouth and whispered into my hands. "No, she can't have been there."

The syla continued to gaze at me serenely. I collapsed onto my knees and stared at the onyx floor in which the dawning comprehension of my folly was reflected. This was a cruel joke.

"Nazkia?" Vasily had finally come after me. He crouched beside me, putting an arm around my shoulders. "What's happened? What does this mean?"

"It means I could have found her," I said hopelessly. "I was there. I went to Solovetsky, and she was within yards of me. She must have been in the monastery. And I just left her there. I could have found her."

He gripped my shoulders tightly and I thought he might hit me, but when he spoke, it wasn't in anger. "You couldn't have known," he said, and I thought my heart would break at the despair in his voice. He looked up at the syla. "Tell us where she is now. Where did she go?"

"Little Queen sleeps in her bed in city of Archangel."

"She's home?" Tears of relief sprang to my eyes.

"Then that's where we're going." Vasily pulled me to my feet. "Right now. We wish to leave. You can't keep us here."

"The syla do not keep." She shook her head as if he weren't very bright. "Those who come to Unseen World come by choice. Stay by choice. The syla provide what is needed."

"We don't need anything," Vasily snapped. "We just need to leave. Where's Belphagor?"

The syla looked at one another.

"What? What have you done with him?"

"The syla do not know if this one wishes to leave. Little Brother takes."

"Little Brother?"

"Mikhail."

"Misha." He spat the name.

I looked from the syla to Vasily. "Who's Misha?"

"He's Yulya Volfovna's son." Vasily's eyes had gone red with fury. "Where did he take him?"

Two syla went before us, a constant dusting of snow powder swirling around them as if kicked up by their feet, though there was none of it beneath them. In a long corridor lined with mirrors etched with intricate, intertwining symbols and bordered by elaborate silver frames, the syla stopped as one before a mirror that looked the same to me as all the others.

"Little Brother is here." Our guide held up a pale blue hand as Vasily reached to push open the mirrored panel. "Little Brother is leshi. Leshi are not like syla."

"So?" His brow knitted with irritation.

"Leshi are…" She turned to her sisters. "How is said?" She nodded at some silent communication. "Leshi like mischief."

Vasily glared and thrust his palm against the panel, pushing it wide. Inside was a marble terrace that looked out over a placid amber sea colored by the golden orb of sun sinking behind it.

Reclining on a luxuriously draped couch, a young man with hair like vines and skin like palest turquoise held Belphagor, asleep and completely naked, in his arms. The leshi regarded us with brilliant green eyes that seemed to light the terrace. He was bare from the waist up, and his unnatural hue covered muscles of such fine definition that I nearly blushed to look on him.

Vasily could barely control his rage. "What have you done to him?"

Misha smiled. "I hardly think you want to hear about that, my friend. The question you should ask is what *you* have done to him. I'm sure you'll find your answer lacking the color of mine."

Before Vasily could attack the leshi, I put my hand on his arm and stepped forward. "Why doesn't he wake? Have you enchanted him?"

"Why, hello, Anazakia." He gave me a friendlier smile. "I'm glad to see you looking well. Your rest has done you good."

I paused, puzzled. "Have we met?"

"You were fevering. At Mother's. I put you into an ice bath."

"Oh." I felt peculiar knowing he'd been by my side with Yulya, tending to me, though I hadn't been aware of him. I'd woken stripped down to my underwear. I blushed and looked away.

Misha answered my question. "He's not enchanted. He's exhausted. I can wake him if you like."

An angry heat radiated off Vasily behind me, and his voice became more gravelly than usual. "Why is he exhausted?"

Misha laughed. "Your mind does go to the most depraved places at the most innocent words."

I blocked Vasily with my outstretched arm.

"He is exhausted from worry and guilt—and shame that should not even belong to him." Misha brushed his fingers through the dark hair that lay across Belphagor's forehead. "Have you even touched him since his celestial ordeal, Vasily? He seemed starved for it."

Vasily emitted a low growl. "You son of a bitch."

The leshi frowned. "I don't think Mother would appreciate that."

"We need to wake him," I interrupted. "We need to go. The syla have seen my daughter."

"Ah, that's right. Your daughter. The one you conceived by his lover while he was recovering from gang rape in the Kresty infirmary."

I stepped back and bumped into Vasily, shaking my head as if my disbelief would make it untrue. Vasily had hinted that Belphagor had been vulnerable in the earthly prison because of the tattoos that marked him, but Belphagor had never spoken of the time he'd spent there.

Vasily wrapped an arm around me as if for his own comfort. "Did he tell you that?" His voice was quiet and had lost its gritty edge.

Misha gave him an accusatory look. "Belyi did not have to tell me. I can feel it in his skin. Didn't you feel it?" He raised a woody eyebrow.

"Oh, that's right. You don't touch him."

"I'm not the one not touching him! He won't touch me!" Vasily swore and let go of me, pacing to control his temper. "Why am I telling you this, you little shit? This has nothing to do with you! And don't you dare call him Beli!"

Misha kissed Belphagor's forehead and Vasily actually hissed. "That is the name he gave when he first came to us. He drank to dull his misery and whispered of you as he took me to his bed. I didn't care because he was beautiful and sad and he took me with such passion. Though why he felt such grief over the loss of you, I can't imagine."

Vasily was beyond words, whether from rage or shock, I couldn't tell.

"And now he's sad again." Misha smoothed Belphagor's hair. "Sadder. Because he's lost his little girl. Only he's not allowed to call her that because you treat him as something intrusive and outside, as if a child were a possession or a trophy of conquest, even though all he has done is love her since the moment he first saw her. He hides his sadness because you feel he has no right to it. Sadness is only for birth parents, apparently."

I'd never seen Vasily at such a loss for words. He looked at me to refute what Misha said, but I couldn't. Vasily recoiled from my silence as if I'd slapped him.

"Shall I wake him, then? Let's find out if he wants to go with you and face your daily blame and scorn or stay with me and be cherished." He bent and kissed Belphagor on the lips and breathed against his ear. "Wake up, Belyi."

Belphagor stirred, snuggling against the leshi's chest, and opened his eyes. He blinked at us for a moment before he sat up swiftly, his face blazing red as he realized how we'd found him. He pulled a blanket over his lap and Misha smiled as if to say it was far too late for such modesty.

I ignored the leshi and the awkwardness. "Belphagor, it's time to go. The syla have seen Ola being taken back to the dacha, and we've lost so much time here. We can't delay."

"Ola's safe?" The relief in his eyes was like a drowning man reaching shore, but as Misha slowly stroked his arm with the tips of his fingers, Belphagor made no attempt to get up. "Thank Heaven you've found her."

"Aren't you coming?"

"Perhaps I should catch up with you later. I'd only be in the way. You need some time with Ola."

"Don't be ridiculous. You're not in the way. Vasily, tell him."

Vasily growled like a bear behind me. "Belphagor seems to have made up his mind to stay."

"Dammit, Vasily. Do you want him to stay?" I was tired of his pouting and his constant assumption that everyone's intentions were the worst. "Tell him how you feel!"

"How I feel?" He threw me a smoldering look. "How I feel about the fact that he'd rather stay in the kingdom of the Unseen than come with me?" He turned his hot gaze on Belphagor. "Or how I feel about the fact that he'd fuck a green forest troll before he'd fuck me!"

"I take exception to that," said Misha, but Vasily spoke over him.

"And that he'd do it while Ola is missing!"

"I didn't fuck him," Belphagor said quietly.

"Like I care what specific acts you've been engaged in!"

"I fellated him," said the leshi.

"For God's sake, Misha!" Belphagor jumped up with the drape about his waist, but Misha was sitting on the edge of it and it nearly slipped off entirely.

"That's an interesting imprecation for a celestial." Misha smirked as Belphagor yanked the drape from under him. Before Belphagor could say another word, Vasily turned and left.

I whirled on Belphagor. "If you're too much of a fool to come for Vasily, come for Ola. You'll break her heart if you're not there."

"That isn't fair."

"Fair? Of course it's not fair. None of this is fair! Now quit feeling sorry for yourself and put your clothes on!"

He reddened and reached for the pile at his feet.

Misha let out a wistful sigh. "Ah, Belyi. Your sadism I can always count on, but I've underestimated your masochistic streak."

Belphagor gave him a rueful smile. "You're not the first."

While he dressed, I returned to the Midnight Court with my *snegurochki* escort, anxious to be on our way. Now that I knew Ola was so close, every moment away from her seemed interminable. As we passed through layers of majestic halls and galleries dusted by their snowy aura, I remembered belatedly why they had brought me here.

"Your autumn sisters spoke of a circle of ice and fire where I would stop the Seraphim. Do you know what they meant?"

One of the ice-blue syla shrugged. "We see no more than they. All syla see together. But fire angels fear the ice. That is why they do not come for *snegurochki*, but they will come again when spring sisters take our place. The fire angels slay when syla walk in world of Man."

"Can't you all stay here? I thought the Seraphim couldn't enter your world."

"Is not in the nature of syla to stay within Unseen World. Syla must breathe the air beyond. Syla must dance under the moon."

"What about your brothers? Can't the leshi defend you?"

"Brothers have no wish to make enemies. Leshi did not hide flower."

We had arrived at the Hall of Echoes, where Vasily paced, almost literally fuming. Belphagor appeared, stepping through the colonnade with his head down and his hands in his pockets. Only one syla remained to see us out.

I pressed her cool, dainty hand. "I still don't really understand, but I promise to do what I can to stop them. You have my word." Whatever it was I must do, at least I had until the equinox to find out.

The syla smiled and held her hand out toward Vasily. "To leave together, you must touch."

Vasily took my hand as she brought it to his, while Belphagor gave him a wide and careful berth as he came around to my other side. The syla began to murmur in her language, indecipherable words that sounded vaguely like Russian. In a moment, the amber walls were shimmering, wavering in their solidity.

My feet grew cold and a chilly wind began to blow as the walls became permeable. We were standing in several inches of snow, the leafless trees of the Alexander Park now surrounding us like graceful skeletons, and the path that had been strewn with leaves of bronze and copper was now sparkling white, fit for a sleigh. Even the clothes I'd arrived in would have been inadequate, but I'd forgotten them. I was barefoot and dressed only in a light gown of silk that left my shoulders bare.

Vasily and Belphagor both removed their coats at once as they saw me shivering, and I took Vasily's before the hatred in his eyes began to encompass me as well. The hall had disappeared completely as we broke the chain of our hands, but the lone syla still stood with us.

She bowed to me. "The syla are grateful to *Padshaya Koroleva* for what she will do." She kissed my hand, a tear of ice on her cheek. "We know to shed blood of one so close will cause you pain."

I stared at her, shocked that she would say this in front of Vasily and Belphagor.

"They cannot see or hear syla outside of Unseen World." The syla smiled. "They are not queensdaughters." A whirlwind of snow spun up around her pale blue body and she disappeared into the leaden color of the winter afternoon.

Belphagor watched me with a wrinkled brow. "Are you all right?"

"Of course she's not all right," snapped Vasily. "She's freezing to death." He nearly took my breath away as he whisked me off my feet into his arms.

Clenching my teeth to keep them from chattering, I huddled against his firespirit-warm chest and couldn't resist a little smugness. "I suppose you believe me now about the syla."

By the time we reached Yulya Volfovna's flat three blocks away, I truly was freezing. She welcomed us as if she'd only seen us yesterday—which was true enough for us, though not for her—and bustled me into the bedroom to dress me in warmer clothing. Plying us with hot tea and biscuits, she asked politely about our visit to "the parks" without making any mention of the Unseen World. Belphagor pointedly avoided the topic of her son and she didn't ask. Vasily barely uttered a word.

Once we'd warmed a bit, Yulya provided us with ample outerwear before we departed for the train station. She blinked back tears as we waved good-bye, as if genuinely sad to see us go, and a tug of regret pulled at me. In such a short time, she had been as much a comfort to me as I had once thought Helga to be.

On the train to St. Petersburg, Belphagor tried to reach Dmitri on his phone but discovered it had no power. I gave him the one I'd brought to Yulya's and he chided me for forgetting to turn it on.

I watched the gloomy landscape through the window as the train passed alongside suburban roads heavy with snow and sleet. The drivers of the cars on the roads seemed undaunted, speeding ahead with almost alarming nonchalance, though a few cars appeared stranded in the deep drifts on the shoulders. It was early afternoon, but with the snow clouds looming overhead and the low angle of the Russian winter sun, it was like traveling through a timeless void.

Though it seemed to take far too long, every revolution of the train's wheels was bringing me closer to Ola. I might be with her tomorrow. Beside me, Vasily seemed to be thinking the same, and he took my hand. Though the tension between him and Belphagor was terrible, he and I had gained some peace between us during our rest in the grassy hall of the Unseen World. Once we were home with Ola, I was sure Vasily would forget his anger at Belphagor.

Seated behind us, Belphagor closed the phone and leaned over the back of the seat, causing Vasily to flinch and let go of my hand. "Dmitri says they know where Ola's been and she's truly on her way home." His voice expressed the release of the dark burden we all seemed to feel, as if we'd been holding our breath, afraid this would be taken from us. "He's been working with an anonymous contact who provided the information for the promise of asylum."

"I don't like the idea of asylum," Vasily growled.

"I know. But Dmitri had to grant it before the contact would reveal the source. It was their nonnegotiable condition for bringing Ola back. The rest of the *Angliski* clan will still be punished. At any rate, they've made arrangements for us to fly into Arkhangel'sk tomorrow afternoon to meet the plane coming in from Solovetsky."

I took Vasily's hand again, my heart lighter than it had been in so long, and he didn't resist.

"But you're not going to like who's been granted asylum."

"Who?" Vasily's eyes darkened toward red.

Belphagor moved back from the seat as if removing himself from the range of Vasily's fist. "Vashti."

I cried out as Vasily crushed my fingers in his.

Desatoe: A Skylark Wounded on the Wing

The plane had taken off from the frozen center of the White Sea at one thirty in the afternoon, dusk already as the sun hugged the arctic white horizon. The tiny vessel shuddered as it rumbled across the frozen runway, lurching its way into the sullen sky, and Love instinctively grabbed Kirill's wrist on the armrest beside her, making him jump.

He'd been in shock since stabbing Zeus, mutely following Vashti's orders as he murmured his prayers. Apparently, she'd arranged everything in advance—except for Zeus's death. Vashti had come to the monastery with plane tickets and forged papers for Love and Ola, and she hurried them out the door, pressing money into Kirill's hand to bribe the airport officials for an extra seat on the plane and insisting it was his duty to get Love and Ola to safety. She would remain behind to report the death after they were safely away. Love didn't ask any questions. She was happy to do whatever Vashti told her to as long as she and Ola were going home.

Ola was quiet and solemn after her prolonged crying episode at the monastery, and Love waited until they were in the air to tell her they were on their way to see Mama. After so many weeks, she wasn't sure if Ola understood who Mama was, but Ola's eyes seemed bright and interested.

"And we'll see Papa and Beli, too," she promised, but Ola only stared at this.

Kirill was equally quiet, fingers counting the knots in his *chotki* and lips moving with his interminable prayer. When they reached the airport at Arkhangel'sk, he tried to stay on the plane, stubbornly insisting he had to go back, but there was only one flight in and out of Arkhangel'sk that day, and they'd been on it.

Love managed to convince him to come with her to the dacha. She would tell them he'd taken care of her in the monastery, that keeping her and Ola there had been against his will and he'd been unable to free them until now.

"This is not truth." He spoke in angelic and then blushed, realizing it was no longer necessary. *"Eto nepravda."*

"It is the truth. You were lied to. I don't believe you would have kept us there if it were up to your own conscience."

Kirill frowned but didn't argue.

They had enough money left for a taxi, and they arrived at last to discover the dacha dark, with no smoke at the chimney. Love found the key they kept beneath a pot in the garden and let herself into the cold, empty house.

She left Kirill to light a fire as she went about with Ola, turning on lights and checking rooms, though it was obvious there was no one there, and hadn't been for some time. Ola became more animated when she saw her crib and toys, examining her stuffed animals with interest as Love handed them to her.

Keeping one eye on Ola as she explored the room, Love stripped out of the hateful black garments, trading them for a thermal undershirt and a heavy T-shirt that fit snugly over it. She pulled on a pair of her own underwear with relief, along with a favorite pair of overalls and the warmest woolen socks she could find. Ola no longer had anything that fit her here, so Love left her in the borrowed clothes from the monastery donations.

In the bathroom, Love took a pair of scissors and trimmed her hair back to the short waves she preferred. The long wisps that kept falling into her eyes had been driving her mad. She freshened up, washing the grime from her face and putting on her moisturizer and deodorant at last. Every step of the routine denied her in the austere monastery made her feel more like herself.

"*Sobaka.*" Ola held out a soft stuffed dog as Love picked her up. Belphagor had given it to her on her first birthday—just a few weeks before they'd gone to Solovetsky.

"That's right. That's Ola's *sobaka*. Beli gave that to you."

"La *sobaka*," said Ola, clearly pleased.

When they returned downstairs, Kirill looked up from warming his hands by the fire and regarded Love with surprise.

She glared at him with a hand on her hip. "I hope you didn't expect me to keep dressing like a nun."

Kirill shook his head almost shyly.

Her computer still sat on the table, and Love started it up and checked her voicemail online. An angry message from Belphagor startled her, left the day after she and Ola had been taken.

"You're going to be sorry you ever laid eyes on that child," his voice snarled at her. "I WILL find you, I promise you that. And by the time I'm done thrashing you, you'll understand that the unseen world is real. You can bet your *tsigane* ass on that."

She stared at the computer, her heart pounding and her eyes burning. They thought she'd taken Ola. They thought she was part of it. Ola was looking at the computer with a puzzled expression, as if she found the voice familiar but couldn't quite place it.

"That was Beli. He was a little angry with me."

"Zoo." Ola's lower lip protruded in worry.

"No, no." Love hugged her. "Not like Zeus. Zeus was a bad man. Beli loves us. He was just angry because he was frightened and didn't know where we were. He won't be angry when he sees us. He'll be so happy." She pulled up the folder where she'd uploaded shots from her cell phone and showed Ola a picture of Belphagor and Vasily. "There's Beli. Next to Papa. Do you remember Papa?"

Ola patted the computer, looking shy. Love opened another picture of them standing beside Anazakia holding a six-month-old Ola.

"And here's—"

"Mama. La's mama."

"That's right." Love bit back tears as she ruffled the burnished hair. "Ola's mama."

"Mama baby." Ola pointed at herself in the picture.

"That's you. That's baby Ola. See, Mama's kissing you because she loves you. I know Mama misses you very much, and we're going to see her soon."

Ola stared at the screen a little longer before squirming to get down. The picture would look nice above her crib, so Love printed it out and slipped it into the wide front pocket of her overalls to find a frame for it later.

While Kirill ignored the meal Love managed to scrounge up, she took Ola upstairs for a bath, leaving him to his thoughts and his untouched plate. Ola splashed about with toys that were novelties to her now as Love luxuriated in the hot water with a profusion of bubbles, not wanting to get out until it was too cool to stay in any longer.

Ola's hair was soft and wispy after Love toweled it dry, the glow of the candles on the counter catching the ruby lights among the darkening curls. She took her in to bed, tucking her under the blankets in the center of Anazakia's mattress, which seemed massive and decadent after the ascetic cot they'd shared. Ola tucked her toy *sobaka* under her arm and was asleep in an instant.

When Love went down to sit by the fire, Kirill finally spoke to her. "You are very kind to offer me hospitality." He stared into the flames. "But it isn't true that I took care of you, and tomorrow I must return to face my crime. I have sinned against God and allowed you to suffer the gravest of abominations. And now I have damned my soul. The blood of God's messenger is on my hands." It was the most he'd spoken since she discovered him standing over Zeus's body.

"He was *not* God's messenger. If anything, he was the devil's."

"Then God has sent temptation to test me and I have failed, falling for the honeyed tongue of the serpent. And I have fled the judgment of my sins."

"You're not to blame." When he refused to look at her, she crouched down in front of him and put her hand on his where it rested on his knee. "If you hadn't stopped him, he would have held me down and done what he wanted with me as Ola watched, and he meant to smother me while he did it."

Kirill shuddered. "I *am* to blame. You would not have been there if I had not allowed it. He would not have touched you if I had not turned a blind eye to it."

"Kirill—"

"No." He pulled his hand away from hers. "I must cleanse my soul of this wickedness. I must beseech the Lord to know how I am to atone." He rose and went upstairs to the bathroom and closed the door, running water for a bath.

Love went up to bed, climbing in beside Ola's sleep-flushed heat, and lay awake, her mind whirling with how changed her situation was since going to sleep the night before. She'd nearly succumbed to a state of resignation and despair at Solovetsky, no longer thinking about when they would be released, concerned only with maintaining some kind of normalcy for Ola and counteracting the detriments to her development.

She'd succeeded in potty training her, and had read to her for several hours a day, trying to make sure her vocabulary didn't suffer for lack of socialization. Ola's health and well-being had become the purpose of her life. Now she felt strangely unmoored, her purpose suddenly removed. She wasn't certain how to go back to being the Love she'd been before—or even if she could. Belphagor's angry voice repeated in a loop in her head.

Just as her mad thoughts were finally wending toward sleep, a sound below made her instantly alert. The door had opened. She slipped out of bed and into her *tapochki* and paused in the hall to look in on Belphagor and Vasily's empty room. Kirill hadn't gone to bed.

The light was still on in the bathroom, but the door was open and the room was empty. His robes lay on the floor next to the full tub—still steaming, which seemed odd for how long it must have been sitting. She dipped her fingers in it and discovered it was nearly scalding, as if he'd used no cold water in running the bath.

A chill was rushing toward her up the stairs; the front door stood open. Love hurried down and grabbed her coat, and she found the monk standing naked in the garden, his skin covered in a thin layer of ice, like a human icicle.

"*Bozhe moi*, Kirill!" She ran to him and tried to pull him toward the dacha. "What on earth are you doing?"

He was beyond responding, his lips already blue, nearly convulsing with involuntary shivers. She took off her coat and threw it over him, and then tried to turn him toward the house, but he stumbled and fell in the snow, his feet too frozen to carry him. He was too heavy for her to try to lift, so she ran back inside and grabbed his *ryasa* and laid it flat on the ground beside him. Shoving as hard as she could, she rolled him onto the robe and grabbed the garment by the collar, dragging it like a sled along the path. It was like pulling a block of ice—which he very nearly was.

At last she got him inside by the fire and covered him in blankets. His beard was a solid icicle extending from his chin, and the hair pulled back in his ponytail was similarly frozen.

"*Kirill.*"

His eyes were open, but he was shaking like a leaf and he didn't respond. Love climbed beneath his blankets and tried to warm him with her body heat, her arms about his chest and shoulders. After several minutes, his shaking began to subside and he closed his eyes.

"Kirill, can you hear me? Don't go to sleep. You're scaring me."

"L-leave me. It's G-god's will. The f-flesh must be mort—" He paused as his chattering teeth caused his jaw to clench. "Mortified." Because of his beard and his air of authority, she'd thought of him as older, but right now he seemed surprisingly young and vulnerable, like a frightened adolescent boy, and she realized he couldn't be much older than she was.

Love shook her head. "I won't leave you to freeze yourself to death. If God wants this, there's something wrong with Him."

"You b-blaspheme!" He shivered and tried to extricate himself, too frozen to properly rebuke her.

"I'll blaspheme more if you don't stop this," she threatened, holding onto him stubbornly. "Then my damnation will be on your head."

Kirill turned his head away but stopped resisting her, and he said nothing more. She laid her head on his shoulder as his body warmed and his shivering stopped, and after a time, she realized she'd drifted off to sleep when his soft voice woke her. He was reciting the Prayer of the Heart again, low and rhythmic, as if it were part of his breath.

Love listened, watching the rise and fall of his chest. He seemed to be able to carry the lilting chant of the prayer indefinitely, as though he was no longer conscious of it, might even be saying it in his sleep.

"*Gospodi Iisuse Khriste, Syne Bozhii,*" he breathed in—*Lord Jesus Christ, Son of God*—and breathed out: "*Pomilui, mya greshnago*"—*have mercy on me, a sinner.* He paused, aware she was listening to him. "I need you to go, Sister Lyubov. You distract me from my purpose."

"What's your purpose?"

"To unite the body and mind with the heart."

Love hesitated. "You're not going to harm yourself again?"

"I give my word that I will not, as Christ is my witness."

She supposed she had to be satisfied with that. Love climbed out from under the blankets, listening to the embers sliding down against each other with a hiss as the log broke apart in the fireplace.

"There's another bed upstairs."

"The floor will do. Please go." He resumed his unconscious recitation as if she'd already done so. Love gave up and went to snuggle under the covers with Ola.

In the morning, Kirill seemed composed once more, dressed serenely in his robes and seated by the fire, though he stubbornly refused breakfast when Love prepared it for them. He insisted this was not an attempt to harm himself, only a temporary fast so he could more clearly hear God's will.

Ola wanted to play with the computer when Love opened it, so Love let her sit on her lap and bang on the keyboard, showing her the pictures of her parents. Ola hadn't let go of her stuffed dog since Love had put it into her hands, and she patted it at the screen when the picture of Belphagor and Vasily came up.

"Beli *sobaka*?"

Love smiled. "Yes, sweetie, that's Beli. He gave you the *sobaka*." She dug around in her rucksack for an uncharged cell phone from her extensive collection for Ola to play with, and discovered three of the prepaid phones and chargers were gone. The others must have each taken one. She had all of the numbers in her contacts, so she plugged in her headset and tried each one, only to get voicemail for all three. There was no telling who had which phone, as they hadn't changed the generic greetings, so she left the same message on each, letting them know she and Ola were safe and home and trying to reassure them she hadn't been involved in Ola's abduction.

As she was leaving the last, she felt a strange prickling sensation at her ear, as if a static charge were building, and then a bright flash knocked her to the floor. She lay there dazed for a moment, the headset clattering across the polished wood. Ola was crying, and with the negative image of the flash burned into her retinas, Love couldn't see.

Kirill cried out and fell onto his knees beside her with a heavy thud. "Have mercy on me, a sinner! I am a humble servant of the Lord!"

"Irrelevant." A strange voice thundered in her head like the roar of a lion. "We are not acquainted with your 'lord.' We come from Heaven."

• • •

They arrived at Talagi Airport an hour before the flight from the Solovetsky Islands was due to land. The weather so far was clear and cold as crystal, and there was no indication the flight from the islands had been canceled, as was often the case this time of year.

Vasily paced, nearly emitting smoke in his pent-up rage, the emotion he habitually projected to cover worry or fear. Belphagor wished he could comfort him, but Vasily was too agitated for even Anazakia to get near him. The angel was quiet, peering out the window beneath the brown-tipped polecat *ushanka* Yulya had given her. He suspected Anazakia had no concept what a gift that had been for a woman of Yulya's means.

Dmitri had come along to take custody of Vashti. He might have granted her asylum, but she wouldn't simply be free to go her way. Asylum meant she wouldn't face death—or the particularly gruesome punishment reserved for violent criminals among the clans: pinioning of their terrestrial wings—but she would be confined at Dmitri's discretion until he determined whether she was a threat to Fallen, Host, or Man.

They'd met up with Dmitri and a Nephil named Nebo in St. Petersburg. Tall and beautiful, with skin as supple and rich as mink, Nebo was Vashti's fraternal twin. He was the contact Dmitri had mentioned to Belphagor before their trip to the Unseen World, who'd arranged for Vashti's surrender. Nebo had been trying to persuade Vashti to turn herself in, but Dmitri had heard nothing more from him until just days ago, when Nebo announced she was ready to come in if Dmitri's offer of asylum still held. She'd promised to bring Ola with her, and Dmitri had readily agreed.

The plane arrived at last just after the early arctic sunset. Anazakia pressed her hands against the icy glass as she watched the passengers emerge. There weren't many who braved the White Sea this time of year, and they soon saw Vashti stepping onto the tarmac. She was alone. Belphagor's heart jolted with alarm.

Anazakia cried out and pounded on the window. "Where is she? Where's Ola?"

Beside her, Vasily lunged for the door, eyes wild with his fire, and Dmitri and Nebo barely managed to restrain him.

Belphagor rounded on Nebo and grabbed him by the collar. "You said she was bringing Ola. What's going on?"

"I don't know. I swear to you." The Nephil's voice shook in his urban London accent. "She said she'd have her."

Vasily swore, struggling against Nebo's grip. "This is the last day of your sister's life."

Nebo looked ill, as if his worst fears were coming true.

When Vashti entered the terminal, she stopped short in dismay, taking inventory of the furious faces awaiting her and the look of dread on Nebo's. She pulled the collar of her fur coat close around her neck as if afraid she was about to lose her head.

Belphagor dug his nails into his palms, ready to oblige. He'd never hit a woman before, but not only did this one have it coming, Vashti was bigger than he was, and trained in combat. He was willing to compromise his principles this once.

Anazakia was the one to dart forward and swing Vashti by the arm to face her. "Where's my baby?"

"It's all right." Vashti, who had nearly a foot on Anazakia and a good fifty pounds, shrank from her. "I sent her with Love yesterday. She's already home." She winced as Anazakia's fingers dug into her arm. "I thought you'd be at the dacha already. I thought you knew."

Belphagor grabbed her other arm. "How do we know you're telling the truth? How do we know your little gypsy friend didn't just decide to take off with Ola on her own? She wasn't offered asylum."

Vashti's mouth hung open for a moment, and then she straightened and took a slow, steady breath. "I didn't realize you weren't aware. Love was a prisoner. Zeus took her." There was something else in Vashti's eyes she wasn't saying. "He thought it would make things easier if there was someone to take care of the baby so we wouldn't have to."

A loud slap rang out through the airport as Anazakia struck her across the face. Vashti took it without flinching but kept her eyes lowered. Nebo was the only one regarding her with sympathy.

Vasily wrenched himself away from Dmitri and the Nephil. "Let's go," he growled. "I want to see my daughter. Now." He shoved past Vashti with a scowl that said he was barely holding back the tightened fist clenched at his side.

As the others turned to follow, the cell phone in Belphagor's pocket chirped, announcing a message. He pressed the voicemail button as they escorted Vashti to the door.

"It's Love," he called out with relief as he listened. "She's at the dacha. Ola's fine." He cringed as he listened to the apologetic voice. She'd heard the threatening message he'd left her and she was trying to assure them she hadn't been part of the conspiracy to take Ola. He'd have to make it up to her. He felt foolish for assuming she would do such a terrible thing. It had never even occurred to him she could have been a victim herself.

"Say hello to Mama," she said.

Ola's little voice piped up from the background, saying, "La's Mama!" and Belphagor nearly wept. She sounded so grown up already.

"That's right. Ola's Mama. We're going to see her very—"

There was a sudden, loud burst of static that nearly split his eardrum, and the phone clattered repeatedly, as if tumbling across the floor. He could hear Ola crying, and someone else he didn't recognize pleading for mercy. Just before the message cut off, he heard it as clearly as if he were standing beside them: the metallic, thundering voice of a Cherub.

• • •

There was something wrong with the man's face. Love blinked against spots in front of her eyes as she looked up at him, but the man standing over her seemed to blur and morph when he turned his head, as if his appearance weren't fully formed. It had to be a trick of the light. A bright, white glow with the bluish hue of ivory under an ultraviolet bulb illuminated his skin where his golden robe didn't cover it, as if he'd painted himself with a phosphorescent substance.

She looked away from him, trying to clear her head. Immense

walls of pale stained blue glass surrounded her, revealing a wavering landscape of pines and hills. Though covered in snow, it wasn't the countryside of Arkhangel'sk. They were no longer in the dacha.

Love was certain she hadn't blacked out, but she couldn't explain how they'd gotten here. Perhaps the lightning that struck her through the phone line had dazed her more than she realized. Her lungs felt peculiar, as if the air she was breathing wasn't the substance she was used to—like the air of a high altitude, only…sweeter. It burned in her throat like ice.

She was lying on her stomach on a cold stone floor carved with curious symbols, and Kirill was beside her, his head bowed to the ground, murmuring his frantic prayer. Realizing she couldn't hear Ola crying any longer, Love sat up, gripping her head.

"Ola?"

"The grand duchess was not appropriately dressed for travel." The strange voice had a disturbingly disjointed sound, like a quartet of voices speaking at once in different, discordant octaves. Love looked at the man sidelong, trying to avoid focusing on the peculiar, unsettling effect of his face. The others had occasionally referred to Anazakia as the grand duchess, so she supposed it stood to reason this title would extend to her daughter as well.

"Who are you? What do you want with us?"

He turned his head toward her and Love gasped as his profile flashed past her peripheral vision. What appeared to be the face of a lion had briefly wavered on his countenance.

"We are the Fifth Order," he said in his disturbing cadence. "We are the Cherubim."

Kirill began to murmur against the stone floor. *"You have sinned, therefore I will cast you out from the mountain of God and destroy you, oh protecting Cherub, away from the fiery stones."*

"Quaint," said the man. "You quote the stories of the Malakim, used to control susceptible Men. But do not mistake us for the servants of your biblical god."

"God tests me because I have sinned against him. He tests me with demons in the guise of angels at the gates of hell."

The man came close to Kirill and bent low. His head turned on his shoulders with the agility of a bird, displaying a third wavering countenance that made Love think of Egyptian gods with the heads of hawks or eagles.

"We are not demons," he shrilled at Kirill. "We are pure! We are the angels of the element of fire. The Fifth Order. The Second Choir. Our brothers are the Seraph and the Ophan!"

Kirill rocked forward against the floor as he chanted, his *chotki* clutched between his fingers.

There was nothing in Love's experience that could explain this. There were no contact lenses or prosthetic devices that could turn a man's head one hundred and eighty degrees and give him the face of a lion or a bird. Nothing in what the others liked to call "the world of Man" could account for what was happening, except that she was no longer in it.

Another being like the first entered through a pair of silver-embellished oak doors that opened in a ponderous arc. At his side, bundled in thick woolen garments like a snowsuit buttoned down the front, her feet laced into little boots of heavy suede, Ola stood holding his hand. Her stuffed dog dangled from her grip.

"Lub!" She grinned happily, and the Cherub released her, allowing her to run into Love's arms, though she moved awkwardly in the heavy garments. Love caught her and gathered her into her lap and Ola snuggled against her, looking shyly up at the Cherubim from the safety of familiar arms.

The two Cherubim spoke to each other quietly in what seemed to be the angelic tongue, though they used words with which Love was not familiar. The one who had just entered nodded toward the doors, and two more of the creatures appeared. These two approached Love and Kirill and pulled them to their feet. Love lifted Ola in her arms and the Cherubim prodded them forward.

Kirill was repeating *"Iisuse Khriste"* with a frantic desperation.

"Enough of that." The first Cherub growled at him, showing the wavering appearance of an ox as he turned his left side toward them. "We are growing tired of your superstitious incantations."

They were led through a corridor lined with the same stained glass under grey stone arches, the pale moonstone hue lending the snowdrifts piled beside the glass an ethereal blue cast. Beyond the drifting snow and the white-draped landscape of pine and cedar lay the stark outlines of high mountain peaks.

The Cherubim stopped at the end of the corridor and directed them into an atrium covered by a sweeping stained-glass dome. An empty pool stood beneath the dome, and the terraced stones around it held small potted fruit trees, out of place in this wintry desolation.

Near the peculiar oasis stood a being so breathtaking Love couldn't be certain whether it was a man or a woman. Long silvery hair hung over one white-robed shoulder, and the eyes focused on her seemed to have an equally silver-grey hue like none she'd ever seen.

"Welcome." The voice seemed to be that of a man. "And how fare our guests?"

"The grand duchess and her companions will not be guests for long, Sarael. We've been instructed to take Her Supernal Highness to the Citadel of Gehenna."

Sarael observed the Cherub with an unreadable expression of calm. "Are you sure that's wise, Zophiel? Why not keep her here at Aravoth where the Virtues will guide and guard her?"

Zophiel made a motion like a shrug, but seemed to involve another bird-like revolution of his head. "Gehenna is where she wants the child to be taken. Gehenna is where we shall take the child."

The graceful Sarael bowed as if deferring to the Cherub.

Zophiel directed Love and Kirill through the atrium to the vestibule of the building, where they were outfitted with heavy ankle-length coats, woolen mittens, and suede boots like the ones Ola had on. Love drew up the hood on Ola's outfit and pulled the drawstring tight beneath her chin before putting mittens on both of them as Zophiel led them outdoors. Two more Cherubim were waiting by a large horse-drawn sleigh at the end of a circular drive.

Love refused to climb up onto the seat when she was bidden. "You haven't told us where we are or where we're going."

One of the Cherubim took Ola from Love's arms. "The Grand Duchess Ola Vasilyevna of the House of Arkhangel'sk is heir to the throne of All the Heavens. Where she goes is none of your concern. You are inconsequential. If you will accompany her, do so. Otherwise, you will be transported to the nearest Relocation Camp."

Love didn't like the sound of that, and she wasn't about to let these brutes take Ola away from her. She climbed into the sleigh without further questions, and the Cherub handed Ola up to her. Kirill followed, sitting next to Love and staring ahead with an expression of shock and hopelessness. She found a somewhat grim, reluctant satisfaction in his misery after the months she'd spent confined in the cell at Solovetsky. Perhaps he'd begun to understand what his complicity in Zeus's plan had meant to her and Ola.

They rode with two Cherubim at their backs and two facing them as the driver took the reins and the sleigh moved forward, pulled by two powerful draught horses with shining coats of black. The horses were a stark contrast to the white, empty landscape and the light colors of the Cherubim and the sleigh itself. Even the garments she'd been given and the blanket provided to cover her lap were a pale, creamy wool. Love tucked the blanket around Ola, who, despite the strangeness of the countryside and the conveyance, was soon fast asleep in Love's lap.

The grand estate behind them became indistinct as Love looked back, and with it the peaks of the mountains beyond. Before them was nothing but a flat, white expanse. Lightheaded from the peculiar air, she soon found herself being lulled to sleep as well by the monotonous white.

After driving all day, they camped at dusk in canvas tents erected by the Cherubim in the midst of the endless ice. A circle of stones glowed with an unearthly golden heat, conjured somehow between a Cherub's hands. Though she'd slept for much of the day, after a bland but filling dinner of smoked venison and a kind of flat cracker bread, Love was more than ready to climb into the tent with Ola and Kirill. The soft murmur of the monk's endless prayer soothed her as she drifted off to sleep.

In the morning, the smell of something cooking roused her early, but Kirill again refused breakfast. Love had seen him consume nothing in two days. When she urged him to eat he turned his back and she gave up and went out with Ola into the bright, white morning. The Cherubim provided a watery porridge and hot water for tea. Perhaps Kirill would at least drink a little.

She left Ola happily working on her porridge and took a tin cup of tea to the tent, but nearly dropped it when she opened the flap. Kirill sat with his robes open, tightening a cord on his upper thigh that held a sort of chainmail garter in place. He tried to cover himself, but Love set the cup down and pulled his robes out of the way. She gasped when she saw the garter was composed of dozens of spiked metal rings forced into his inflamed skin.

"*Kirill!* What the hell are you doing?"

He frowned at her language as he pulled his robe away from her and covered the device. "Mortification of the flesh."

"Where did you get that thing?"

"It's a cilice. I found it in a drawer in the bedroom at the dacha." Kirill stroked his beard and refused to look at her. "Someone there apparently understands the need for penitence."

Love knelt down beside him. "Kirill, please. You have to stop this."

He raised his pale aquamarine eyes to her, full of anguish and terror. "I have been brought to hell for what I've done. I am tormented by demons—though I can't understand why God has brought this upon you and the child as well." He shook his head. "The flesh must die so the spirit may live."

"This isn't hell." Love rubbed her hands against her arms as she shivered. Wasn't hell supposed to be hot? "The Cherub said it was Heaven."

Kirill buttoned his robes with the cilice still biting into his flesh. "Would God's kingdom be populated with such terrible creatures who deny Him?"

"Drink this, at least. You need something in your stomach." She picked up the cup and handed it to him, and he took it and sipped reluctantly. "You promised me you wouldn't hurt yourself again," she reminded him, but he'd already tuned her out, his pale eyes staring at the canvas.

The sleigh carried them onward into the frozen wilderness for another day, and then another. The flat whiteness stretched for miles around them in every direction, as if they were adrift in the White Sea in winter. Love had no idea how the driver knew his course.

Late on the third day of travel, a low range of jagged mountains at last broke the monotony, growing steadily larger until they were passing between its peaks through a narrow gorge that seemed nothing more than a frozen river—though this desolate country didn't look as though it ever reached thaw. Within a plain of ice beyond the mountains, something was giving off steam, a faint orange glow visible in a line along the horizon.

"What is it?" she asked the Cherubim.

Only the one called Zophiel bothered to speak to them. "The Pyriphlegethon. The source of Heaven's elemental fire."

As they drew closer, she saw what looked like molten lava flowing as if from a volcanic eruption, but it didn't seem to melt the snow around it. When they drew up beside it to make camp as dusk approached, Kirill became agitated.

"It's as I said! We are in hell!" He leapt from the sleigh, and Love watched helplessly as one of the Cherubim knocked him to the icy ground. Kirill rose on his knees and began to cross himself. *"Though I walk through the valley of the shadow of death, I will fear no evil."* When the Cherub turned its lion face to him, Kirill raised his voice. *"The devil prowls like a roaring lion, seeking someone to devour!"*

The Cherub made a sound like a metallic growl. "If you do not wish to be devoured, priest of the Malakim, you will not call us devils again."

Kirill bowed his head and resumed his prayer. While the Cherubim made camp around him, Love lifted Ola onto her hip and went to his side. He'd thrown off his coat and mittens, and would soon freeze if he remained this way.

"Kirill, you have to get up. It's too cold for you to kneel on the ground." She took the coat and handed it to him, but he ignored her, closing his eyes as he rocked forward in his prayer.

"Ki'ill sleepy," said Ola.

Love placed the coat around his shoulders, and at least he didn't resist this. She brought him some food, but there was no reaching him, and when it was time to climb into their tents for the night, he wouldn't budge. Love put Ola to bed with her stuffed dog and told her she'd be right back. Outside, Kirill's rocking motions had ceased and he was trembling, his lips quivering and blue as he tried to continue his prayer.

Love knelt down beside him. "Kirill, listen to me. This is not what God wants."

His eyes remained closed, but he paused to answer her. "How do you know what God wants? You don't even believe in God."

"But you do. And you must believe he's sent you here for a purpose."

"For my iniquities. I am cast into the outer darkness."

"But what if he's sent you to be a guardian to Ola? She's become very fond of you, and if something happens to you, I don't know what it will do to her after everyone she's lost. She's depending on you. We're both depending on you."

When he raised his head at last, the pain in his pale blue eyes made her heart ache.

"And I've become very fond of you myself, despite your foolishness," she said. "Now come on." Love held her hand out to him, and he rose unsteadily and stumbled with her to the tent, falling onto his knees when they were inside. Ola was already fast asleep.

Kirill bowed his head as if he meant to go back to his prayers, but Love knelt down in front of him, and he looked up at her in surprise.

"Will you do something for me, Kirill?"

"If I can." His eyes were puzzled as she removed her mittens, and he flinched when she laid her hand gently on his thigh. She could feel the cilice beneath the robes.

"Please take this off."

"The flesh must die," he began, but Love was working her cold fingers through the buttons of his outer robe. He shook his head at her and tried to push her hands away as she moved to the inner buttons, but his own fingers were numb. Love opened the *podryasnik* and stared at the spikes in his inflamed flesh.

She looked to him for permission as she took hold of the knotted cord, and Kirill didn't stop her. He breathed in sharply as she tugged at the knot, but remained stoic as she untied it and worked the spikes out of his thigh ring by ring. Trails of blood extended from the tiny prick-marks like the stigmata of a saint.

She set the cilice aside, her hand against the mutilated skin. "Why did you do this?"

He avoided her eyes. "Because the flesh is weak. And I am easily tempted."

"Tempted by what?"

Kirill's voice came out in a harsh whisper, as if it hurt his lungs to admit it. "By you."

Love reached up and touched his flushed cheek. His beard was soft against her palm. As he blinked his haunted eyes at her, she moved her hand to his chest, feeling his heart pounding softly in the dark, before buttoning him up and pulling her mittens back on.

"Good night, Kirill." She kissed him on the cheek and climbed between the covers, snuggling close to Ola. As she closed her eyes, she could still feel Kirill staring silently at her.

In the morning, Love woke to find him gone. She scrambled out of the tent and left Ola sleeping, afraid he'd walked off into the snow, but Kirill was kneeling by the fiery river with two of the Cherubim standing over him.

"I will ask you one more time, 'holy' man." Zophiel grabbed him by the beard. "What are you doing outside your tent?" When the Cherub got no response, he forced Kirill to his feet. "Perhaps you came out for a swim?" The Cherub shoved him toward the river.

"Don't!" Love ran forward as Zophiel held Kirill's head twisted at an awkward angle to keep him from sliding into the molten river. "He was only praying! Kirill, answer him!"

Kirill met Love's eyes. "As you say." He answered in angelic. "I pray to God."

Zophiel pushed him away with disdain, and Kirill caught himself as he swayed on the bank. "There is no 'God' here," the Cherub said.

"I pray to God for deliverance." Kirill stared at him defiantly. "From the Evil One."

Zophiel's lion countenance turned toward him. "I've warned you not to insult us again."

Without flinching, Kirill began to recite another piece of scripture. *"And the* Devil *was thrown into the lake of fire and sulfur where the beast and the false prophet were, and they will be tormented day and night forever!"* He stepped forward and shoved the furious Cherub toward the river with all his might.

Zophiel shrieked with the voice of the eagle as he stumbled backward. Two sets of enormous golden wings that had seemed to be a part of his garment a moment before were flung wide, and he rose from the riverbank before he ever touched the river. The amber eyes in his human-like face appeared to burn as he focused them on Kirill. He flapped his upper wings toward the monk, and with a blinding flash of light and a crack like thunder, Kirill was gone.

Odinnadtsatoe: Seraphic Light
from the memoirs of the Grand Duchess Anazakia
Helisonovna of the House of Arkhangel'sk

The others were surprised when it was I who tried to kill Vashti.

The moment Belphagor stopped dead in the lobby of the Arkhangel'sk airport, fingers white around his phone, I knew. Something else—something worse—had happened, and Ola, so close at last, had been snatched from within our grasp. He'd passed the phone to me, and I had listened to Ola's voice, happy and eager one moment, wailing and frightened the next against the mocking voice of a Cherub.

We hurried home in a hired taxi, but our heavy hearts already knew what we would find there. The door stood open, with snow piling on the inside mat, the light from the kitchen casting a pale yellow triangle across the entryway. There was no one there.

It was then I had calmly walked to the kitchen, taken a fish-scaling knife from the drawer, and turned and plunged it into Vashti's flesh. I was aiming for the gut, but her reflexes were quick, and instead I buried it in her upper thigh.

Only the others were stunned by my actions; Vashti didn't seem surprised.

Vasily pulled me away while Dmitri and the Nephil's twin tended to her leg. A great deal of blood seemed to be flowing, but I apparently hadn't severed the crucial femoral artery, and she would live. After

Dmitri managed to stanch the blood, Nebo sewed her up. There was no anesthetic.

I watched all this, and watched Vashti's stoic response to it, from the chair by the fire where Vasily held me down. He didn't chastise me—no one did, not even Nebo—only kept me from doing her further harm. His eyes, however stunned they appeared to be, nevertheless seemed dark with satisfaction. I suppose if I hadn't done it, he or Belphagor would have, and they would have been more efficient at it. In the end, her death would have served nothing but to remove our only source of information, so it was just as well I was unaccustomed to killing.

At my request, Vashti was given my bed in which to recover—not because I gave a damn about her comfort, but because I couldn't bear to look at her, and being kept from the fireplace while she convalesced beside it would have driven me into a rage. Nebo would bunk with her, and Dmitri with Belphagor, while Vasily and I would sleep by the fire as Love used to do.

Love was another matter that made my heart heavy. I was dismayed at how quickly we'd jumped to blame her, even assumed the Nephilim had been doing her bidding. Twice I'd failed to follow my gut, sending Ola farther from my arms. Out of heartbreak, I'd ignored what I knew and believed of Love's nature, choosing instead to think the worst of her. And on the isle of Solovetsky, I'd thought myself foolish when my heart had told me Ola was there.

I'd never been so immersed in darkness in my life as I was now, not even after the loss of my family and all I'd known when Kae took them from me. The short, dreary winter days of Arkhangel'sk were a just accompaniment to my mental state.

In brief sessions of lucidity and wakefulness between the fog of painkillers upon which her brother Nebo insisted despite my heated disapproval, Vashti told us what she knew, though she was reticent to speak of Love. The *Angliski* clan of Nephilim were not in league with the Malakim, she said, but against them. She explained, to Vasily's dismay, that it was a barroom brawl he'd provoked last summer that had prompted the clan to take action. Through the Night Travelers, they'd learned that the Malakim had been alerted to his presence by Seraphim in the region who had caught his scent. With a sick feeling in the pit of my stomach, I realized the Seraphim who had murdered the syla had been much closer than I'd dreamed. Vasily was quiet, avoiding Belphagor's eyes.

Knowing it was only a matter of time before the Malakim discovered the dacha, the *Angliski* had taken Ola to keep her from falling into Aeval's hands, believing we couldn't be counted upon to do what was necessary to prevent it. What was necessary, as perceived by many in the clan, was apparently the death of my child.

I flew at her throat at this suggestion, once again held back by Vasily and Belphagor overriding their own instincts to strangle her. Vashti claimed she'd swayed Zeus from his intentions and insisted Ola be kept alive, but I wasn't about to give her the benefit of believing anything that put her in a better light.

When she said she'd arranged to get Love and Ola off the island, I didn't believe her, but Dmitri confirmed that Nebo himself had worked with Vashti to obtain the aliases and plane tickets necessary for their escape. When we asked how she managed to deceive Zeus, she replied that she'd killed him. She broke down when she said this, grieving her lover, and it was the first thing out of her mouth I believed.

She had no knowledge of the Cherubim, however, and we could only conclude that the Malakim had staked out the dacha, waiting for Ola's return. Using the Cherubim, they'd been able to circumvent the careful surveillance of the Watchers. With nearly five months to come up with a way to spirit Ola into Heaven despite the vigilance of the Grigori and Nephilim, "spirit her" turned out to be exactly what they'd done. The Cherubim alone among the Host had the power to assume other beings directly into Heaven.

I fell deeper into despair. If Vashti spoke the truth—and I hadn't yet conceded that she did—we had no way of finding out where in Heaven Ola had been taken. What little contact we still had with the underground told us her presence in the Firmament hadn't been mentioned. She wasn't in the palace. She hadn't been seen. It was Solovetsky all over again.

Dmitri gathered us together, and I stared in open hostility as Vashti, with the help of Nebo, came downstairs to join us, but the Grigori chieftain asked for my forbearance. When we were seated about the kitchen table, he looked at me grimly. A wave of dread washed over me. I was certain he had news of Ola.

"I've spoken with the clan heads. We're in agreement. An expedition must be taken into Heaven to get your daughter back."

"An expedition?" This wasn't what I'd expected. "You mean another breach?" The breach they'd opened to storm Heaven to rescue Belphagor and me had taken two hundred Fallen bursting onto the palace square, with the benefit of the element of surprise and the fortuitous convergence of a general strike among the demon workers. Afterward, Dmitri and the others had conceded it was the pandemonium created by the striking workers that had allowed a frontal assault to work.

"Not a breach. The Queen's forces would be ready for that. I propose we take a small contingent up through the portals at Baikal and try to blend in as Raqia locals. We'll infiltrate the ranks of the queen's workers on her Urban Renewal projects. And then we'll get ourselves sent to work among the camps."

I stared for a moment, realizing what he was suggesting. I'd spent time in Aeval's first House of Correction, the model for her Relocation Camps. It was time I didn't like to remember. Pregnant with Ola, believing Belphagor had betrayed me, I'd been at the mercy of Aeval's dehumanizing system. If Ola was there—I could barely stand to entertain the thought. We had to get her out.

I began to plan at once. "We'll need the badges the Fallen are made to wear. Red disks of felt embroidered with black pentacles. And I'll need some of the potions they sell in the Demon Market to disguise myself."

Dmitri frowned at me. "We can't allow you to do that, Anazakia. It's too dangerous. We mean to take a small group of our people."

I stood up and dared him to fight me on it. "She is my child. I have wasted enough time being safe." I looked to Vashti with bitterness. "And I'm afraid my faith in your people has been rather damaged." I stared the same challenge at Vasily and Belphagor, waiting for them to oppose me on this, but Vasily's grim expression conveyed no objection.

Belphagor glanced at Vasily before responding. "If something happens to you, Nazkia—"

"Nothing will happen to me if I'm with Ola. When I held her, Aeval couldn't touch me. Her Seraphim couldn't touch me. It's why Aeval wants her. She knows that without Ola I'm powerless against her." I sighed at their doubtful expressions. "You didn't see what happened. You weren't there. Ola's radiance combined with mine."

"Her radiance?" Vasily gave me a dubious look. "Ola hasn't shown any sign of her element yet. We don't even know which of us she favors. And even if she had, how much radiance could she actually manifest in Heaven? How much could you? Certainly none that was visible."

"I saw it." Vashti had remained silent beside Nebo, avoiding drawing attention to herself until now. For the first time since stepping off the airplane, she met my eyes straight on. "You don't even know what it was, do you?" Her voice was soft, almost awed.

Dmitri frowned at her. "What are you talking about?"

Vashti kept her eyes on mine. "The radiance. The baby's radiance... it's seraphic."

This was preposterous. I had no idea what game she was playing at now, but I wasn't about to stand for it. I came around the table, and Nebo stood up and stepped between us. The expression on his face was sorrowful, as if he was compelled to defend her though even he knew she didn't deserve it.

"It's all right, Nebo." She waved him away, her eyes still on me. "The Queen knew. I could see it by the way she behaved—as if she feared you."

"There's just one problem with your theory," I snapped. "Ola's father is not a Seraph."

"Not entirely. But I'm guessing half." She looked at Vasily as if expecting him to confirm this.

He burst out with a laugh of utter amazement. "You're completely insane."

"You don't see it?" Vashti appealed to the rest of us. "The fire inside him? The heat he radiates? He smells like a chimney, for Heaven's sake!"

"I'm a firespirit!" Vasily shoved his chair back from the table in exasperation.

The rest of us were regarding Vashti as if she'd truly lost her mind, but Belphagor's expression was peculiar.

Vasily scowled at him. "Don't tell me you're entertaining this nonsense. My father was no Seraph."

"How do you know? You never met him." Belphagor ignored the withering look Vasily gave him, the flames burning deep within his pupils as they did when he was furious or aroused. "You can light a cigar with your tongue. You can breathe glowing embers. And you are extremely…warm." Heat rose in his own cheeks as he said this, and I felt a corresponding heat in mine.

"Obviously, I have a Seraph somewhere in my line." Vasily was dismissive. "Generations ago. Just as one of your ancestors was from the First Choir. But neither of us bears any resemblance to those creatures."

Vashti shook her head at him. "No. You're a true hybrid, just as we are. The Nephilim have a special interest in celestial genetics. We strive for purity."

This struck me as an odd phrase. It was the same spoken by the Host. How could a being whose blood was by nature mixed aspire to genetic purity?

"It's what Zeus's clan has devoted itself to." She spoke his name with a mixture of sorrow and shame. "They keep meticulous records of our bloodlines, going all the way back to the Nephilic Genesis. Most

Nephilim regard those who are more than once removed from a full-blooded Grigori-*humani* pairing as diluted. For Zeus's clan, only those descended from successive nephilic pairs are pure."

Vasily rose and pushed away from the table. "This is *derrmo*. Ola is not Seraph. I am not Seraph. I can't believe any of you are listening to this for one minute. She's obviously deranged." He turned his back on her and addressed Dmitri. "What do we need to do to make this expedition happen? I want it to start yesterday."

"You're not going." Dmitri held up his hand as Vasily's eyes flared with anger. "I won't have both of you at risk. And you're far too recognizable. I'll put a team together and we'll move out first thing in the morning."

Dmitri had underestimated the firespirit stubbornness. I knew immediately that Vasily would not abide by his ruling. Certainly, Belphagor knew it. Early the next morning, when Vasily crept out from under the blankets he shared with me by the fireplace, I lay awake and watched him quietly put together a bag for travel. After leaving a note on the kitchen table, he glanced over and realized he hadn't been quite as stealthy as he'd hoped.

"Nazkia." He started guiltily. "I'm just going ahead by a few hours so Dmitri can't object when I'm already there."

I sat up and hugged my knees. "Take me with you. He'll try to keep me back when he finds you gone. He thinks one of us needs to be here, safe for Ola if something happens to the other. But it's a suicide mission. There's no getting her out. We both know that."

His face twisted with emotion.

"I want to see her again, Vasily, even if it's the last thing I see. I want to say good-bye to her."

He nodded, unable to speak, and I rose and pulled some traveling clothes together. As an afterthought, I packed the knife Knud had bequeathed to me. Vasily added my name to the note before we slipped out, letting the others know we meant to see them in Heaven.

As we stepped into the frozen darkness of the winter morning, he turned to me suddenly and gathered me into a rough embrace, kissing me with an almost desperate passion. I melted into him like a bit of supple wax beneath his heat, tasting the charged particles of our radiance between our tongues. He released me all too soon and I slipped from his arms with reluctance.

"I love you, Nazkia." He whispered it fiercely, words he'd never said before. "Whatever happens to us now, I wanted to tell you—"

I put my fingers on his lips. "I know, Vasya. I know."

With his large hand enveloping mine, we walked the three miles into town in our felt *valenki* designed to keep our feet dry, the only sounds the crackling of tree boughs laden with snow and the crunch under our feet among the deep drifts. The verdant, wood-paved walks that bordered the rows of wooden houses in the azure light of summer were now but icy trails lined with naked trees in the dark.

The train to Moscow took twenty-four hours. From *Yaroslavsky Vokzal*, we boarded the Trans-Siberian to Irkutsk—the same train that had once brought from the portals of Heaven a destitute and frightened girl in the company of demons.

Vasily carried a large cache of bills, and he purchased tickets for us in a private *spalny vagon* compartment. We spent the three days on the train in near silence, but it wasn't the bitter quiet in which we'd spent the months since Ola's disappearance. It was the silence of needing no words.

I lay against Vasily's warm chest while the train pulled us onward through the frozen world, wondering if what Vashti had said could be true. When Helga had told me of Vasily's parentage, she'd seemed angry about his mother Ysael's familiarity with the demons of Raqia. Vasily hadn't known either of his parents, but Helga remembered, having grown up in Raqia. She considered Ysael's relationship with the unidentified demon father to have been an unforgivable transgression, trespassing into territory that wasn't hers. If a Seraph had fathered

Vasily instead of one of the Fallen, was it possible Helga hadn't known? As before, I shuddered at the thought of intimacy with a full-blooded Seraph, even in their non-lethal celestial form.

Vasily tightened his arms around me, thinking I was cold. As the motion pushed up my sleeve, the violet charge of our combined radiance jumped from his arm to mine, and I found my whole being tingling with it. We would be in Heaven tomorrow, where we were almost certainly headed for a fatal rendezvous. Just as I wanted to say good-bye to Ola before we were separated from each other forever, I needed to say good-bye to Vasily, and there was one language between us we both understood without words.

I unbuttoned my flannel shirt and shrugged it off as Vasily loosened his arms around me, watching me with a gentle fire deep within his eyes.

I whispered the words I'd once uttered to set us irrevocably on this path: "Share your heat with me."

The fire quickened in his eyes and his voice became gruffer than usual. "I don't have any protection."

I colored slightly. "Belphagor went to the druggist. I've been taking a pill."

Before he could recover from his surprise, I pushed up the cotton T-shirt that was the only one he wore even in winter and pressed myself against him, sending the radiant aurora skipping along every surface where we touched. He traced my flesh, watching the strange violet light follow his finger. On the first ride we'd taken together on this route, his fire had healed the hole torn in me by my cousin's sword.

Now he filled the empty hollow where Ola had been torn from me as surely as her unborn cousin had been torn from my sister for whom she'd been named. I wept softly as we rode the waves of our radiance, and I could feel the wetness on his own cheeks as he kissed me, hot tears that turned to steam. I held him while he poured his sorrow and despair into me, as he'd poured out his grief over the loss of Belphagor the first time we came together. I could feel that, too, even now—how desperately he missed what they'd shared. If circumstances were different, I knew Vasily would have forgiven Belphagor anything. If only they'd had time. If only we had found our daughter.

We grieved together and whispered our good-byes with our bodies, making peace with what was to come, and at last we fell asleep in the waning glow of an unlikely alliance of the opposing cardinal elements of water and fire.

When we arrived in the southern Siberian city of Irkutsk, we had to board yet another train, the local Circum-Baikal rail that took tourists up along the shore of the frozen lake and through the old railway's many tunnels. Here at Lake Baikal, the Heavens touched the world of Man.

At one of the tunnels, the few winter tourists were encouraged to get out and walk, exploring the impressive construction through the layers of rock. Vasily and I trailed the group, and when their attention was occupied by their surroundings, he showed me the gap in the wall that went unnoticed unless one was looking for it. We passed through and disappeared into the dark, ancient tunnel only cross-dimensional tourists ever saw.

Vasily used his breath to light the way. I'd forgotten this, having been in a drugged stupor and a state of shock when we'd descended the winding stone staircase—only three years ago, though it seemed like a lifetime.

As we climbed, he exhaled rings of glowing vapor as if smoking a pipe, though the heat was coming from deep inside him. The stairs seemed to go on forever, closing in from behind with the passage's claustrophobic magic as we ascended. It was designed to confound and even sicken those who might find it by sheer chance, ensuring they would never make it to the top. The ascent itself, of course, was an illusion, as there was no literal vertical climb to the realm of Heaven, as if it were situated above the sky. It was, as the syla might put it, always there, merely unseen.

When we reached the landing where Vasily expected the portal to be, he paused and turned about as if lost. "It ought to be here. I don't understand."

"Belphagor said The Brimstone had burned down. Could they have closed it from above when they rebuilt?"

"Shit. I'd forgotten." His eyes glowed with worry behind his glasses. "Bel must know other portals…but I've only ever used this one."

I thought for a moment while we stood in the disorienting absence of direction. "Helga sent me to another one. I'm not sure how to find it from below, but it was in the storm drain at the end of a long street in the eastern end of Raqia."

"A storm drain? We ought to be able to see the light filtering down from the street." He turned in a slow circle, already apparently losing his bearings—such was the danger of this place's magic. Then he took my hand, leading me decisively toward a passage to our right. I saw nothing, but Vasily swore there was a barely perceptible difference in the level of illumination. The only illumination I saw was what he emitted.

We walked for what seemed like hours. It could easily have been days, or only a moment. The passage of time in this place was more confounding than that of the syla's Unseen World.

At last Vasily pointed toward the edge of the ceiling over a curve we were approaching. "There. That thread of light. That could be it."

I wasn't sure I saw anything, but as we drew closer, I found it easier to see my way, as if the passage was becoming gradually lighter. He stopped and pointed it out again, standing almost directly beneath whatever he was seeing, but I shook my head.

"You're too short." Without warning, he lifted me with his firm hands around my waist, holding me aloft as if I were a ballerina. At my new eye level was a long, flat plank of ice, just high enough to be covering the opening of a storm drain. Light indeed was somewhere behind it.

I put out my gloved hand. "It's frozen. It must be the snow piled against the drain."

Vasily lowered me to the ground and reached up, feeling along the ledge that had hidden the opening from me. He took a utility knife from his pocket and began jabbing it at the ice like a flat pick, loosening shaved bits that sprinkled down over us like snow. He pounded at it steadily and methodically, but he seemed to be making little progress.

"Why don't you use your heat?" I suggested, and he laughed at the simple solution that hadn't occurred to him.

Vasily bent down and kissed the side of my neck above my scarf, imparting some of that heat to me with a touch that made me shiver. He took his knife and held it to his tongue until the metal glowed. When he resumed his picking with the red-hot knife, the ice began to melt, trickling down over the stone in a steady stream.

When he'd melted all the solid ice away, he stretched his arm farther across the ledge and brushed at the loose snow packed behind it. All at once, a rush of cold air struck us and the low light of a celestial afternoon was clearly visible above. Vasily boosted me up with the same effortless grip around my waist that made me wish we'd had more time on the train, and I scrambled through and climbed out onto an empty street in Raqia.

The space was tight for Vasily's broad chest and shoulders, but after removing his coat, he managed to get through. We stood beside each other in the snow, staring at the seemingly deserted street. Now that we were in, we had no plan for how to proceed. I wondered if we ought to wait below for the others, but Vasily explained the stairs wouldn't remain in the same apparent place for long and we'd have to find the portal all over again.

Helga's apartment wasn't far. Though I was certain to receive a poor reception if I brought Vasily to it, there was a chance she might have heard or seen something of Ola. Whatever unfriendly welcome we might receive was worth the possibility of news.

On the block where Helga's building stood, I hesitated, uncertain which was hers. A curtain moved in one of the windows above, and after a moment the sash was thrown open. A harried-looking woman peered down at us.

"We have no bread. Go on. Beg somewhere else."

"We're not beggars. We're looking for Helga…" I paused, ashamed as I realized I'd never known her father's name. We'd called her only by her intimate given name, as though servants were unworthy of the common respect of a patronymic or a family name. The window slammed shut, and I stared up at the closed curtain in surprise. Perhaps my bad manners had offended her.

In a moment, however, one of the unmarked doors opened, and the woman glanced nervously up and down the street. She pulled her shawl over her head and drew it tight against the cold. "Haven't you heard, then?" She spoke in a conspiratorial whisper. "Are you up from Arcadia?"

I opened my mouth to deny it, but Vasily stopped me. "We've come from the southern lands." Arcadia was the capital of Vilon, often referred to as the southern lands, but the phrase was also a euphemism for the world of Man.

"You've come too late." She kept her voice low. "The queen has issued a warrant for her arrest for anti-celestial activities. She's gone into hiding." The woman nodded at my widened eyes, as if agreeing with my expression. "We were all shocked. The Ophanim Guard came to take her to the camps, but someone had tipped her off and she was already gone." She perused the street once more. "Word is she may have gone north to join the Makhon cell in Zevul." She pulled her shawl down low. "I'm sorry, now, but you'll have to move on. It doesn't look good, you standing in the street. You don't want to be picked up for loitering or soliciting." She stepped back without another word and closed the door.

Speechless, I exchanged a look of astonishment with Vasily. What could Helga possibly have done to earn Aeval's attention?

He regarded the closed door with a frown. "Raqia's changed. Of course, I've never been to the respectable end before." He sighed. "I suppose she's right. We shouldn't linger." A light snowfall had begun, and he smudged a flake across my cheek.

Something fluttered under my eye and I blinked and ducked my head instinctively, thinking something had flown at me. Vasily was staring at me strangely.

"What?" I brushed at my face, my nerves spiking with anxiety.

He held his bare palm to my cheek—he rarely bothered with gloves or mittens—and the source of the fluttering became clear. Our radiance was visible in Heaven. Though it wasn't the brilliant aurora our touch produced in the world of Man, a distinct, pale lavender glow wavered like a field of static electricity in the dark. There was no mistaking it.

I clasped my mittened hand around Vasily's bare one on my cheek. "I told you I'd seen it in Heaven." I brought his warm palm to my lips, placing a kiss in the center and watching the feathery luminescence.

Vasily shivered and snatched his hand away. "Don't. You'll drive me mad." He gave me a rueful grin. "I'm sure the good folk of reformed Raqia would be alarmed if I ravaged you in the street." He examined his hand once more, turning it about as if he might see his own radiance. "How is it possible?"

I shrugged, covering a shiver of my own as I tried to put the image out of my head of being ravaged by him in the street. "How are we possible at all?"

Vasily put his hand in mine again. "Let's get you to the market so you can buy your potions." He shook his head as he observed me, a slight glimmer of flame in his eyes giving away his own preoccupation. "Even in those clothes, you look like an angel."

It wasn't the marketplace I remembered. The Demon Market had been a lively gathering place at any time of year, with vendors of every description and hawkers at every intersection. Games of dice and cards had spilled onto the sidewalks among the kiosks and curtained tents, and musicians had played for money on the street corners, while ladies of the evening called provocative greetings to male patrons of the marketplace—whether it was evening or not.

There was none of that here now. The stalls were orderly and quiet, and they seemed to belong to only vendors of practical things, such as dry goods, textiles, and household services. We found a booth selling fresh meat pies, and Vasily bought one for each of us.

He crossed the vendor's palm with crystal after he'd already paid for the pastries. "We're looking for…salves and elixirs. Do you know where we might find any?"

"I have no idea what you're talking about, sir." The vendor eyed our unmarked coats. "You're not Fallen. What would decent Host be doing in Raqia?"

"We are *not* Host." Vasily took off his spectacles for full effect as he flashed the red of his eyes.

"Could've fooled me." He eyed me suspiciously as I ate my pie. "Though it isn't wise to be practicing folkery on the street."

"Folkery?"

"Peasant magic," he snapped. "Watch your eyes." The vendor looked us over once more, again lingering on me. "You've been below."

Vasily put his spectacles back on and folded his arms. "So?"

"Should've stayed." He leaned over the ledge of his stall and muttered as he glanced about. "North end of Lethe. Where The Brimstone used to be."

Vasily nodded grimly. "I know it."

"They can set you up with your badges." He tapped his own on his sleeve. "You'll need them if you intend to remain in the Firmament."

Vasily thanked him and we hurried away.

Lethe was the last street between the border of Raqia and Elysium proper. It was where I'd first met Belphagor in our fateful game of wingcasting. He'd beaten me effortlessly, taking every crystal facet I had. I wasn't a novice to the cards, but I'd never made it to the master table before that night, and I hadn't known whom I was up against. It was also there at the wingcasting table that Helga had found me to tell me my family was dead.

On the site where The Brimstone used to sit was a much smaller, unassuming building of brick. A sign hung over the door announcing we'd come to the apothecary. Vasily looked sad as he lifted the latch and stepped inside.

An elderly demon, his age a sure indicator he'd spent many years in the world of Man, stooped over the counter, measuring powder into a jar. He adjusted his wire spectacles and observed us, paying particular attention to me.

"We've come from the southern lands," said Vasily. "A vendor in the markets mentioned you were the place to go for our badges."

He barked his reply with a harsh voice. "Her Supernal Majesty's Admiralty is the place to go for your badges. But then you'd be arrested for violating Queen's Order Five-Twenty-One."

"What's Queen's Order Five-Twenty-One?"

"That the Fallen abstain from the world of Man." He chuckled to himself. "Don't know what you'd call Fallen that never fall." He rang a bell on the counter. "Lively!"

I jumped at the unexpected shout, while a mousy demon girl hurried from the back room and dropped the apothecary a halfhearted curtsy.

"Take the lady's and the gentleman's coats in back." He winked at us. "She's nimble with a thimble." He chuckled again as she slipped our coats from our shoulders.

I peeled off my icy mittens and shoved them in the pockets before she scurried away.

Pushing up his spectacles, the old man squinted at me for a moment while we stood awkwardly before the counter. "And I suppose you expect to be taken for a demon bitch." He snorted at my expression. "It's not meant as an insult, my good woman, just a technical term. It's not as if we're Host, after all, putting on airs. We recognize our animal nature."

I looked helplessly at Vasily, no idea what to say to this, but the old man continued while he took bottles down from his shelves and checked labels.

"Don't waste my time denying you're Host. Anyone can see it. That's why you've come. I won't ask what foolish situation you've gotten yourself into that hiding among the chattel race in Queen Aeval's Heaven seems like a good idea to you. I don't care." He set an empty vial on the counter next to the items he'd selected and glanced at Vasily. "Though I expect this tall, fiery buck is good enough in the sack to make an angel do foolish things."

"That's enough," snapped Vasily. "We're just here to do business."

"Business. Business." The man muttered to himself as he measured liquids into the vial. When it was filled, he screwed a metal cap onto it and slid it across the counter to me with his finger on the top. "For my investment in your business—" He paused, and his eyes fell on my signet ring. "I'll take that."

Too late, I hid my hand behind my back. The blue celestine was a symbol of the House of Arkhangel'sk and a protective charm against the elemental firespirits who served the crown. I'd meant to keep the ring in my pocket and had forgotten. "No. I need it."

The apothecary shrugged. "That's the price."

Vasily was outraged. "Then we'll go somewhere else."

"There is nowhere else."

The girl returned with our coats emblazoned on the arms with red and black pentacles.

The elder demon gave an exaggerated click of his tongue. "Lively's done the work already. If you won't pay, I suppose I'll just have to keep your coats for her trouble." He jerked his head at the girl to take them away, and gave Vasily a vulgar wink. "I expect you keep her warm enough."

With a sigh, I brought my hand from behind my back and slipped the ring off my finger.

Vasily grabbed my hand. "No, Nazkia."

"We need the glamour."

His eyes were flickering. "We *need* to keep you safe from the

Seraphim."

"It's not going to matter."

"I'll give you twenty facets," he offered the demon, an outrageous sum the man couldn't have earned in a month, but the demon shook his head stubbornly.

I pulled my hand from Vasily's and handed over the ring. This was a suicide mission, after all. I wouldn't be needing it much longer.

"That's for the vial," said the demon, taking his finger from the lid as he pocketed the ring. "I'll take twenty facets for the badges."

Vasily grabbed our coats and pushed mine onto my shoulders. With a glower, he shoved his arms into his own and pulled a pouch from his inside pocket. He shook twenty facets into his palm.

The demon sighed. "Should've looked in the pockets, Lively. I keep telling you."

After I'd shrugged into my coat, I picked up the vial and turned it about. A dark, greenish liquid sparkled inside it. "How much do I take?"

He was busy counting his facets. "Take it all. Don't take any of it. I don't care."

"Well, what will it do?"

"Darken you up a bit." He regarded me as if I were stupid. "What did you think it would do, give you horns and a tail?"

"I thought there would be gemstone oils. I used to use them to color my eyes. And there were herbs to take the color from my skin, not to darken it."

"Obvious folkery. Tinted eyes will get you slapped in irons faster than you can blink them. And dulling your color? Did that fool anyone? With your porcelain skin, and hair like spun honey? Darkening is the only thing that will work. Unless you'd rather just have your man here rough up your face. A few good punches to the snout ought to do it."

Vasily was ready to leap over the counter in a rage, but I pulled him toward the door. "Never mind," I said. "We got what we came for."

"*Mudak*," snarled Vasily as he slammed the shop door.

I opened the vial and drank half the draught, grimacing at the bitter taste, and we headed back toward the portal to wait for Dmitri's expedition to arrive. Vasily watched me while we walked, pulling up his collar against the wind rising with the approaching evening.

After a moment, he reached out and touched my hair beneath the fur *ushanka*. "I don't see any difference." He glared toward the apothecary's shop. "That son of a succubus!"

"Wait." I grabbed his arm. Ahead of us, an unnatural light threw shadows across the snow. "Ophanim. I think we're out past..." The ground swayed beneath me and I clutched at Vasily, who caught me as my legs gave way. "Curfew," I finished, as the light of the Ophanim disappeared into a warm and pleasant darkness.

Dvenadtsatoe: A Pale Horse

"Nazkia!" Vasily scooped her up as the cold glow of the Ophanim Guard illuminated the end of the dusk-shadowed street. He considered for a moment letting the Ophanim apprehend them. It would be a quick way to get into the queen's camp to find Ola. But the thought of Anazakia waking in such a place was more than he could stand. He turned and hurried back to the apothecary's door.

When he tried the latch, it was locked. He banged on the thin wood, but there was no response. The Ophanim patrol would soon be upon them. Vasily had the advantage for the moment, but even cloaked in shadows, he'd be spotted in a few more feet.

"Damn you, demon!" He pounded the door. "Let us in or I'll show the Guard where we got this bottle!"

The door opened so swiftly he almost fell into the shop. The demoness Lively was staring up at him in wide-eyed fear.

"Lively!" The old man snarled at her from behind the counter. "Get them in!"

The girl stepped aside and Vasily hurried in.

"What the devil do you mean," the apothecary demanded, "shouting in the street like a madman?"

"What the devil do *you* mean by drugging my girl?"

"Nobody drugged anyone. It's not my fault she's a lightweight. She shouldn't have drunk so much."

The heat in Vasily's eyes flared at the old man. "You wouldn't tell her how much to take!"

The apothecary waved his hand with a grunt of dismissal.

"As if it mattered anyway. Your elixir's useless."

The apothecary lifted a bushy white eyebrow. "Seems to be working fine to me."

Vasily glanced down at Anazakia and nearly dropped her in surprise. She'd taken on the appearance of the girl who stood behind them.

"Worked a little too well, maybe. Suppose I shouldn't have used so much of Lively's blood."

"Blood?" Vasily looked from Anazakia to the demon girl. It was uncanny. Both faces were a wan olive with a softly pointed chin, and both had tresses of a dull nut-brown, though Anazakia had retained a slight wave to hers if one looked closely. Her full, rose-hued lips were now a thin, colorless line, and the color had also gone out of her cheeks.

"Lively," barked the apothecary. "Give the girl your bed to sleep it off." He nodded to Vasily. "Might as well tuck in for the night anyway. Curfew won't lift until dawn."

Vasily followed Lively through the partitioning curtain and set Anazakia down on the straw tick mattress the girl indicated on the floor. After covering Anazakia with a blanket and tucking it beneath her unfamiliar chin, he returned to the front of the shop.

"How long will the other effects last?" he asked the apothecary. "Will she have to take more in the morning?"

"Nyet. Nyet." The old man lapsed into Russian easily, as if he'd spent more time below than above, and from the looks of him, he might have spent the equivalent of a human life below. "Won't wear off until she takes the antidote."

"What antidote?" Vasily demanded. "You didn't sell us an antidote."

"Well, you didn't ask for one, did you?" the old man grumbled as he pulled out another bottle from beneath the counter, filled with a clear fluid. "Twenty facets."

Vasily yanked the pouch from his pocket and counted out another twenty. The crystal facets used for money in Heaven were worth plenty here, but far more in the world of Man. Below, they called them diamonds.

The apothecary took his crystal and handed over the bottle. "Bit of a problem now, though, isn't it?"

"Why's that?"

"Needs a drop of your girl's blood. Hers has Lively's in it now." The old man shrugged. "Won't be of much use unless you've stored up some of her pure angel blood somewhere else."

• • •

The expedition came to a dead end with the discovery of the closure of the Brimstone portal. They'd ended up with a late afternoon arrival at Lake Baikal, having fallen behind at every step of the trip. It started with arguing over who was to stay behind with Vashti now that Vasily had given them the slip and gone ahead. The Nephil's twin couldn't be left in custody of her, regardless of how helpful he'd been in her surrender. It was simply unwise to pit his loyalty to one against the other.

Belphagor had flatly refused the duty when Dmitri suggested that as Ola's only other earthly connection, he couldn't be risked on the expedition. Dmitri had called in Lev to take the task, and he was only too happy to be included. Though he was Dmitri's partner, Lev was an ordinary demon. Born to a Grigori father and a demon mother, without the human blood, he was as unremarkable as Belphagor. As a result, Dmitri—in Belphagor's opinion—was overprotective, trying to keep Lev out of clan business as much as possible, though by birth he was an Exile himself.

After Lev's arrival, however, Nebo insisted he wouldn't leave his sister, and Dmitri gave up and decided Vashti would be brought along. Her injury could work in their favor. They needed someone on the inside at the Relocation Camp to be on the lookout for Ola, and turning in a known fugitive to the authorities in Raqia would help earn their trust to get the group a spot on the local work crew. They'd planned for that someone to be Belphagor, as his infamy would make him difficult to disguise among the demon population, but how much better to have two fugitives to turn in than one? Bringing the Nephil who'd stolen Ola from the queen in the first place would be sure to seal the deal.

In addition, the camp was likely to be segregated, and it would take someone on the women's side of the complex to find the child. With this in mind, Dmitri called in Margarita Pavlovna from the Muscovite Nephilim to infiltrate the women's work crew. A graceful redhead in her late thirties, Margarita was petite for a Nephil, but she possessed a surprising mastery of the traditional Russian martial arts known as *Systema* from her years in special forces. If Belphagor hadn't known otherwise, he would have taken her for a dancer.

With the addition of Margarita, the expedition was complete. Only now, with the former Brimstone portal sealed, the six of them were stranded in the damp stone passage affectionately known as the "Hell Stairway."

Belphagor felt like a fool. He should have known the Host wouldn't have left the portal open once it was discovered. "I don't suppose one of you could just blast through it somehow. Being earthspirits."

Lev snorted. "Oh, sure we can, Bel. Just like you can float through it, being an airspirit. It's actually *that* easy for Exiles to get back into Heaven. We're just that lazy."

"No need to be testy, sweetheart." Belphagor squinted under the sudden glare of Dmitri's flashlight. Dmitri had been more forgiving of Belphagor's intimacy with Lev than Vasily had ever been, but the Grigori chieftain had always been somewhat irritated at their easy banter, preferring to make himself scarce when the two of them were together. They were in a tight space now in more ways than one. It would be wise not to exacerbate his annoyance.

Nebo lowered Vashti onto the steps to rest her leg, while Margarita observed the rest of them with mild disdain, though she was careful not to direct her condescending looks toward the chieftain.

She gave Belphagor a dismissive once-over. "So you don't know any other portals? Just the one under your gambling hall?"

"It was more than a gambling hall." He tried to keep a lid on his temper. "It was home for a great many demons."

"Demons who are dead because of your involvement with angelic royalty, if I'm not mistaken."

Belphagor cast an angry look at Dmitri. "Are all of your Nephilim such bigots? We don't need another ignorant purity queen who can't stay on mission."

"I'm not some sex-starved simpleton who sells out my entire race for a bit of Nephil cock," Margarita countered. "I know where my loyalties lie."

"I'm sitting right here," said Vashti. It was the first hint of resentment she'd displayed since turning herself in.

Margarita regarded her coolly. "How clever of you to recognize yourself in that description."

"That's enough," snapped Dmitri. "Belphagor's right. The Grigori have agreed to defend and protect the offspring of Vasily and Anazakia, and I've done a poor job of keeping our people on mission. There is no room for delusions of ethnic or social superiority here. If there's anybody on this team who isn't prepared to die for the child of an angel, you can leave now—with the exception of Vashti, of course."

"I'm on mission now," Vashti said in a quiet voice. "I don't expect anyone to believe that, but I'll try to earn your trust."

"Thank you, Vashti. I appreciate that." Dmitri gave her a stern look. "And yes, you will have to earn it. I don't know that you can." He looked at the others. "Well? Are we clear?"

"Yes," Margarita answered a little stiffly. "My apologies."

Nebo nodded. "Absolutely."

"Lev?" Dmitri prompted.

"Are you joking?" Lev's lifted eyebrow dropped at the disapproving glare. "Of course, yes."

Dmitri sighed. "Now that we're clear on our mission, Bel, what do you propose we do about getting into Heaven?"

Belphagor considered for a moment. "Well, it's got to be past curfew in Raqia now, so I suppose we're stuck here for the night. We can look for an alternate portal in the morning."

Margarita groaned, but the general mood was one of reluctant agreement. After eating the last of the food they'd brought for the train trip, they curled up on the landing and steps with their packs for pillows and tried to catch a few hours' sleep.

Belphagor found himself sharing a corner with Margarita, their backs together for warmth. The red ponytail hanging over her shoulder reminded him of Vasily, and he dreamt he was with him on Misha's terrace in the Unseen World. Instead of Misha touching him, it was Vasily with his warm firespirit hands, kissing Belphagor's scars and then kneeling before him. On his face was the penitent expression of need and desire the novice pickpocket had shown after the thrashing Belphagor had given him on the night they'd met.

"Moi sladostny malchik." He whispered the endearment after Vasily had earnestly pleasured him without being asked. *My sweet boy.* He reached down to stroke the matted red locks Vasily wore tied together on his crown, but instead Belphagor's hand rested on soft, pale golden curls.

He yanked back his hand as if he'd been bitten. The head in his lap belonged to the former principality of Heaven. Kae lifted his head and laughed, grey eyes twinkling with the same sadistic merriment that had so often danced in the quicksilver eyes of the queen. In his hand, Kae held the *knut*, Belphagor's blood dripping from the cured leather thong at its tip.

"Come back for more, I see." Kae grinned. "So have I. What can I say? It's in my blood."

Belphagor woke in a cold sweat and sat up with a start. Margarita curved away from him with a murmur of half-conscious complaint. The walls and ceiling surrounding them weren't the same as when he'd gone to sleep. As the staircase was prone to do, it had changed locations under Raqia—or Raqia had changed its location over the staircase. A crossbeam of early winter light was clearly visible at the top of the stairs before the next turn of the spiral. Wait long enough in the Hell Stairway, it seemed, and Raqia came to you.

• • •

Vasily had prepared her, explaining how the elixir worked, but Anazakia still stared in shock into the mirror over the washbasin.

"What do you mean I don't have my own blood anymore?" She brushed her fingers against her lips. "You mean I have to stay this way?"

"He says we should have taken a drop of your blood before you drank it. When your blood was still pure."

"Nice of him to tell us afterward!" Tears wavered against her lashes—lashes that were no longer the long golden ones turning up subtly at the ends, but dark, thin, and straight. Vasily reached out to comfort her and saw Lively standing behind them just inside the curtain. Anazakia jumped, her olive cheeks burning a deep crimson.

"Don't trouble on account of me, miss. I don't take it personal." Lively's voice was nearly as nondescript as her appearance. At least Anazakia had retained her own. Lively pulled a moth-eaten hat down low over olive-green eyes that matched Anazakia's, wearing a tightly buttoned, patched coat. "Master Apothecary says you're wanting the queen's labor camp. I'll take you." They'd decided to head to the camp directly, since there was no chance of rendezvousing with the expedition now.

"Master?" Anazakia picked up her coat. "He doesn't *own* you?" She asked the question in a tone of disbelief, as if expecting an answer in the negative.

Vasily suppressed the urge to roll his eyes. Anazakia seemed forever naive about the ways of her own erstwhile princedom.

"I work for him." Lively shrugged. "Master Apothecary paid my family a goodly sum."

As they followed Lively out, the apothecary, finishing a transaction with another patron, grunted at them from the counter without looking up. Vasily glanced at the female patron with interest. Down her back hung a neat queue of hair in a rich, natural red like his own when it wasn't enhanced with his element. Anazakia noticed his look, and he ducked his head awkwardly. He'd never experienced the jealousy of a lover before—Belphagor had practically passed him out like a favor to men who expressed an interest in him—but he was certain he was seeing it now in the cool look from her foreign grey-green eyes.

Lively led them out onto a street that was at least less deserted than it had been the afternoon before, though it was a far cry from the bustling district Vasily remembered. The brothel that had stood beside The Brimstone was gone, as was the tavern across the street. The flophouse on the corner—he'd roomed there briefly after his return to Raqia following the "misunderstanding" between him and Belphagor—still showed a vacancy sign in the window, but across from it had been a cabaret that rang with bawdy music and bawdier company at all hours of the day. It was silent now. Judging by the ragged souls hanging about outside, a soup kitchen had taken its place.

Though the Demon Market had once extended from the Devil's Doorstep at the south end of Lethe Street to its glittering lanterns on the embankment of the River Acheron, it was now a single lackluster block. Past the anemic remnants of the former marketplace that had drawn angels both genuinely bohemian and scornfully curious, the streets of Raqia grew progressively shabbier as they neared the perimeter of Elysium. It was as if its proximity with the city of the ruling class had left a stain of sin upon the city's edges.

Crossing the Acheron over the bridge that demons and angels alike called the Hell Gate, they entered the capital of the Firmament of Shehaqim. Anazakia seemed tense. Vasily took her hand, hesitating for a moment to glance from her face to Lively's to be sure he was taking the right one. Eyeing the red and black badges on their sleeves, angelic mothers and nannies crossed to the other side of the street with their prams as they approached. It was nothing new to Vasily. When he'd bothered to set foot in the sterile domain of the Host, his appearance had always elicited such reactions, but this was a world in which Anazakia had once been used to drawing attention of a different kind.

He'd seen the supernal family himself once on his way out of Elysium, as he'd left Belphagor to seek "higher learning" in Araphel. The four girls were much younger, before Grand Duke Azel was born. Anazakia was the youngest, so she must have been the child in pigtails tucked in layers of furs between her mother and a sister in the front of a gilded red sleigh, while the older girls rode behind them. All four of the grand duchesses were honey-haired beauties with the same porcelain skin, and all had bright, joyful eyes in varying hues of summer sky. They'd smiled and laughed with one another as the sleigh passed by. It was a joy he hadn't seen in Anazakia since he'd known her—except perhaps when holding Ola.

Lively led them from the southern end of Elysium along the main thoroughfare of Palace Avenue, the "Nevsky Prospekt" of the celestial realm. The camp, she said, was situated on the northern boundary of Elysium on the shore of the Gulf of the Firmament, the spot where Vasilevsky Island lay across the Neva from *Dvortsevaya Ploshchad* in the world of Man. In Heaven's geography, a startlingly similar River Neba separated the two. To reach it from the south, one had to pass by the Palace Square or take a long detour around it.

Anazakia gripped his hand tightly as they neared the newly constructed Winter Palace. It was much like the one that had stood on the spot when they'd last been here—the one in which Anazakia had spent her childhood—only grander in scale and embellishments. She paused for a moment and looked up at the gilded gates spanned by two golden, four-winged Cherubim. In front of them, some black-robed, bearded fool was ranting and waving his hands. A lone protestor, Vasily supposed, although he resembled in habit and manner a monk from the world of Man. Perhaps he was a Dominion, one of the angels who dedicated themselves to art and philosophy, though a protesting Dominion seemed unlikely.

A small crowd had gathered to gawk at the man, and at its perimeter,

Vasily realized with a start, stood Belphagor, alongside Dmitri and Lev dressed in celestial garb. Behind them, with her hand around one of Vashti's bound arms, was the redheaded demoness who'd visited the apothecary this morning.

Anazakia saw them as well. She started toward them, and Vasily followed, raising a hand when Belphagor looked up. The warmth of his recognition tugged at Vasily's heart.

"Where are you going?" Lively called out. "That's not the way."

"Some friends," said Vasily over his shoulder. "We've been looking for them."

Anazakia pulled ahead through the crowd, but Vasily stopped in alarm. A horse-mounted company of the Queen's Army was clattering onto the square from the direction in which they'd come. The gathered crowd parted as they approached, isolating Dmitri's expedition and the bearded man beside the gate.

Flanked by four Ophanim on foot, the field marshal of the Armies of Heaven rode at the head of the company on a magnificent bone-colored stallion. The whiteness of the Ophanim's luminescence and their traditional dress was a stunning contrast to the severe black of the field marshal's uniform and his high, polished boots. A heavy cape of grey wool draped the back of his mount, and on his face he wore a strange mask that covered more than half of it, including his left eye, while what remained uncovered appeared badly disfigured. He signaled to the captain of the company, who approached the raving man.

The captain struck the man across the shoulders with his crop. "For what cause do you disturb the peace?"

"D'yavol!" the man cried.

"Just whom are you calling devil, Raqia dog?" The captain raised his crop in outrage, poised to strike again.

The strange man whirled and pointed at Vashti. "There is devil!" he shouted in stilted angelic. This was no Dominion or Raqia demon.

Vashti took a limping step back.

"And there!" The man pointed into the crowd. "And there!" He seemed to be targeting everyone around him. The more Vasily observed him, the more certain he became that this was indeed a monk from the world of Man. What he was doing in the middle of Elysium's Palace Square, Vasily couldn't imagine.

"Enough!" The captain turned his horse toward two of the Ophanim. "Arrest this fool."

As the Ophanim came forward and took the fellow by the arms, the monk howled in fear, jerking under their grip. Vasily couldn't blame him. He'd done battle himself with a pair of Ophanim during the assault on the palace. Their touch had sent a current of unpleasant sensation crawling along his skin, as if he'd stuck a fork in an earthly electrical socket.

"Devils steal the angel child!" the monk cried out in Russian, twisting in their grasp. He pulled one arm free to clutch at the golden Cherubim that graced the gate. "Devils of the fourfold wings!"

Vasily pushed through the crowd and caught Anazakia's sleeve.

Wide-eyed, she turned to him, mouthing, "Ola?"

Belphagor must have had the same thought. He stepped toward the monk, unwisely coming between him and an Ophan. The Ophan grabbed Belphagor around the neck. Like Vashti's, Belphagor's arms were bound behind his back, and he jolted, unable to pull away.

The added commotion caught the single, watery eye of the dark-clad field marshal. He leaned down and spoke to the captain, who turned toward Belphagor, still arching against the Ophan's grasp.

"You! Demon!" The captain gestured with his crop to the Ophan to bring him closer. "Your papers. Identify yourself before the field marshal of Her Supernal Majesty's Army."

Belphagor spat at the ground and the captain raised his crop to strike him, but Dmitri stepped forward to hand up an identification card. Vasily was close enough to hear his calm announcement in the deeper intonation the Powers possessed within celestial air.

"This man is the demon Belphagor who escaped from Her Supernal Majesty's House of Correction. My friends and I are bringing him in for the reward, along with this Nephil who participated in the escape of the grand duchess. We caught them sneaking into Raqia from the world of Man." Beside him, Lev also handed up his papers.

As the captain examined their identification, the earthly monk lunged forward against the grip of his captors with a look of madness.

"The grand duchess!"

Anazakia froze beside Vasily, but the monk wasn't looking in her direction. He focused on Vashti, whom the red-haired woman had brought forward at Dmitri's words.

"You lie to me!" he shouted in angelic. "You tell me you protect, but you are demon! You lie and send to *nechiste angely*! You give to unholy devils!"

The field marshal looked at Vashti shrewdly and beckoned the captain closer with two gloved fingers to murmur something else to him.

The captain tucked the identification papers into his coat. "Place them all under arrest." He addressed the prisoners as the Ophanim surrounded them. "You are hereby charged with conspiring against the throne of Heaven."

• • •

It seemed their plan to get inside the Relocation Camp had worked a bit too well. Belphagor didn't dare look back at Vasily as the mounted company turned at the field marshal's orders and moved out toward the wide Celestial Boulevard bordering the embankment.

There'd been no sign of Anazakia in the crowd. Belphagor had no idea whether they'd been separated or if she was just well hidden, but he was relieved that the two of them had defied Dmitri and gone ahead to Raqia. It would have been a hopeless disaster if all of them had been caught up together. He only hoped Nebo had seen Vasily.

They'd decided before venturing into the capital that with Vashti as a prisoner, her twin would be too conspicuous traveling with them. Nebo had donned a hooded cloak to hide his striking ebony skin and followed at a distance, with the intent of meeting up with the others once Belphagor and Vashti were inside the camp.

Beside him, the monk suddenly broke free of the Ophanim and ran toward the field marshal at the head of the company.

"Are you angel or are you devil?" he entreated as the Ophanim caught him beside the field marshal's horse.

The field marshal stopped and regarded him. "Angel," he said gruffly.

"You will rescue child from four-winged devils?"

"What child is that?" The field marshal's voice had a peculiar roughness to it. Like Vasily's, it gave the impression of one who smoked excessively, though it had less strength to it than Vasily's did, as if the field marshal had a bad case of laryngitis.

The monk's eyes were wild. "Grand duchess!" he exclaimed in a voice of vexation. "The child, Ola!"

Belphagor cast a glance behind him at Vashti, who was making a great effort not to meet his eyes. She knew who this man was and she'd kept it from them.

The field marshal stared down at the monk. "You've seen Her Supernal Highness?"

"Nogi yee niskhodyat k smerti, i yee shagi idut nastol'ko, naskol'ko ad!" He recited the words as if from some earthly scripture.

" 'Her feet go down into death,' " Margarita translated. " 'And her steps go in as far as hell.' "

The field marshal gave the Nephil a dismissive look and started forward again.

The monk was persistent. "Devils called Cherubim. They take child to Gehenna."

The field marshal fixed his single eye on the monk. "Gehenna? The child is in the Empyrean? She's here in the Heavens?"

The monk began to rave once more in the language of Men. *"The Son of man shall send forth his angels and shall cast them into a furnace of fire: there shall be wailing and gnashing of teeth!"*

The field marshal growled at the captain next to him. "Shut him up."

The captain dismounted and struck the monk, and when the poor fool continued to rail, he stuffed a handkerchief into the monk's mouth and tied it in place with a leather strap from his horse's pack.

The field marshal brought his ivory champagne mount around to face the company. "Turn about!" he ordered in his strained voice. "We're bound for the Empyrean."

· · ·

It was Lively who determined their next step. As Vasily stared after the mounted soldiers, she grasped Anazakia's hand beside him and implored her earnestly. "Are you the daughter of Sefira?"

Anazakia's face, in Lively's image, went pale.

"I've been asked to bring you to Aravoth," said the girl.

"Asked by whom?" Vasily demanded, keeping his voice low. "Your Master Apothecary?"

"By the Elohim."

It didn't seem prudent to continue this conversation in the square. He jerked his head toward Palace Avenue. "I saw a café a block from here. Not another word until we're off the street."

As they made their way across the square, Vasily noticed a hooded figure following them at a distance. He continued calmly toward Palace Avenue, then ducked into an alley between the rows of businesses that lined the block beyond the square. With a warning sign to keep quiet, he pushed Anazakia and Lively behind him against the wall.

When their pursuer entered the secluded alley, Vasily leapt on him, concentrating the heat of his element into his hands as he grasped the figure by the throat. As they struggled, the hood fell back, and Vasily saw it was the Nephil's twin.

"Sukin syn!" Vasily exclaimed as he let go. "Sonofabitch, Nebo. I thought you were a fucking Seraph!"

Nebo pressed his fingers to the red welts on his throat. "You were going to attack a Seraph with your bare hands?"

"I didn't have anything else," Vasily grumbled. "Why are you skulking behind us? Where were you when the others were being arrested?"

"Dmitri thought I'd give them away. He wanted me to lie low until they'd gotten Vashti and Belphagor into the camp. Don't think this was exactly the plan, though." He lowered his hand and examined it as if expecting to see blood. "Who are the twins?"

"It's me," said Anazakia. "I've taken a potion. And this is Lively. She's…"

"She's going to explain after we're off the street," said Vasily.

They found a quiet booth in the café, and after the waitress left them with coffee and pastries, Vasily turned to Lively. "So. Explain."

Lively warmed her hands on her coffee and looked at Anazakia. "The Elohim wish to speak with Your Supernal Highness. They'll give you asylum if you satisfy them that you aren't mad." She lifted her coffee mug to her lips. "You don't seem mad to me."

"I'm sorry," said Vasily, "but who exactly are the Elohim?"

Anazakia answered. "They're an elite sect of the Order of Virtues. Aeval pretends to be one, in fact, but she isn't."

"That's why they joined the Party," said Lively.

Anazakia looked at her blankly. "The Party?"

"The Social Liberation Party," said Nebo. "The group Vashti joined."

"*Khristos.*" Vasily scowled. Now the revolutionary fools were overrunning the world of Man.

Lively nodded at Nebo. "But the Elohim—and many of us—don't agree with the Party on the aims of the revolution. They've split off into the Party of the Socialist Host."

Vasily clenched his hands into fists. "You belong to the group of revolutionaries who stole my daughter. Before the queen stole her from you."

"Not anymore. That's why the Socialist Host was formed. We found such actions unacceptable." She looked away as he continued to stare at her with his eyes burning. "But the queen didn't take her. We don't think the queen even knows she's here."

"What do you mean? Her Cherubim burst into our home!"

Lively nodded. "Yes, and the Cherubim are working with the Social Liberationists."

Vasily leaned back on the bench, shaking his head in disbelief. There had been talk of revolution as long as he could remember. He'd even been fool enough to get caught up in it for a while after he'd left Belphagor. There were always small groups of angels, generally students, who joined in the militant calls for reform, but he'd never heard of higher-order Host such as the Virtues backing such radical ideas, let alone pure elementals like the Cherubim.

"Then you know where she is." Anazakia grasped Lively's hand. "Tell me where she is!" Lively tried to pull away, but Anazakia yanked her forward by the wrist and spoke in a deadly whisper. "Have they put her in that awful place or not?"

Lively seemed to be reconsidering her assessment of Anazakia's sanity. "If you mean the camp—" She winced against the pressure on her wrist. "No, she isn't there. I don't know where she is. But the Elohim know." She gave a startled gasp as Anazakia released her abruptly.

Anazakia drew herself up as she regarded Lively, and she seemed a different person for a moment, more than just in physicality. It was as if the Anazakia who'd been raised to be a queen had emerged from inside her and usurped the gentle, uncertain woman who contained her. As at Arkhangel'sk, when she'd unexpectedly and coolly attacked the Nephil nearly twice her size, Vasily was at once aroused and alarmed by it.

"Then you will take us to the Elohim," said Anazakia. "Immediately."

***Trinadtsatoe:* The Virtuous Court**
from the memoirs of the Grand Duchess Anazakia Helisonovna of the House of Arkhangel'sk

Traveling to Aravoth this time of year, even if I were not Heaven's most wanted fugitive, was a risky prospect. Not only were the northern winds through the mountain pass treacherous and the ridges over which we would have to cross to reach the isolated mountain city covered with ice and snow, but we would have to pass the Summer Palace where, Lively informed us, the queen was still in residence.

The road between Elysium and the Mountains of Aravoth was well maintained and relatively flat until we reached the foothills, but it was also crawling with the Queen's Army. Every inn-and-tavern town along the way seemed to house a garrison of soldiers. Like the company that had swept through Palace Square and apprehended Belphagor and the others, each comprised conscripted Fallen, enlisted Host of the Fourth Choir, commissioned officers of the Order of Powers, and a small number of foot soldiers from the Ophanim Guard.

"There were not so many when my father was in power," I murmured over my hot cider to no one in particular, watching the soldiers carousing at a nearby table in one of the taverns where we'd stopped for the night.

"They keep the people in mind of the queen's rule," said Lively, cautious around me since the café on Palace Square. "Ever since she issued the decree that she was sovereign to all princedoms."

"But the principality of the Firmament has always been sovereign—*Principality of All the Heavens*."

"In name, yes. But the other princedoms were never challenged in their authority before. The Firmament has had little to do with the governing of Aravoth or Zevul. Ma'on and Vilon have always given tribute but were left to their own rule. And the Empyrean…" She shrugged. "Well, no one even really knows what goes on there."

"Let's not forget Raqia." Vasily spoke with a touch of vitriol.

"Raqia?" I paused over my cider, baffled. "It's just a district. It's always been subject to the Firmament."

Vasily observed me over the tankard of his harder drink. He, too, seemed cautious of me. I could see he was holding something back, as if I'd irritated him with my lack of political acumen, but he was afraid to say it.

It wasn't the first time I'd seen this expression on his face. When it came to questions of angelic rule and the oppression of the Fallen, I had to concede I was exceedingly ignorant. Until a chambermaid told me during my imprisonment under Aeval, I hadn't even known the Fallen were largely the property of the Host who employed them. My surprise at Lively calling the apothecary her master wasn't because I remained unaware of the practice, but because I hadn't known a demon could enslave another demon. It was a strange and unsavory world that lurked beneath the gilded surface of the Heaven in which I had been raised to believe.

Vasily threw back the rest of his drink—not cider, like mine, but hot just the same, yet it didn't seem to bother him. "Raqia is a princedom."

I stared at him blankly. Raqia was barely large enough to be called a town. It was most certainly not a princedom.

"Every demon knows it. Every demon remembers it. And yet the daughter of the *Principality of All the Heavens* has never heard of it." His tone was disdainful and incredulous.

"You're not making sense," I said a bit tersely. "How can Raqia be a princedom? That's like saying this tavern stop is a princedom."

Vasily sighed and set down his tankard. "The Princedom of Raqia once stretched from the River Lethe to the Acheron along the Gulf of the Firmament and from Ma'on to the coast. Arcadia was the capital."

I laughed, thinking he was joking, but the glimmer of orange in his pupils said he was serious. "But that's impossible. Arcadia is the capital of Vilon."

"It is now." He spoke patiently, as if I were a slightly dim child. "Aden used to be their capital. The Firmament annexed Arcadia and gave it to Vilon when Mikhail I redrew the borders to erase Raqia. It was a concession for their grab of the entire coastline of the gulf along with Erebus on the coast. They had to give Vilon something to ensure their cooperation."

I looked at Lively to see if Vasily was making this up for some reason I couldn't fathom.

She nodded. "The Firmament subsumed Raqia. And that's what Aeval intends to do with the rest."

I was astounded that knowledge passed down through nothing more than oral tradition among the Fallen was simply absent from the angelic histories. Of what else was I still ignorant about the world that had been my father's domain? He had been the sovereign of a princedom in which a large number of its subjects had no voice at all, and now I learned those subjects should not even have been our own.

But it was one thing, however base, to invade a princedom and divide the conquered lands among its neighbors. It was quite another to claim absolute rule over an entire world. If the queen was now exercising total authority over all princedoms, it meant she had subjugated not only the Host of the Second Choir—the firespirits who, despite their greater physical power, had always served the lesser Order of Principalities—but the Third Choir as well. The Second Choir angels were presumed to serve their inferiors because their strength lay in brute force and not in mental faculties, but the Third Choir was the intellectual elite of the Heavens.

Among their Orders, the Dominions were the philosophers and

scholars who'd founded the universities at the city of Araphel where all angelic nobility studied, and from the Powers came the military strategists of the Armies of Heaven. It was from this order the Grigori themselves had fallen. The Virtues I couldn't imagine bowing to a lesser order. They were seekers of truth in all things, lending themselves to celestial investigations and contemplating the nature of the universe.

A commotion beside us jarred me from my troubled thoughts, and I looked up to see two officers swaggering toward our table—or perhaps *staggering* might have been a better term, as they'd clearly been imbibing for hours. I ducked my head instinctively, though no one would recognize me now.

One of the officers stepped behind me and put his hand on my shoulder, turning me about on my chair. "Don't be coy now, madam." He gave me a wink and an exaggerated flourish as he took an unsteady bow. "We've seen you looking at us."

"I don't know what you mean."

"He's partial to twins," said the other with a smirk, and put his hand over Lively's as she shrugged away from him. "What say you give us a dance?"

Vasily and Nebo pushed back their chairs and stood at once. Had the officers been slightly more sober, I'm certain they would have backed away at this, particularly when Vasily straightened his spectacles in the way he had that managed to make him look more menacing instead of less. It was like watching another man crack his knuckles or his neck.

"What's the matter, demon?" said the officer beside me. "I always heard your kind believed in sharing. Surely your orgies can spare at least one twin."

I shook my head in warning at Vasily as his eyes blazed red, but he was beyond exercising discretion. The officer moved his hand from my shoulder to my neck, and Vasily charged him like a bull.

The surprised man went down without a fight, while the other swung foolishly at Nebo and found himself being tossed across the bar, but their comrades at the other table came quickly to their aid. Lively and I leapt out of the way as the tavern descended into chaos.

"We'd better pack," she whispered. I agreed. Whatever the outcome, it was certain we wouldn't be welcome here for the night. Our belongings had already been dropped off in our room, so we hurried up the stairs and stuffed what little we'd unpacked into our bags.

Before I turned to head down, Lively stopped me and nodded at the window. "The stable is right below us."

I shrugged. "What's that to us?"

"The army horses. They're bred for the ice and the snow. We could ride straight through to Aravoth."

"You must be joking. You want to steal horses from the Queen's Army? The soldiers would be after us in an instant."

Lively looked at me slyly. "Not if someone were to release the rest of their horses."

I shook my head. "What makes you think they'd go? Horses won't just run off on their own in the snow. They know where their feed and shelter are."

"They might if their feed and shelter were on fire."

I stared aghast as she began to pry open the icy window. "That's someone's property. The innkeeper's done nothing to us."

Lively thrust open the sash. "You are a prim, sheltered thing, aren't you?"

An unexpected fury took hold of me, as if she were an insolent maid and I were still a revered grand duchess in my father's house, and I swung her by the arm to face me, but this time Lively stared me down.

"Do you want to find your child or not? There's a revolution afoot and the inhabitants of Heaven are choosing sides. There's no longer any place for what's proper and what's right. The world has changed."

The world has changed. It was the same thing Helga had said to me the last time I'd seen her. She'd called me spoiled, and it was true. I'd been reacting to the events in Heaven as if they affected only me, as if it were a game of noughts and crosses and the other players were treating me unfairly. I was waiting for some supervising grownup to step in and make the others abide by the rules. But this wasn't noughts and crosses; it was chess, and I was fretting over pawns.

Tossing her bag onto the roof of the stable, Lively crawled through the window and lowered herself beside it. I glanced back at the door before I gave up and followed. Lively shimmied down the side of the building and swung herself into the stable through an unshuttered window. When I jumped down beside her, a young stable hand sleeping in the hayloft scrambled to his feet and spun toward the door as if to shout for help, but Lively grabbed his hand.

"Please. Don't turn us in. We've run away from our master."

The stable hand looked doubtfully toward the exit.

"He beats us," she pleaded. "Just make yourself scarce for an hour and we'll be gone. No one will know."

"I'll be beaten myself, miss," the youth said reluctantly. "If anything were to happen…"

Lively's wheedling tone changed swiftly as she turned to me. "Pay him."

"Pay him?" I exclaimed. "I haven't any crystal!"

Lively sighed and began hitching up her skirt. "Come here, boy. Unless I miss my guess, you've not had a woman before."

"No, mum." He blushed, and I blushed with him.

I gaped as Lively rapidly unlaced the stable hand's pants and pulled him up against her while she scuttled back onto a bale of hay.

"Come on, then. Quickly. We haven't got all day."

The stable hand fumbled beneath her skirt, and Lively rolled her eyes and helped him get what he was after. She wrapped her legs around his bare behind as the youth groaned and pumped frantically against her.

His wide-eyed initiation was over in a minute, and Lively pushed him off, straightening her garments as she jumped down from the hay. He staggered back, staring for a moment, damp and exposed, before turning beet red and hitching up his pants.

"You'll keep quiet," Lively ordered, and he nodded as he fumbled at his laces. "If you don't, I'll curse you and you won't be able to use that thing again."

He nodded more vigorously, his eyes huge.

"Go on, then."

The stable hand scurried out the door.

Lively gave me a challenging look, but I didn't say a word. We opened the stalls one by one and led the horses out into the yard, reserving four of the finest to saddle up for ourselves.

"Take ours out to the road and hang onto them," she said when they were ready. "I'll get the other horses moving and then sound the alarm after I've set the fire. When the innkeeper and the rest run to put it out, I'll bring Nebo and Vasily through the front."

I wasn't sure how she intended to pull this off, but after what I'd seen with the stable hand, I wasn't sure I wanted to know.

I walked the horses to the road as she'd instructed and waited nervously. Smoke rose over the top of the inn as the fire started to burn, and then the horses in the yard began to run, as if something besides the fire had spooked them. Fortunately, Lively had sent them in the opposite direction, but it still took everything I had to calm our four and keep them from joining the rest.

Shouting erupted from the tavern as the doors flew open, and people ran in every direction from both ends of the building. In the darkness, I could see the glow of flames leaping onto the tavern roof. The wind had picked up and carried the sparks. For several agonizing seconds, there was no sign of my companions, and then Lively came tumbling out onto the tavern steps beside the lamppost as if thrown, with Vasily and Nebo close behind her.

"And if I see you here again, I'll run you through myself!" the innkeeper shouted after them.

Lively dragged Vasily and Nebo into the dark toward me, but a pair of soldiers had come after them from the yard, and one of them gave the alarm.

"They've stolen the horses!"

Another pair gathering snow to put out the fire dropped their pails and joined the pursuit.

Lively reached me first and mounted one of the horses. "Come on." She took off down the road without waiting. I was an adept rider, but I was barely able to swing up into my saddle before my horse began to run at a whistled signal from the demon girl, and the others with it.

"Wait, Lively! We can't leave without Vasily and Nebo!"

"They'll catch up!" she called back without slowing.

I looked over my shoulder and saw Nebo pulling ahead of our pursuers with Vasily close behind him, but there was little I could do as the horses thundered over the hard-packed snow after Lively. Whether she was a horse charmer or had used some demon trick, it didn't matter, as they had decided to follow her lead.

We rode hard for nearly half an hour before I convinced Lively to slow to a walk. At last, Nebo appeared over the crest of a hill. A stutter of alarm raced through my heart.

I stopped and dismounted as he took one of the loose sets of reins. "Where's Vasily?"

"They caught him. He told me to run." Nebo paused for breath. "To protect you."

"Protect me?" I looked toward the horizon in dismay, hoping Nebo was somehow mistaken, and silenced my fear with anger. "And just who is going to protect *him*?"

Lively drew her horse up beside me. "He does seem fairly capable of protecting himself." There was another, subtle implication in her words: that I was not.

"Well, thanks to you, I suppose he'll have to be!" I looked out over the empty lane of snow, contemplating the hint of sunrise painting a cool line of blue on the eastern horizon. We'd said our good-byes on the train from Arkhangel'sk, prepared for the probability that we wouldn't make it out of Heaven, but I was unwilling to leave him like this. We would both see Ola again if it was the last thing we did. We'd promised each other.

I blinked away tears. This couldn't be it. "I'm going back for him."

Nebo put his hand on my horse's lead as I stepped back into the stirrup. "With all due respect, you'll only get yourself caught. What good will that do your daughter?"

Lively nodded. "The Elohim are waiting. Time is of the essence."

I hesitated. Ola was what mattered most. Vasily had sacrificed his freedom to make sure I reached her. "You're certain the Elohim know where Ola is."

"That's what they said. Virtues aren't known for stretching the truth."

That much I couldn't argue with. The only thing I couldn't be sure of was whether Lively herself could be trusted. Pushing down the ache in my gut at going on without Vasily, I mounted my horse. There was only one way to find out.

Luck was with us, and we encountered none of Aeval's soldiers as we spent the day heading north. With the aid of the horses, we were able to cover more ground without tiring, and we reached the rolling foothills of the Mountains of Aravoth before nightfall. Unfortunately, this also marked the boundaries of the Summer Palace estate. We couldn't afford to linger here, but the horses couldn't be pushed much farther. The road to the palace itself was heavily guarded, and the glow of Ophanim was visible at the gates, but the private road to our mountain—the Queen's Mountain now—was hidden from the highway by a grove of pines, deserted in the twilight. There was nothing along this road but our hunting lodge. With no one in residence at this time of year, the private road was left unprotected.

"This way." I turned my horse into the grove where the snow-cloaked trees would hide us from the palace grounds. Ghosts seemed to walk beside us as I led the way toward my father's hunting house, and one ghost in particular rode beside me as we went farther along the path. This was where I'd ridden with my cousin Kae on a winter's morning and doomed us all.

It was dark by the time we reached the spot where Kae had claimed to see the wild white steed. The little grove was the best place away from the road to make camp, with winter sage still green beneath the snow for the horses to graze on, but its dark memories troubled my sleep.

• • •

The game had become hide-and-go-seek. I thought myself quite clever for evading Maia as I heard Tatia squeal at the collar full of snow Maia gave her upon her discovery. Warming my hands under my arms, I closed my eyes and waited, believing I was alone in the grove until I heard my sister's voice.

"Nazkia, what are you doing up here? I told you it was too cold to go riding." Ola regarded me reproachfully from her mount. Hoofbeats sounded on the road below and I realized I, too, was on horseback.

A white steed thundered past us into the gloomy, mist-shrouded path in the distance. It was the wild horse Kae had seen on that winter's morning.

Ola's expression grew grim. "I told you he was seeing someone else." She turned her horse about in pursuit and broke into a gallop as the grove dissolved into an open plain of ice. Another rider was behind me as I raced after her, and the horse gained on me steadily until I caught the dark profile of the queen's field marshal as he galloped past.

I tried to reach Ola, spurring my horse onward, but the field marshal caught her and swung her from her mount by the hair, tossing her to the icy ground. Ola's horse reared up over her in a panic, and I scrambled from my mount as the steel-clad hooves descended. One hoof struck her stomach before I could drag her from its path, and blood began to spill over the pristine white of winter.

"Ola!" I cried. "The baby!"

"It's all right." She smiled as I cradled her head. "I'm not pregnant anymore." Blood was trickling from the side of her mouth.

The masked field marshal looked down at us from his pale mount, his sword drawn, ready to fall upon both of us.

Ola shivered. "It's so cold. Maybe you should light a fire." She stared up at the sky serenely, and I realized she was no longer breathing.

In a rage, I leapt up and wrenched the sword from the field marshal's grip with both hands. He lunged toward me in his saddle to try to take it back, but I had turned it toward him and he fell on it instead and I drove it deep. As his one eye stared at me in shock, the sword seemed to catch fire in his belly. It consumed him, though the horse remained unscathed.

• • •

I woke, trembling with a cold more keenly felt for the loss of Vasily, to find our small fire had gone out. It was just as well, for when I rose to rekindle it, the glow of torchlight winked through the trees on the road below us, accompanied by the pounding of hooves. I woke Lively and Nebo; there was no need to tell them why. Voices carried up to us with the jangling of metal as the riders drew closer, and we scrambled to saddle the horses and gather our gear.

"I think we should leave this one." Nebo patted the extra horse when he'd finished saddling his own. "We don't have time to take her. She'll just slow us down."

I paused over the saddle I'd picked up.

"If that's the Queen's Guard behind us," he said, "they'll take her along. She'll be in good hands."

I nodded and left the equipment where it was. There was no point in trying to take an extra horse into the rocky, frozen terrain we would have to flee over. The only way out was to keep on through the mountain and rejoin the Aravoth Pass between the sharp peaks of the range on the other side.

Unlike our pursuers, we didn't have the advantage of torches, but we were swifter with three. We made our way carefully over ground not meant for travel in any season. The mountains surrounding Aravoth had protected her small capital in ancient times, in turn protecting the borders of the Firmament from northern invasion. But there had been peace between the neighboring princedoms since before the rule of the House of Arkhangel'sk, and the border at Aravoth was merely a formality.

Morning dawned as we made our way through the winding heights, and I could no longer hear the riders behind us. We all relaxed, thinking we'd lost them, and even indulged in a rest for the horses beside a partially frozen stream. Shortly after midday, however, we descended the far side of the Queen's Mountain toward the northern portion of the Aravoth Pass and saw what had become of our pursuers. A small patrol of the Queen's Army was advancing through the pass from the Firmament border and was nearly upon us.

"Go!" cried Nebo. "I'll take the rear!"

Lively and I spurred our horses on as we reached the bank of the Gihon River at the bottom of the ravine, with Nebo at our heels. The horses had already gone several miles over the rocky mountainside without adequate rest, but they were rugged and built for war, and seemed to take to the sudden burst of action almost eagerly. Unfortunately, their compatriots in pursuit were of equal measure and hadn't spent the last hours climbing over rocks and ice on unmarked paths. I heard them gaining on us, though I didn't look back.

On the other side of the pass, the gates of Aravoth City sparkled in the rare winter sun, but the famous winds of the rock-walled ravine were screaming through as the passage narrowed, driving a heavy mist against us. Lively was ahead of me and had almost reached the end of the pass when her horse stumbled and she went tumbling. Trying to rein in my mount, I narrowly missed her, but Nebo shouted at me to keep going as he came up behind. Lively got to her feet, though her spooked horse barreled past me, and Nebo shouted at me again as he reached down to pull Lively onto his horse. I straightened my mount and rode hell-for-leather, while the supernal cavalry overtook them.

As I came through the ravine, the gates of the city loomed at the crest of the pass, the road from Elysium ending here in the last habitable enclave before the Empyrean began. I thundered over the snow-covered cobblestones of the bridge and through the arched gate of the walled city as the riders of the Queen's Guard at last surrounded me. Slowing my horse, I clung exhausted to her mane, and one of the soldiers grabbed the reins from me and drew her toward him.

Before us on the snow-swept road, another horse and rider approached from the north. Tall and statuesque in the saddle, with hair like the snow itself streaming behind him beneath his fur cap, the white fur of the great cloak that enveloped him fluttering in the wind, the rider advanced on us rapidly. The Virtue pulled up his horse before us, prancing sideways to block the way, and studied me intently. Like Aeval's, his eyes seemed to sparkle like the silver surface of a lake.

"Do I address Her Supernal Highness the Grand Duchess Anazakia Helisonovna of the House of Arkhangel'sk?"

I couldn't imagine how he knew me in my glamour, but there seemed no better answer than the truth. "You do."

The soldiers beside me exchanged looks of disbelief.

"I am Sar Sarael of the Virtuous Court of the Elohim." The Virtue lowered his head. "It is an honor." He turned to the soldier who held my horse's reins. "Release Her Supernal Highness at once. You tread on Aravothan soil."

The officer protested. "This girl, duchess or not, is riding on the stolen property of Her Supernal Majesty the Queen of the Firmament of Shehaqim. Furthermore, if she *is* the fugitive Bloody Anazakia, she is wanted for crimes of high treason against the crown."

"And I repeat, you are not within the Firmament, but on Aravothan soil."

The officer released my reins as a troop of Aravothan cavalry arrived behind Sar Sarael. "Perhaps you are not aware, Your Serenity, that Aravoth is subject to the Queen of All the Heavens."

"We are well aware of the queen's authority." Sarael nodded his head toward the horses drawing up behind me. "And are these Her Supernal Highness's companions whom you have in your custody?"

"They were with her." The officer glanced from Lively to me, obviously still doubtful of my identity. "But they're also under arrest for crimes against the crown."

Sarael was unmoved. "You will leave them here at our Court. You may take the queen's horses back with you, but the prisoners stay here."

"You realize this is in direct defiance of the will of Her Supernal Majesty." The officer lowered his voice in warning. "This will be taken as a declaration of war."

"I suppose the queen shall make of it what she will. But we are a sovereign nation and you are on our soil, and the Queen's Army has shown no respect for it." He gestured to his men. "Take custody of the prisoners."

I dismounted while they led Lively and Nebo forward, and as the queen's soldiers turned about with our horses, I caught a flash of red in the rear of the formation outside the gate. Among the pack animals carrying their supplies, Vasily sat, hands bound before him, upon the back of a mule. His head was covered with a cloth sack, but the locks hanging down beneath it were unmistakable.

"Please, Your Serenity," I appealed to Sar Sarael. "That demon with them—he's my companion also."

"Demon?" Sarael followed my gaze. He frowned, and for a horrible moment I was certain he would disregard my request, but he nodded to his men. "Bring that one to me as well."

Vasily stood blinking in surprise once the soldier had removed the sack from his head and unbound him to bring him forward. "Nazkia?" He looked from Lively to me, and I held out my hand. In the presence of the Sar's entourage, a silent squeeze was all I could give him to convey my relief.

The commanding officer threw one last warning to Sarael as they moved out. "Her Supernal Majesty will not be pleased."

Sarael shrugged. "I've no doubt."

We were escorted through the walled mountain city to the Hekhaloth of the princedom, the great hall of the Virtuous Court. Like the austere and awe-inspiring terrain upon which the city was built, the architecture of Aravoth seemed stark and oversized, as though built for giants. Great edifices of grey stone and marble lined the winding street, soaring several stories overhead in competition with the jagged peaks of the surrounding mountain range.

The Hekhaloth itself, built into the solid rock, was immense. Two dozen columns at its front supported a pediment with a broad tympanum carved with scenes of Cherubim and Seraphim extending their many wings in a display of power and grace. Beside these figures were carvings of robed Virtues in poses of study and contemplation.

Between the columns that supported this, heavy doors that seemed to be inlaid with platinum opened onto a soaring atrium that held an improbable summer garden in the midst of winter. The tiled floor appeared to be heated from below, and as the doors closed, it was like entering another world. We peeled out of our heavy outer garments, and a servant came to take them from us.

A fountain splashed and sparkled at the garden's center in the marble pool that served as a collector for rainwater in the warmer seasons. Reminded of the silver fountains that had been commissioned to decorate the Winter Palace for the last Equinox Gala of the House of Arkhangel'sk, I looked away with a pang of nostalgia.

"We've met before." Sarael spoke quietly to me as he led us past it.

I glanced up at him, puzzled, and then remembered: He'd been a guest at that very gala. Maia had teased me, playing her favorite game, and declared I would marry the next gentleman we saw whose name began with *S*. She had merrily pointed out Sarael, whose Virtuous beauty had made me blush at the age of seventeen. I frowned as I remembered something else. He'd been seated next to none other than Aeval herself, though I hadn't known her identity. She had held the rapt attention of my cousin Kae even then.

"Yes." I gave him a guarded look. "I remember you. But how did you know me?"

Sarael smiled. "News within the cause travels faster than angels. We were told to expect you—and that you might not look like yourself."

We were received in the tablinum, a secluded den on the other side of the atrium, where a dozen Virtues sat around a long stone table. Like Sarael, they all had shining hair like snow, and eyes like lakes of silver, and their skin seemed to reflect and refract wavelengths of light not normally visible to the naked eye.

One of the seated Virtues glanced from me to Lively. "Which one is Her Supernal Highness?"

"I am." I stepped forward. "I took a potion to disguise myself."

He rose and bowed to me, with a glance toward Vasily. "And who is the Seraph's son?"

Vasily's face was red with annoyance that this story had apparently spread. "Whom do you mean?"

"You, sir, of course."

"You're mistaken." Fire deep in his eyes blazed up to make his protest seem mere modesty. "My name is Vasily of Raqia. My father was a demon and my mother was the Grand Duchess Ysael of the House of Arcadia, or so I'm told. But I can assure you neither was a Seraph."

The Virtues whispered together for a moment before the one who'd addressed Vasily bowed to him as well. Vasily, in a manner I have seen neither before nor since, blanched completely white.

"I am Sar Tzadkiel." The angel spread out his arms to encompass the assembly, the sleeves of his robe giving the impression of terrestrial wings. "The Virtuous Court of the Elohim welcomes the son of the House of Arcadia, His Supernal Highness the Grand Duke Vasily."

"Grand—Grand *Duke*?" sputtered Vasily. "No, you misunderstand me. I'm...I'm a *polovina-d'yavol*."

"If by that you mean you are the son of an angel and a demon, it is assuredly not so. We see no demon blood in you. We do, however, see seraphic blood."

"Excuse me." Lively's informal address seemed to startle the Virtues. "What is demon blood? Are we not all of the same four elements? Are not the Fallen simply those whom Heaven chooses to marginalize and oppress?"

Tzadkiel inclined his head. "It is the contention of the Socialist Host that there should be no distinction between the Host and the Fallen. We are one race. Nevertheless, there are genetic traits that identify one's heritage, and it is in our nature to see them. When we say that the grand duke has no demon blood, we are merely affirming what is clear in his physical makeup: his mother and father are both of pure, unmixed elements, and one of these is the fire of a Seraph." Tzadkiel motioned to us to sit down at the table. "Just as it is clear that your other companion is a son of the Fallen Powers and of Men."

Nebo looked uncomfortable as he took his seat between Lively and Sarael.

"Yes, we are aware that you are an Exile. There is some debate among the Party as to whether this restriction should be removed from your people and our former Watchers. But what is foremost now is removing the current threat to Heaven. Sarael?"

Sarael turned to me. "Your Supernal Highness, the Elohim have brought you here to determine whether you are culpable in the deaths of the House of Arkhangel'sk and of the demon workers, as the queen claims."

"She is not." Vasily made a move to jump to his feet in my defense, but I pulled him back.

"It's all right, Vasily. No, Sar Sarael, I have murdered no one. In the first instance, in fact, I was murdered myself."

The Virtues exchanged looks with one another that said they thought I might be mad after all, and even Lively and Nebo looked dubious.

"I was breaking the law. I had conjured a shade simulacrum so I could sneak out of the palace to play cards with demons." This confession was met with disapproving frowns. "My simulacrum was murdered along with the rest of my family."

Tzadkiel regarded me doubtfully. "We are no experts in peasant magic, but would that not have killed you also as soon as your shade was reunited with you?"

"It would have, except—"

"Except then I broke the law." Vasily pushed up his spectacles as if in challenge. "I used my element to repair the damage."

Tzadkiel observed him for a moment. "You can use fire to heal a mortal wound?"

"In the terrestrial plane."

"Still, that is an unusual skill." The Virtue studied him with interest. "Seraphic fire is usually a destructive force, not a constructive one."

Vasily shrugged. "Perhaps they've just never tried."

"And so who was it that killed your shade?" asked Sarael. "Do you recall?"

I nodded to him. "Oh, yes, I recall it very well. It was my brother-in-law, the Grand Duke Kae Lebesovich of the House of Arkhangel'sk." I raised my voice over their exclamations of surprise. "Aeval had bewitched him and driven him mad." They were still buzzing over Kae, but I noticed no one expressed shock at that part of my story.

Sarael interrupted the murmuring among them. "That is a most serious accusation. How do you know it was Aeval, and what makes you certain the Grand Duke was mad?"

"Anyone could see he was mad. I spoke to him myself a number of times when I was a prisoner in Aeval's palace, and he was—" My breath caught in my throat as I remembered Kae begging me to help him in a brief moment of lucidity. "He was completely without memory or understanding of what he'd done, and his mood was subject to wild swings. While he was raving, he told me Aeval had called his blood. She used the same words when she bragged of it to me. She said he was her slave."

This shocked the Virtues, and one even jumped to her feet with her hand to her chest. "Called his blood?"

"I have seen her call the elements in others. She said she could call them all, and she spoke as if blood were one of them."

"Be seated, Sar Sophia." Tzadkiel turned to me with a solemn expression. "Blood is the alembic of all elements. In it, the four exist in their purest forms. One element predominates in all celestial beings, and thus, a firespirit can manipulate fire, a waterspirit can manipulate water. For someone to be able to manipulate them all—well, it is nothing any of our Choir has ever mastered." He lifted his shoulders. "Perhaps the First."

"She is certainly not of the First." Sophia sniffed as she took her seat. "And if they do possess such knowledge, they would not have shared it with a lesser angel."

"She's not an angel at all." Once again, I'd shocked them.

"How can that be?" Tzadkiel looked at Sarael. "You knew her, did you not, Sar Sarael? Was she not a Virtue of the House of Merkabah?"

Sarael looked distinctly uncomfortable. "I did vouch for her, Sar Tzadkiel, as you rightly recall, but I'm afraid I…cannot quite remember how I met Her Supernal Majesty." A profusion of pale coral pigment bloomed in the shining complexion as the others stared at him. "She was for many years on the Council of Ethics, which I oversaw, and the last Sar of Merkabah, whom she claimed to be her father, was known to my predecessor, but when and how I made her particular acquaintance is…fuzzy." It seemed my cousin wasn't the only angel who'd fallen prey to Aeval's glamour.

Tzadkiel frowned. "Fuzzy?"

"I believe she can manipulate the elements of her physical appearance," I said. "For the present, she's adopted the appearance of a Virtue, but she was once the queen of the realm of the Unseen in the world of Man."

This time no one stood or gasped. The room simply went silent, as if they didn't know whether to react with shock, outrage, or utter disbelief.

"I take it you refer to Mankind's fae." Tzadkiel's tone was somewhat condescending. "What makes you think Her Supernal Majesty once ruled a place no one can see?"

"Because they told me. I've been there."

It was clear I'd suddenly lost whatever credibility I had gained during this interview.

"It's true." Vasily came to my defense. "I've seen them myself. They speak to Nazkia—to Her Supernal Highness. We spent some time in the Unseen World before we returned to Heaven."

I threw him a grateful look, and he smiled reassuringly from behind his spectacles. The Elohim rose as if they were dismissing us and Vasily took my hand apologetically, stroking his thumb idly against my wrist. A pale glimmer of radiance followed the path of his touch, and every eye turned to us. Vasily snatched his hand away, embarrassed, but the Virtue next to me grabbed my wrist and turned it about, staring at it.

"What was that?" he demanded.

"Sar Vretil." Though he seemed just as curious, Sarael gave him a stern look. "You are accosting a grand duchess of the House of Arkhangel'sk."

Vretil let go. "My apologies, Your Supernal Highness. But…what was that light we saw?"

All the Virtues seemed to be holding their breath for an answer.

I blushed, uncertain how to respond, and uncomfortable with their probing eyes on me. "I—my radiance. *Our* radiance."

Tzadkiel approached me from the head of the table. "Do you mean to tell us that Your Supernal Highnesses produce this 'radiance' together?"

I nodded silently, thoroughly embarrassed, and didn't dare look at Vasily.

"I beg Your Supernal Highness's forgiveness for such an impertinent request, but—may we see it again?"

I was mortified by all of this attention to something so linked to our intimacy, but Vasily reached for me and boldly clasped his fingers about my wrist as if in defiance of any Virtuous sensitivities. The lavender glow played between our skin, a pale echo of what appeared in the world of Man, but nonetheless an unmistakable display.

The Elohim sat slowly back in their chairs, unable to take their eyes from it. I pulled my arm away.

"Sarim." Tzadkiel quietly addressed his colleagues. "Do you realize what we've witnessed?"

The other Virtues nodded. I looked at Vasily, and he shrugged, as in the dark as I was.

Sarael turned to us. "Your Supernal Highnesses' elements of water and fire apparently react together in a rather unusual way, whether because of His Supernal Highness's seraphic blood, or something in Her Supernal Highness's blood of which we are unaware, or both. Whatever the reason, your combined radiance seems to have formed the quintessence."

"Quintessence?" Vasily looked baffled, but this was a part of every angel's education, and I knew it well. It was theoretical, mythical— mystical, even—as arcane and improbable as the earthly concept of God.

"Aether," I said to Vasily, shocked to hear myself utter the word aloud, as if what the Virtues were saying could possibly be true. "The fifth element."

Chetirnadtsatoe: The Fires of Gehenna

The fire demon had slipped through her grasp. Aeval had been anticipating meeting the father of Anazakia's child. When her scouts had informed her that Vasily had been seen in the Firmament, she'd ordered him brought to her. She wanted to see this Fallen firespirit who was lover to both the grand duchess and to her own reluctant pet. Obtaining the child had thus far proven elusive; the father was the next best thing. And now her reporting officer informed her that though they'd apprehended the demon, they had lost him to a disloyal Virtue when pursuing the demon's fellow horse thieves into Aravoth.

It was troubling enough that a prince of Aravoth would defy her authority, but the report had come with altogether more disturbing news: Anazakia Helisonovna was among the thieves. Her reappearance in the celestial plane could only mean one thing. The pockets of rebellion Aeval's field marshal had quashed, and to which Aeval had given little credence, were more serious than she'd believed. These ignorant revolutionaries meant to usurp her and return the throne of the Firmament of Shehaqim to the misbegotten House of Arkhangel'sk.

All the fuss the Grigori had been making in the world of Man, accusing her Malakim of abducting Anazakia's daughter, had been a ruse meant to throw Aeval off the scent of what they were actually planning; the child was most likely hidden away by Anazakia's own cohorts. She hadn't believed the self-absorbed little princess had it in her.

Aeval was not about to lose everything she'd worked for. The grand duchess was unfit, as her progenitors had been. She would only be a figurehead for the treasonous demon riffraff. Like the Bolsheviks before them, they were incapable of comprehending the natural order. Aeval's Heaven would be a pure Heaven whose authority in the world of Man would once again be felt.

It was time to call her field marshal to her side. He excelled at hunting things down.

• • •

By all accounts, a journey to the Empyrean in the midst of winter was madness, but they were clearly being led by someone mad enough to pull it off. Without question, the field marshal knew his celestial terrain. Instead of due north through the impassable mountains of Aravoth, he took the eastern road that led on a slow but steady northerly incline into Ma'on, through Zevul, and terminated at the northern border city of Makhon, where the icy plains of the Empyrean began. Once they had crossed into the Empyrean, the road to the Citadel of Gehenna would be little more than a path over the ice, but for now, the route was a broad, well-traveled highway.

The company, with its odd collection of prisoners, reached the Zevulian capital of Araphel in twenty days. It was a city almost entirely devoted to the accumulation and dissemination of knowledge. Ancient towers and halls of stone dominated the landscape, their soaring spires and bell towers seemingly aspiring to a Heaven already attained. Belphagor found the symbolism a bit heavy handed.

With the university students on winter break, the queen's field marshal commandeered the mostly empty dormitories on the vast campus of the Academy of Celestial Philosophy. This was a world Belphagor had never seen before—though Vasily had come here without him. Imagining his *malchik* in this scholarly capital as a plaything for angels was a painful kick in the gut.

The field marshal's entourage wound through streets heavy with slush, while frigid sleet poured down onto the winter's accumulation of snow, melting as it reached the ground. It was a testament to Aeval's expanded influence throughout the Heavens that the presence of the Queen's Army in the streets among these learned halls attracted little attention. Of course, with the students away, the population of the city automatically decreased by nearly sixty percent. The one thing that did attract attention was the presence of the bound and gagged Holy Fool.

Vashti had admitted to knowing who he was; she'd sent Brother Kirill from the monastery with Love and Ola for some reason she wouldn't explain. There was little opportunity for speaking privately, so Belphagor had to be content with this information for now, but he intended to get the full story out of her. She'd done enough damage; he wouldn't allow her to do more with sins of omission.

At least, if this Kirill spoke the truth, they were one step closer to Ola with every passing day. What they would do when they got there, he wasn't sure. He only hoped Vasily and Anazakia were aware that the company had changed course instead of taking their prisoners to the Relocation Camp. If they'd met up with Nebo and followed at a distance, there might be some hope of an escape before the company reached the Citadel of Gehenna, and an attempt could be made to reach it ahead of the queen's men.

Belphagor planned to take the monk along with them if the opportunity arose, even if they had to keep him bound. He was the key to finding out what they were up against with regard to the Cherubim—though getting lucid answers out of Kirill would certainly be challenging. The air of Heaven seemed to have driven him completely mad.

By the luck of the draw, Belphagor was garrisoned with the monk. It was the first time they'd been given actual beds to sleep in, and Belphagor was grateful to be out of the cold, if only for a night. The inns where they'd stayed along the road barely accommodated the soldiers, even with the company occupying every inn in the vicinity, and the prisoners had been forced to sleep in the stables, while the Ophanim, who needed no sleep, stood guard.

Such lodging was in fact the sort of opportunity Belphagor hoped to exploit to make their escape, but not yet. It was prudent to take advantage of the resources of the Queen's Army for as long as possible. The last inn would likely be just outside Makhon before they entered the Empyrean.

To prevent their escape from inside the dormitory, the prisoners were fitted with ankle manacles and shackled to the masonry. The Ophanim only needed to occupy the corridor outside the dormitory rooms; the bars on the windows would do the rest. Unless the students were kept here under duress, it seemed housing prisoners in the empty dorms was not a novel event.

Belphagor fell onto his bed. He was exhausted enough from a full day's slog through the snow to sleep immediately, but the monk was kneeling on the floor making strangled noises against his gag as if trying to recite a prayer, crossing himself awkwardly with his bound hands.

Sighing, Belphagor got up and dragged his chain across the floor to where the bearded man rocked back and forth in his attempt at devotion. When he put his hand on Kirill's shoulder, the monk scrambled back with terror in his eyes.

"Ne bespokoites, Brat Kirill." Belphagor spoke in Russian, as it seemed the monk's angelic was only rudimentary. "No worries. I only want to help you."

The monk calmed at the sound of his own tongue and the mention of his name. Belphagor reached around him to release the leather strap that stretched between his lips, which were parched and chapped from being forced open in the cold. The monk spat out the handkerchief, coughing wretchedly, and Belphagor brought him a glass of water from the pitcher on a table near the door.

"Why are you helping me?" Kirill demanded after slaking his thirst. "You are a demon like the rest, yes?"

Belphagor regarded the monk still kneeling on the floor. "I am a demon, yes. As for the rest, the ones who've been abusing you and who've taken you prisoner, they are angels. They regard your kind as little more than demon, in point of fact." He gestured to his manacle. "You may have noticed I'm shackled just as you are."

"Yet you do not untie my hands."

"I've no wish to be strangled in my sleep."

Kirill studied him for a moment more and then resumed his awkward, two-handed genuflection, murmuring the words of an Orthodox prayer as he rocked forward.

"You were the one who guarded my daughter when she was imprisoned on Solovetsky."

At Belphagor's words, the monk stopped and stared at the ground without straightening.

"Not *my* daughter," Belphagor amended. "Not exactly, but she means as much to me."

Kirill looked up, his wild blue eyes stricken. "And now I am punished for my sins! I have put my faith in the false prophet. I am taken down into the bowels of hell."

"This is Heaven, actually." Belphagor sat on the edge of his bed. "Not exactly what you envisioned, eh, Brother? One does not get into Heaven through any sort of good works or divine grace, I'm afraid to say. It's as full of despicable people as the world of Man."

Kirill was giving him a doubtful look. He was a demon, after all. To the monk, he supposed, it was just as likely that Belphagor was a minion of the Father of Lies sent to tempt him from the path of righteousness.

"At any rate, I'm not interested in your crisis of faith. I want to know about Ola. Was she well when you saw her last? Is she still with the gypsy girl?"

The monk stood and stared down at his bound hands. "The child was very well. She is too young to understand she is a prisoner. She is happy. Bright." He seemed to choke back tears. "She misses her mother."

Belphagor swallowed roughly before he could speak. "You cannot imagine how her mother misses her. Or her father. This has nearly destroyed him." He fixed his gaze on the monk, who kept his eyes lowered. "And the gypsy?"

"Sister Lyubov?" Kirill raised his head, and there was a hint of redness in his cheeks, as if the mere mention of her name were a transgression. "She was with the child when I was sent away by the demon of light. Sister Lyubov has cared for her with great devotion, despite…" He paused and looked down again. "Despite adversity."

Belphagor didn't like the way the monk said this word. "What sort of adversity?"

"Ola has not been harmed. She has been safe."

"What adversity, then?"

Kirill's face had gone white as the winter fields. "The false prophet. The one called Zey-us."

"What about him?"

Kirill shook his head as if he wouldn't say, but then answered anyway. "He abused Sister Lyubov." Kirill's eyes went dark with passion. "And so I killed him."

· · ·

The Elohim had granted Anazakia conditional asylum. They were satisfied of her innocence of the crimes of which she'd been accused, but they were still uncertain about her mental state. Until they ruled on her claim of communication with the syla, they were reserving judgment.

If they deemed her fit, they pledged they would fully commit the Virtues, the Princedom of Aravoth, and the Party of the Socialist Host to restoring Anazakia to the throne of the Firmament. Though she hadn't accepted this offer, they were of one mind about Ola's legitimacy, and they promised to expend all their resources to extract her from the Social Liberationist forces.

Ola, the Virtues informed them, had been taken by the Cherubim into the Empyrean. The leader of the Social Liberation Party had issued orders to deliver her to the northernmost settlement of the celestial realm: the Citadel of Gehenna.

Sar Sarael, whose estate lay beyond the mountainous terrain on the northern boundary of Aravoth, agreed to outfit Anazakia and her companions with all they needed for the expedition into the Empyrean. Because it would take a day to reach his manor over treacherous ground, the four of them were given rooms at the Hekhaloth for the night. Vasily, to his dismay, was treated like a prince.

He couldn't reconcile himself with the revelations about his nature that the Virtues had thrust upon him. They were the second to insist he'd been fathered by a Seraph. Vashti he could have dismissed, but there was no motive for the Virtues to invent such an allegation, nor did they seem prone to flights of fancy.

If it was true, it made his already complicated feelings about his parentage more complicated still. He'd grown up on the streets of Raqia believing his mother was a demon whore who'd thrown him away at the earliest opportunity. He'd been stunned to learn she'd been of noble birth. Ysael, by Helga's account, had been indiscreet with one of the Raqia players. Like Anazakia, she'd apparently been the adventurous sort who sought the thrill of hobnobbing with the hoi polloi.

If his father had been a Seraph, however, this put Ysael in a different light. Anazakia had told him members of the angelic royalty were often assigned a personal Seraph guard. She herself had been obliged to give her bodyguard the slip on the night she'd come to Raqia and unwittingly escaped assassination.

From his own experience, he knew that outside of their unfailing loyalty to their royal charges, Seraphim were not particularly intelligent and were possessed of a rather sadistic nature. Such unappealing personalities, combined with the off-putting nature of their physical form, wouldn't seem to make them attractive choices for intimacy. As hurtful as his thoughts had been about a demon mother who sold her body on the street, the idea of an angel mother lying with a brutish Seraph slave was hardly more comforting. Could she have done it out of the same rebellious compulsion that made her sneak about in the underbelly of Heaven? He was compelled to assume she had. Any other possibility was too unpleasant to contemplate.

Whatever the truth of his history, he had suddenly become "His Supernal Highness the Grand Duke Vasily of the House of Arcadia." He had no idea what to make of the personal attendant the Virtues sent to him. The youth was exceedingly beautiful in the chilly manner of the Virtues, and so deferential and unfazed by his unlikely "superior" that when Vasily burst into nervous laughter at the suggestion that the attendant take his clothes, the young Virtue had simply bowed and stepped aside to wait patiently for Vasily to undress himself. The long woolen gown he held draped over his arm was apparently something Vasily was expected to wear for sleeping.

"I'm a firespirit," Vasily said gruffly. "I sleep in my skin. I don't think I'll be needing your assistance." He paused and added, "Thank you," having no idea what the expected interaction was between them. That seemed to have done the trick, and the servant bowed and went out.

He undressed in the glow of firelight before the unrelenting mirrored glass that spanned the walls on either side of the room. The spike-capped piercings above his collarbone caught and bent the light, and Vasily touched his hand automatically to the uneven right side where there were three instead of four. They were mementos of his time with Belphagor before their argument and long estrangement, one for every year, placed there by Belphagor on each anniversary. Bel had promised him the long-missing eighth when Vasily had rescued him from Aeval's prison, but once he was well, he hadn't mentioned it again.

The heavy oak door opened a crack, and Vasily thought the servant had returned to offer him some other service, but it was Anazakia peering around the door, the long gown she'd been given trailing behind her. Vasily pulled her inside and closed the door, pushing her back against the wood to kiss her hungrily.

"You don't know how badly I wanted to see you." He grinned, his body punctuating the statement as he pressed against her. "I don't think you need this." He unbuttoned the gown and let it fall onto the floor as he swept her up in his arms and carried her to the large bed piled high with luxurious blankets and topped with a wide, creamy fleece.

Anazakia pulled off his glasses and set them on the side table as he crawled over her, her legs wrapping around his as he kissed her breasts.

He murmured against the soft flesh. "It's a little strange seeing you in someone else's skin."

She moaned as he took one of the unfamiliar breasts into his mouth. "Does it matter?" she whispered, arching beneath him as he shook his head without taking his mouth from her.

He consumed her, desperate to anchor himself as the Vasily he'd always been, desperate to bury his fear and the persistent ache for Belphagor's hard hand upon him. Anazakia seemed to understand his need and she received him more roughly than usual, driving herself against him as she rolled him onto his back.

He curled into her arms when they were spent, both exhausted from several days of long travel and nights of hard beds, and they slept immediately, a deep and satisfied sleep they'd sorely needed.

In the morning, Vasily was awakened by his personal attendant. He sat up swiftly to cover Anazakia—they'd gone to sleep on top of the covers, since Vasily's heat had been enough for them—but she was gone.

When he arrived at breakfast, Nebo and Lively were already dressed for travel and Sarael was waiting, but Anazakia hadn't come down. By the time she arrived, Sarael told her apologetically that they needed to leave at once, but he'd instructed the chef to pack something she could eat on the road.

Anazakia was gracious and formal among her element. "No need to apologize, Sar Sarael. I'm the one who's tardy. I decided to take a bath last night because it smelled so wonderful when I passed it. It relaxed me so much I slept like a stone and your chambermaid couldn't wake me."

"A bath, eh?" Vasily grinned at her as they were heading out. He kissed her neck and smelled a delicate aroma of petals and resins. "You do smell like a bath. I suppose you slipped away this morning to take one."

"No, I took one last night. I told you. I nearly fell asleep in it."

"When?"

Anazakia eyed him peculiarly. "What do you mean, when? When I went upstairs for bed, of course. There's a tiled bath just beyond the room I slept in that's kept constantly steaming with sweet herbs and oils. It was, if I may say it, heavenly." She smiled. "How did you sleep?"

He expected her to wink, to let him know she was toying with him, but she was perfectly sincere. Vasily glanced at the others coming down the steps. Lively met his eyes indifferently, but he knew as soon as she looked at him. It had been Lively in his bed.

It took every ounce of restraint he possessed to keep his pupils from burning with anger as he answered casually, "Well enough."

Lively rode beside Nebo, as cool as Aravothan ice, as they set out on the frozen path through the mountains. Vasily couldn't imagine what her motivation could have been except sheer maliciousness. Or perhaps desperation. She wasn't a homely girl, and wasn't nearly as bland and expressionless as she'd seemed at the apothecary's, but she was no great beauty. Perhaps she felt the only means she had for obtaining what she desired was trickery, but he doubted this was the case. She seemed too self-assured for that.

Whatever the reason, it was an unpleasant feeling to realize he'd let himself be so vulnerable, so fully himself, with a near-stranger under false pretenses. But worse, he couldn't quite escape the nagging feeling he ought to have known. That perhaps on some level, he *had* known.

There was no time to dwell on this, however, as the narrow, winding path took all his concentration. The ravine that led into Aravoth had now become a steep canyon below them, and they were forced to travel single-file around the mountain. The horses were surefooted and well used to this precarious route, but it was painstaking and nerve wracking. Chunks of frozen rock broke off and plunged to the iced-over riverbed as they disturbed the untouched ground, and Vasily had no wish to join them.

He wasn't the best of riders. No celestial demon was, he supposed, though Lively seemed to be fair enough at it. It wasn't as if they grew up with their own personal stables and a professional trainer. Most demons, unless employed in such a capacity by the Host, learned to ride through thievery and necessity.

Around midday, Sarael found a small clearing, thick with virgin snow, where they stopped to feed and water the horses, as well as themselves. Vasily was only too happy to be off the path, and off the horse. Every part of him ached as if he'd been in a bad fight—which he had, he realized. Only two days ago, he and Nebo had cleaned the clocks of those insufferable angelic soldiers. The demons had managed to keep the upper hand, but Vasily had been roughed up a bit when the soldiers caught him.

He smiled to himself as he ate his cold pork, remembering the looks on the soldiers' faces when Nebo had tossed them on their backs like scrawny adolescents. There was something to be said for the superiority of mixed blood. Vasily himself had used the advantage of his element, though he normally considered it not quite sporting. The average enlisted man in the Heavenly armies, after all, was a twelfth-order waterspirit who had never so much as broken a legitimate sweat, let alone manipulated his own element. The officers, of course, were Powers from the Third Choir, and as their element of earth implied, were built more sturdily than mere angels. But like the rest of the purebloods, they shunned the cultivation of elemental "peasant magic."

The winds picked up when they set out after lunch, and it took all Vasily's concentration to follow the horse ahead of him while snow whipped across the trail. He only hoped the horse ahead of him wouldn't plunge suddenly into the abyss.

Their descent began when the sun was hanging low in the sky, and by the time they reached the bottom and the relatively flat ground of northern Aravoth, there was nothing but shadows. Sar Sarael's manor was little more than a dark shape hulking against an even darker sky by the time they arrived.

This time, Vasily asked Sarael discreetly if he might share a room with Anazakia. The Virtue was happy to oblige, and Anazakia was pleased that he'd thought of it. They were too tired to do anything but sleep, but at least he knew whom he held in his arms.

By daylight, Pyr Amaravati Manor was like a world under water, its immense windows of pale bluish glass blocks keeping out the cold while still filtering in a warm and calming light. Like the Hekhaloth, the manor was heated by some kind of pipes beneath the tiled floors, with hollowed columns along the walls to carry the heat through the rooms and out the chimneys.

Vasily's inexperience on horseback had caught up with him, however, and he woke too stiff to move. Sarael insisted that he partake of Pyr Amaravati's bath and his personal masseur to ease his muscles, and would take no argument. Vasily felt guilty indulging in such luxury while being the cause of even a slight delay, but he had to admit there was nothing else like it in the Heavens.

Luckily, the morning's pampering did him good, and they were able to start for Gehenna before midday. A horse-drawn sleigh carried Anazakia and Vasily, along with Nebo and Lively, who insisted they would see the mission to its end. Vasily was grateful for Nebo's presence but could have done without Lively's. Along with the driver of the sleigh, four dozen mounted Virtues from Sar Sarael's personal guard accompanied them to challenge the Cherubim and the leader of the Social Liberation Party for Ola's return.

It took them approximately three days to reach the southern banks of the fiery Pyriphlegethon across the Empyrean's empty white expanse. Anazakia was quiet, looking into the orange glow with a solemn expression as the Virtues set up camp beside the flaming river. When Vasily pressed her, she at last admitted that according to Helga, this was where his mother had taken her own life.

She was tender with him as they lay together in the tent, her soft touch, though it belonged to another woman's hands, as healing as it had once been to his Seraph-ravaged flesh.

"My angel of mercy," he whispered to her as he traced her flesh and watched their light illuminate her skin. He tried not to think of where the light came from, or of the river of fire winding past their tent, and when he was sure she was sleeping, he held her to his chest and wept.

They would be another eighteen days on the gruesome river's bank, following it northward until they reached their destination. The solitary angelic habitation in the Empyrean, the Citadel of Gehenna was situated at the very pinnacle of Heaven. Surrounded by the ever-circling Pyriphlegethon, it could only be reached by a high stone bridge across the river, as if the Pyriphlegethon itself were its mote. The bridge crossed the river at its northernmost point so that those who wished to reach Gehenna had to follow the outer bank until it turned and circled back on itself toward the south like a fiery snake swallowing its own tail.

They had all grown weary of the bleak, monotonous landscape by the time they saw the citadel at last. Its high, imposing walls were made of massive blocks of stone carted from the southern princedoms over the miles of ice long before recorded history. The bridge was composed of several tons of the same stone and spanned the half-mile of burning river in a road wide enough to accommodate an army of Empyreanese. No one had seen the Empyreanese in modern times, of course—if any still existed. The airspirits of the First Choir who were said to have built the citadel had long been absent from celestial discourse.

The closest thing to locals now were the Seraphim born of the flaming Pyriphlegethon itself—a sort of reincarnating bath of celestial fire from which they rose like phoenixes—but they loathed the cold and flew to warmer climes as soon as they emerged from it.

One such fantastically born creature must have been his own father, Vasily reflected. He shivered beside Anazakia in the sleigh as they approached the bridge. She gripped his hand, her borrowed olive skin pale with anxiety as they came close to finding Ola at last. The horsemen went before them, trotting carefully over the ice-slick stone, and at the opposite end of the bridge, they pulled up before the towering grey walls, where a single Cherub stood before the gate tower. From the rear of the procession, they couldn't hear what was passing between the Cherub and Sarael's men.

"I can't stand this." Anazakia threw off the lap blankets and grabbed Vasily's hand as she leapt down from the sleigh. He allowed her to pull him with her toward the front, vacillating between a rage that made him want to grab the Cherub and throw him into the river, and a terrible fear that Ola wouldn't be here after all, which threatened to freeze him in his tracks.

The towering Cherub turned its angelic face toward them as they approached. "Who are these?" The fourfold voice grated as the Cherub spoke from each of its mouths at once.

The Virtue Haniel, who led their expedition, answered. "Eager revolutionaries, Zophiel. They wish to see the heir for themselves and have come all the way from Raqia to dedicate themselves to the cause."

"We were not informed of any reinforcements coming." Zophiel's eagle eye regarded them doubtfully. "I understood this was all to be kept quiet for now."

"Well, apparently, someone has let the cat out of the bag. Might as well allow these eager youngsters in, as they've come all this way. And surely you see why you need the reinforcements. Sarael sent us specifically to help defend the citadel now that word has gotten out. There are only four of you, are there not? All alone up here in the unpleasant cold?"

"We are not alone." The Cherub corrected him with a tone of annoyance. "The Party Leader is here with a company of her advisers. One hundred in all, including my brothers."

"Well, that's a relief. Still, one hundred men against the Queen's Army is hardly a defense, particularly men not trained in war. We'll send two of our men back with word to Sarael that you need as many as Aravoth can spare, but the rest of us are at your service immediately." Haniel signaled to two of the riders, and they turned and headed back the way they'd come.

Zophiel signaled to the demon in the gate tower to raise the portcullis as if he were not quite sure when he had agreed to do so, and Sarael's men rode forward into the Citadel of Gehenna. Lively and Nebo came up beside Vasily and Anazakia as they entered on foot, and the sleigh was left on the bridge.

"One hundred men to our fifty," Nebo murmured to Vasily as they marched through the ward. "Those are not good odds. I wish we'd been better informed. I don't like the idea of having to maintain this charade for a month while we wait for Sarael's reinforcements."

Vasily whispered to him as they continued walking. "This has always been a fool's errand, Nebo. Nazkia and I don't expect to return. We only want to see Ola while we can. It might be better for you if you head back with the scouts. We won't think poorly of you."

Nebo stopped and gave him a deeply offended look. "I made a promise to my sister. She did you a terrible wrong, and I vowed to right it. I always keep my promises to Vashti."

Vasily stared at the Nephil a moment. He'd almost forgotten about Vashti, and that Nebo was her twin. As Anazakia dropped his hand, anxious to keep moving, he contemplated what to say, contemplated whether this man was a friend, as Vasily had come to regard him.

Before he could speak, however, an entourage emerged from the inner ward of the citadel to greet them. Among them was a handsome older woman who exuded authority. This was surely the Party Leader of whom the Cherub and the Elohim spoke. As she drew closer, her gaze moved from the mounted Virtues toward the four on foot, and she stopped and smiled. He'd seen her somewhere before. Anazakia gasped.

"Lively Ivovna." The woman greeted Anazakia warmly, holding out her hands.

"I'm over here." Lively stepped from behind them.

The older woman glanced at Anazakia a moment and then took Lively's hands and embraced her, kissing her on both cheeks.

"Hello, Auntie Helga. I've brought them, just as you asked." She folded her hands over her belly beneath her navel and looked at Vasily with a smirk. "And I've brought some of his seed."

Pyatnadtsatoe: **Within the Keep**
*from the memoirs of the Grand Duchess Anazakia
Helisonovna of the House of Arkhangel'sk*

The scene was simply incomprehensible. My childhood nurse could not
be the Leader of the Social Liberation Party. This could not be Helga.
She could not have kidnapped my child. And what in Heaven's name
was Lively doing? The demon girl's words throbbed in my head. *I've
brought some of his seed.* I stared at Vasily, hoping to see the same
confusion in his eyes, but he'd lowered them, his skin more flushed than
usual. Had everyone betrayed me? Nebo, at least, looked baffled, and
the Virtues seemed angry.

Helga turned to the uniformed men beside her—her advisers, if
she was truly who she seemed to be. "See to our Aravothan friends'
needs. I'm sure they're all very tired and hungry after their journey."
She smiled at me as they carried out her orders. "My goodness, how
like Lively you look. She's my brother's daughter. But of course you're
not interested in my family, dear. Come, let's see to your own." Helga
turned, tucking Lively against her with one arm as they walked, carrying
on the intimate conversation of relatives who had much to catch up on.
I had no choice but to follow.

Vasily stepped up beside me as we passed between two Cherubim
at the entrance to the keep. "About what Lively said…I can explain."

I turned on him. "Do you really want to? Right here? Right now?
Is that really what concerns you most at this moment, when you are

finally so close to your daughter—what I think about whom you bed?"

Vasily stared at me, stung, but I wasn't in the mood to prance about his delicate feelings. He wasn't what was important now.

Helga led us up a winding stone staircase into the foretower of the keep, dimly lit with torches. At the top, another Cherub stood before an iron door, and he opened it for Helga with a large iron key. Inside the tower room, a delicate beam of winter sun from the window illuminated the dark hair of a woman seated on the bed, her head bent over a book. On her lap, intently interested in what she was reading, sat a pale red-haired child—not an infant, but a child. This could not be my baby, not already, not so big without my having seen a moment of it.

Love looked up and dropped the book from her hand. "*Bozhe moi*! Vasily, you're here!" For a moment, I couldn't understand why she was ignoring me, until I remembered I no longer had my own face.

"We'll give you some time to get reacquainted before dinner," said Helga, and she closed us inside.

Ola looked at us with interest, her blue eyes bright and intelligent. She rested those wide, beautiful eyes on Vasily's flame-red bound locks and said with solemn certainty, "Papa."

The tears of pain and joy in Vasily's eyes made me ashamed that I'd spoken to him so scornfully. He went to Ola and bent down on one knee, putting his hand on her head as if to be certain she was real.

"Yes, sweetheart, it's Papa," he rasped, his voice rougher than usual. He looked up at Love. "I was afraid she wouldn't remember me."

"I printed out a picture for her at the dacha." Love took a folded piece of paper from the large front pocket of her overalls. "I show it to her every day."

Ola took the worn sheet and pointed at Vasily's likeness in it. "Papa," she said again. "Ola's Papa." She pointed then at the rest of us in the photo. "Ola's Mama. Baby Ola. Beli." She looked up at Vasily, proud of her recital, and he swept her into his arms, unabashedly weeping.

Love glanced toward Nebo and me. "Where are Anazakia and

Belphagor? Aren't they with you?"

"I'm here," I said, feeling like a ghost among them. "I drank a glamour."

"I'm sorry," Vasily gasped, standing with Ola in his arms. "I'm so sorry, I should have said at once." He brought Ola to me. "It's your mama, darling. She's been looking for you for so long."

Ola stared at me as at the stranger I was to her and shook her head. She held her paper up to Vasily and pointed again as if he were not quite bright. "Ola's Mama."

Vasily handed her to me and I balanced her on my hip—so much heavier than I remembered. I was trembling now that I held her at last. Tears rolled down my cheeks and I could think of nothing to say to her. With everyone else aware of my identity, it was a bitter sentence to be forever glamoured with Lively's face, unrecognizable to my own daughter.

Vasily took something from his pocket and held it out to me: a glass vial like the one that had held the glamour, filled with clear liquid. "There's a way to restore you. The apothecary told me."

I looked at the vial doubtfully. "You said we needed a drop of my own blood, and mine is spoiled now—by Lively's," I added bitterly.

"A drop of your 'pure angel blood stored up someplace,'" the apothecary said." He looked at Ola significantly.

I pulled her away from him to my other side, horrified. "You will not take a drop of my baby's blood!"

"Nazkia—"

I shook my head vehemently, holding her away. "Besides, it's no more my own than what I have in my veins. She's both of us."

"But you're the source of her, Nazkia," Vasily insisted. "Every cell of her body was fed by your blood for nine months. I believe it will work."

"No. I won't do it. You can't ask me to."

"Then I'll do it." Vasily stared me down as he took the pocketknife from his belt.

I stepped back, holding Ola tightly against my chest.

"Nazkia, Ola needs the mother she remembers. She can't understand." His eyes flashed a bit of fire and his voice dropped to a growl. "And if you think I want to keep touching that bitch's body when I touch you, you're out of your mind." He pulled the cork from the vial and held out his hand for me to give him Ola's. "I'll be the monster. It's only fitting. She'll associate me with the pain."

I refused to hold out her hand, but I didn't stop him, and Ola whimpered in surprise when Vasily pricked her index finger with the sharp tip of his knife. Her little lower lip protruded in a wounded pout as he held the finger over the vial and squeezed a single drop of blood into the clear liquid. It swirled and dissolved colorlessly. Ola buried her head against my chest, and Vasily handed the vial to me. With an accusing look, I snatched it from him and drank.

I felt no different, but Vasily breathed a sigh of relief at once. "There, sweetheart," he said to Ola. "See? It's Mama."

Ola peered at me with one eye and then sat up, looking pleased. "Ola's Mama." She patted me decisively.

"I'm here." I wiped my eyes and kissed her. "Mama's here."

Wiping tears from her own eyes, Love hurtled toward me from the bed and threw her arms around me. "I was afraid we'd never see you again. But you're here…is Belphagor with you? Are we going home?"

I hugged her tightly, too overcome to speak, and Vasily answered for me.

"Belphagor and the rest of our party were detained by the Queen's Army," he said soberly. "We managed to escape to Aravoth, and we brought a small company of men with us, but I don't know if it's enough to get us out."

Love's hopeful expression faded as she stepped back, and I noticed how pale and thin she'd become, though Ola looked healthy.

I squeezed her hand, searching for words. "I can't begin to tell you how sorry I am, Love. You've been taking such care of Ola, and all this time…well, we thought…" My voice failed me and I couldn't meet her eyes. "I can't imagine how hard this has been."

Love shrugged, the sort of gesture one made to avoid crying, though she still clung to my hand. "You look familiar," she said to Nebo, who'd stood so quietly behind us that I'd forgotten his presence.

Vasily nodded grimly. "Nebo is Vashti's brother."

Love dropped my hand and recoiled, hugging her arms to her chest with a guarded expression.

"You must be Love." Nebo's warm brown eyes were full of guilt, as if he'd been the one to wrong her. "My sister spoke of you. She very much regrets everything that's happened."

Love's expression didn't change. "Oh, well, that makes it all better, then."

The key turned in the lock as she spoke, and the heavy door opened. One of Helga's lackeys had come to bring us down to dinner.

The meal was held in the central hall of the citadel, a vast room with sweeping ribbed vaults built to accommodate the high windows that in daytime would capture the cold northern light. It was lit now by numerous candelabra and torches held in iron sconces in the shapes of the elemental firespirits of Heaven. At an ancient oak table that must have been cut from a single massive trunk, the Virtue Haniel sat with a handful of his men, along with a dozen of Helga's advisers. Lively sat smugly beside her aunt.

"Nenny." Helga greeted me with my childhood pet name as we sat, and then corrected herself. "Anazakia Helisonovna. You look more yourself." She directed a pointed glance at Ola's bandaged finger as if she knew precisely how it had been accomplished, and I reddened. "And you." She greeted Vasily less cordially. "I must say I was a bit surprised to hear of a man of your nature taking such an interest in his get."

"And what nature would that be?" growled Vasily.

"A Raqia street rat, of course."

"Don't you mean *polovina-d'yavol*?" I spat the word at her. "Isn't that what you told me? That he was a half-devil?"

She raised an eyebrow at my tone. "I believed he was. I have come to realize I was mistaken about his paternity."

"Is that why you kidnapped Ola? For her paternity?"

Helga sighed. "This is neither the place nor the time for this discussion. You are guests at our table, and we are here to partake of the fine meal our staff has provided while we all get acquainted." She began to eat her dinner and then waved her fork at us as we sat motionless. "Eat," she ordered in the practiced voice of the palace nurse, and like chastised children, we ate.

It was a plain but satisfying meal of smoked mutton and boiled potatoes—a welcome change from the endless meals of beans and hardtack we'd been eating for days.

Helga glanced with curiosity at Nebo. "I've not been introduced to your friend."

I gave her a cool glance. "This is Nebo. I believe you know his sister, Vashti."

"Ah." Helga frowned. "What a disappointment that one turned out to be." She turned toward Love before Nebo could say a word. "And Love, I trust your meal is satisfactory?"

Love glared at her as she cut Ola's meat. "You mean is it better than stale bread and water in my cell? Why yes, in that case, it's quite satisfactory."

"Don't exaggerate," Helga said in a tone I remembered all too well. "You haven't been kept on bread and water, and you and the child have only been here under our protection."

I set my fork down with a snap reminiscent of her own signature mark of irritation. "Then I suppose we're all free to go."

Helga gave me a stern look. "I really hoped we could have a nice meal, but I see you're still the rude, spoiled girl you've always been. You are under our protection. It would be inadvisable for any of you to leave. If the queen were to discover little Ola's whereabouts, the revolution would be over before it began."

"Why?" I wasn't about to make this easy for her. "What does

Ola have to do with your revolution? And since when are you a revolutionary, let alone the leader of a Party?"

Helga frowned. "I told you to take those herbs, Nenny, but you've never listened to anyone but yourself. I realized as soon as you told me you were carrying his child that I must have been wrong about Vasily's father."

I was still fuming at her reference to aborting Ola. "I don't understand. How could that have changed your mind?"

"Male firespirits of mixed blood are very rarely fertile, my dear. All that heat seems to burn up the diluted seed. As a consequence, it's only those with the highest concentrations of fire in their makeup who seem to overcome the other elements within them enough to reproduce." Helga took a sip of her wine as if we all understood this. "It puzzled me when Vasily was born and we saw he was firespirit. I couldn't imagine who among the young men we knew could have been so powerful."

"But what made you think it was an actual Seraph? Why not some firespirit demon you weren't acquainted with?"

"Because Vasily's mother was pure waterspirit," Helga said pointedly. "If her offspring was not only firespirit but fertile, well, Vasily certainly couldn't have been less than half fire. And there was only one way for that to happen." Helga set down her glass. "I also had other reasons to believe it."

"You knew the Seraph," said Vasily. "You know exactly who my father was."

"This isn't really a conversation for the dinner table. I doubt you want to dredge up such unpleasantness in front of strangers."

"I've been the demon bastard of a street whore all my life," Vasily scoffed. "Everyone knew it. They could see it by looking at me. And now suddenly you tell me I'm not. Whatever you know about it, I doubt it could be worse than what I've always believed."

Helga turned to her advisers and the Virtues. "Would you excuse us?"

They rose and filed awkwardly from the hall while the rest of us stared at her. Lively had stayed, as if what Helga was about to say was something she knew already.

Helga eyed Vasily. "Are you sure you want all of your companions here?"

"I'm sure." His growl was low and threatening, but she was unmoved.

"Well, I suppose the child won't understand." She sighed and addressed him resolutely. "Ysael was disowned by the House of Arcadia when it was discovered she was pregnant. Few of us wanted anything to do with the sort of trouble a girl like her would bring in Raqia, and since she wouldn't say who the demon was she'd been with, and he didn't come forward, she had to make her own way on the streets until her confinement. That much I suppose Anazakia has told you."

Vasily looked at me, his eyes unreadable. I'd spared him the details of how his mother had been forced to make her way. "Not all of it. But enough. Go on."

"Ysael confided in me shortly before you were born. I saw her on the street and gave her some food to eat. She looked very hungry, and no matter how disgraced she was, I didn't think it was right that an expectant mother should go hungry." Helga paused, and for a moment she almost looked sorry for Vasily—or perhaps it was only for Ysael. "She told me it wasn't for the pregnancy she was disowned. She hadn't even known about it yet. Her disgrace was allowing a Seraph to defile her."

"And who was the Seraph?" Vasily demanded with disgust. "Her personal guard, I suppose?"

Helga acknowledged this with a curt nod. "She said whenever she snuck away to play in Raqia, she tricked him into thinking she was in the library of her family's manor. He caught her, apparently, the last time she'd come, as she was sneaking back in through the window. He told her he'd followed her and saw a demon touching her, and it outraged his seraphic sensibilities." Helga hesitated and looked at Vasily as if to see if she needed to go on. My stomach clenched and I reached for my glass of water.

Vasily was still puzzled. "So he told her family because he was jealous? Because she cheated on him?"

"She wasn't having an affair with him, Vasily."

I looked away. How easily Ysael's fate might have been my own. Love pulled Ola toward her, as if to protect her from the ugliness of the world, and I wished I could as well.

Helga saw Vasily was stubbornly refusing to understand. "He wanted to teach her a lesson about what ought to be allowed to touch an angel," she said finally, a bit terse, as if annoyed at having to spell it out. "He raped her."

Vasily stood up as if he meant to strike her, the deep fire in his eyes throwing sparks of reflection from the lenses of his spectacles, but Helga went on.

"The House of Arcadia, in their infinite angelic grace, didn't believe she'd been unwilling. She had her ring, after all—the ring he threw at her afterward, having found it where she'd left it behind for safekeeping when she went to Raqia. Still, despite what happened to her, we never thought for a minute he could be the father. We didn't think it was possible to conceive after such…damage—"

"*No.*" Vasily interrupted her. "No. No, that isn't true. You're a despicable creature."

"Vasily." I put my hand on his arm, but he shook me off and shoved back his wooden chair, knocking it to the floor as he left the table.

Nebo stood and pressed a reassuring hand to my shoulder as I started to rise. "I'll talk to him. The Nephilim are well acquainted with the shame of birthright." He bowed and went out after Vasily.

Love whispered to me while Ola fussed to be released. "The Seraphim…didn't you guys tell me they're made of fire?"

"It doesn't burn in Heaven. Not exactly." Love was no longer the naive skeptic she'd once been, though it was little wonder.

"It's hot enough." Helga was merciless now that Vasily was gone. "You can hardly look at them. They've been the punishers of law-breaking Fallen for thousands of years, and they can cause a great deal of pain if they wish to. And this one wished to."

I didn't want to think about Seraphim anymore. "What does any of this have to do with the revolution? What does Ola have to do with it?"

Helga gave me a disapproving look. "Don't be disingenuous—it's unbecoming. I'm well aware of what the Virtues told you about the element you and Vasily produce; you forget that Lively was there. Vashti told us what the child could do; the Virtues have only confirmed how." She gave me a satisfied look when I said nothing, and then handed Lively the bottle of wine to refill our glasses. "The Queen has certainly guessed it, which is why she instructed her Malakim to fetch the child from the world of Man. She may not have guessed precisely what Ola is—I wasn't sure myself what would result from your union, but I knew the child would be powerful, and I'm sure so did she. Controlling Ola's element would give the queen unstoppable power. And that cannot happen."

"So you wanted her for yourself." I felt bitterly betrayed. Helga had once been family to me, the only family I'd had left.

"I wanted to keep her out of the queen's clutches." Helga took up her glass. "Something you were woefully unprepared to do—as became painfully obvious, given how simple it was to take her from you." The truth of this stung like a physical blow. "As for wanting her power myself..." She sipped her wine. "I don't need it." Her fingers rested on the locket that hung at her breast. It was the locket she'd taken from me, the one that held the flower of the fern.

Lying beside Vasily later, I couldn't help but think of all the mistakes I'd made that had brought us to this pass. When Helga had taken the locket from me on that afternoon in Raqia, I'd given her the means to control the Heavens. Somehow I'd let her take it from my hand, though even now I couldn't remember that moment clearly. Had she already been working the flower's influence against me? Even if she had, I ought to have guarded it more carefully. I hadn't taken the responsibility the syla gave me seriously enough. Nor had I taken the threat to Ola seriously enough, playing house in Arkhangel'sk and pretending I wasn't the last heir to the throne of the Firmament of Shehaqim.

In the heady afterglow of our escape from Heaven, I'd told Belphagor I was its rightful queen; the Grigori and Nephilim had treated me as such, and even the syla had called me one. But if I was a queen, I was surely the worst in Heaven's history. Every step I took simply endangered everyone I loved and anyone I came into contact with—from my childish whim to go riding in the snow on my seventeenth birthday, to the moment I'd taken the apothecary's elixir without weighing the consequences.

Vasily whispered beside me from the darkness. "Whatever you're thinking about, stop it." The edges of his pupils glowed softly, like a predator in the moonlight. "I can hear you sighing. It's like having a small storm lying beside me."

"I didn't know you were awake."

"I have a lot on my mind, too."

"I know. I'm sorry."

"Nazkia, about Lively… She pretended to be you." He stroked a finger along my wrist and watched the lavender luminescence. "I swear to you, I would never have taken her to my bed."

"Did her skin glow like that when you touched her?"

Vasily paused. "No, I…I don't think it did."

"And yet you thought she was me."

He was silent, and I rolled onto my side and pulled up the covers, not wanting to argue about it, not wanting this between us. We'd found Ola at last, even if we were prisoners here. That was what was important.

We spent the next few weeks getting to know the child Ola had become. It wasn't the worst existence. She remained with Love in the tower room at night at Helga's insistence—for her own safety, Helga claimed—but was allowed to share her meals with the rest of us and to run and play about the citadel, which Love told me hadn't been the case before we came. She was more comfortable with Love, as was only natural after so much time, so she wasn't the least bothered by going to sleep at night without us. It was Vasily and I who missed her when she slept.

Helga's Party believed in egalitarianism, and every inhabitant of the citadel shared chores equally. I found it pleasant to partake in the daily workings of a communal household, and I began to believe Helga's Heaven might not be so bad. The only part of the citadel that wasn't in our routine was the main tower of the keep itself, where the Cherubim stayed, and I was more than happy to stay clear of them.

"I hate them," Love confided to me one afternoon. One of the large, glittering angels had crossed the doorway of the laundry while we sat on the floor folding the washing. She looked around to see that Ola was occupied with Vasily, who was teaching her to put socks into pairs, and lowered her voice to a whisper. "They murdered Kirill."

"Who's Kirill?"

She'd barely spoken of the time she and Ola had spent in captivity before we came, sharing only Ola's developmental milestones we'd missed.

"He watched over us at Solovetsky." Her eyes misted with tears. "He was the kindest, gentlest man."

"Solovetsky." I remembered with a pang the day I'd spent on the island, when I'd dismissed the certainty that my daughter was near. Love and Ola had been only yards away from me within the monastery walls. How much had I missed of Ola's life because of that mistake? "I went to Solovetsky," I confessed as I focused on my folding. "I wanted to see the last place Ola had been seen. I thought I heard her crying and I thought I must be going mad."

Love's face twisted with emotion when I looked up. "In September? Just after the equinox?"

"Yes. How did you know?"

Love began to cry. "She said you were there, and I didn't believe her. We were outside—Kirill let us take a walk—and she suddenly pointed toward the sea and demanded to go to you. It was her first real sentence. I said she was wrong and took her inside. She cried for hours." Love took a handkerchief from her pocket and wiped at her eyes and nose, trying to keep Ola from seeing her cry, and I wondered how many times she'd put on a brave face for Ola in the past several months. "I'm so sorry, Anazakia."

"Don't." I took her hand, trying not to cry myself. "Don't torture yourself. It wasn't your fault; you couldn't have known. I should have listened to my instincts. It's my fault you had to stay there longer. It's my fault you're here."

Love laughed weakly, blowing her nose. "Now you're doing it. I guess we should both stop it."

We'd drawn Ola's attention, and she came over to me and held out a sock she'd been folding. "Here, Mama." She smiled and tried to wipe a tear from my face with it. "Don't cry."

I laughed and gathered her in my arms, smelling the sweet scent of her. I didn't care how long we stayed here or what the Social Liberation Party or Aeval did in their battle over Heaven. As long as we were together. That was all that mattered.

Shestnadtsatoe: Chain of Command

The monk was falling behind, and the company's captain had no sympathy for weakness. Belphagor tried to keep him moving, but the soldiers didn't care for them "fraternizing," and with his hands bound and his feet becoming frostbitten, the monk simply couldn't keep up. The leather strap cutting into his cheeks from the gag didn't help matters any, but he refused to keep quiet without it.

Belphagor had hoped to make a break for it when they garrisoned at Makhon, but the dreary little burg turned out to be a stronghold of the Social Liberation Party, and its inns were mysteriously dark when the Queen's Army arrived.

There were no more warm beds or damp stables once they struck out into the Empyrean, only a caravan of tents with layers of rough blankets for padding and cover. They were nearly four weeks on the flat, frozen plains. The first five days there'd been nothing at all on the horizon, and then the Pyriphlegethon with its shocking red fire appeared and they'd followed it ever since, using it to light the kindling they carried and huddling beside it for warmth when they stopped for the night. They lost two horses along the way, and there had been fresh meat on those occasions.

The soldiers had begun to harass Margarita and Vashti as they got farther from civilization, and Belphagor feared for them until Margarita challenged one of the soldiers to hand-to-hand combat and wiped the Empyrean ice with him. Vashti's leg had healed, and she made it clear that she, too, could handle herself in a fight. Dmitri and Lev just tried to lie low, refraining from any signs of intimacy—though now that the four of them shared a tent at night, they were allowing themselves the comfort of snuggling together until just before dawn.

Kirill saw this and doubled his strangled attempts to recite his prayer. Belphagor had tried to unbind him at night again and had gotten a black eye from one of the soldiers for his effort when Kirill was heard chanting early in the morning.

He hadn't had a chance to find out more about the monk from Vashti, and Kirill hadn't elaborated on his claim that it was he who'd murdered Zeus, but it seemed highly unlikely. For a human of such slight build—taller than Belphagor, but even thinner—to have taken down a Nephil of Zeus's size would have required years of specialized combat training—or a very large gun. Neither was likely to have been in great supply in a Russian monastery. More likely the monk was being gallant. Or was simply mad.

The monk stopped eating, and the soldiers stopped bothering to remove his gag to attempt to feed him. Belphagor kept him hydrated—breaking off icicles from the opening of the tent and forcing them into his mouth past the gag so that he swallowed involuntarily as they melted—but by the time they reached Gehenna, the monk had to be hauled behind the supply carts on a strip of hide.

Just shy of eight weeks after they'd left Elysium, the field marshal and his company arrived at the long stone bridge that connected the island fortress of Gehenna with the rest of the Heavens across the protective barrier of the Pyriphlegethon. The forces that occupied the Citadel of Gehenna were waiting for them.

• • •

Her field marshal was supposed to be within a day's ride of Elysium, but she had sent word to him after the defiance of the princes of Aravoth, only to learn he'd taken his entire company north on some undefined mission. Aeval was beside herself with fury. She hadn't given him command of the Armies of Heaven so that he could pursue his own agendas. He ought have no other agenda than what she gave him, no other thought than what she put into his head, no desires but her own.

Like everyone else, he failed and disappointed her.

A full regiment of four hundred men, twice as many as the company he rode with, was dispatched to retrieve the field marshal. He would turn straight around and head back to report, no matter how far he'd gone, or she would have his head. If there was a legitimate need for the troops where he'd taken them, the extra company would more than make up for it. But she could not imagine why troops would be needed on the route he'd chosen.

Aeval commanded that a single rider be returned to Elysium each day to report on their progress so that she would never be more than two days without word. When the fifteenth rider returned to her in a month's time to report that the company had been seen heading out of Araphel into the barren northern quadrant of Zevul, Aeval was through waiting for reports. They could only be headed for her Pyriphlegethon—she had come to think of it as hers after the time she'd spent there planning her conquest of Heaven—and the field marshal had no business there.

Aeval had come to Heaven long before the fortuitous meddling of the impertinent syla had provided her with inspiration in the form of the daughters of the House of Arkhangel'sk. She'd wandered the earth aimlessly for a time, having left the Russian lands in the world of Man once they ceased to be Russia. The nonsense of the Bolsheviks had been disappointing. That was the trouble with revolution; it encouraged the lowest common denominator, the least qualified, to think they had what it took to govern a nation. Invariably, the most opportunistic rose to the top of the precarious structure left in the wake of the heady thrill of having overthrown the Powers That Were.

The lofty aim of equality that drove such revolutions was meaningless. There were simply some who could never govern themselves, those who needed to be ruled, and there were others who had ruling in their veins. Men had called it Divine Right, having been subjugated themselves by the opportunistic forces of Heaven and the Unseen World, allowing themselves to be governed by myths. Whether the syla and their kin had begun to spin the cords of the royal courts in response to the rise of such notions or whether their spinning had engendered the myths was immaterial. The end result was that rulers were bred and cultivated.

The price they paid for power was something the masses never thought about. They saw the world in simple terms of Haves and Have-Nots, and assumed that all that was necessary for the Have-Nots to become the Haves was to overthrow the ones who had it now.

That was why Heaven was ripe for Aeval's designs. She had channeled the restless energy of the masses into projects of reform rather than waiting for another revolution to brew. If it hadn't been Aeval who had taken down the House of Arkhangel'sk, the discontent of those masses would have boiled over on its own and the throne would have been forever lost in a chaotic attempt by fools to govern themselves. The fact was that Heaven needed her.

When she'd abandoned the *Polnochnoi Sud* and then abandoned her plans for ruling in the world of Man, Aeval had remembered the syla's talk of Heaven. It was a place she'd never been, and the idea that these impertinent wood spirits dared consider her to be unworthy of something had made her more determined than ever to have it. She studied Heaven and its Choirs, biding her time, learning where the most likely weakness was that she might exploit.

The Virtues, soft and senile in their moral purity, had been the ideal place to get her foothold. They were so obsessed with form that they had never looked beyond hers. Once she settled on the Virtues as her way in, she styled herself as one of them and they took it for truth — of course, this made their recent insubordination particularly galling. It meant they'd chosen to turn against not just their queen, but one of their own.

Aeval had set up her base in the empty Empyrean, observing

Aravoth and the Firmament in turn. First she discovered the source of the Seraphim in the lovely Pyriphlegethon, and then she learned to play with their element. It was they who told her about the Citadel of Gehenna hidden at the center of the eternal river. Built by the airspirits of the First Choir and then abandoned when the mysterious caste of angels disappeared from Heaven, it had proven an ideal spot in which to practice her control of the elements. The Pyriphlegethon and the Empyrean were rich in pure, elemental energy easily accessible in three of the four elements, and in Gehenna, the stones provided the fourth.

There was nothing else but these in the North Country, and an empty palette for elemental transformation could not be of any use to her field marshal. Whatever he was up to, Aeval would have to put a stop to it herself.

· · ·

The massive fortress at Gehenna, practically a town unto itself, was over a millennium old, and the field marshal couldn't even recall why it had been built. It seemed an unlikely — and pointless — place to defend against siege. Heaven had seen little warfare in nearly as long, and as far as anyone from the other princedoms was aware, the walled village of Gehenna hadn't been occupied in centuries.

Yet today, in front of it, a line of two dozen mounted Virtues blocked the access to the bridge, preparing to defy the Queen's Army at ridiculous odds. If the human monk spoke the truth, Cherubim were involved in this rebellion as well. They must all be mad to go against their queen, who had done nothing but unify the Heavens and work toward the improvement of the lot of the unfortunate Fallen — though, of course, many were beyond help.

The field marshal called his captain to his side and advised him to bring the leader of this defiance to explain himself. It wasn't that he couldn't give such orders himself, but the chain of command was important. Captain Jusguarin was in command of this company, and the field marshal had only joined it in routine inspection as they arrived in Elysium. He had no wish to usurp the captain's authority among his men. As leader of his company, Jusguarin was, after all, only an extension of the field marshal's authority, just as the field marshal was an extension of the queen's. Through him, her reach stretched throughout the Heavens.

There was also the matter of his damaged voice that didn't carry. He'd had to prove himself worthy of the queen's commission and earn the respect of his men without the benefit of an imposing physicality or a booming, authoritative voice barking orders. Instead, his shrewdness in battle had earned their admiration—and if it hadn't, his unpredictable cruelty when his orders were defied had at least earned their fear.

Not that there had been much battle for any of them to prove themselves in, but there were always enclaves of revolutionaries and rebels in the smaller communities upon whom their skills could be honed. Thus far, no princedom had resisted Queen Aeval's demands for fealty or tribute, and until now, none of the Host had participated in any rebellion.

Captain Jusguarin returned to his side, the look of irritation on his face almost certainly masking an underlying dread that the field marshal wouldn't like what he was about to tell him. "They say they have no leader and there is no defiance. They claim they're merely defending their property from unreasonable search and seizure." He backed up his horse a bit after delivering his news, a wise move learned from experience.

The field marshal unsheathed his sword. "Perhaps they'll elect someone leader if I start killing them one by one. Bring me the first one from the left."

The captain took two of his men and rode off to the end of the line, hauling the first angel from his mount and dragging him before the field marshal. The other Virtues drew their weapons in a pitiful display of force. The long silver hair of the angel before him was tied up in a traditional Aravothan queue bound into a knot at the top of his head. The hairstyle looked quite nice against the snow when the field marshal struck the man's head from his body with a quick swing of his sword. The blood, of course, was far more striking as the headless torso dropped to the ground.

There was a commotion as the Virtues started forward in shock and anger, and then pulled back, aware that they were hopelessly outnumbered.

One of them held his hand out beside him, instructing the others to stay back, and brought his horse forward from the formation. "I am Sar Haniel. I answer for these men."

The field marshal's lip curled in a smile that pulled against the stiff scar-tissue of his right cheek. It always paid to be direct.

• • •

Love had taken Ola to the tower for her afternoon nap, and Vasily seized the opportunity to screw up his courage and attempt to work things out with Anazakia.

He cornered her in the pantry as she took inventory of the dried goods. He blocked the light from the windows in the kitchen beyond, and she glanced up from where she knelt on the floor. A scarf bound her hair, a smudge of dirt marked her cheek, and the sight of her made his heart beat faster. Damn, he was far gone. How the hell had this happened?

Vasily cleared his throat and rubbed his palms against his pants. "We haven't talked about what happened with Lively, and I mean to do it now. I know neither of us wants to," he added as her face clouded. "But you keep turning away from me at night, and I know it's bothering you."

"There's hard work during the day. Naturally, I'm tired."

He crouched down to her level. "Please talk to me. I know you're angry and I don't blame you—"

"I'm not angry."

"—But you know I would never have done it if I'd realized it wasn't you."

Anazakia went back to her counting.

"Nazkia."

"You could have asked," she said without looking at him. "You would have known if she'd spoken."

He opened his mouth to protest, and then closed it. She *had* spoken, he remembered. It had been a whisper, but it was one more thing he might have paid attention to, like the absence of what he now thought of as their seraphic light.

"I'm sorry. I was stupid. I don't know how to take it back or make it up to you." He lifted her chin to look into the ocean of her eyes. The light danced palely at the tips of his fingers. "I've missed your face."

She lowered her eyes, trying to hide the moisture that had swum across them.

"Please forgive me," he whispered. He kissed her and at least she didn't pull away. "And I've missed this." He watched the light trail his touch along her jaw to her throat. "I think I let myself be fooled because it *wasn't* there. All that talk of quintessence and grand dukes and Seraphim…I just wanted to believe I was still me, nothing more than an ordinary demon."

"I like our light." Her tone was slightly wounded, but she was no longer resisting him.

"I like it, too." He grinned. "Let's make more of it."

She couldn't hide her smile, and he took advantage of it, pulling her close and teasing the pale fire between their lips until she was squirming against him, trying to get closer. Tumbling together among the sacks of grain and legumes, each grappled at the other's clothes, releasing just enough to reach what they needed. They stroked each other like frantic teenagers until they both climaxed quickly and fell back against the sacks, breathing as if they'd just run a race and laughing at the absurdity of it.

As pleasant as it was, he wished they had more privacy, and some "protection," as their old friend Knud had called it—Anazakia had run out of her pills weeks ago. What he really wanted was to be inside her.

His cock twitched as if it agreed and was already eager to go again.

"I wish there were condoms in Heaven," he murmured. "As much as I love Ola, I don't think I want any more surprises just now."

Anazakia pulled her clothes together. "Well, don't speak too soon." There was a note of bitterness in her voice.

His brows drew together in consternation. Surely she didn't want another? "What do you mean by that?"

Anazakia sighed as she buttoned up her shirt. "Lively's been looking a bit green around the gills."

• • •

Blood spattered the white, fleecy greatcoat of the kneeling Virtue, and flecks of it peppered the silver hair that had slipped from its topknot. The field marshal observed these details almost philosophically, detached from any sense of empathy by which a lesser man might be bound. His reputation for brutality was built upon his unflinching and emotionless execution of justice. Hesitancy and lenience were excesses he could not indulge in, or the queen would be seen as weak. He was her emissary.

He struck Haniel once more with the back of his gloved hand. "I want to know what you're keeping here, and I want to know on whose command you're doing it. The Empyrean is the domain of Her Supernal Majesty, Queen of All the Heavens. This citadel belongs to Her, and if you continue to defy the authority of Her agent, you will watch as I line up every pretty little Virtuous head in your sad platoon here in the snow." He thrust his sword into the eye of the first dead Virtue for emphasis, pinning it to the frozen ground.

As he waved his hand toward the captain to bring him another, Haniel spoke quickly, if grudgingly, to prevent it. "Sar Sarael of Pyr Amaravati sent us."

"Ah. I see you're a reasonable man after all." The field marshal lifted the bruised face. Haniel's silver eyes were dull with shame. "Don't torture yourself with conscience, Sar Haniel. After all, you've acquiesced to save your men, not your own head." He squeezed the bloody cheeks between his gloved fingers. "He sent you to do what?"

Haniel's eyes flitted to the headless corpse at his feet, but he said nothing.

The field marshal shoved him over onto the snow. "Bring me the next."

When Captain Jusguarin signaled for another to be dragged from the line, Haniel whispered from his place on the ground. "For a summit with the leader of the Social Liberation Party."

Gripping the Virtue by the loosened topknot, the field marshal pulled Haniel back up to a kneeling position. "Thank you, Sar Haniel. You've been most accommodating." He pulled his sword from the dead man's skull and slashed into Haniel's gut, twisting the blade and spilling his viscera onto the snow.

With a startled, gurgling shout, the angel grasped for his own intestines as he crumpled, as if he could put them back in. It would have made a striking painting.

The field marshal wiped his blade on the Virtue's white coat. "Kill the rest."

• • •

A great commotion in the common hall met Vasily and Anazakia as they emerged from the pantry. Demons were running from every direction, while Helga shouted orders. The Queen's Army was at the gate.

The Virtues Helga had stationed on guard to prevent intruders from reaching the bridge had already been lost, while the others, stationed along the battlements, were taking heavy hits from the queen's archers. The rest of the population of the citadel was a motley assembly of demons untrained in the art of war.

Despite his hatred for the Social Liberation Party, Vasily had no desire to let the citadel fall to the queen. He offered his services, such as they were—he'd fought in the skirmish on the night of the Solstice Conflagration—but Helga would have none of it. He and Anazakia were among what the queen was seeking and must be kept from her soldiers at all costs. For their own protection, Helga had them locked in the tower room with Love and Ola—and Lively—leaving them with a cache of nonperishable food and water to last several days. There was no telling how long the Queen's Army might assail the citadel's defenses before they risked running out of their own supplies.

Lively, as Anazakia had said, was visibly under the weather. She sat by herself, looking miserable, and though he wasn't pleased at the probable cause of it, Vasily couldn't help but take a certain amount of satisfaction in her misery. Anazakia, however, astonished him by going to Lively and holding her hair out of the basin when she was ill. Luckily for the rest of them in the enclosed room, Lively was only vomiting small amounts of an odorless, clear yellow bile, but Anazakia confirmed this was a likely indication of morning sickness. She encouraged Lively to eat small pieces of cracker bread at frequent intervals to keep the nausea at bay.

"Why are you being nice to me?" Lively asked with suspicion.

Anazakia's answer was simple. "Because no one was nice to me when I was pregnant."

• • •

The petty magic of the demonic revolutionaries was easy enough to evade once they were familiar with it. The field marshal had the company's supply carts emptied to use for cover against the bolts of cherubic energy, along with two Aravothan sleighs that had been left on the near side of the Pyriphlegethon as if docked on a frozen sea. The green hides of the horses that had been slaughtered on the march were stretched across these to keep them from catching fire. Beneath one of the overturned sleighs, a group of soldiers was hard at work drilling into the mortar between the thick stones with a mechanical bore to make a breach in the wall. By the third day, the outer wall began to crumble, and by the fifth they had breached the inner.

They took Gehenna in less than a week, quickly overtaking demons armed only with knives once the walls were breached. The field marshal did not feel inclined toward mercy, and he permitted the soldiers to slaughter as many demons as they wished, provided the leader of the insurgence was captured for interrogation. The Virtues his men hadn't dispatched he ordered lined up on their knees in the snow-covered yard to be dealt with once he determined the full extent of their princedom's involvement in the rebellion, while the prisoners they'd brought from Elysium were bound and taken with him into the keep in the custody of the Ophanim.

As for the Cherubim, there were none to be found. As soon as the traitors had seen that the citadel was lost, they'd risen on their fourfold golden wings and fled like cowards.

The field marshal was somewhat surprised when a middle-aged demoness was brought before him and identified as the demons' leader. She smiled at him as if he were a guest in her castle and she was merely welcoming a weary traveler.

The field marshal's expression remained flat. "By what authority do you claim possession of Her Supernal Majesty's property?"

"Which property would that be, dear?" Her matronly smile gave him an unpleasant feeling, as if she knew something about him.

When he struck her for her insolence, his hand stiffened up and began to ache as if the joints were suddenly swollen. Perhaps he'd used too much force on the Virtue Haniel in beating out his confession.

He flexed his fingers within the glove. "The dominions of all celestial princedoms belong to Her Supernal Majesty."

"They should belong to the people." She seemed unmoved by his correction. "After all, it's the people whose labor builds the manors and the palaces and the fortresses throughout all of Heaven. It is the sweat and blood of the people who maintain them."

"And I suppose by 'people,' you mean demons."

"Are we not people?" She wiped the blood from the corner of her mouth and held her hand out. "Do we not bleed?"

"You'll bleed more if you don't answer my question. By what

authority have you occupied this estate?"

"By the authority of the people. I represent the people's Social Liberation Party."

The field marshal made a dismissive noise. "All such parties crumble under the weight of their own folly. What I want to know is who has fomented mutiny among the Host against their queen. They would not have bowed to the authority of a Raqia bawd. I believe there is someone of importance here in the keep."

He turned to the Ophanim that held the earthly monk. The creature looked beyond mad now. Trails of frozen spit stained his beard from having his mouth forced open by the leather bit, and he was unable or unwilling to stand on his own.

"This terrestrial claims you're harboring the last heir of the House of Arkhangel'sk."

The demoness looked upon the mad monk with disgust. "This is why the queen has sent you to attack us unprovoked? Preposterous. I know nothing about this person."

"Yet he spoke the truth about the presence of the Cherubim. How do you suppose he knew about that?"

"I haven't the slightest idea. Lucky guess?"

The field marshal raised his hand to strike her again, but the ache throbbed in it once more, like daggers thrust between his bones. He looked at the drooling monk and began to doubt himself. Something about the man had convinced him he spoke the truth and caused him to turn his men around for this foolhardy trek to the north in the midst of winter, but he felt none of that certainty now. He was not used to doubt, and it wormed inside his veins like a prickling heat.

The Cherubim and Virtues were here consorting with demons, however. It had to mean something. He would have the remaining Virtues tortured until they told him what he wanted to know.

He turned to give orders to one of his men but was interrupted by a pair of soldiers coming down the steps of the keep's tower.

"There's a locked room at the top, sir."

"Well, break down the door." What *were* they teaching at the Academy these days?

"It's iron, sir."

"What's in that room?" He turned to the demoness, but she pursed her lips stubbornly. "Search her for the key."

They probed her unceremoniously until a key was found on a chatelaine beneath her skirts.

A dozen soldiers mounted the steps, and within minutes they returned escorting a tall, fiery-haired brute, along with three women and a young child. The demon buck glared at him defiantly as he was brought forward, but the field marshal was uninterested in him. It was the child he'd come for.

He ordered the dark-haired maid holding the child to be brought to him, but one of the other women, clearly an angel, stepped forward and took the girl from her arms.

"You will not touch her." Her tone reminded him of the queen and there was something in her azurite eyes that unnerved him. Another unfamiliar feeling fluttered in his breast—a trickle of fear.

He nodded brusquely to the Ophanim who held the monk, and they dropped him to the floor and stepped forward, reaching for the child.

Two peculiar things happened at once. An arc of light in the color of an Aravothan sunset over Lake Superna in summer jumped from mother to child, causing the Ophanim to fall back as if stung, and the dark-haired maid cried out at the same moment and ran to the monk before anyone could stop her.

Semnadtsatoe: **The Man in the Leather Mask**
from the memoirs of the Grand Duchess Anazakia
Helisonovna of the House of Arkhangel'sk

Love fell on her knees before the madman we'd seen ranting in the
Palace Square. "Kirill! What have they done to you?"

This was her Kirill? She lifted his head into her lap, stroking the
matted hair. His mouth was bound with a cruel leather strap, and Love
began to work at the buckles to remove it. One of the Ophanim reached
to stop her, and Love gasped and jerked at the touch, her hands flying
away from the buckles.

"Let her go," I ordered, holding Ola tighter.

The Ophan hesitated, looking to the masked field marshal, who
was staring intently at me with his rheumy eye.

"He's no longer of any interest to me." The harsh growl of the field
marshal's voice sounded almost painful. "Leave the girl."

The Ophan backed away and allowed Love to remove the strap,
along with a damp rag that had been stuffed against the monk's tongue
as a gag. The poor man looked much the worse for wear, his lips cracked
and bleeding and his skin nearly colorless. He also looked as if he hadn't
eaten in days. If this was Kirill whom Love had thought dead, I wasn't
certain she'd been wrong.

Though I tried to hold her still, Ola turned in my arms and looked
down at Love. "Ki'ill," she said a bit mournfully, and sucked on her fist.

The field marshal reached out as if to touch Ola, but then jerked his hand back, rubbing the palm between stiffly curved fingers as if he couldn't quite spread them. The fourth finger of his glove was empty.

"So it's true." He turned to me, his voice more gravelly than Vasily's when he was angry. "She has seraphic blood."

I gave him no answer, and he didn't seem to expect one. There was something familiar about his face despite the knot of scars that marked the only visible part of it, but before I could dwell on this, my gaze focused on the prisoners standing behind him in the great hall, escorted by his Ophanim. Belphagor and the others were here.

Ola apparently noticed them just as I did. She pointed with certainty, announcing, "Beli."

Belphagor looked as close to tears as I had ever seen him. Beside me, Vasily smoothed Ola's wispy curls, but his eyes were on Belphagor as well.

"Well, now." The field marshal looked from Ola to Belphagor. "This is interesting." He raised his single patchy eyebrow toward Belphagor. "How does the Seraph-blood know Her Supernal Majesty's favorite pet?"

The way he said this phrase arrested me. It wasn't possible. I stared at the scarred face, searching for evidence of what might have been there before the tissue was damaged. The hair was swept back tight and slick, making it look darker than it was, making it look straight. But as it reflected the torchlight, I could see it was a pale golden blond.

"It can't be." As the whisper escaped my lips, the field marshal cocked his head at me in a gesture that was unmistakable. *"Kae?"*

Vasily gripped my arm, hard enough to bruise.

The field marshal looked as if I'd slapped him. "What did you call me?" He flexed his gloved hand once more in my direction, still not quite daring to touch me.

I shook my head, unable to repeat it.

"She called you," said Belphagor, "Your Supernal Majesty the Principality Kae Lebesovich of the House of Arkhangel'sk."

The field marshal turned slowly toward him, the long curls of his unmistakable ponytail slipping out from beneath the collar of his cape.

Belphagor met his gaze and added with a sneer, "Her Supernal Majesty's eternal slave."

With a swift and brutal gesture, my cousin—there was no mistaking him now for anyone else—loosed an instrument of knotted hide and lead from his belt and struck Belphagor across his collarbone with it. Belphagor stumbled under the weight and force of the blow, and before I could stop him, Vasily hurled himself forward and tackled Kae to the ground.

The Ophanim leapt upon Vasily and dragged him off, tossing him onto his back against the stone tile. Kae jumped up as swiftly, and the heel of one tall, shiny black boot struck Vasily in the head. I screamed, and Ola began to cry, frightened by me, I think, more than anything else. She twisted away from me and reached out her arms and wailed plaintively, "Lub!"

Love jumped up and took Ola, soothing her as I relinquished her. "It's okay, sweetie." We had both acted automatically, and I realized too late what a foolish thing I'd done when my cousin turned and swept Ola away from Love.

"Hold her," he ordered his Ophanim before I could take a step, and two smooth hands that seemed both cold and hot at once gripped my arms. I'd felt their unpleasant touch once before, apprehended in Raqia after Helga sent me away, but it wasn't a touch one got used to.

A field of current prickled at my flesh like a swarm of fire ants, and the shifting impression the Ophanim gave when they stood close, like something seen out of the corner of one's eye not quite in focus, made my stomach churn. Beside Kae, the other two Ophanim had dragged Vasily to his feet. Blood was trickling into his eye from the cut where Kae had kicked him, already swelling at his brow, and he looked as ill as I felt.

In all the years the Ophanim had guarded the palaces in which I'd lived, they'd never laid a hand on me. Like the Seraphim who had guarded our persons, they had stood in their places and done their duty, decorative complements to the splendor of their surroundings. They were both unobtrusive and unimportant. I'd never given a thought to the power that surrounded us. It had seemed benign.

I tried to focus on Kae. "Please. Don't hurt my baby."

He was holding Ola up as if examining an interesting artifact, and she'd gone quiet, as uncertain what to make of him as he seemed of her. "Why in Heaven would I hurt the child? I've come all the way from Elysium to find the last scion of the House of Arkhangel'sk." Apparently satisfied by his examination, he set Ola down and held her hand to keep her next to him. "And if such she is, then you must be Bloody Anazakia." He spat the words as if they dirtied his mouth. "You and your accomplices will answer for your crimes in Elysium."

"Nogi yee niskhodyat k smerti." The monk murmured the strange phrase from the floor and began to cough.

"He needs water." Love knelt down to him once more. "Please, can't we give him some water?"

"Bring it," Kae ordered one of his men.

The soldier went to the pump at the other end of the hall that brought water up from the cistern and filled a skin for the monk, bringing it to Love reluctantly. She lifted Kirill's head and encouraged him to drink. I had the feeling he wouldn't have done so for anyone but her.

"Ki'ill." Ola pulled on Kae's hand as if to go to him.

Kirill sat up with Love's help and smiled at Ola. "Hello, little one." A cloud came over his expression and he repeated in angelic the phrase he'd said in Russian: "Her feet go down into death." He paused to control his ragged breathing. *"And her steps go in as far as hell."*

The captain of the company entered the hall at that moment and signaled for Kae's attention. "What should we do with these?" He held up something that my mind at first simply refused to comprehend. "They're becoming defiant."

"Oh my God," said Love.

Behind me, Lively turned away and vomited onto the stones. The object the captain held was the severed head of a Virtue.

In a gesture that made me forgive just the tiniest piece of his cruelty, Kae dropped to his haunches and swiftly covered Ola's eyes. "What in the name of the Firmament is wrong with you, man?" His rasping voice couldn't quite yell. "Get that thing out of here!"

The captain balked, staring at his commanding officer as if he were a complete stranger before handing the head to one of his men, who took it out into the yard.

As the captain surveyed the rest of us, he paused when his gaze fell on me. "So you *are* alive, Your Supernal Highness." He gave me a slight, unconscious bow. "I've never quite believed the stories." He shook his head as if he still didn't. "You look just like your mother."

I realized with a shock that I'd danced with this man once, had flirted with him on several occasions during the single season in which I'd been presented to society before my life had been forever changed.

"Shall we bring her a dance card for you to fill your name in?" Kae delivered this drily as he stood, and for an instant, he was the Kae I knew.

Embarrassed, the captain drew himself up and saluted the field marshal as if he'd only just entered. "The Virtues, sir. They're pushing the men to the limit. I believe they actually wish to join the rest of their platoon. Seems to be a matter of honor." He glanced at Vashti and the red-headed woman standing next to Belphagor. "And I think we've found another Nephil."

Vashti made a movement toward the captain, but the soldier who held her jerked her back.

Kae noted the movement. "I believe there is more going on with this rebellion than it would seem. We'll set up operations here for now, and I'll question the Virtues at my leisure. Put them in irons for the time being and throw them in the dungeon—and make sure they have no means of taking the coward's way out before I've had my turn at them. As for the rest…" He paused and looked us over, and as he did so, Ola pulled from his grasp and ran to Love.

One of the Ophanim who held me let go and moved to take her, and I grabbed his arm. A shock went through me that left me rigid and unable to move.

"Never mind." Kae waved the Ophan back. "You can let her go as well." He looked at me as the other Ophan stepped away. "It doesn't matter if she touches the child and activates her element. If she opposes me when I decide to take the child from her, I'll simply start beheading her friends one by one until she gives me what I want."

We were returned to the tower room, but Kae had Vasily taken with the men to the dungeon. At least I was with Ola, though I didn't relish being stuck with the company of Helga and Lively—or Vashti—for any length of time. The latter pressed me for news of Nebo until I gave her a look that seemed to remind her where she'd gotten the limp that had yet to heal completely.

I was surprised to learn that the redhead, Margarita, was Nephil. I wondered at Dmitri's choice. I couldn't imagine her being useful in combat.

Ola seemed enamored of her hair. She climbed into Margarita's lap without hesitation and tugged on her ponytail, and Margarita was kind enough to indulge her. Ola's hair had darkened since the summer, and while it was more golden than Margarita's, it had taken on a decidedly red hue. It made me wonder about Vasily's natural shade, though of course I'd seen the muted reddish blond of his body hair. The thought of this made me blush, and I turned away to talk to Love.

"So that was your Kirill." I sat beside her on the bed.

She nodded. "I thought the Cherub had killed him. I guess he only transported him somewhere else." She dabbed at her eyes with the corner of her sleeve. "It looks as though they've been starving him. Or he's been starving himself." She blinked away the tears almost angrily. "This has been very hard on him, coming here. Seeing these creatures. He's a very simple man who believes deeply in his faith. He thought he was doing God's bidding, that he'd been visited by his messenger." Love directed her angry gaze at Vashti. "He was completely taken in by Zeus."

Vashti rubbed the red marks on her wrists where they'd been bound with rope. "I'm very sorry, Love." The small, penitent voice seemed utterly unlike her. She looked up to meet Love's eyes. "You have to believe I didn't know."

"Oh, I have to, do I?"

"He was my lover." Vashti's eyes were rimmed with red. "You can't think I would have been with someone who would—"

"Don't," Love snapped. "Don't you talk about that in front of Ola. There's been enough in front of Ola."

As I watched the look that passed between them, I knew suddenly it wasn't Vashti's relations with Zeus that Love didn't want her to speak of. There could only be one thing Vashti had been about to say that would put that look into Love's eyes. It struck me like a weight in my stomach.

"Oh, Love." I took her hand, and she looked away from me, but I pulled her into my arms, and she cried silently against my shoulder. I gave Helga a dark look. "This is what you've done. All of this is on your head."

"Sacrifices must be made for revolution." Her voice was cold and emotionless. "You have no idea of the sacrifices I've made."

"Sacrifices *you've* made?" I held on to Love to keep from leaping up and striking my former nurse, the woman who'd cared for me through childhood illnesses, who had bathed and clothed and fed me when I was small. I had once trusted her more than anyone in my life, as Ola now trusted Love. I shook my head at her in disgust. "You are well and truly mad."

"I'm fighting to save this world from a tyrant," she said haughtily. "Fighting to free my people from centuries of bondage. Something Vashti's kind ought to appreciate. As should your little gypsy." Helga gave Love a scornful look. "Yet she does your bidding like a happy little slave."

Love took a sharp, shocked breath and drew back, wiping her eyes.

Vashti, who'd risen and crossed the room as she spoke, stopped before Helga, her six feet towering over the shorter woman. "And just what the hell do you mean by 'my kind'? You know bollocks about my kind." She slapped Helga with the full force of her nephilic strength, and the older woman buckled at the knees but caught herself and stood upright. Vashti gripped her palm as if the blow had hurt her hand, and Helga smiled, fingering the locket at her breast. Vashti drew the hand to her waist. "As for Love, you don't know bollocks about her kind, either, so don't you talk about her or even speak to her. Anyone who insults Love or so much as touches her or Anazakia or that baby will answer to me." She looked embarrassed as she turned away from Helga and saw that Ola had scrambled up from Margarita's lap into Love's, regarding her warily.

"Remind me not to get on your bad side," Margarita murmured as Vashti sat down next to her at the little table that clearly had not been designed for someone of her size.

"Remind me to shut up." She gave me an apologetic look. "I didn't mean to scare her. Don't mind me, kid," she said to Ola, attempting a smile. "Vashti is very naughty."

I looked away from her. If she thought changing her allegiance now was going to make up for her part in this, she was as mad as Helga.

From the bench by the door, Lively watched with curiosity, apparently unperturbed by Vashti's assault on her aunt.

"What about demons who enslave one another?" I asked Helga. "Where do they fit in your revolution? Or was that just one more thing Lively was lying about? Did your family actually sell her?"

Helga shrugged. "People do what they must to survive. I passed for angelic. My brother wasn't so fortunate. He was more like your Vasily, wearing his demonic persona with defiant pride. My sister-in-law was rather fecund and they couldn't afford to feed all those mouths. But most of them found decent posts." She smiled at Lively. "Lively will inherit the apothecary when her employer passes on. There'll be no need to sell her baby. Of course, her baby will be very special."

"Yes," I said. "It will be *polovina-d'yavol.*"

Helga glared at me.

"It will be Ola's little brother or sister," Lively said smugly. "Then you won't be the only one with something special."

"Don't ask," I said as Vashti and Margarita exchanged looks of surprise.

Lively didn't wait for them to. "I'm carrying Vasily's baby." She cupped her stomach with a smile.

Love, who hadn't known about Vasily's part in Lively's condition, seemed particularly offended by the notion. "*Eto fignya.* He would never cheat on Nazkia."

"I wouldn't call it cheating," I reminded her. "He belongs to Belphagor."

"Beli," said Ola, pleased with herself for recognizing this name.

Love put her hands over Ola's ears as if she would understand what was being said. "But while you were searching for Ola?"

"He thought she was me." I was irritated at having to go over this and even more irritated that Lively was obviously enjoying it.

Love looked confused for a moment before the realization dawned on her. "Oh. The glamour. You looked like her."

"Believe whatever you like about how it happened." Lively took a bite of one of the pieces of cracker bread she kept in her pocket. I'd never seen anyone look so pleased with herself in all my life. She was like a cat fat with cream. "The fact remains that his seed is in my belly."

"Beli," said Ola. She slipped from Love's lap and went to pat on the door. "Go see Beli."

Vosemnadtsatoe: Wild Card

The monk spent nearly every waking moment murmuring the words of an Orthodox prayer about the Christian god Jesus. He knelt on the floor of the dungeon with his face pressed to the ground—something Belphagor considered inadvisable—holding a rope of knotted wool that he worked in his fingers with each iteration of the prayer. At least he was eating now, if only small pieces of bread. It seemed his brief reunion with Love had given him the will to live.

Belphagor stole a glance at Vasily on the cot beside him. He could understand the sentiment.

Vasily nodded toward the monk. "Does he ever stop that?"

"Not so you'd notice."

"It's the Prayer of the Heart," said Lev, leaning against the bars. "I learned it in church."

Belphagor regarded him dubiously. "You've been to church?"

"Why not? Churches are pretty." Lev shrugged. "I like the sense of ceremony, the peaceful meditation."

Dmitri smirked at Lev. "I keep telling him he's going to burst into flames one of these days."

"I prefer the church of chance myself." Belphagor clasped his fingers in front of him and cracked his knuckles as he stretched, glad not to have his wrists bound. "I could do with some 'ceremony' right about now. Can't remember the last time I partook of a good game of wingcasting."

Nebo, at the other end of the cot, pulled a leather bag from his coat pocket and held it up. "It just so happens I've got a deck right here." He grinned at Vasily. "Took it from a fellow along the road to Aravoth who didn't seem to need it."

Vasily laughed and Belphagor raised his pierced eyebrow. Apparently the two of them had shared a bit of adventure.

The graceful Virtues, shackled in the cell across from them, watched with curiosity as Belphagor and Vasily turned the iron cot into a wingcasting table. Stretching a coat across the frame for a surface to cast the die and deal out cards, the five players sat around the table while the monk continued his devotion unperturbed.

"Teams?" asked Belphagor as he dealt.

"With you and Vasily together?" Lev rolled his eyes. "We've met you, you know. I think we'll stick to single-player."

Belphagor shrugged and dealt out seven cards to each of them. "Aeons wild."

"Just a minute." Dmitri grabbed up his cards. "You can't call a wild card after you've already looked at your hand."

"I hadn't looked." Belphagor tried to maintain a straight face and then grinned as the others stared him down. "All right, nothing wild for this hand. Your cast, Dmitri." He set the die before him.

Dmitri threw the twelve-sided die lightly across the makeshift table, and Nebo, to his left, called out "Ptarmigan." The die landed on the Phoenix.

"What are we betting?" asked Nebo. "Rubles? Facets?" He looked into his pocket. "I've also got euros."

Belphagor laughed. "We're betting you won't notice we're all broke. Go ahead and throw in. We'll be happy to take whatever you've got."

"How 'bout we play for who has to sleep next to the piss-pot tonight," Lev suggested, wrinkling his nose.

"Was that piss-pot or piss spot?" asked Vasily. "The cot seemed a little damp after you had it last."

"Oh, ouch." Dmitri examined his hand. "That was the wet spot, not the piss spot."

Nebo laughed. "You're the craziest bunch of demons I've ever played with. I'm not putting down anything."

"Doesn't matter." Belphagor dropped his cards onto the cot in front of them. "Full choir plus a full sphere." The complete Second Choir—Seraph, Cherub, and Ophan—in the suit of facets was neatly arranged next to the Aeon, Seraph, Dominion, and Principality of tricks, the first orders of each choir.

"You dealt yourself a Scarlet Wing on the first round?" Lev tossed down his cards. "You are so cheating, Prince of Tricks!"

Belphagor grinned. "There's no need for name calling."

Vasily was smiling at him over his black-rimmed spectacles, and Belphagor's pulse picked up a beat. Vasily had always been aroused by his antics at the wingcasting table. There had been more nights than he could count, back in the day, when he'd gotten up in the middle of a game to take Vasily back to his room at The Brimstone to "punish" him for his own misdeeds. It was an agreement they'd come to early on in their relationship that seemed to suit them both. Despite his temper, Vasily was generally too well behaved to earn the sort of treatment he craved from Belphagor, while Belphagor, by his nature, was as Lev had said: the Prince of Tricks.

It was a double-entendre on Belphagor's wandering eye. Punishing Vasily for such wanderings as well had made the wandering and the punishing that much more exciting. Lev, in fact, had been a bit of that wandering when they'd first met. Because of the natural aging that occurred in the terrestrial sphere, Dmitri and Lev appeared some years older than Belphagor and Vasily now, but they'd been a perfectly matched foursome for a time.

"How nice to see you amusing yourselves." The field marshal stepped into the torchlight from the darkened passageway in his trademark black, right down to the leather mask that covered his disfigurement. Looking at him now, Belphagor was surprised he hadn't seen it before. As principality, Kae had dressed always in black, presumably at the desire of his queen. She'd found it amusing to dress Belphagor in ivories and creams so that when they encountered each other, the effect was that of two pawns on a chessboard. Indeed, that was exactly what they'd both been.

He wasn't sure to what extent Anazakia's cousin was under Aeval's control, but he suspected the principality hadn't even been aware of his state. Even now, the field marshal seemed unaware of who he'd once been, which made his disguise all the more convincing.

Clearly, however, he remembered something of Belphagor, even if he wasn't certain why. He walked slowly along the corridor of the dungeon with the *pleti* in his hand, running it along the bars. The knotted leather-and-lead flogger was an antique instrument from the brutal history of Russia's prison system. Aeval had procured it for Kae, wanting to see it used on Belphagor, and Kae had taken to it like a natural—Belphagor was enough of a connoisseur to know.

"Who is that for?" Belphagor nodded at the *pleti*. He felt Vasily's fury rising beside him and he touched his hand lightly to calm him.

Kae noted the motion. "Charming." He looked at Dmitri and Lev as he stopped before the cell. "Are you all...*that way*?" He smiled as Lev betrayed his surprise. "Yes, I've noted your unnatural tendencies, though you were wise to try to hide it. My men have been growing restless after so long on the road—and you do look like you'd put up less of a fight than those two toms." He cocked his head. "Is it a demon thing? Do you simply fall to depravity despite yourselves?"

"What do you mean by 'tom'?" Nebo looked as if he was about to rise and challenge the field marshal. "If you're implying my sister is a dyke—"

"It's really best not to engage him," Belphagor murmured, and then ignored his own advice and gave Kae a contemptuous look. "Certainly not to disagree with him. He gets quite testy if you challenge his world view."

Kae stood perfectly still for a moment. His silence was like that of a sleeping Vesuvius, deceptively tranquil until it went off.

"Of course she's a dyke." Belphagor gathered up the cards. "We're all dykes. Just a bunch of happy little dykes. She's just better groomed than you are."

"What is it you think you know about me, demon?" Kae stroked the *pleti*.

Again, Vasily tensed beside him, and again Belphagor stilled his hand. "What is it you think you know about *me*? Why did you call me the queen's pet?" He dug his nails into the back of Vasily's hand this time to stop him from reacting. Instead of his murderous fury at the angel, Vasily's breath quickened with the more familiar outrage that Belphagor's seemingly arbitrary acts of cruelty always inspired in him. As much as Vasily desired it, it always infuriated him at first when Belphagor appeared to abuse him without cause. Indignant resistance and a sense of being unfairly wronged seemed to be a key ingredient in Vasily's eventual surrender and release.

Belphagor was actually surprised and touched to have elicited such a reaction. Perhaps Vasily had forgiven him for his unconscionable stupidity now that they'd found Ola. Perhaps he was feeling just a little bit of fear at how far over the line he'd stepped—not that Belphagor hadn't deserved it.

He deliberately broke the skin as he squeezed Vasily's hand behind him, feeling the thrill of the hot blood against his fingers. He hoped he'd have the opportunity to make good on the implied threat—as well as the energy and fortitude to carry it through.

Kae looked unnerved. "Your reputation," he answered vaguely. "Every man in the Queen's Army knows about you."

"Do they really?" Belphagor pretended to be flattered. "The queen actually shares such intimate details with the enlisted men?"

Kae struck the bars with the *pleti*. "You will not speak of Her Supernal Majesty with such insolence!"

"Me?" Belphagor released Vasily's hand to shuffle the deck. "I believe it was you who were being indelicate and discussing Her Supernal Majesty's private business in front of your entire company."

He shrugged. "Though how you'd know about it, I can't imagine." He cut the deck. "Shall I deal you in? We could use a little in the pot." He glanced up at the field marshal, gauging the level of rage that was building in his cold veins. "You know the game, don't you? Or haven't you figured it out yet?"

The field marshal raised a cool eyebrow at him. "Your game, sir? No, I have not. But I intend to."

Belphagor had lost the moment. Kae's volatile blood, held in check by the queen who commanded it, was no longer threatening to rise out of control. They'd done it once, he and Anazakia, nearly driving the man out of his mind, and might have killed him in the process. The heat of Vasily's child inside her womb had seemed to spark an answering heat in Kae's blood when he'd grabbed Anazakia after Belphagor had driven him to a frenzy. Belphagor wondered what would happen if he let Vasily at him.

Once the angel's frozen blood had begun to heat, his temperature couldn't be brought down. Only Aeval had been able to return him to equilibrium. Without her to cool him once driven to fever, Kae would likely die. Belphagor shrugged, unable to see a downside.

"However." Kae pulled his eyes away as if Belphagor had mesmerized him. "Figuring out your game is not why I came down here." He moved to the opposite cell and unlocked the door. Pulling one of the shackled Virtues to his feet, he led him out into the corridor with the chain dragging between his ankles. The Virtue looked barely old enough to hold a sword.

"What is your name?" The field marshal observed him as if with idle curiosity.

"Loquel."

Kae turned him about and hooked the shackles that locked his wrists together on a peg protruding from the cell bars above his head, so that Loquel had to stand on the balls of his feet.

"Well, Loquel." Kae tore open the jacket at his back. "I intend to have more names from you before I'm through." He swung and struck the Virtue with the *pleti* before he'd even given him a chance.

Loquel cried out in surprise, scrabbling with his feet to remain standing.

In his head, Belphagor heard the sound of Aeval's melodic laughter the first time Kae had beaten him with that same weapon, with an equal lack of warning. Her delighted voice echoed in his memory. *Oh, if you could only see your face!*

"That was a warning." The field marshal turned Loquel's head toward him. "A taste of what you can expect if you defy me." The path of the lead balls in the leather thongs was already livid against the Virtue's back.

Virtues were not normally warriors. The Powers of their choir had that distinction, while Virtues studied the law and used their intellect and wisdom to enforce it. They didn't seem built for war, and certainly not to withstand the sort of abuse a man like Kae Lebesovich took pleasure in meting out.

"Your leader told me before he died that he'd come from the estate of Sar Sarael."

The Virtue said nothing, and Kae struck him again. The other angels turned their heads away, evidently unable to look Loquel in the eyes as he was suffering.

Loquel swung forward off his feet before catching himself with difficulty, his knees bashing against the bars. "Yes, sir! We came from Pyr Amaravati!"

"Good." The field marshal nodded. "And for whom does Sar Sarael procure such forces?"

"For whom, sir?" He gasped as Kae struck him again, his legs trembling as he tried to remain on his toes. "Please, sir, I don't know what you mean."

The next blow landed on his lower back and curled around his side. The luminous Virtuous flesh was already scored with ugly welts, and this drew blood. Loquel lost his footing and howled when one of his shoulders was dislocated as his arms were forced to bear his weight.

When the field marshal struck him again, he made a sound like a beaten dog and wet himself as he dangled from his shackles, the silver-white hair falling over his face from its queue.

Inside their cell, the monk had begun whispering his prayer more urgently, crossing himself and bobbing forward and back in agitation. Belphagor was methodically shuffling cards, while Dmitri and Lev stared down at the wingcasting table, and Nebo stared ahead with outrage in his eyes. Vasily had turned pale.

Belphagor placed his hand on Vasily's forearm and Vasily stared at him, ashen. "You know it wasn't like that for me," he murmured to the backdrop of helpless whimpering to which the Virtue had been reduced. "Demons are made of tougher stuff."

Vasily continued to stare at him, as if Belphagor himself had beaten the young man.

Belphagor sighed. "He doesn't know what you want," he said loudly when Loquel's breathing started to come in ragged moans.

The field marshal turned around and fixed him with his unnerving, clouded eye. "Are you telling me how to do my job?" His voice was dangerously flat.

"No, sir." Belphagor met his eye. "I'm simply telling you that this Virtue you're beating the hell out of will probably die before he answers you, and not out of pride or valor, but because he simply doesn't understand what you're asking him. I'm certain he would have told you after the second blow if he had."

Kae sneered. "I think I've made myself perfectly clear. Sar Sarael cannot be mobilizing forces against the queen and committing treason on his own. The Virtue knows who is behind this."

"He might." Belphagor shuffled the wingcasting deck. "But his head isn't clear enough to make that connection with what you've offered him, and I think he's beyond answering now." He gave the field marshal another even stare. "Perhaps one of the others." He hated the idea of watching another man beaten, but he knew this one couldn't take another stroke.

Kae regarded him with mistrust, flicking his wrist in a figure-eight motion with his flogger as he practiced his stroke. Returning the handle to its hook on his belt, he lifted Loquel's shackles from the peg. The young Virtue groaned as Kae opened the cell and shoved him inside. Two of the other Virtues caught Loquel with their shackled arms before he collapsed.

"Who's next? Or will you all just watch as I beat you one by one?"

A more seasoned-looking Virtue stepped forward, his eyes defiant. "Gereimon."

"Is that your name or are you giving me one of the names I've asked for?"

"That is my name," said the Virtue. This one wasn't likely to give the field marshal the answer he wanted either, and not because he didn't know it.

Kae led Gereimon out and hooked his shackles to the peg. This time, he pulled the man's jacket up over his head. This kept both the fabric and the long Virtuous hair out of the path of his flogger. Ripping a man's clothes off before beating him might be satisfying, but as Belphagor knew well, it wasn't always practical.

As the field marshal pulled back his arm and raised the *pleti*, Vasily jumped to his feet. "The Elohim," he said loudly. "They're the ones you want. They're the ones behind the Aravothan rebellion."

"What are you doing?" Belphagor tried to pull him back.

Vasily gave him a dark look. "I'm trying to keep a score of Virtues from being beaten to death in front of our eyes. I suppose it's easy enough for you to watch such brutality, but not for the rest of us." He was still in the defiant mode that so often led to their intimacy. Belphagor was beginning to wish he hadn't provoked him.

The field marshal approached their cell, leaving Gereimon in suspense. "The Virtuous Court has participated in this mutiny?"

"It's not a mutiny; it's a damned revolution." Vasily stared him down with fire in his eyes. "The Elohim belong to the Party of the Socialist Host. Maybe the queen had better start taking notice, because they're not the only ones in it."

• • •

Vasily supposed it should have come as no surprise that his confession hadn't earned him any points with the sonofawhore. The field marshal had demanded intricate details about the revolutionary party, though Vasily hadn't bothered to tell him there was more than one. Was it only the Elohim who were behind it? Had it spread beyond Aravoth and this small pocket of demon riffraff? Whom besides Sar Sarael could Vasily confirm was a member of the Elohim?

When Vasily couldn't answer, Kae, in a rage, had struck him with his flogger through the bars of the cell, catching him with the leaded thongs on the side of his cheek, and turned to beat Gereimon after all. This Virtue, at least, seemed better able to withstand it—or at least had been better prepared.

The field marshal returned to the dungeon day after day, promising to beat another man each time they refused to give him more information on the Elohim and the Party of the Socialist Host. He worked his way through the Virtues, targeting young Loquel twice more out of spite, and then started on the monk, who of course knew nothing. Kirill ranted and recited strange scripture and the repetitions of his prayer, reaching a kind of trancelike, ecstatic state. Perhaps, like Vasily, he was a natural masochist.

It was Belphagor who noticed the marks in his flesh when Kae tossed him back into the cell, throwing his robes in after him. Around the monk's right thigh were recent scars from something that had pierced his flesh—four rows of marks too regular to be anything but deliberately inflicted.

"This is from a cilice," said Belphagor, crouching down to inspect them. He eyed the monk shrewdly. "*My* cilice."

Vasily grew warm as he remembered it. Belphagor had tied the belt of barbed chain lovingly onto his thigh when they were first together, telling him the constant irritant of the little hooks would remind Vasily whom he belonged to. Vasily wore it while they sat at the wingcasting tables, quietly fuming as Belphagor utterly ignored him for hours. Whenever he tried to speak, Belphagor silenced him scornfully, much to the amusement of the other players, dismissing him when he lost his temper at last with a curt command to wait for him in their room while Belphagor finished his round of wingcasting.

He was gone far longer than a round, and had come back smelling of absinthe.

Vasily had been furious and humiliated, demanding to know what Belphagor had been doing at the tables so long, hurt that he'd been forgotten. Belphagor had caned him for his attitude and then wound Vasily's locks viciously in his fist as he had his way with him. Railing and cursing him, Vasily had borne it bitterly as the hooks of the cilice jabbed into his thigh with Belphagor's rough motions, only to have Belphagor whisper to him at last that he'd followed him straight back to the room a few moments later and had been sitting outside the door for three hours with a bottle of absinthe, thinking how lovely Vasily had looked when he'd tied the cilice in place. Three hours, Belphagor had whispered, was all he could stand before he had to have him.

As Belphagor untied the cord at his thigh, Vasily, somewhat subdued but still hurt at Belphagor's treatment of him at the table, had asked why he'd ignored and humiliated him. Belphagor replied that he'd made him wear the cilice so Vasily could feel his love with every moment of discomfort, that no matter how unfeeling Belphagor seemed to be toward him outwardly, he could take secret pleasure, as Belphagor had, in knowing he was Belphagor's.

"How did you get these marks?" Belphagor asked the monk as he helped him pull on his robes.

"Mortification of the flesh." Kirill hissed against the pain of the stripes on his back as he pulled the rough wool garment into place.

"You wore a cilice?"

The monk nodded and told him God had placed it in a drawer in "Sister Lyubov's dacha," leaving it for him to find.

Belphagor murmured in Vasily's ear as the monk resumed his bobbing and bowing recitation, "I've never been called God before. We'll have to remember that one."

Kae slammed the door of the cell and locked it. "Perhaps you'd do better to remember the members of the Elohim the next time you see me."

When the field marshal returned, however, he made the mistake of choosing Belphagor as the next to be flogged. Vasily wouldn't have it. Belphagor tried to calm him down, but he was through being the "good boy" to Belphagor's bad. The soldiers waiting in the corridor were called in to drag Vasily out, and he went kicking and screaming. It took four of them to subdue him and they had to beat him to keep him down.

The field marshal snapped his fingers at Belphagor, who went all too willingly for Vasily's taste. He even did the bastard the favor of removing his own shirt and laying it neatly aside before he left the cell. Vasily cringed as he always did at the sight of the scarred flesh while Belphagor helpfully leaned forward against the bars and grasped them high and wide. Kae paused as his eye fell on the one clear tattoo that still remained, the tips of the red crown that marked Belphagor as "the king of bitches" in the language of thieves.

"What's the matter?" Belphagor turned his head. "Surely you've seen your own work before?"

"What work?"

"You don't remember, Your Supernal Majesty?"

Kae swung the flogger with a swift, vindictive stroke, and Belphagor took it without so much as a flinch of his skin. "Whatever you're playing at, you will soon be sorry."

"I wonder what *you're* playing at. Do you really not remember me? Is it possible you truly can't recall all those intimate moments we shared?"

"There were no intimate moments!" Kae swung the flogger again. "I've never seen you before."

"Shame on you to say such a thing, Your Supernal Majesty."
Belphagor breathed into the pain, the way he'd taught Vasily. "After I
spent so much time letting you cheat at cards."

Kae struck him again.

"I did let you win, you know," said Belphagor when he'd steadied
his breath. "Aeval told me your tempers needed to be indulged. I must
say, I was surprised at how delicately she treated you."

Kae exploded with fury, slamming Belphagor's head into the bars.
"What in hell's name are you talking about?"

Vasily struggled, but the soldiers held him tight.

"You were her pride, Your Supernal Majesty." Belphagor spoke
casually. "Did she toss you out because you lost your looks, or is she the
one who took them?"

The field marshal stood deadly still for several seconds. What little
expression the mask afforded, Vasily couldn't see from his position.

Then Kae took three deliberate steps back. "Take all of them to
the yard."

"All of them, sir?" asked one of his men.

"ALL OF THEM!" The shout seemed to tear his throat with its
rage. It wasn't loud, but it carried the weight of a much stronger voice.

• • •

In the cold yard of the inner ward, the field marshal lined up the
prisoners on their knees with their hands bound before them. He was
through being mocked by these petty upstarts. He would take the
company to Aravoth and deal with the Elohim himself. Any Virtue who
refused to cooperate in identifying the traitors would meet the same
fate as these: a swift and merciless execution.

He sent Captain Jusguarin to bring the female prisoners down
from the tower room as well, leaving only the child and her nurse, along
with the matronly demoness; that one would be publicly executed in
Elysium as an example to the rest of her followers.

The field marshal ordered the Virtue Loquel to be brought to him first. The angel moved awkwardly, not having taken his beatings well at all. The young Virtue—almost a boy, really—knelt before him and looked up to meet his eye, his face sad but resolved, as if a bit relieved to be joining his fallen comrades. An instant of compassion struck the field marshal, and then he shook himself out of it, more furious than ever, and raised his sword while Loquel was pushed forward. One of the soldiers yanked Loquel's silvery queue to the front to bare his neck.

The demon Belphagor called out from in front of him before he took his swing. "Why not just execute me? I'm the one you want dead."

The field marshal stared at the miserable little demon. He ought to make him watch every last execution before he had his turn. And then the field marshal had a better idea.

He spoke quietly to the soldiers who'd brought Loquel. "Bring me the red demon. I'll deal with this one later."

Loquel looked stunned as he was pulled to his feet and returned to the row of Virtues. The demon Vasily was brought forward, and the field marshal was pleased with the effect this had on Belphagor, who leapt to his feet and struggled as the field marshal's men restrained him.

The larger demon stared at the field marshal, his eyes red with defiance, and had to be forced to his knees. As the thick red tangles of hair were pulled out of the way, the field marshal paused momentarily, noting the metal spikes protruding through the flesh on either side of the demon's neck like rows of cravat pins.

"Do those come out?"

One of the soldiers pulled on one of the spikes, and the demon thrashed and nearly bit him. Several men had to hold the demon down before his man could determine that the spiked caps unscrewed.

"Take them out," he ordered.

"Don't you dare!" the demon roared. "Get your fucking hands off me!"

Several of the men jumped back as the firespirit's flesh grew suddenly hot, and it took another minute for them to get hold of him once more without touching bare skin.

The field marshal stood over the demon when they'd subdued him. "Unless you want my blade catching in them halfway through your neck, you had better hold still."

"I don't give a damn what the blade does," the demon growled.

The field marshal shrugged. "Earthly damnation is immaterial. But I've seen a man's spinal cord severed by a blade while his head was still attached. It was extraordinarily unpleasant for all involved."

The soldiers held the demon securely, though he hissed breath hot as steam through his teeth, while they unscrewed his decorations and tossed them on the ground. The demon's bare neck was positioned for the blow.

Belphagor appealed to the field marshal once more as they readied his paramour. "Spare him, and I can guarantee he'll tell you anything you want to know about the Elohim. He's bound to me and has to obey."

The field marshal raised his eyebrow at this.

"Not anymore," said the fire demon, his voice dull. "My bonds are lying in the snow."

"Was that the only thing that bound you to me, Vasya?" The smaller demon spoke quietly. "Just pieces of metal? Was our bond so weak?"

"No." The demon sighed. "But it doesn't matter. I don't know anything about this stupid revolution. All I wanted was Ola."

For no reason at all, the field marshal felt ill. His blood was pounding in his ears, he felt as if his gut were being torn in two, and he'd broken out in a sweat.

The smaller demon was staring at him shrewdly. "*Ola*. That's the child's name. I thought you knew your cousin had named the baby after your wife."

The field marshal staggered back, resisting the vertigo that pulled at him. "Stop speaking nonsense! There is no cousin! There is no wife!" He put one hand to his throat as his voice strained muscles that still felt as if black smoke were coursing through them.

"Anazakia is your cousin. You delivered the baby yourself at the

Winter Palace."

The field marshal reeled. In his head, he saw three things at once that he couldn't make sense of. He was in the Winter Palace carrying a newborn baby away from the sobbing grand duchess as she lay shackled to a wooden camp bed. He was a young boy standing over a beautiful blond woman whose eyes were closed and whose dressing gown was soaked in blood, while in his arms he held a stillborn infant. He was a man holding a gore-soaked sword before a woman with azure eyes whose rich honey curls were spattered in blood, her stomach laid open like the abdomen of an autopsied corpse.

He dropped the sword and covered his ears as a chorus of voices he couldn't understand overwhelmed his head, screaming at once. "It's not me!" he cried. "It's not me!" He spun around as if someone had touched him. "Where's the baby?"

Jusguarin was just arriving from the keep with the four female prisoners, and he stopped and stared at him. "You told me not to bring the baby. She's upstairs with the nurse and the old maid."

"The nurse," the field marshal gasped. "The old maid is the nurse."

The captain gave him a peculiar look. "I'm sorry, sir, but I don't know what you mean. The nurse is a young woman, no older than these two." He nodded his head toward the demon girl and the grand duchess.

Bloody Anazakia. She was staring at him as if she knew more about him than he knew himself. In her azurite eyes, a couple danced: the grand duchess in a ball gown with her hair swept up in ringlets about her head and a gaily dressed young man with hair like his own, but a face the field marshal didn't recognize.

"Who is that man?" he asked, transfixed.

She gave him a puzzled look. "What man?"

"The one in your eyes! The one you danced with!"

Her face went pale and he remembered that he hated her—*hated her!*—and wanted her dead. "You're next!" he shouted. He grabbed her by the arm and swung her around to retrieve his sword. They were dancing, forever dancing, and he meant to put an end to it.

Devatnadtsatoe: **Tears and a Kiss**
from the memoirs of the Grand Duchess Anazakia
Helisonovna of the House of Arkhangel'sk

He had once been my cousin, my brother-in-law, and my friend. The man who looked at me now through a single watery eye full of rage and hate was none of these. He threw me to the frozen ground as he took up his sword, and I was vaguely aware that Vasily knelt in the snow beside me, held fast by Ophanim.

"On your knees!" Kae ordered hoarsely.

As I drew myself up, I felt something hard inside my coat against my thigh. *Knud's knife.* The soldiers had never bothered to search me for weapons. I let my coat fall open and moved my hand up to my pocket. Behind me, Kae grabbed the hair at my forehead and jerked my head back, bringing his blade in front of my throat as if he meant to slit it instead of beheading me.

There was a scuffle in the snow beside us as Vasily sprang forward, his hands suddenly free, and I could smell burning rope. It was a futile effort, however, as the Ophanim yanked him back.

"Son of a whore!" Vasily growled. "Let her go!"

"From what I understand, it was your mother who was the whore." Kae ignored Vasily's further curses and crouched behind me to speak in my ear almost intimately. "Is there anything you wish to say before I cut you open?"

"Yes," I whispered. The sound of the folding knife ratcheting open seemed horribly loud and I was certain he must have heard it, but he took no notice. "I'm sorry." I drove the blade back with my fist, fighting tears as it sank into flesh.

The sword at my throat slipped loosely in his hand as if he'd lost his grip, and Kae fell forward onto his knees, grasping my shoulder as if he were embracing me. I don't think he quite understood at first that he'd been stabbed, and in the position where he crouched, it had been visible to no one else.

"You're sorry?" He sounded dazed. "For what?"

"For taking you up the mountain on my seventeenth birthday." Tears slid down my cheeks in the cold as I hardened my resolve. "For not being able to save you. And for this." I twisted the knife inside him and dragged it sideways, and his sword dropped from his hand as he fell back onto his heels. I grabbed for his blade before anyone moved, jumping to my feet with it clutched in both hands. "Back away." I waved it at the Ophanim holding Vasily's arms, but they were unimpressed.

The soldiers began to move in, but their field marshal rasped out the last order he was likely to give. "Stand down!"

"Sir, you're wounded." His captain eyed the blood seeping around the handle of the blade in Kae's abdomen. "I'm not sure you're thinking clearly."

"Am I not—still the field marshal—of the Armies of Heaven?" A weak cough broke up his words. "You—will obey me!" He looked down at last at the knife handle protruding from his flesh and pressed his fingers to the blood, staring at it as if uncertain what it was. His one eye was as wide as a child's when he raised his head. "Nenny? What have you done to me?" He pulled the knife out and stared at it as his blood began to flow freely from the wound.

He had spoken our special name. It was what my brother Azel had called me when he was too young to pronounce "Nazkia." Helga had continued to use it throughout my childhood—I'd thought it a sign of her affection, but it was clear now it was a sign of her disdain. Only Kae had used it as a kind of special code between us, spoken with a fondness that conveyed an acknowledgment of our bond, deeper than his love for my sister Ola, though it was not romantic. It was a sign that we understood each other without words, that he knew me better than anyone, and he had used it in his lucid moments in Aeval's Winter Palace, begging me for help I could not understand how to give. I had left him to her. I had abandoned him to let him become...*this*.

I fell on my knees before him, the sword gripped at my side. "Don't," I pleaded under my breath.

He tilted his head with a sad half-smile that was so fully Kae that my heart stopped for an instant. "I think," he said, his voice a hoarse whisper on the labored edge of a breath, "it's too late."

"No." I dropped the sword and pressed my hand against the wound to stop the blood, but pulled it back as quickly. The blood wasn't right. It was cold as the ice and snow around us, and it moved like sap dripping from a tapped maple. I covered my mouth with my hand, staring at him, while tears poured down my cheeks.

Kae reached out and startled me by taking my hand away from my mouth. "Ola, darling. I didn't mean to make you cry." He lifted my hand to his lips and kissed my knuckles. "Salty," he said with a smile as he tasted my tears, and then he dropped my hand as if it were a hot coal. "Nazkia?" Though he knelt in Empyrean snow, sweat began to drip from his temples. This had happened before.

He took up his sword and staggered to his feet, shoving his captain backward when he caught him as he stumbled. "You have my orders! Why are your men still—standing about me—like vultures? Keep away! I can't breathe!"

The captain and his men retreated several steps, exchanging glances.

"Is this mutiny?" Kae accused, gasping for breath. "Put your swords away! Get back!"

They retreated still more, sheathing their swords after the captain nodded. A wide circle had opened around us. Only Vasily and the Ophanim remained within it.

Kae's eye fixed on Vasily. "You're the devil—come to finish me."

Cold blood still dripped from his gut like treacle, though his skin was flushed with fever. "What took you so long?" He staggered toward Vasily and raised the sword, and for a terrible instant I thought he meant to run him through, but Kae jabbed it at one of the Ophanim. "I said—get back. Leave him." When the Ophanim obeyed, he turned the hilt of the sword toward Vasily.

Vasily gave me only the briefest hard glance before he took the sword and moved in with purpose to do what I knew he had long dreamed of. But before he could follow through, Kae's eye rolled back in his head and he toppled backward and hit the ground. Like Vasily, the soldiers stared dumbstruck as their field marshal shook in the grip of a fit.

"It's a febrile seizure," I heard myself say. "We need to cool him down." My sister's voice from my own fevered dream echoed in my head. *You'd have to bury him in the snow to cool his blood.* I dropped to my knees beside him and began unbuttoning his double-breasted coat. "Someone hold him still," I cried as his thrashing hampered my efforts.

After a stunned moment of inertia, two officers knelt down beside me and held their field marshal while I bared his chest and began covering him in snow. I piled it around his head and pulled his arms from his sleeves to cover them as well, and then packed him in snow from head to foot, as if preserving a corpse.

As his convulsions stopped, his temperature dropped and his erratic breathing steadied, but strangely, his blood seemed to heat even as the rest of him cooled. It flowed more like normal blood, and was now rapidly coloring the snow at his midsection as it poured from the wound. It looked as if the snow itself were bleeding.

The two officers rose and stepped away as they saw there was nothing more they could do.

"Nazkia." Vasily crouched down beside me. "Let him die."

I shook my head, my heart aching at how I must be hurting him. "I can't. He knew me. He knew me and he knew I'd left him to her. What he is—I did this to him." I pressed the heel of my hand into the snow against the wound, trying to stop it, and a weak bluish trickle of my radiance glowed for a moment.

Vasily yanked my hand back and turned me toward him. His eyes were full of angry heat, but the flame faded as I stared up at him, weeping and mute with guilt. Pale lavender flickered beneath his fingers against my skin.

He slid his hand down to mine and locked our fingers in a painful grip, staring into me as if he might see my soul if he looked hard enough. "Dammit," he murmured and pressed both our hands against Kae's bleeding gut.

The lavender flame rose up instantly and flowed from our hands to the blood. It licked across Kae's body like a hungry fire, as if we'd doused him in lamp oil and he was the wick. The radiance melted the snow as it surrounded him, swirling in a continuous circular path like the boiling surface of the Pyriphlegethon. It was burning brighter now than it had in the world of Man and I looked at Vasily, stunned by its intensity. It surged up as if drawing all the aether together before it flashed in one bright, violet point above Kae's heart and was gone.

When we pulled our hands away, Kae was whole.

I searched Vasily's eyes, astounded that he'd helped the man he hated more than anything, and whispered, "Why?"

Vasily let go of my hand. "Because, Nazkia." He sighed and thumbed a tear across my cheek. "You've bewitched me as surely as Aeval has bewitched him." He took the sword and stood.

Kae had begun to shake once more, but it was from cold now, a natural cold that any man would feel half buried in snow. I brushed the remaining powder away and pulled his coat over his shoulders, and his uncovered eye opened and focused on me. He stared as if at an apparition, shaking his head.

"N-no," he stammered with the cold. He curled onto his side away from me, so I could only see the mask. "Oh, please, no." Kae covered his ears as if trying to shut out something he couldn't bear to hear. "Not this." He rocked forward. "Not you. Not here." He shook his head again.

"No. No, no, no, *no*!" He punctuated each denial with a violent blow of his head against the frozen ground, until I thought he would crack open his own skull. "In the name of Heaven, Nazkia," he moaned at last. "Why didn't you let me die?"

I stood and backed away, nearly falling into Vasily, who put his free arm around me and pulled me close. His fierce grip was a silent I-told-you-so.

The captain was eyeing him warily. "What are your orders, sir?"

Kae slipped his arms back into the sleeves of his shirt and coat, and climbed slowly to his feet, looking down at the bloodstained scar where the garments hung open. He raised his head to the captain and held his arms wide.

"My orders? My orders are to run me through at the end of your sword. I am the enemy of the queen of Heaven."

The captain moved his hand away from his hilt and stared aghast.

The sound of the portcullis being raised broke the tension of the moment, accompanied by the rumble and jangle of riders on horseback. For a brief instant, my hopes surged, thinking it must be the Virtues Sar Haniel had sent for—but of course the field marshal's men wouldn't have simply raised the portcullis for them. It was unlikely they were coming anyway. I'd begun to suspect weeks ago that Helga's henchmen had followed Haniel's riders the day we arrived and had them killed.

As the newcomers advanced through the gate tower of the outer ward, it was clear it was more of the Queen's Army, and on a large white steed at the front of it sat the queen herself. She observed the scene, the field marshal's soldiers and the Ophanim bowing low before her, and her piercing silver eyes fixed on the three of us who hadn't bowed.

Though she'd been too far away to have heard him, she focused on Kae with a dark smile and addressed him as if she had. "Are you really, my pet?" Her voice was like the dangerous purr of a large cat. "The enemy of the queen of Heaven?" She signaled to the waiting Ophanim. "Bring Our field marshal to Us."

Kae didn't resist or show any sign of discomfort at their touch when they escorted him to her side, though he flinched slightly when the queen reached down and gripped his jaw.

She turned his head, examining him. "You seem to be running a fever, my angel."

His face remained expressionless. "I feel quite well."

Aeval looked at me with naked malice. "You mustn't touch other people's things. I warned you he would die without me. How far do you think you'd get if you took him from my influence?" She didn't bother with the supernal "We"; there was no pretense of formality between us.

She snatched Kae's gloved hand from where he rested it on the horse's neck. "You may have been able to keep his blood from boiling over for the moment, but it will not last." Pulling off his glove, she held up his hand and revealed his missing finger. "This is what it takes to soothe him when he is out of sorts. Can you do that? Can you cut your precious cousin?"

Aeval dropped his hand and laid one of her own white-gloved palms against his cheek. "His blood belongs to me." Her voice was soft and seductive. She kissed him and he recoiled, but she grabbed both sides of his head to keep him from pulling away.

I remembered how her kiss had made him cold once more, his skin pale and bloodless, after his fever had raged out of control the last time. I remembered the look of wild adoration in his eyes her kisses had brought. I remembered how he'd told me—before I ran from him and left him in the burning Winter Palace—that she had kissed him and called his blood.

There was none of this now.

When she released him, Kae pulled away and spat upon the ground. Aeval's crystalline Virtuous complexion turned red with fury. She removed her right glove and held her cupped palm in Kae's direction, and it filled with the undulating liquid I'd seen once before when she'd called my element.

"Don't," I pleaded. "It's not his fault."

Kae stumbled, clutching at his stomach, as Aeval began to squeeze the substance in her hand. Water was pouring from her clenched fist—water she was drawing out of him. Like all Fourth Choir angels, Kae was a waterspirit.

I ran through the snow to where he stood frozen in her grip and put my hands over his as if I could protect him somehow. The ripple of lavender flame that engulfed our hands shocked us both. The pain seemed to have left him and he straightened, clutching my hands, and stared at the radiance that surged between us.

Aeval dropped her hand as if stung. "That is not possible." For once, I had to agree with her. "Who has tainted you with Seraph blood?" She looked accusingly from one of us to the other.

Vasily stepped forward. "I believe I did. I believe I must have tainted them both." He looked devastated as he met my eyes. Somehow, I'd given a precious gift to Kae that ought to be ours alone.

I let go of Kae's hands as if Vasily had caught me in the act of infidelity, severing the conduit of radiance.

"I touched their blood." Vasily was still staring at me.

"You are the half-Seraph Vasily." Aeval's voice was tinged with both fascination and disgust. She dismounted her horse, swinging her leg over it in a pair of wide, voluminous pants made to look like a skirt beneath a silver fur-trimmed coat of palest wool. Beneath the matching fox fur hat, her silver-white hair was done up in a knot behind her head in a manner reminiscent of a Virtue's queue, but more compact and stylish. She was a woman who never went anywhere, apparently, without considering these things. She certainly didn't look like someone who'd just ridden for weeks over the permafrost of the Empyrean.

She circled Vasily, studying the wild red locks and the rough beard on his cheeks and jaw that ended at his chin, amused as she took in his spectacles. Her eyes stopped on his neck, and I realized as I followed her gaze that his piercings were gone. Only the rows of small holes with a slight indentation from the spikes remained.

"So you're the one who made that baby. You're the '*malchik*' Our pet demon cried out for in his sleep after We exhausted him."

Vasily's eyes glowed with anger. "So you're the bitch who touched my Belphagor."

Aeval laughed her delicate laugh, like crystal goblets filled with water being jostled together, and then struck him with force. He brought the sword up swiftly, but Aeval's Ophanim were faster, and as they shocked him with their grip, she took the sword from his hand.

"Now, what can you be doing with this?" She turned it in her gloved palm. "This belongs to Our field marshal, does it not?" She tossed it unexpectedly to Kae, who easily caught it by the hilt with his maimed hand. "Put it away." The order was curt. "You are still in Our employ."

He hesitated before sheathing it, his expression grim. Though he was no longer under her control, it seemed he was too accustomed to taking orders from her to disobey.

Something caught the queen's eye and she walked over to the row of kneeling prisoners. She smiled as she stopped before Belphagor. "So here you are as well. I should have known that where your 'boy' went, you would be."

Belphagor said nothing as she nudged the toe of her silver fur boot against his thigh and slid it down between his legs. Vasily jerked beside me in the Ophanim's grip.

"I do so love to see you on your knees." Aeval withdrew her foot and looked at Kae. "Pray tell, field marshal, why are all these prisoners kneeling in the snow?"

When Kae didn't answer, the captain came forward and bowed before her. "They are all to be executed for treason, Your Supernal Majesty. The Virtues were in league with a group of demon revolutionaries who had occupied the citadel."

"And these are all the demons?" She regarded them doubtfully.

"Most of the demons were killed in the siege, Your Supernal Majesty. We've dumped the dead into the Pyriphlegethon. There were nearly a hundred all told, plus a few dozen Virtues."

Aeval sneered at the group. "Four men and a girl, and a handful of—" Her preternaturally bright eyes fell on the monk kneeling behind the Virtues, his mouth once more bound with the strap of leather, and she scowled with distaste. "Exactly what is *that* doing here?"

"It's a human holy man of some kind, Your Supernal Majesty."

"We know what it is, fool." She gave the captain a look that made him take an unconscious step back. "We wish to know why it is in Our Heavens."

The captain looked to his field marshal, clearly uncertain how to answer, but Kae seemed determined to be of no help to him. "He was with the demons, Your Supernal Majesty."

"Then it can stay with the demons!" Aeval spat. "Throw it into the Pyriphlegethon."

No one moved at first, and then the displeasure that emanated from her prompted several officers to step forward at once to take hold of Kirill. I bit my lip and took a step forward myself, though I couldn't possibly have stopped them, but Kae had moved at the same time, and as he stepped in front of the monk, the officers fell back. He grabbed Kirill by the scruff of his robe and turned toward the gate tower.

Aeval watched him with a pleased look on her face as he marched the monk out through the ward between the lines of her cavalry to the open gate. When he reached the bridge over the Pyriphlegethon, however, he tossed Kirill onto the snowy bank instead of plunging him into the fires, and signaled to the man in the gatehouse to lower the portcullis.

Aeval gave him a dark look as he returned. "That was not the order We gave."

"What difference does it make?" Kae retorted. "By ice or by fire, he'll be dead by morning."

Aeval regarded him, apparently as uncertain of his motives and loyalties as I was by now, before turning away to scan the faces of the kneeling prisoners once more. "A hundred demons and a few dozen Virtues. This cannot be an isolated incident." She turned to the captain. "Did you interrogate the leader?"

"We did, Your Supernal Majesty. But she's told us little. The field marshal intended to return her to Elysium to be questioned further."

"She?" Aeval frowned, looking at the assembled prisoners, and her eyes rested with suspicion on me. "And which is she?"

"The name she gave is Helga Semyazovna of Raqia, Your Supernal Majesty. She's locked in the tower. With the child."

Aeval turned her sharp attention on him, and my heart leapt with fear. "The child? *The* child? The grand duchess?" When he confirmed this, she picked up her garments and marched resolutely toward the keep. "We wish to see this child. Take the rest of the prisoners in for now. We shall deal with them later."

We were ushered inside to the great hall while Aeval and the captain mounted the tower stairs with a retinue of soldiers and Ophanim. Kae followed on his own. They separated us by sex once more, taking the men back to the dungeon, while the women remained in the hall, our "cell" occupied for the moment.

Behind Margarita and Vashti, Lively stood beside me looking ill. The soldiers guarding us began to joke among themselves about whether they'd rather have a mad grand duchess or a pregnant demon. She was not yet showing, but Lively had made no secret of her condition. I ignored them. I was busy steeling myself to bargain for our lives with everything I had.

If Aeval would spare Vasily and Belphagor, I would promise her anything, even if it meant confessing to the crimes of which she'd accused me. I would relinquish any claim to the throne for Ola or myself and accept permanent exile from the celestial sphere. And in exchange for my child, I was prepared to offer Aeval what she most desired. I would tell her Helga's locket held the flower of the fern.

I couldn't let myself think about what this meant for Heaven.

As for Kae, at that moment, I was willing to sacrifice him. By his own admission, he would be better off dead than living with the knowledge of what he'd done. And the others…I couldn't think of them. I had to think of Ola.

Angry shouting carried down to us from the tower room. Helga wouldn't bow to Aeval easily, I was certain. As they descended, I heard Love sobbing, and I wondered what Aeval had done to her. Love appeared first at the foot of the stairs, propelled by an Ophan, her eyes red and swollen as if she'd been crying for some time. Aeval swept down behind Love, her face white with rage. Helga and Ola were not with them.

The Ophan shoved Love forward and she fell weeping at my feet. "I'm sorry. I'm so sorry."

Fear hammered in my chest. I knelt down and lifted her shoulders. "For what? What's happened? Love!"

"Helga," she gasped between sobs. "I couldn't stop her."

"What do you mean? What has she done?" My heart stopped when her brown eyes looked up into mine, drowning in grief. "Where is Ola?"

"The Cherub." Love choked back her tears. "Helga conjured him somehow. I begged her to take me with her. I didn't want Ola to be afraid."

"No." My fingers went numb and Love slipped from my hands onto the ground. "No! She can't be gone again!" I jumped up and ran for the stairs, but the Ophan pulled me back with an arm around my waist. "Let me go!" I screamed.

He lifted me off the ground, but the painful prickling of his touch meant nothing to me in the face of losing Ola. I railed against him, pulling at his arms and beating uselessly at his chest, until the ophanic current rendered me insensate and he dropped me to the floor.

Aeval crossed the room, garments swirling about her white fur boots against the stone, to challenge her Ophanim Guard. "What do you know about the Cherubim? They are your choral cousins. Are you part of this sedition?"

"We know nothing of it. The Ophanim serve the throne of the Firmament of Shehaqim." The voice crackled in my head like a burst of static on a telephone in the world of Man, and I tried to cover my ears, but my hands wouldn't move as I wished.

Beside me, Lively was ill, and I almost joined her. Someone gave her a cloth to wipe her face and she knelt down and cleaned the stone floor with it in an almost automatic gesture, as though used to scrubbing on her hands and knees.

"She left me," Lively murmured to herself. "Auntie left me to die."

Love pulled me up to lean against her, and I sat shaking in her arms while my muscles recovered from the Ophan's touch. "Please forgive me," she whispered.

"No," I slurred. "Not you…" I couldn't organize my thoughts or speech enough yet to tell her she needed no forgiveness.

"We will have an answer." Aeval paced with a careful fury, a lioness who had already cornered her prey and was now determining the best way to take it down. "Where are Our Seraphim?" She flung out her hand with a sweeping motion, and an arc of flame seemed to soar from it across the stones. Where it touched, Seraphim materialized, and I turned my head away from the brightness.

Aeval stalked the room. "Your cousin Cherubim have betrayed the throne of Heaven. They have stolen the child We sent you to find." She stopped and scrutinized one of the Seraphim, having no difficulty looking him in the eye despite the brightness of his countenance. "How did the Cherubim know about the child?"

"All of Heaven knows about the child," answered the Seraph in his devastating voice.

"All of Heaven does not know she shares your blood. But it would seem this peasant Helga knows it and intends to use it to rule Heaven."

"She was the mother's nurse," said the Seraph. "Perhaps the mother told her."

Aeval turned on me, incredulous. "This Helga was your *nurse*? The nurse of the House of Arkhangel'sk is leading a peasant revolt against my throne?" When I said nothing, she crossed the floor with swift, furious strides and hauled me to my feet. "Is she your nurse!"

"Yes." I nodded, dizzy. "Helga—my nurse."

"And so the two of you planned this together." She shook me hard enough to rattle my teeth.

"Stole her. She stole my Ola."

"You expect me to believe you just happened to be here with the leader of the rebellion, yet you are not in league with her." Aeval shoved me away and I crumpled back to the floor.

Love caught me and glared up at Aeval. "It's your fault."

It was hard to say which of us was the more startled at Love's tenacity. Aeval simply stared, as if a piece of the furniture had begun to speak.

"It's because she found out you wanted her stupid flower."

Aeval focused on Love with deadly calm. I grabbed at Love's shirt, shaking my head in desperation, but it was too late. She would not be deterred.

"I heard her talking to the Cherub. Because of a 'fern' flower, Ola and I have been prisoners for two hundred and forty-two days. And now…" She trailed off as her voice broke.

Aeval's silvery eyes narrowed on me, taking on a feral, preternatural glow. The lioness was about to pounce. "That—*peasant*—has the flower of the fern? How did she get *the flower of the fern*?"

"She took it from me," I managed.

An expression of such utter astonishment crossed her face, it was almost comical. "And how did *you*—?" Aeval paused, the feral silver of her eyes shadowing over with outraged understanding. "Those little bitches."

She hadn't known. I swallowed a nervous burst of laughter that threatened to erupt from my throat. Despite himself, Belphagor had been right all along. She hadn't known about the flower at all.

But something was puzzling me. "Why?" I made a weak attempt to sit up as my coordination began to return. "Why are you punishing them?"

Aeval gave me a perturbed glare. "What *are* you babbling about?"

"The syla. If you didn't know they'd given me the flower, why are you tormenting those defenseless creatures?"

"Tormenting the syla?" Aeval looked baffled. It was clearly not an expression she was used to wearing. "I haven't the slightest idea what you're talking about, though I can assure you those 'creatures' are far from defenseless."

"Then why are your Seraphim killing them?"

It was hard to be certain in the brightness of their countenances, but it seemed the Seraphim cringed.

Aeval's baffled expression slowly hardened as she turned toward the firespirits, biting out each word as a carefully enunciated barb. "What have you done?"

The seraphic radiance wavered. "Her Supernal Highness is mistaken." The Seraph's tone betrayed nothing, though with a voice like a steel hammer to the skull, intonation was largely irrelevant.

"I am not mistaken. I saw them burn." I rose unsteadily. "The *snegurochki* told me in the Midnight Court—"

"What were you doing in my Midnight Court?" Aeval's eyes flashed with outrage.

I stared down her challenge. "The syla invited me there, and from what I understand, it hasn't been your Midnight Court in some time. They said the Seraphim had destroyed the summer and autumn syla and were waiting to destroy the spring." I looked at the Seraph who'd spoken. "They destroyed them by forcing themselves upon the syla."

The Seraph stepped close to me, his radiance flaring brightly. "The grand duchess lies."

I stood under his glare without flinching. "They told me the Seraphim claimed to have been sent by you, Your Supernal Majesty. To punish them."

With a swift motion like a striking snake, the Seraph raised his wings and slashed out at me with an arc of fire. Behind me, Love screamed, and I whirled to try to evade it, taking the brunt of the strike against my shoulder. A searing pain shot through my skin, like being struck with a skillet pulled from the fire. At the same instant, the Seraph made a grating roar of pain. He twisted around to locate the source of his agony. Kae stood behind him, his sword embedded in the Seraph's back.

"Enough!" Aeval's anger echoed from the stone walls.

Kae retreated smoothly, unseating his sword, and the Seraph stumbled to his knees in front of me with a sort of molten ichor flowing from his wound.

Aeval rounded on Kae and shoved his chest. "Don't forget you take orders from me. And you—" She circled the Seraph. "You have no will but mine. If you have taken it upon yourself to act of your own accord in the world of Man, I promise you shall never have freedom. I have not convened the Midnight Court in a century." She turned her gaze on me. "But it is still *my* Midnight Court. And it seems even in Heaven there are claims in need of judging."

The queen circled the room, observing the other Seraphim who had offered neither to confirm nor refute the wounded Seraph's denial. "Will you make the case for your innocence? Do you stand with your groveling brother and swear you have no knowledge of what the grand duchess claims?" Her eyes darkened dangerously. "Or are you part of this conspiracy with a pack of lowly demons?"

They remained stubbornly quiet.

"One of you will answer me, or I will drain you of your element one by one. Have you or have you not attacked my wood spirits?"

"They are not your wood spirits," one of the Seraphim replied.

"That was the wrong answer." Aeval pierced him with her stare, and his radiance flickered. "You were bound by celestial oath to obey the rulers of Heaven."

The Seraph at my feet coughed up more of the glowing ichor as he fell forward onto his hands. "You are not a celestial. And you have allowed this one to live too long." One of his upper wings slapped out toward me, and the heat of it struck me before the wing itself, but again Kae moved swiftly, this time slashing off the tip of the Seraph's wing and darting forward to plunge his sword into the glowing heart of the creature.

Aeval's angry shout was swallowed up into the Seraph's horrible shriek. Both her fists were outstretched in a familiar motion, one dripping seraphic ichor and the other dripping water. Kae stumbled against the Seraph as she began to squeeze the life from him.

After everything she'd done to him, I would not cede his life to her. I leapt forward to close my hand over Kae's on the hilt of his blade. The spark of radiance between us before had been no fluke. A vivid amethyst surged around our hands, traveling up the steel of his sword to connect with the Seraph's fire, and it was as though our radiance became a solid wall of water. The luminous amethyst wave rushed over the Seraph, the surface of him roiling with the contradictory elements, and it seemed to pull away his fire, taking the radiance with it as it rolled over him.

When the wave receded, it left him gasping on the ground, Kae's sword still glowing with a field of light where it pierced him, and the Seraph's glorious flame a pale, wan flicker. Around us, the other Seraphim glowed with the same sickly light. Kae pulled out the blade, and I shuddered and let go of him, realizing with a sickening start that the same blade had once been buried in me.

Aeval, livid a moment before, stood with a look of frank curiosity on her flawless features as she gazed about the room. "You've... *neutered* them." She lifted her hand, her fingers pulling at the air as if experimenting with an element we couldn't see. The remaining seraphic radiance flowed toward her like ghostly threads with her motions.

She smiled at me unexpectedly. "It seems the two of you in your joint folly have inadvertently saved me the time and effort of a messy castration." She regarded me with a gleam in her eye. "You may yet prove useful to me. And you, my darling angel"—she shook her finger playfully at Kae—"you, I shall deal with later." Aeval's expression turned hard, and she extended her arms to encompass the room, fingers curled into the invisible seraphic radiance. "As for the Seraphim, you five have damned your race." She yanked the ghostly threads into her fists. "I will stop the Pyriphlegethon. You will never leave the Empyrean again."

The Seraphim wailed miserably as what little remained of their fire began to dissipate, and this time I managed to cover my ears. They were so wretched I almost felt sorry for them for a moment, until I remembered what they'd done to the syla.

Dvadtsatoe: **A Thief in the Night**

One moment, the Seraphim were burning through the green wood of the leshi's cordon around the fairy ring at Tsarskoe Selo, and the next they'd vanished in a cloud of steam, as if doused.

Misha had stood beside his half brothers as long as he could, but his human side couldn't withstand the flames. Where the charred flesh on the limbs of full-blooded leshi would peel away and be renewed, he would be permanently scarred if the fire burned deeply enough.

As a rule, the leshi felt little obligation to assist in the matters of the syla. They might be siblings of a sort, and they were more than willing to share each other's beds, but they occupied themselves with very different concerns. Normally, however, the syla were quite capable of taking care of their own matters; the power to entrance and confound was not something to be taken lightly. But nothing like this had ever happened before in the Unseen World. The Seraphim had threatened its very existence.

As predicted, the firespirits had returned to the world of Man at the vernal equinox and lain in wait. The syla could not remain unseen. It wasn't in their nature—particularly on their birthday—and they had stepped from the arms of the leshi into the world of Man in their quaternary dance. The leshi posed as trees, hoping to catch the Seraphim as they came to accost their sisters, but they weren't expecting the sudden violence that descended.

Misha had never seen anything like it. The syla had believed the

Seraphim to be acting as agents of the queen, yet the firespirits now seemed to be taking out their hatred for the queen herself on the syla they considered to be her kin. This conception wasn't entirely correct, as Aeval had merely styled herself as the Unseen Queen as she now styled herself Heaven's, but it was a distinction that mattered little to the single-minded Seraphim. In the time-honored tradition of conquering invaders, they invaded the personal and profaned the sacred, violating that which they couldn't subdue.

It was the epitome of all that Misha abhorred in Men and could never comprehend. The burden weighed upon him personally as a descendant of Mankind, but to see it among the celestial Host was a first in his experience. He'd observed with horror the injuries of the syla who'd escaped below. The syla were less substantial, less earthy, than their male counterparts—less substantial even than humans—and it hadn't taken much to damage them. Like the leshi, their tissues could be renewed, but when the burns were so extensive, the syla couldn't heal. The fire continued to burn and simply consumed them from within.

The leshi surrounded as many syla as they could reach for their protection, but even leshi burned, and in some ways burned more efficiently. They were forced to retreat, and they fled with the injured to take them below. The Hall of Echoes had always been sacrosanct, and they believed they were safe, but something had opened the doors to the Seraphim, allowing them to cross the threshold, and it could only have been the flower of the fern. Whoever possessed it had unleashed its power to disrupt the barriers of the spheres.

That was when the leshi had banded together on the mound and blocked the Seraphim's way, and Misha was certain they wouldn't have held for long. Green or not, they had an inherent and inevitable inflammability. He'd retreated to the Hall of Echoes to tend the wounded, when finally the raging sound of fire above their heads simply ceased.

Misha went up alone, fearing the lack of sound indicated something ominous had happened to his brothers, but instead, he found them

ಠाा

standing speechless in the dissipating steam. One of the syla joined him, and she stood beside him as the leshi puzzled over the Seraphim's sudden disappearance.

She seemed unfazed and smiled at their bewilderment. "It is as we have seen. *Padshaya Koroleva* has stopped the fire angels."

Misha shook his head with a wry smile. Belphagor's little blond angel had come through.

• • •

Kae stood at the top of the dark lookout watching the monk huddle against the bastion below. He'd come here to throw himself into the fires aeonian. Aeval had tested him, calling him to her bed after the Seraphim were dealt with, and he'd gone, not out of desire, but out of an unquenchable hatred for himself. She seemed particularly pleased that he came to her by choice, taking it as evidence that he was still her agent, and she'd ridden him harder than one of the horses from her stables.

He lay staring up at the ceiling, his body participating, while his mind was full of violent images. He thought of taking her delicate neck in his hands and squeezing the life out of her, of gutting her on the end of his sword, but if it were possible to overpower her, he knew the demon Belphagor would have done it at his first opportunity, instead of spending nearly a year as her kept whore.

Kae left her satisfied and sleeping soundly, giving him the luxury of carefully executing his plans for his own death without fear of interruption. He'd contemplated falling on his sword, but the chance of missing a vital organ, however slim, deterred him. The last thing he needed was Anazakia healing him again. The sensible thing would be to fling himself into the Pyriphlegethon, and to ensure his nerve didn't fail him, he climbed the lookout tower and relieved the man on duty in order to throw himself from a height.

But now, looking down, he was gripped with a terrible compassion for the mad monk, so much so that he almost fell down weeping against the parapet. It was as if the part of him Aeval had frozen—his conscience, his heart—could suddenly feel all that it had been denied under her spell. Every coldly calculated action he'd taken as her field marshal struck him with the full force of the anguish that had been bottled up inside him where his dormant self had watched in mute horror.

In defiance of Aeval's will, he had left the monk outside the citadel to give him a fighting chance, but Kirill hadn't taken it. Perhaps he was too weak to attempt to flee. Kae's plans would have to wait. He couldn't leave the man suffering.

He descended the tower, taking the blankets and hardtack left there by the sentry, and relieved the man at the sally port. When the soldier had gone, Kae unlocked the gate and slipped out.

Walking softly along the snowy embankment, he rounded the ancient stone bastions toward where Kirill huddled. It was the quietest moment he'd ever experienced. No sound carried from inside the walls of the citadel—no jangling of tack or whicker of horses from the stables, no muted conversations from the soldiers inside, not even the hushed sounds of servants going about their jobs. He stopped for a moment and stared at the profusion of stars soaring over the black canopy of Empyrean sky above the eerie glow of the Pyriphlegethon, wishing his head could be as empty as this silence. If he could just forget again, forget everything.

The monk startled at his presence and leapt up in fear. It took Kae some time to convince the man he meant him no harm. As a gesture of goodwill, he took out his knife to loose the ropes that bound Kirill's hands, but the monk was clearly convinced he'd come to slit his throat, no matter what Kae said to the contrary. When he'd cut loose the ropes without burying the knife in him, Kirill relaxed a bit, rubbing his numb wrists while Kae unbuckled the strap that stopped his mouth. When Kae handed him the blankets and food, the monk stared back at him out of a pair of unusually blue-green eyes.

"You are madman," he said in his broken angelic.

"I take that as a compliment, coming from you."

Kirill didn't seem to follow this. He held up the blankets. "You wish me to die or you wish me to camp?"

"I do not wish you to die," Kae assured him. "I've come out here, in fact, to jump into the flames myself."

The monk's eyes grew wide and outraged. "You must not! Is mortal sin!"

Kae gave him a cheerless attempt at a smile. "What hell do you imagine I'd go to that could be worse than this one?"

The monk frowned as he considered this rhetorical question. Kae looked away from Kirill's troubled eyes and stared into the river, mesmerized by the ever-changing shapes that moved within it. As he watched, dark silhouettes began to resolve on its perimeter, not part of the river's edge. He strained his lone eye in the darkness. There were men on the bridge.

Kae drew his sword and waited while the figures advanced. As they approached the near bank, they slowed, and he heard the sound of metal being drawn. The sharpening figures revealed a small party of Virtues traveling on foot.

He called out softly, "Are you loyal soldiers to the queen?"

"Who asks?" countered a Virtue when they came close.

One of the others murmured beside him. "It's the queen's field marshal." As the man raised his sword, Kae put his away, and the Virtues stared at him, perplexed.

"What's your name?" he asked the first.

"Vaol." The Virtue lifted his chin with an air of defiance.

"If you were loyal to the queen, Vaol, you would have saluted me and addressed me with the respect due the supreme commander of the Armies of Heaven."

The Virtues exchanged glances and Vaol nodded slightly to one who was trying to conceal a dagger in his hand.

"Fortunately for you, I've come outside this fine evening to put an end to my career." He opened his coat and unbuttoned his shirt, baring his chest over his heart. "Come on then, I haven't got all night."

"Is this some kind of joke?"

"If you consider my having disemboweled your Sar Haniel and beheaded more than twenty of your compatriots before whipping the rest to be a joke, then I suppose you may laugh if you like." He continued to stand with his shirt held open, and the Virtue holding the dagger lunged forward in outrage to plunge it into his breast.

Kae waited for the blade to sink into him, but as the Virtue made his move, the monk darted forward and threw himself in front of the knife. Before Kae could stop him, the blade struck Kirill's shoulder and the monk fell bleeding to the snow, while the stunned Virtue stood over him.

"You mad fool!" Kae knelt down, tearing a strip from the bottom of his shirt. "What in the name of Heaven were you thinking?"

"You shall not kill," the monk admonished as Kae bandaged the shoulder. "Is God's commandment."

"And you shall not die," Kae retorted. "That's my command. No one else will die because of me, do you hear?" He glanced up at the Virtue still holding the bloody knife. "Have the five of you walked from Aravoth for a midnight constitutional or have you brought an army?"

The Virtue looked as if he'd been startled awake, and he bent to clean his knife in the snow while Vaol answered. "We are four hundred men."

"The Queen has nearly six hundred." Kae stood. "But you have darkness and surprise on your side, and an unguarded postern." He looked at the younger Virtue settling his knife in its sheath. "You must be more decisive if you intend to succeed in battle. Follow-through is essential. Who told you to put that knife away?"

Vaol regarded him steadily. "Suria's action was rash. But you will pay for your crimes against Aravoth. I'll make sure of it." He paused. "Did you say an unguarded postern?"

"The fool has left his post. As has the fool meant to man the lookout. Send one of your men back to camp and tell your troops to be ready to advance. I'd leave the horses on the other side of the river and send your men through the postern in pairs. And take this man with you." He nodded toward Kirill and turned to head back.

"I will not leave without angel child," the monk insisted as he got to his feet.

Kae paused. "I'm sorry to tell you, Brother Kirill, but the child is no longer here. The Cherubim have come and taken her somewhere else."

Kirill's eyes smoldered. "And Sister Lyubov? They take her, too?"

"No. They left your friend behind. But I'll send her to you shortly."

Vaol called after him. "Where are you going?"

"To get the rest of your comrades. And to show you where the postern is, unless you'd rather find it yourself in the dark."

. . .

Love woke to the sound of tumblers turning in the iron lock. It was a sound she was attuned to now. Her sleep was never deep. She sat up with a racing heart, grasping Anazakia's hand on the floor beside her. Anazakia had insisted on giving that pregnant slut Lively the bed. Love couldn't fathom how anyone could be so gracious in the face of what Lively had done. It came of being raised a grand duchess, she supposed.

Anazakia stirred beside her, but Vashti and Margarita were already awake. They positioned themselves flat against either side of the door before it creaked open in the dark. Vashti pounced and hooked her arm around the neck of the intruder, slamming him back against the wall with her elbow at his throat. It was the field marshal in his creepy mask, and he relaxed his head against the stone without expression, swinging a ring of keys on the end of his finger.

Anazakia stared at him with the same look she had in her eyes every time she saw him, a pained expression as if she'd been gutted, with a pinch of fear, as though she were staring at a walking corpse. She wouldn't speak to Love of who he was to her, but she clearly knew him.

"What do you want?" Vashti punctuated the words with a jab of her elbow.

He answered in his perpetually hoarse voice. "I want you to get out. Before the fighting starts."

Anazakia hugged her arms against the cold. "What fighting?"

His single eye never focused on her when he spoke. "The fighting between the Queen's Army and the four hundred troops from Aravoth across the bridge." He remained in his unperturbed stance while Vashti relaxed her arm against his neck and looked at Anazakia as if for orders. "Do you know where the sally port is?"

"Of course."

"Get there as quickly and quietly as you can. I'll take care of the sentries in the hall."

"What about the others? I'm not leaving without them."

The field marshal sighed. "Why does everyone insist on someone they won't leave without?" He held up the keys. "I'm on my way to open the dungeon now." He pushed himself away from the wall as Vashti stepped back.

"I'm not leaving without you this time, either." Anazakia's voice was solemn.

He paused in the doorway with his back to her. "Nazkia…"

"I think you owe me that." There was a long silence before she spoke again in a voice that was as hard as Love had ever heard it. "You were never a coward before."

He breathed in sharply and continued down the stairs without turning back.

• • •

Vasily lay awake beside Belphagor on the floor of their cell, maddened by an itch he couldn't scratch with his hands tied together. They had all been left bound, as if there were any danger of their escape. Belphagor lay with his back to him against the wall. He hadn't said a word to Vasily since they'd been returned to the dungeon, not a word since Vasily had lost his mind and used his element to heal that bastard Kae.

"Are you awake?" he whispered.

Belphagor didn't reply, but after a moment, he turned his head, his dark eyes sparkling like polished onyx in the gloominess of the cell.

"You don't have to say anything. I just wanted you to know, in case we die tomorrow, that I'm sorry I blamed you when…when it all happened. Deep down, I knew it wasn't your fault. I just—I thought I was going to die, it hurt so much." Vasily took a breath to keep from blubbering like a fool. "But I treated you horribly when you were in just as much pain as I was. I know how much you love Ola." He brushed Belphagor's arm with the tips of his captive fingers. "You *are* her father, Beli." He looked down at his hands, blinking away the tears. If he cried, he'd get his glasses dirty and he wouldn't be able to see a thing.

Belphagor was still quiet.

"And I don't blame you for being angry with me for helping that *sukin syn*." Vasily growled the words. "I should have put his sword through his heart for what he did to you. I should have cut out his entrails and let him bleed to death. I don't know what got into me. Anazakia just seemed so heartbroken…" He looked up at Belphagor, who was staring at him silently with a peculiar expression, after Vasily had poured his heart out. His temper flared. "For the love of Heaven, Bel! Say *something* at least."

Belphagor chewed on the inside of his cheek a moment and then looked down as if trying to hide a smile. At last, he opened his mouth, but instead of speaking, he bared his teeth, and Vasily saw something shining between them.

"What the hell?" He squinted in the dark.

Belphagor pushed the shining object forward with his tongue, grinning around it. It was one of Vasily's piercing barbells with the spiked end screwed on.

A flush of unexpected pleasure accompanied the realization that Belphagor had cared enough to retrieve it. "How did you get that?"

Belphagor moved his tongue about and pushed a second one through his teeth, and then another, and another. Five of the seven— complete with their spiked caps, as if he'd screwed them all on with his tongue—were clutched between his teeth.

Vasily laughed softly, wishing he could get his hands free to do more than brush Bel's arm. He leaned in and brushed Belphagor's lips with his instead, and Belphagor pressed closer to him, opening his mouth to let their tongues wrap together around the steel. Vasily was becoming pleasantly uncomfortable.

Belphagor pulled away at last and left the barbells in Vasily's mouth. "I actually got them all. But I may have…swallowed two of them."

When the door swung open at the top of the stairs, Vasily nearly swallowed a few himself. Torchlight bloomed into the darkness, revealing Kae's masked face, with the two dungeon guards following close behind him.

Kae put the torch into the sconce on the wall at the foot of the stairs. "Bring out the dark one."

So he was going to pick up where he'd left off. After everything, he was as mad as ever. Vasily sat up, intending to say something caustic, but remembered he had a mouthful of metal.

The guards unlocked their cell and hauled Nebo from the iron cot. Kae stood back while they brought the Nephil forward and hung his bound hands from the whipping peg. Vasily held his breath as Kae took out his sword instead of his flogger, but the angel leaned in and spoke in Nebo's ear for a moment, and then brought his sword up unexpectedly and sliced it through the bonds on Nebo's wrists with a jerk. Nebo turned too swiftly for the guards to react and grabbed them both by the neck. With perfect coordination, he slammed their heads into the bars and stunned them before whisking their swords from their scabbards.

"Interesting tactic." Kae observed the dazed guards. "I only meant the one sword, but I suppose you're right. We can always use more." He dragged one of the guards to his feet while Nebo hoisted the other, and shoved them both into the cell. "Untie the others."

"Sir." The guard protested with a grimace as he rubbed his head. "Her Supernal Majesty will not be pleased."

"I rather doubt she will. But she's sleeping fairly heavily tonight and I can almost guarantee she won't wake for hours."

From the look on Belphagor's face, this meant something to him, and Vasily was certain he didn't want to know what.

The guards reluctantly followed Kae's orders. When his hands were free, Vasily spat the jewelry into his palm and then pocketed it. Belphagor gave him a wink as they stepped out into the corridor.

"Nice move." Dmitri nodded at Nebo as the Nephil handed him the extra sword, and Nebo flashed him a broad smile. The Nephilim were always pleased by praise from the Grigori, as if from a parent. Dmitri held his hand out to the sullen guards. "Scabbards."

They hesitated until a look from Kae persuaded them.

Kae locked the guards in and turned to unlock the opposite cell, where the Virtues were watching the drama in amazement.

One of the guards hooked his hands around the bars while Kae released the Virtues from their manacles. "How far do you think you're going to get before you're caught?"

"Me?" Kae shrugged. "I'm not going anywhere. And you would do well to remember that I am still the field marshal of this army until the queen chooses to say otherwise." He pulled the young Loquel forward to unlock him and the Virtue flinched, his eyes flickering between humiliation and hatred. Kae addressed him gruffly as he unlocked the irons. "If you want revenge, you'll have to get in line. I've wronged many others far worse than you."

• • •

Inside the keep, all had gone well until Lively fell faint at the bottom of the stairs.

Anazakia caught her before she dropped, whispering in concern that Love simply couldn't fathom, "When did you last eat?"

Lively shook her head, looking disoriented.

Love regarded her with disgust. "I told you we shouldn't have brought her, Nazkia. Let's just leave her here. Let her fend for herself."

"Love!" Anazakia gave her a stern look. "We are not leaving her."

"Give her to me." Vashti stepped in, scooping Lively into her arms, and Love stared after her with grudging admiration at her strength. The tall woman went ahead of them toward the far end of the great hall where Kae had left the doors unbarred and two Ophanim dead beside it. Pushing the door open with her shoulder, Vashti turned to hold it for them.

There was no time to cry out a warning at the sudden movement in the shadows. A soldier waiting just outside the door lunged forward and swung a heavy object at Vashti's head. The *crack* was loud in the empty hall.

Margarita moved before anyone else reacted, and with a swift motion that made it look as if she were flying, she landed a kick to the inside of the assailant's knee and a blow to his neck from her fist at the same instant, incapacitating him instantly.

Vashti fell to her knees, dropping Lively almost gracefully onto the floor. Blood was pouring into her eyes as she slumped back against the door. "I'm…so sorry…" She looked as if she were about to say something else, her eyes still open wide, but her body had gone slack.

Beside her, Margarita felt for her pulse and shook her head.

"What happened?" Lively reeled and caught herself against the stone.

Love moved toward her guiltily, a moment too late, as Anazakia crouched down and helped her up.

Anazakia looked to Margarita as she steadied Lively. "She's dead?"

Margarita nodded sharply with the stoic detachment of a soldier, and Anazakia gave a sigh of weariness and regret. Love hugged her arms in the cold, staring at the empty amber eyes, feeling nothing. She took no satisfaction in the woman's death, but after what Vashti had done to her, it simply wasn't in her to be sorry.

"We have to go." Margarita took the truncheon from the unconscious soldier, along with his belt and sword. "This one won't be out for long." She extended the hilt of the sword. "Can either of you wield one?"

Love stepped back. "Don't look at me."

Anazakia also shook her head. "Can't you?"

"Of course I can." Margarita's voice held a note of irritation. "But I don't need it." She started to sling the belt around her hips, but Lively stepped away from Anazakia and held out her hand.

"I'll take it."

Margarita frowned at her. "You can barely stand up."

"I feel a little clearer now." She looked down at Vashti staring sightlessly at the wall and bit her lip. "I'll be fine."

Margarita gave it to her with a shrug and handed the truncheon to Anazakia. "You can at least swing this if you have to."

They moved quietly out into the yard, following Anazakia through the ancient stone fortress. North of the keep, a complex twice the size of the keep itself housed the stables and the barracks where nearly six hundred soldiers lay sleeping. The sally port was situated just beyond its perimeter.

They were almost past the complex when a door opened a few yards ahead of them and they stopped dead in their tracks. A soldier stepped out and stood in the snow relieving himself. He didn't look in their direction until he'd finished his business and set a cigar between his teeth, glancing up at last as he struck his match.

Margarita charged him before he had a chance to go for his sword. His cry was cut short when Margarita snapped his neck. She glanced at the three of them as she dropped his body, just as lamplight bloomed in the barracks beside them.

"*Run.*"

• • •

From the dungeon, they heard shouting in the yard. Kae took the stairs two at a time with Dmitri and Nebo at his heels.

"Weapons—trunk." Kae barked the words at Vasily as they emerged into the anteroom and tossed him a ring of keys as he dashed outside.

Vasily turned, at first seeing nothing resembling a trunk. "Where?"

But Belphagor had spotted it and was sweeping a pile of plates and tankards off the surface of a large iron coffer. Vasily stabbed keys at the lock, swearing as he went through half a dozen before he found the right one. Inside appeared to be everything Kae's men had taken off the Virtues when they stormed the citadel.

Once the Virtues had armed themselves, Vasily grabbed one of the extra swords and tossed another to Belphagor, who caught it doubtfully.

"I'm not much of a sword man," said Belphagor.

"How about a Kalashnikov?"

"Seriously? There's a Kalashnikov in there?"

"No." Vasily slammed the lid. "Just take the damn sword. It's sharp. Poke people with it."

Belphagor glared, but he took the sword from its sheath and swung it in his hand experimentally. As Vasily turned to follow the Virtues into the yard, Belphagor paused and popped the trunk open again to grab another sword, this time slinging the Virtue's baldric over his shoulder.

"Suddenly you like them so much you want two?"

"It's for Lev. I think he followed Dmitri out before we got the trunk open, and he wasn't armed." He frowned as Vasily bristled reflexively. "Don't do that. Not now. Not over this."

Vasily reddened. Belphagor was right. He couldn't remember seeing Lev after Kae had thrown him the keys.

. . .

Love was the only one who reached the opening the others called the sally port.

Margarita had taken down the first few men to wake at the noise, but a second door had opened as they ran for the wall. As Anazakia tried to swing her truncheon, a soldier grabbed hold of her scalded shoulder, while another caught her around the waist. Lively turned back with her sword gripped in both hands, and Love hesitated, but Anazakia screamed at her to go, so she ran for all she was worth, slipped into the narrow passage between the inner and outer walls of the citadel, and rounded the corner to the gate on the other side.

She nearly screamed when she burst out onto the embankment and collided with one of the white-haired angels. Beside him stood two more—and Kirill, wrapped in a blanket. Love gasped and threw herself into Kirill's arms.

"Sister Lyubov." His voice was deep and warm, but he was wincing at her touch, trying to hide a blood-soaked bandage beneath the blanket.

"*Kirill.*"

The angel she'd run into spoke beside her. "He insisted on waiting for you. We tried to send him back to our camp to have it looked at." He turned with a swift flourish as one of the queen's soldiers barreled through the gate, and he caught the soldier by surprise on the end of his sword.

Staring in shock, Kirill began to cross himself and pray over the dead body.

"Kirill." Love put her hand over his as he touched the dead man's shoulder. "He's already in Heaven."

He cut short his prayer and looked at her with the haunted look he'd worn since they arrived.

"Time to go." The angel hurried them toward the bridge. "We've been waiting for the field marshal's signal, but from the sound of things in there, it looks like you're it."

"The others." Love tried to turn back. "They were caught…"

The angel motioned toward the bridge with his hand, and a mighty silhouette rippled against the starlight behind them as hundreds of angels began to move toward the citadel. "They'll take care of it."

Dvadtsat Pervoe: **Surrender**
from the memoirs of the Grand Duchess Anazakia Helisonovna of the House of Arkhangel'sk

The ground rushed up at me. I'd thrown out my hands to brace my fall, but my right wrist struck at an awkward angle, and I cried out as my weight fell against it. The soldier who had tossed me to the ground straddled me and pinned me down with a hand on my neck, and I winced against the pain of the seraphic burn.

"Well, that settles it." He laughed, his breath hot against my ear. "I'll take the mad grand duchess over the pregnant demoness."

"Think again." Lively spoke from behind us, and something sharp grazed my side. The soldier fell against me like a dead weight and when I turned my head, I saw the point of a sword sticking into the ground beside me. Blood was dripping down the shining steel. I couldn't help wondering if Lively had intended to put the blade through both of us.

Before she could wrest the sword from the dead man, another soldier appeared from the barracks, and with a loud *smack*, he knocked her off her feet. Margarita charged the angel and dropped him to the ground beside me with a quick motion.

"What kind of asshole hits a pregnant woman?" She helped Lively up and yanked the sword from the dead man, tossing it to Lively as she kicked him away from me. The two of them held off the soldiers as I staggered to my feet, but more lamps were coming on around the barracks and we'd soon be surrounded.

Margarita looked at me awkwardly holding my wrist. "Go on," she urged. "You can't help here."

Reluctant to abandon them, I backed toward the eastern wall, feeling useless, and nearly stumbled into someone behind me. I whirled around, thinking the man Lively had skewered wasn't dead after all.

A Virtue I'd never seen before gave me a quick bow. "Your Supernal Highness." He hurried past to help fight the growing army. Behind him, a score of Virtues was flooding in through the sally port, and I stepped out of the way against the wall to let them pass.

Across the yard, the shimmering, silver white of another small band of Virtues approached, with Kae's black coat standing out among them as he raced over the snow-covered stone, leading the way. They met the queen's soldiers from the other side, pressing them toward the oncoming Virtues as they fought, but the queen's ranks were swelling as they poured from the barracks, and the Virtues couldn't come in quickly enough through the narrow postern. It was horrible to watch and worse to know I could do nothing.

I looked to the north entrance of the stables. The road to the gate tower was clear. The citadel hadn't been on guard against invaders; Aeval had vastly underestimated the growing rebellion in Heaven. Steering clear of the fighting, I made my way toward the exit and ran for the gate tower as fast as I could. There was no one in the outer ward to protect the portcullis.

I dashed up to the top of the gatehouse unnoticed and began to turn the wheel on the heavy spool of chain. It was properly a two-handed job and I had only the use of one, but I raised it by inches, glad of the noise in the yard to mask the sound as it cranked slowly upward. When I paused a moment to rest, I looked out over the gallery and saw it had been enough. The Virtues on the bridge had seen it rise, and they were already ducking in under it.

The Empyrean wind whipped up, and I pulled the hood up on my coat while I hurried back to the stables at the perimeter of the advancing Virtues. The scene there was chaotic, and at first I couldn't see Lively or Margarita, but they spotted me.

Margarita ran from the cover they'd taken behind the inner wall of the sally port and dragged me away from the fighting. "Where have you been? I was about to go back to the keep to look for you!"

I nodded toward the influx of Virtues surging from the outer ward. "I let them in."

My heart leapt at the sight of Vasily and Belphagor pushing toward us through a group of Virtues. We weren't their goal, however. On the south side of the stables, Dmitri and his friend, Lev, were backed against a wall. Dmitri kept pushing Lev behind him as he fought, and I couldn't understand why until I saw Lev was empty-handed.

As Dmitri turned to block a sword on his right, another soldier dashed in and swung at him from his left. I screamed in vain as Lev sprang forward between them and caught the blow. Vasily and Belphagor reached them moments later. I held my breath as Belphagor gored the soldier who'd cut Lev, and Vasily helped Dmitri dispatch the other.

Lev staggered against Belphagor, and he and Dmitri each took an arm before Lev's weight collapsed between them. While Vasily covered them, they dragged the demon at a run toward our shelter. Nebo had seen them also, and he slashed his way from the center of a group of the queen's soldiers, swinging his sword two-handed, and met them as they reached us.

Margarita jerked her head toward the sally port, abandoned by the Virtues for the wide-open portcullis at the gate. "The postern's clear now. Let's get out of here." She and Lively dashed for the opening.

I was behind them when Nebo caught my arm. "Where's Vashti?"

I couldn't bring myself to tell him, but I didn't have to.

"No." He turned around, staring at the fighting as if he might see her in it. "Oh, Ti, no." His eyes darted about anxiously. "In the yard?"

"In the keep."

Vasily put a hand on his shoulder, but Nebo didn't seem to notice. "Nebo, we have to go."

The Nephil shook his head. "I'll stay with her." And he was gone, running through the clashing soldiers toward the keep.

Deep in the center of the fighting, I saw Kae's dark coat swirling among a shining field of Virtues. When all was said and done, he was a stranger, whether or not he was Aeval's puppet. Under her influence, he was as despicable a man as Heaven had ever known. But I had left him to her once when my conscience urged otherwise—and how much more twisted and dangerous he had become as a tool in her hands. Yet through it all, through the darkness she had cultivated or created, some little part of him—whatever was left of the man I had once called *friend*—had remained aware, and had suffered the knowledge of his fate.

To that little remnant of Kae Lebesovich, I was Nenny. I was the girl who had gone riding in the snow, thinking of no one but myself, and led my dearest friend into an unthinkable captivity that would sunder the House of Arkhangel'sk. However foolish it was that I had spared him when his life was in my hands, I had done it; he lived. And he was a son of the House of Arkhangel'sk. He did not belong to Aeval.

Vasily had gripped my arm and I tried to pull away.

"Kae!"

My cousin turned and looked as if he'd heard my frantic shout. He shook his head.

"You owe it to me!" I screamed at Kae as Vasily picked me up and carried me bodily to the sally port. "Coward!"

Outside the wall, a group of Virtues waited to take us to their camp, and I let them lead me through the driving wind, wondering bleakly what all this had been for. We'd come for Ola and lost her again, and though I'd broken Aeval's hold on my cousin, I hadn't freed him at all. Instead, he seemed a captive to his own dark conscience.

We had Love, at least. When we reached the Virtues' base, she was waiting with her monk beside the bank of the glowing Pyriphlegethon, and she jumped up and embraced me.

Vasily looked around. "Where's Ola?"

Kae hadn't told them. I sank to the ground and burst into tears.

Love explained while she comforted me, her voice trembling as if she feared Vasily might hit her, but he was speechless, staring at us with his hazel eyes empty of fire. Belphagor, still supporting Lev with Dmitri, looked utterly lost. He hadn't even had the chance to hold her.

Lev coughed, groaning as the motion jarred his wound. There was no more time to think of Ola. Dmitri and Belphagor sat him down against a cart on a blanket one of the Virtues supplied. His coat was sticky with blood and his face was grey.

"Lyova." Dmitri knelt beside him and took his hand. "Why did you do this?"

"Bastard was going to cut you," gasped Lev.

"So you thought it would be better if he cut you instead?"

"Pretty much." Lev grimaced as Belphagor unbuttoned his coat and pulled it open. Inside, the right flank of his shirt was soaked. Belphagor stripped off his own coat and pulled his shirt over his head, his tattoos stark in the firelight against his winter-pale skin.

He pressed the shirt against Lev's wound. "Hold it there. We have to stop the bleeding."

"Can't you fix him?" Dmitri's eyes were dark as he appealed to Vasily. "You did it for that *zhopa* Kae."

Vasily glanced at me. "I think it must have been Nazkia. It's never worked for me in Heaven before."

Clasping hands, we knelt over Lev and covered the wound. The aether flared but didn't seem to catch. The glow was a pale flicker, weak and consuming nothing. The bleeding seemed to slow, but it appeared the radiance could do nothing more.

I let my hand fall away at last. "I don't think it works on ordinary wounds."

"I don't understand." Dmitri regarded me angrily. "How was the field marshal's wound any less ordinary? You stabbed him with a knife."

"It was his blood. The queen did something to it. He was—cold." I left unsaid the words that followed in my head: *like something not alive.*

I longed to know if he'd stay warm, if we'd truly undone what Aeval had called. She hadn't been able to reassert her hold on him with a kiss, but she'd cut him before, and if he became her prisoner tonight, she might cut him again—if she allowed him to live.

"But the wound," Dmitri insisted, as if I were simply being stubborn about healing Lev. "That was ordinary, just a knife."

"I'm sorry, Dmitri. I wish I understood how it works. I never even knew it could do that until yesterday." Had it only been yesterday?

"Your Supernal Highness." One of the Virtues interrupted us, and I recognized him as Gereimon, one of the original four dozen of our escort to Gehenna. "I'm sorry to have to rush you, but we need to move out now before we're seen." As if to demonstrate his point, the sky was growing pale along the eastern horizon. He nodded toward Dmitri. "We'll see to the wound, sir."

Heaven's greatest physicians came from the Order of Virtues. Lev was in the best hands possible in the celestial sphere. After cleaning and bandaging his wound, they helped Lev into one of the two sleighs packed with supplies for the trip back to Aravoth. Belphagor and Vasily would ride with him and Dmitri, while I rode with the others. The howling wind that had begun the night before was a driving wall of swirling snow at our backs by the time we set out. We'd been lucky on the trip to Gehenna to have had such clear weather. We would have no such luck now.

Beneath the blankets tucked around us, I huddled out of necessity with Lively and Margarita, while Love soon fell asleep in Kirill's lap in the seat across from us. Margarita had told me that Kirill's kind took a lifelong vow of celibacy, but watching him with his arm over Love while she slept, it was obvious he adored her. Something in the monk's aquamarine eyes made it the most desolate and heartbreaking adoration I'd ever seen.

With the wind behind us, we reached Aravoth in little more than a fortnight, though every moment of the trip was cold and wretched. The wind wracked our tents at night, and we had only the peculiar heat of the Pyriphlegethon to warm our bodies and our food until we turned south toward Aravoth. With the help of the Virtues, Lev held on, though he had a high fever for several days and didn't seem well, while Lively took ill and was weak and thin by the time we arrived.

We pulled into Pyr Amaravati just as the spring snow squalls that had been driving us ushered in a miserable ice storm. Sar Sarael and his staff welcomed us with Virtuous hospitality. Four walls, a ceiling, and a warm bed had never seemed more wonderful.

In the morning, as I eased away the ache and insensibility of the frigid Empyrean in the healing waters of Sarael's bath, I had to face the hard reality that we were further from finding Ola than we had ever been. Helga's Cherub might have taken them anywhere in the Heavens, or even to the world of Man. We had been lucky to make it to Aravoth in the midst of its most turbulent season. Even if we had some way of tracking Helga or gaining intelligence from the SLP, there was no passage from the mountain princedom until the late spring thaw.

After my soak in the aromatic water, I wrapped myself in the thick cashmere robe and boots provided by Sarael's staff and went down to breakfast, though it was surely some hours after Pyr Amaravati's accustomed lunch. Vasily and Belphagor were seated at the table with Sarael, and I noted with a mixture of relief and jealousy that Vasily was almost blushing with pleasure and Belphagor wore a certain air of pride and contentment, as though they'd at last resumed their intimacy. Margarita and Love joined us shortly afterward, while the rest were sleeping or convalescing. The ice storm howled against the pale blue glass, but with the thermal pipes that heated the place beneath the floors, it was as warm inside as if fires blazed in every room.

A bountiful breakfast of a thick egg bread, fried and dipped in sugar with preserves of every description, soft-boiled eggs in silver cups dabbed with sweet clotted cream, and piles of steaming curls of bacon, was followed by a kind of bittersweet hot cocoa. As we sat sipping our drinks, we heard a small commotion in the outer rooms of the house. Sarael excused himself and went to investigate. When he returned, he apologized for the interruption but said my presence was needed.

Puzzled, I set down my drink and followed him through the manor. In the vestibule, the heavy doors were open and sheets of ice were battering the tiles. A handful of anxious servants were standing about as if uncertain of their roles, and two heavily wrapped Virtues stood in the doorway. Between them, they gripped a kneeling man who could barely hold himself up on his own, a soaked and ice-crusted black coat upon his back and his bare head bowed. He raised his head and stared at me out of a red, watery eye beside his leather mask.

"Kae." I looked to the Virtues. "What are you doing? Let him in!"

"He will not come in, Your Supernal Highness."

"I've come to surrender myself." His rasping voice paused as he gasped for breath in the cold. "To the rightful queen of Heaven."

I put my hand to my throat, shocked by the sound of him. "Please, Kae. Just come inside." I reached down to him, but he refused.

"Wherever the Sar keeps his prisoners. Take me there."

Sarael frowned beside me. "I do not keep prisoners. If you will come in, we will arrange a room for you—"

"The stables, then." It seemed he was using the last of his voice before he lost it.

Sarael looked at me. "If he will not go anywhere else..."

"All right." I pulled my robe close. "Please, just get him somewhere dry." As the Virtues led him away, staggering between them, I hurried upstairs to change into my outdoor clothes.

When I returned, Sarael was waiting with a bundle of warm clothes and blankets. "There's a passage from the house to the stables. You won't need to go out into the ice." He led the way through a subterranean tunnel, lit by oil lamps, to the large covered buildings at the other end of his estate. As he opened the door into the main stable, he handed me the bundle and gave me a key. "Just use this when you want to come back. I'll leave you alone with him."

The building was also lit with lamps along the stalls, as though the servants came through to check and fill them at all hours. I found Kae huddled in an empty stall at the far end, where the Virtues waited with him.

"I'll take care of him, thank you." I nodded to them, and they bowed and went out. "Take this off," I ordered, crouching down to unbutton the frozen coat and pull it from his limbs. He was soaked to the skin, and he shivered uncontrollably as he allowed me to take off his shirt and wrap him in a blanket. My eyes lingered on the scarring that followed the knotted flesh on his face down the side of his neck and over his shoulders. "When you've warmed up, I want you to put these on." I set the clothes beside him on a bale of hay. "But I wish you'd come inside the house. Sarael has a soothing bath—"

"No," he croaked. "Not a guest. Your prisoner."

I shivered. "I don't understand."

He looked at me piercingly with his single eye. "You do." He mustered his resources to force his voice through his larynx. "I am a traitor to the throne of the Firmament of Shehaqim and the House of Arkhangel'sk. I am a murderer. I have struck down His Supernal Majesty the Principality Helison Alimielovich of the House of Arkhangel'sk and Her Supernal Majesty the queen Sefira Huzievna, as well as His Supernal Highness the Grand Duke Azel Helisonovich, the heir to the throne."

"Stop it." I backed away from him.

"I have murdered in cold blood Their Supernal Highnesses the Grand Duchesses Maia and Tatia Helisonovna."

"Stop it!"

"I have murdered—my Ola!" His voice cracked and broke as he said her name. He threw himself at my feet, and I couldn't bear to look at him a moment longer. I couldn't be sure I wouldn't grab a pitchfork from the wall and run him through with it. I turned in a manner as unlike the rightful queen of Heaven as could be, and fled.

Dvadtsat Vtoroe: **Crime and Punishment**

The wretched grand duchess had proven a much greater thorn in Aeval's side than she'd ever dreamed. She had stolen Aeval's angel.

The queen had woken in the middle of the night to the field marshal's Second pounding on her door. She hated to be disturbed after such complete satisfaction, and she'd nearly dashed his head into the stone walls of Gehenna's ancient corridor before waking enough to realize Kae was gone.

When Captain Jusguarin informed her of the breach of the citadel by a regiment of mere Virtues, she stormed down the stairs of the tower. She needed her field marshal to keep these fools in line. But he was nowhere to be found.

From the dungeon, the guards assigned to watch it were brought to Aeval, having been found locked in the very cell they were charged with guarding. She had them beaten, and while they pleaded in vain for mercy, they told her the field marshal himself had locked them in and had released the prisoners.

She'd doubted his loyalty when he failed to follow her wishes with regard to that foul monk. She hadn't been able to stand the sight of that breed since the miserable Rasputin had ruined her plans, and the presence of one in her Heaven was like the presence of a cockroach.

But Kae had fucked her when she'd ordered it, and she was thrilled by his willing submission. As with her demon Belphagor when she'd possessed him, she'd believed she now owned Kae fully. It was something she'd long dreamed of, but it hadn't been practical: to see him fully cognizant of what he did, fully debased, her willing slave. And unlike with the demon, there was no need to call his blood to even one part of his body to obtain his compliance. He serviced her with consent. But all the while, he'd been planning to betray her.

Facing no resistance to their occupation of Heaven's princedoms, her troops had grown lazy and indolent, and though they outnumbered the Virtues overrunning the citadel by three to two, what should have been a rout became a draw. The Virtues eventually retreated to Aravoth, but not before annihilating nearly a third of her forces. She had half a mind to annihilate the rest herself.

Gehenna was worthless to her as a stronghold. It was a place where angels of old had fled conflict and hidden like cowards. She gathered what remained of her regiment and returned south toward Zevul. Their number was inadequate for an assault on Aravoth, but when she assembled her army in Elysium after the spring thaw, they would head north to the Aravoth Pass and Aeval would make certain there was not a Virtue left in Heaven.

• • •

It wasn't until Belphagor ran into the Virtue Loquel that he discovered what had called Anazakia away. Hoping to distract his mind from the hopeless impotence of being unable to do anything to find Ola, he'd gone to Sarael's impressive library in search of something to read. The young Virtue was alone when he arrived, and he stood with a slight bow toward Belphagor.

"Your Supernal Highness."

Belphagor laughed, and the Virtue gave him a look that was slightly surprised and slightly wounded. "I'm not anybody's highness. Just Belphagor of Raqia—demon, cardsharp, and common thief, at your service." He gave the Virtue his own impish bow.

"I apologize. I knew one of you was the grand duke; I just assumed it was you. I wanted to thank you for your kindness at Gehenna."

He shrugged. "It was only common decency. I really didn't do much—and I might have done nothing had Vasily not chastised me." He started to ask whom the Virtue meant by "the grand duke," but Loquel went on, seeming anxious to speak.

"My brother-blades and I would like to offer ourselves in your service. It is our custom to die together if our troop is disgraced…and we have been much disgraced. But the feeling of the troop is that we are in your debt, and we would like to repay it."

Belphagor was baffled by this entire exchange, as if he'd somehow walked in on the middle of it.

"If our offer doesn't please you, we're prepared to dispatch ourselves as planned with no ill feelings toward you."

"I'm not sure I understand you." Belphagor blanched at what he thought he understood.

Loquel looked down at his feet. "I am not the best elocutionist. The others thought it ought to be me who presented our offer, as your kindness to me was great, and my failure as a soldier greater." He colored, an impressive thing in a Virtue, whose skin was like the surface of a pearl.

"Loquel." Belphagor rebuked him kindly. "You did nothing to disgrace yourself."

The angel raised his head, and the depth of pain in his eyes stunned Belphagor. He took Loquel's hand and sat down in the armchair he'd been occupying, pulling Loquel gently onto his lap. He hoped this wouldn't be further humiliation for him, but the young man seemed to be crying out for it.

"It is no failure to be unused to pain. I can tell you this because I've been a master at it." He lifted Loquel's chin. "I've broken one like you before, and I didn't start so crudely. Young flesh requires conditioning." He smiled. "And even an old dog like myself can be pushed beyond his limits, especially when taken by surprise." He was gratified to see his instincts were still good. Loquel had calmed at his touch instead of expressing discomfort. "That very tool was used on me once," he admitted. "And though it took a few more blows, I was screaming and begging for mercy before it ended. When I was beaten again on top of those same wounds, I was willing to debase myself, to do anything to make it stop. Compared to what I did—what I was made to say—you behaved more than admirably."

"Those scars on your back." Loquel spoke with awe.

"From that implement and another I wouldn't wish on my worst enemy." As he said the last, he realized it wasn't quite true. He had dreams of using it on Kae.

"But when the field marshal struck you, you hardly seemed to notice it."

"Because I knew what was coming. I used my breath to transform the pain, dispersing it, like oxygen through the blood."

Loquel lowered his voice. "Could you teach me that?"

Belphagor smiled. "I would love to. To be able to," he amended. "I'm not certain I can any longer." It occurred to him he was contradicting within himself the very thing he was telling Loquel. He was unwilling to be as kind to himself as he was to this Virtue he hardly knew, refusing to forgive himself for having broken under Kae's *knut*. He drew Loquel forward by the hand, subtly guiding him to his feet, and stood to relinquish the chair to him.

"This offer," he said. "You're not telling me the entire unit will… kill yourselves…if I don't accept?"

"Not *because* you don't accept. But yes. That is our wish, to join our fallen brothers. We only mean to defer it out of a debt to you and the grand duke."

Belphagor was still baffled. "And whom do you mean by the 'grand duke'?"

"His Supernal Highness, of course. Grand Duke Vasily of the House of Arcadia."

Belphagor gaped at him.

"I thought that you and he—are you not—?" Loquel began to blush again.

"We are," Belphagor assured him. "But Grand Duke—the House of Arcadia...I'm not sure where you heard that."

"From Sar Sarael. I asked him your names. Was he mistaken?"

Belphagor shook his head ruefully. "It seems I may have missed more than one thing while I was on the march with the Queen's Army."

Though he'd admitted with great embarrassment how Lively had come to be carrying his second child, Vasily had seemed reluctant to discuss his first trip to Aravoth, and conversation had been difficult enough on the Empyrean plains that Belphagor hadn't pressed.

He supposed it was time he and Vasily had a talk. "Tell your brothers we accept your offer. I'm not sure I understand what it means yet, but absolutely, we accept it." He paused. "And I'll give serious thought to tutoring you." An old familiar warmth spread through him at the thought.

Loquel smiled. "I'd like that. Especially with that—unpleasant man here."

"What unpleasant man?"

Loquel gave a slight shudder. "The field marshal. He followed us through the ice storm. He arrived this morning."

• • •

Love stretched her arms against the tile of the Virtuous bath and closed her eyes, breathing in the scented steam. It was the smoothest water she'd ever felt, like bathing in baby oil—but the comparison brought to mind the baths she'd given Ola and the sweet scent on her afterward.

Tears rolled down Love's cheeks in the steam. The arduousness of the journey across the frozen Empyrean had occupied her mind until now, but here at Pyr Amaravati there was nothing but time and quiet. She could barely look at Anazakia—at any of them. Everyone was haunted. It was a bitter irony that after all this time as a prisoner, all she wanted now was to be with Ola, wherever that miserable Helga had taken her.

If only she'd had some of that magical fire. Love had seen it on

Anazakia's skin when Vasily touched her, back at the dacha before all this, but it was one of the many things she told herself was just a trick of the light or the power of suggestion. She wished she could go back to that simple denial.

But Kirill was having much more trouble, for the very fact that he believed. Love ached to be able to help him. He was so lost. She'd long since stopped feeling any sort of satisfaction at his anxiety, any feeling that he was reaping what he'd sown. He had the purest heart and the most guileless of motives. Zeus had violated Kirill's innocence as surely as he'd violated Love. She couldn't be anything but glad the bastard was dead, but his killing was the irreversible step that had damaged Kirill beyond repair. He was so certain everything that had happened since was his punishment, that God had rightly abandoned him.

Love had always been a bit derisive of religious faith. Every believer she'd ever known had been betrayed in some sense by the arbitrary nature of the world, holding out faith as if it could make them immune to life's cruelties, and when it didn't, finding themselves shocked and appalled. But Kirill didn't deserve this rude awakening.

She went looking for him after her bath as the manor began to quiet for the evening and found him in his room. In the grip of the storm, Pyr Amaravati felt like Arkhangel'sk in winter, where the daylight hours seemed dreamlike and evening came not long after midday. He was praying, as usual.

She said his name softly from the doorway, reluctant to interrupt him, but pained at the futility of his devotion.

Kirill looked up and dropped his *chotki* into his pocket. "Sister Lyubov." His face lit up in a smile. "Please come in."

"It's Love, if you don't mind." She sat beside him on the bed. "No one has ever called me that but my family—and Zeus."

Kirill's blue eyes looked stricken. "I apologize. Of course." He observed her. "Your family. They must be worried about you."

Love sighed. "No, not really." She'd left home when she was fourteen, preferring life on the streets to dealing with an alcoholic stepfather and a mother who thought he could do no wrong. Her brothers and sisters had always seemed like strangers. "Anazakia and Vasily and Belphagor…they're my family."

"And little Ola."

Love nodded, not trusting her voice to talk about Ola. "I wanted to check and see how your shoulder was healing." She touched the collar of his robe. "May I?"

He shrugged and she unbuttoned it enough to reveal his bandage, lifting it to see that the flesh looked pink and healthy beneath it.

"I don't think you need this anymore." She began to unwrap his shoulder. "There's a lovely bath just at the end of this hall. You should take a soak in it. It will do you good."

"Sister Love." He placed his hand over hers against the bandage.

"Just Love." She tried to continue, but he stopped her.

"Love." His expression was earnest. "You mustn't touch me like this."

"Why? I'm just taking off the bandage."

"Because." He looked pained. "Because—when your fingers touch my skin, I desire it."

Love studied him for a moment. "And desire is wrong?"

"I have taken a vow before God."

"Kirill." She wasn't certain if what she was about to say to him was kindness or cruelty. "Where is God if he isn't in Heaven?"

Kirill jumped up from the bed and went to the door, holding it in an invitation for her to leave. "You don't know what you're saying." His aquamarine eyes flashed with anger.

"I know exactly what I'm saying. Was God at Solovetsky when he allowed a demon to trick you into imprisoning an innocent child? Where was he, Kirill? Was he there watching when Zeus hurt me?"

"Men—*sin*!"

Love had made a mistake. He'd never been angry with her before. He had been her friend, and she was being cruel to him, taking the only thing he had left.

"I'm sorry, Kirill." She stood up. "I'm very sorry." Though she tried not to, she was crying as she hurried past him, and he caught her by the arm.

"No." He shook his head when she looked up, his sea-blue eyes also full of tears. He closed the door. "No, I'm sorry. I have wronged you. That is why God has abandoned me, because of what I let happen to you in His house." Kirill sank to his knees before her and held her hand in both of his. "Please forgive me." He wept openly. "God cannot forgive me for what I've done."

"Please don't. I shouldn't have said that." She knelt down with him. "You're not the one who hurt me, Kirill."

He sobbed and kissed her hands like a penitent, and like the saint to whom he prayed, she kissed him on the forehead, hoping this wouldn't offend him.

"I am a sinner." He lifted his head, his eyes deep with sorrow. "I am just like him—for wanting you."

"You are *not* like him. He didn't want me. He wanted to hurt me." She smoothed her fingers against his hair, pulled back in its ponytail. "I'm the sinner." She regarded him sadly. "Wanting you to break your vow." She started to get up, but he pulled her back.

"Then God forgive me," he whispered. "Let me break it."

• • •

Kae's arrival changed things. The talk with Vasily would have to wait. Belphagor went to check on Lev, hoping he was feeling well enough to be a sounding board for his anxieties, and found Dmitri reading to him from the Aravoth *Verity*.

"Ah, the celestial *Pravda*." Belphagor winked from the doorway. "What news today?"

Dmitri straightened the paper in front of him with an exaggerated flourish. "Apparently, Pyr Amaravati is the talk of the town. Did you know demons were overrunning the place?"

"Shocking. Speaking of which, how is my favorite little demon doing?" He sat down on the side of the bed and took Lev's hand.

Propped against a nearly decadent pile of pillows, Lev struggled to sit up straighter and Dmitri rearranged the pillows behind him. "That can't be me." It was worrisome how weak his voice sounded. "Surely Vasily is your favorite little demon—or big, anyway."

"Apparently, Vasya is my favorite little big something else."

Dmitri and Lev exchanged puzzled glances.

"I think it's clear that Vashti was right about his father being a Seraph. But apparently we've been misinformed about his other half as well. Loquel tells me the Virtues were introduced to him as His Supernal Highness the Grand Duke Vasily of the House of Arcadia."

"Arcadia?" Dmitri folded the paper. "How the hell—?"

"How the hell, indeed? I'm as baffled as you are. And it seems our grand duke already has his own little army of angels."

Dmitri dropped the *Verity* in his lap. "How's that?"

"The Virtues who shared Gehenna's dungeon with us. They've signed on to do...what, exactly, I don't know. But they've offered their services to Vasily. Well, to me, but only because they thought I was him—the 'grand duke.' "

Lev shook his head. "You've lost me."

"Yes, I'm right there with you in the dark. Marco."

"Marco?"

"You're supposed to say Polo. Then I grope about for you."

Lev squinted at Belphagor as if he was hurting his head.

"It's a game from the Americas. Never mind. Point is, I'm feeling more than a little lost this morning. Particularly now that Anazakia's 'unpleasant' cousin is here."

Dmitri rolled up his paper and wagged it at him. "None of this is in the *Verity*. I don't know if I believe you."

"Kae's here?" Lev frowned. "I thought we'd seen the last of him. Are you all right with that?"

"Not really."

Dmitri rose and picked up a breakfast tray from the nightstand that looked like it had hardly been touched. "I'm sensing you're about to do some of that 'processing' the two of you are so fond of." He smiled and kissed Lev. "I'm going to return this to the kitchen and see what's left of lunch."

Belphagor took the seat Dmitri had vacated. "I should be letting you rest."

"*Bozhe moi.* Please. I do nothing but rest. It's not as if I can do anything more fun in this bed at the moment." He made a rueful face. "And it's been a ridiculously long time since I have."

Belphagor smiled. "Try two years. Then we'll talk."

"Two years?" Lev looked horrified.

"A bit more, actually, but who's counting?" He laughed at the expression on Lev's face. "It's my fault, really. First I went off and got myself imprisoned. And then beaten. And then I lost my nerve." Gratefully, he took the hand Lev held out. "But I think I found it again last night." He grinned. "At least some of it."

"Well, that's a relief. You were scaring me there for a minute. If you're not getting any, the worlds might be ending."

"It's the 'some of it,' though, that troubles me." Belphagor sighed. "Last night I thought I might be able to get it all back. Don't misunderstand; it was good — more than good. But I couldn't give Vasya what he really needed. I couldn't be the person with him I need to be. Every time I think of touching him that way, I remember how I groveled and begged when Kae did it to me."

"I don't know exactly what you went through, but that was hardly the same thing. What Kae did to you was no more like what you do with Vasily than being raped is like having a good fuck."

Belphagor was dismayed to realize this was exactly how he'd been treating it. Well aware of the difference between consensual exchange of power and having one's power robbed, he'd nevertheless fallen into the bland, angelic way of thinking that equated eroticizing pain with abuse.

"Maybe you need to confront the bastard. He may have been

under the queen's control, but he's still responsible for what he did to you. I don't know what he's doing here, but he doesn't have the right to take away something so special between you and Vasily."

Belphagor pressed Lev's hand on top of the thick Aravothan fleece. "Why are you so smart?" He kissed Lev's pale cheek. "You need to get well so I can show you how much I appreciate you."

Lev grinned. "That's what I like about you, Bel. You never miss an opportunity to put the moves on a fellow."

Sarael confirmed it was Kae's arrival that had called Anazakia away at breakfast. He showed Belphagor the tunnel that led to the stables where Kae had been detained, but Belphagor hadn't quite worked up the nerve or determined what he'd say to him when he did.

He was wandering the corridors of Pyr Amaravati while ice rained down on the glass bricks, trying to decide whether to talk to Vasily first, when Love stepped out of one of the rooms and nearly ran into him. She was dressed in a robe from the bath but was coming from the opposite direction. She looked up at him, her cheeks pink with heat from the bath or embarrassment—or some other blood-warming activity. He raised an eyebrow, fairly certain it was the latter when she glanced back at the door with a guilty start. The monk might be mad, but he was apparently no fool.

"Quite rejuvenating, isn't it?" He smiled at her furious blush. "The bath. I wanted to stay there all day."

"Oh…yes. Very." She nibbled her lip and turned to go, walking in the direction of the bath and not away from it.

He remembered something that had been nagging him for some time. "Love."

She turned back, her face even pinker than before, as if she thought he meant to call her out on where she'd been.

"I've been wanting to apologize for that horrible message I left you."

"Message?"

"On your cell phone. Back home."

"Oh." She looked intensely uncomfortable. "No, you don't have to apologize."

"I do. It was ugly. I insulted you and threatened you. I should have known better than to think you were part of it. You've always taken the best care of Ola."

Her lip trembled and she blinked back tears. "I tried to. You don't know how I tried."

"You did. We all know what you've done for—for our family."

Love looked away, wiping her eyes.

"She looked well," he said wistfully.

Love's eyes widened. "Oh, Belphagor. You didn't get to spend any time with her." She touched his arm. "I'm sorry. She really wanted to see you, too. She kept asking."

"She remembers me." He was enormously consoled by that.

"She does. She's very smart." Love paused a moment. "Wait, I have something for you." She went down the hall to her room—not the room she'd come from, he noted—and he followed, waiting outside her open door. As he watched, Love dug in the pocket of her overalls lying on the bed and pulled out something that looked like a worn and dingy sock.

He regarded her quizzically as she handed it to him, and then he saw one button eye on it and a felt nose. It was a stuffed dog he'd given Ola on her birthday.

"She picked that up when we stopped at the dacha. She never wanted to put it down. She slept with it."

He clutched the little toy, his heart aching as if the cilice Kirill had taken from the dacha were being tightened around it.

"Belphagor?"

He hugged her, and then put the dog in his pocket and turned away before Love could see the tears in his eyes.

Belphagor found himself walking toward the passage Sarael had shown him, his sorrow turning to anger at being robbed of Ola, and his anger turning toward the only object he had to project it onto. Kae might not have taken Ola from him, but he'd taken enough.

When he arrived at the stables, he found Kae easily. Vasily had gotten there before him. He had the angel by the throat, slamming his head against the wooden stall. Blood ran down the angel's face beside his mask, and he didn't appear to be resisting.

"You may have helped us escape," Vasily was snarling, "but you're still the son of a bitch who took Belphagor from me."

"Nobody has taken me from you." Belphagor spoke from behind him and Vasily whirled around. He could see it in the smoldering eyes: he was no longer the Belphagor Vasily needed and hungered for. As far as Vasily was concerned, his words to Kae had been nothing but the truth. "Let him go," he said as Vasily's grip on Kae's throat tightened.

"I should have let him die that day at Gehenna." Vasily shoved Kae away from him.

The angel fell to the dusty floor, catching himself on his hands and knees. "Yes." He coughed wretchedly. "You should have."

Belphagor took Vasily by the hand and led him out into the corridor to speak to him quietly. "If you had, we would still be the queen's prisoners." He reached up to put a hand on Vasily's angry cheek. "I want you to leave him alone."

Vasily pulled the hand away. "I can't just pretend it didn't happen. I'm the one who found you, remember? That image is burned into my head. And if you don't have the *yaytsa*—" Vasily cut the sentence short, his face flushed with anger and embarrassment. *Yaytsa* was a Russian colloquialism for testicles. "I didn't mean that."

"Of course you did. Do you think I don't understand why you're so angry? You're not angry at him, you're angry at me. And I don't blame you for being angry. I know I'm no longer the man you need me to be."

"That's not true." But he was avoiding Belphagor's eyes.

"Vasya, promise me you'll leave him alone. You know Nazkia would never forgive you if you went too far." He gave Vasily's hand an affectionate squeeze. "I'm going to talk to him, and I want that to be the end of it."

"Talk!" Vasily yanked back his hand. "You do that, Bel. You and Kae just have your little talk and I'll never mention it again." He left Belphagor in the cold light of the stable lamps.

Belphagor sighed and returned to the stall, where Kae remained on his knees. What showed of the angel's face was a swollen mess, as if Vasily had punched him repeatedly and he'd put up no fight. "Why did you come here?"

Kae looked up at him, his eye watering. "Because I didn't have the stones to throw myself in the Pyriphlegethon. Nazkia was right. I'm a coward."

Belphagor was struck by how pathetic the former principality had become. For a moment, he almost pitied him.

"Why did *you* come here?" Kae countered. "Back for more?"

It was the same thing he'd said in Belphagor's nightmare in the Hell Stairway. Rage surged up inside Belphagor. He yanked the *pleti* off Kae's belt.

Kae sat blinking that wretched eye at him as Belphagor raised the flogger, and he seemed almost eager for it. "What are you waiting for? I beat you half to death and you can't even bring yourself to hit me once?" He was goading him, desperate for a beating that would somehow absolve him. Or maybe obliterate him.

Belphagor lowered his arm and shook his head. "You must truly be Heaven's most pathetic creature." He echoed the words Kae had once said to him. He clutched the handle of the *pleti*, aroused by the feel of it in his hand. "I can't give you what you want. When I use pain to transform a man's suffering, it's because I love him."

Kae stared at him wordlessly. It was no longer rheum running from the swollen, clouded eye. Belphagor hooked the *pleti* on his own belt and left the angel in the grip of pain far greater than anything he could administer.

• • •

Inside the manor, Vasily lay on the bed he shared with Belphagor, staring at the ceiling and seething with pent-up anger alternating with a feeling of hopeless oppression. When Belphagor had unexpectedly woken him in the middle of the night, kissing his neck where his piercings ought to be, he'd nearly wept with relief. Belphagor had finally come back to him. But Bel had shied from any aggression, almost passive in his touch. It was all the tenderness of Belphagor, but completely robbed of passion.

Vasily felt awful for wanting more, and when he found out Kae had joined them at Pyr Amaravati, he was overcome with rage at the one who'd taken what he loved. When he'd beaten the angel, his anger at himself for blaming Belphagor and all the anguish over losing Ola again poured out of him through his fists. It was as much a catharsis for that pain as for anything to do with the change in Belphagor. But Belphagor was the place he'd always taken his grief and rage. Belphagor's ruthless possession of him was what made him feel whole, and safe, and loved.

He hated what he'd said to Belphagor. He was lashing out, as he always did, at the one dearest to him. In the past, it had almost been a kind of mating ritual, with his smart mouth provoking Belphagor into reminding him whom he belonged to. It was going to be a hard habit to break, and knowing that every unkind word he uttered from now on would lie between them instead of earning Belphagor's firm hand was all the more depressing.

One of Sarael's servants came to fetch him to dinner and Vasily rose with a sigh. He was heading for the dining room when Belphagor appeared in the atrium and seized him by the upper arm, turning him toward their room.

"I need to talk to you."

Vasily tried to still the rush of longing this stirred in him. Belphagor was only angry with him over his abuse of Kae, and they were only going to argue, and he hated that.

"You were out of line." Belphagor pushed him into their room and closed the door.

"So you told me." Vasily sighed. "Look, Bel, I don't want to fight over this. We're never going to see eye to eye on it."

"We don't need to see eye to eye. You just need to do what I say."

Vasily was indignant. "I told you I'd never mention it again. Why can't we just leave it at that?"

"Because." Belphagor grabbed him by his locks and twisted him about. "The correct response is, *'Da, ser!'*" Belphagor shoved him to his knees and Vasily gasped as he yanked his hair. "I don't hear anything."

Every inch of Vasily's skin was tingling. He answered slowly and deliberately. *"Pashol na khui."* He cupped himself with a rude gesture on the last syllable.

Belphagor was deathly quiet for a moment, and then he leaned down next to Vasily and whispered into his ear. "Oh, I'm going there, *malchik*. But not just yet." He hauled Vasily to the bed and pushed him forward onto it, and Vasily shivered as Belphagor reached beneath him to jerk his belt from its buckle, and then yanked his pants down to his knees. Belphagor pulled off the long undershirt Vasily was wearing and tossed it on the bed before laying something carefully in front of him. It was the tool Kae had worn on his belt.

"Do you know what that is?"

"Yes."

Belphagor struck his face with it lightly, just enough to sting.

Vasily jerked his head to the side, a bit offended that Belphagor would hit him with such a thing on his face. *"Da, ser,"* he snapped.

"Ah, you're angry." Belphagor trailed the leather down his back and drew a delightful shiver from him. "What's the matter? Too good to be hit with such a common instrument?"

"No." Vasily jerked and cried out, *"Nyet, ser!"* as Belphagor struck him across the shoulders. The sting of the lead balls was surprisingly intense.

"You've been angry with me for a long time."

Vasily answered with reluctance. *"Da, ser."*

"That's my *malchik*," Belphagor whispered, stroking the leather thongs gently against his cheek. Vasily bit his lip to keep from weeping at the tenderness of this word. "You have every right to be angry, *dorogoi moi malchik*. I haven't been here for you. I've been feeling sorry for myself." He ran the flogger down Vasily's spine, setting off an uncontrollable trembling. "I made a promise to you long ago. That I would always punish you for both of our transgressions. And I've failed to do that. Which is just about the greatest transgression I can think of." He put his hand on the small of Vasily's back to still the shaking, and then without warning, he began to flog Vasily with swift, alternating strokes.

Vasily cried out into the blankets, shocked by how strong the sensation was. He'd been one of the few who hadn't received one of Kae's beatings while they'd been at Gehenna. He tried to breathe as Belphagor had taught him, but he was becoming rapidly overwhelmed, his chest tightening and his breath becoming shallow, and the pain increased dramatically as he lost his focus. He was hyperventilating, and Belphagor stopped and stroked his inflamed flesh with his hand.

"This is too much for you."

Vasily shook his head and then began to weep. "I'm sorry," he gasped.

Belphagor sat down on the bed and put his arms around him. "Sshh, *malchik*, it's all right."

"It's not that it's too much," Vasily wept, clinging to Belphagor. "I just can't stop thinking of him using it on you."

"I see. I've messed this up rather badly."

"No." Vasily shook his head, afraid he'd ruined everything, undermining Belphagor just when he'd finally regained his confidence. "No, I'm sorry. I'll be good."

"There's no use making excuses for me. I've done a terrible job of this." He stroked Vasily's hair gently as Vasily cried into his lap. "And the punishment for that will have to be quite severe."

Vasily inhaled sharply, instantly silenced. Belphagor slipped the tear-splattered glasses from Vasily's face and set them aside before he rose and opened the bureau drawer. Without the glasses, he couldn't see what Belphagor was getting, but apparently, in the few minutes he'd been absent from the room, Belphagor had made preparations. The thought made him weak in the knees.

"Kneel and face me."

Vasily slipped to the ground and waited.

Belphagor stepped before him, holding something that looked like a length of rope. "Hands."

Vasily held out his arms with his palms together, as if in prayer.

Belphagor bound his wrists, pulling the rope tight, and fastened the other end of the rope to the bedpost. He positioned Vasily facing the bed and said, "Open your mouth."

When Vasily did, Belphagor slipped something over his head with a piece of metal attached. It was a horse's bit. Vasily jerked back and closed his mouth.

"What are you doing, *malchik*?"

"You're not putting that in my mouth," Vasily growled through his teeth.

Belphagor sighed with displeasure. "Open it or I will open it for you."

Vasily refused, so Belphagor grabbed him by the jaw and forced his thumb and forefinger between Vasily's lips. He dug the fingers in until they were behind Vasily's molars, then pried open Vasily's mouth, shoved the bit in with his other hand, and yanked it back with his thumbs in the rings. He ran another length of rope through the rings and pulled it tight behind Vasily's head, then tied the ends together and hauled back on the makeshift bridle, forcing Vasily to look him in the eye.

"I love you," he said, and Vasily jerked his eyes away.

The last thing Belphagor took from the bureau drawer turned out to be a slender carriage whip. He let Vasily feel the braided thong and fall of the whip snake across his skin so he could be certain what it was. Vasily squirmed at the bedpost, but there was no escaping it, and the lash came down on his back with a sharp crack. He arched against the sting, and his jaw clamped down on the bit.

"Don't do that, love. Breathe. Do you think I enjoy watching you suffer for my mistakes?"

"Yeshhhhhhhhhhh!" Vasily growled the word around the bit, and the lash came down again.

"I won't deny you look very pretty with your mouth forced open." Belphagor snapped the lash this time against his thighs. "But I want you to breathe with the blows and let the pain ride through you."

"*Na khui,*" Vasily managed, and Belphagor struck him again between the shoulders. Vasily found his breath hissing out of him with the impact despite himself.

"That's it. Good boy."

The whip came down on his thighs again and Vasily felt the pain like a wave that was almost sensual as he breathed with it.

"There's something I want to say to you, *malchik.*" The tone of Belphagor's voice sent an icy tingle up Vasily's spine, in curious contrast to the heat of the lash as it struck his shoulder. "I abandoned you, however temporary I intended that to be, when I went to negotiate with the queen and left you and Nazkia at Arkhangel'sk."

He struck the opposite shoulder as if in recompense, and Vasily moaned into the bedding, breathing out the physical pain along with the deeper pain he'd held onto for so long.

"I will never do that again." The whip sliced the air and struck between his shoulder blades with a heavy *thud*. Belphagor leaned close and whispered against the heat of the stripe as it bloomed across Vasily's muscles. "Every stroke is a promise to you. I will never leave you." He stepped back and struck again. "You are mine."

Vasily groaned, the sound rising from deep within him, not caring if anyone could hear.

Belphagor stroked the fall of the whip over the burning skin, and his voice came in a more ordinary tone. "But you abandoned me, too. You took comfort with someone else. That's been bothering me more than I realized."

The swift bite of a blow across the center of Vasily's glutes took him as much by surprise as the simple, blunt confession. It had none of the finesse of Belphagor's usual skill, though it had managed to wrap from one hip to the other in a spectacular single landing that stung like fire. But the realization of how much he must have hurt Belphagor for him to make such an ordinary admission was far more painful.

Belphagor let out a long breath as if he were the one struck, and then began again with his customary precision before Vasily could catch his own breath enough to say something. "But I guess it's been bothering you more than you realize, too." His voice slipped back into the deeper octave of the disciplinarian. "So I want you to let it go. This is our punishment, and then it's done." He delivered the blows almost casually, with no interruption from his words, though he was clearly expending a significant amount of effort. "And no more tiptoeing around a relationship for which I've given my consent. You're *my* boy, and if I want you to service a supernal grand duchess, you'll do it and like it. Is that understood?" He paused to give Vasily a chance to answer.

"Da, ser," Vasily managed in a small, taut voice as the sting of the whip shuddered through him.

"Khorosho, malchik." Belphagor's hand lingered on Vasily's head before he resumed the strokes of the carriage whip with an almost matter-of-fact manner. A steady throb was building in Vasily's muscles, his raw nerves nearly overloaded with sensation, like the prelude to an orgasm.

The blows and his breathing began sharing a rhythm and he let his head hang forward loosely, no longer cognizant of his ordinary frets, as the pain ebbed and flowed with the rise and fall of the lash. The *crack* of the leather in the air and the snap of it against his back formed a comforting meter, and he swayed with it, anticipating the latter in the split-second preceding beat of the former. Heat and vitality spread through his flesh like a sexual release. He was Belphagor's medium, a composition in the hands of a maestro.

Before he realized it, the blows had stopped, and he looked up in confusion.

"Are you all right, *malchik*?" Belphagor was whispering at his side. Vasily nodded.

"I need you to answer out loud."

He laid his cheek against the mattress, content. *"Da, ser."*

Belphagor kissed the top of his head. "That's my sweet boy." He stepped back. "I have something for you."

Vasily felt a pinch at his neck where Belphagor pushed one of the stainless steel barbells through the holes that had begun to heal over. Belphagor alternated between one side and the other, turning Vasily's head gently from side to side as he replaced all of the missing bars in order and screwed on the spiked caps.

When he got to the fifth one, he kissed Vasily on the back of his neck between the rows. "I managed to…recover…the other two." He turned Vasily's head and held them up, the blurred shapes refracting the light.

Vasily narrowed his eyes at him. Surely he wouldn't.

There was an amused grin in Belphagor's voice. "Sarael has an autoclave. They're all sterile." Before Vasily could protest, Belphagor had fitted the last two into the holes. He ran his fingers over them, making Vasily's flesh ripple with goose bumps, and leaned down to whisper in his ear. "Close your eyes."

When Vasily obeyed, Belphagor kissed his eyelids, drawing his attention away from whatever he was doing with his hands. Vasily inhaled with a shock as a sharp needle went through the skin above the seventh piercing. He opened his eyes and found Belphagor's glinting with tears.

"I've had this one for a long time." Belphagor held up an eighth barbell. He unscrewed the cap and fitted the metal bar into the hollow end of the needle, passing it through to the other side. "You've been so good." He screwed the cap into place. "I couldn't wait a moment longer."

Tears slid down Vasily's cheeks as Belphagor untied his hands. On the floor, Belphagor pulled Vasily into his lap and kissed him over the bit while he released the bridle from behind his head, then drew the bit away in his own mouth and set it aside.

"I love you, Beli," Vasily moaned as Belphagor showered his face with kisses.

Belphagor twisted his fingers in Vasily's locks and ran his tongue over a row of spiked steel. "You'd better."

• • •

In the morning, Belphagor woke feeling anything was possible. He stretched under the soft blue light that filtered in, announcing the ice storm had passed. They would find Ola. The Virtuous army would return from Gehenna with Aeval's head on a pike. Even Anazakia's miserable cousin could be redeemed. Perhaps, he laughed to himself, the angel could join the monk's order and spend the rest of his days on Solovetsky not bothering anyone. His clothes already had the proper somber air.

Beside him, Vasily was sleeping with the relaxation of utter trust, and the room was almost steamy with his firespirit body heat—*his seraphic body heat*, Belphagor amended. He smiled as he breathed in the firewood scent. His own Seraph. His own supernal grand duke. It added a new layer of erotic complexity to Vasily's submission.

He kissed the warm forehead and got up to take a bath before breakfast. It was a very civilized ritual these Virtues endorsed and he heartily approved. Afterward, wrapped in his sweet-smelling robe, he stopped in to see Lev, eager to tell him how wonderfully things had come together last night.

When he arrived at the room, the door was open, and Dmitri was on the floor holding Lev in his arms. The Grigori chieftain looked up at Belphagor, his face streaked with tears, and Belphagor tried to comprehend why Lev was leaning against him with his head at such an awkward angle.

Dvadtsat Tritya: After the Storm
from the memoirs of the Grand Duchess Anazakia
Helisonovna of the House of Arkhangel'sk

Lev's death came as a terrible shock to all of us. With Margarita at his side like a loyal lieutenant, Dmitri was inconsolable, insisting he was responsible and refusing to accept any assurance that he was not, even though Lev himself had been unaware of the infection that had been slowly killing him. Belphagor, too, seemed devastated, and Vasily hung back, watching him with concern as Sarael's staff discussed with him and Dmitri what was to be done with the body. There was some argument about whether Lev ought to be laid to rest in the vault at Pyr Amaravati or cremated. Burial at this time of year in Aravoth was impossible.

I took Vasily's hand, watching with him from the hallway, and he pulled me close, trembling, as if the sight of another man losing his lover frightened him. I rested my head on his chest and noticed he was once more adorned with rows of spikes above his collarbone. Where there had been only three on the right, there were now four, with a bit of redness and swelling marking the newest addition.

I touched my fingers to it lightly. "He gave you the eighth."

Vasily nodded with a sad smile and a slight blush, and I didn't pry.

The monk appeared at the commotion with Love at his side, and I noticed with surprise that she was holding his hand. He hadn't seemed the sort who was comfortable with physical contact. As he saw what was happening, he stepped forward and knelt near Lev to pray over him. Dmitri stared at Kirill without comprehension but didn't try to stop him.

Belphagor came away at last, and I let go of Vasily as he stepped in to embrace him. Vasily looked enormously relieved by some silent communication that passed between them, and I realized Belphagor must have had some relationship with Lev beyond friendship. But though his eyes were red from crying, he looked at Vasily with the sort of adoration I'd once seen in my cousin's eyes for my sister Omeliea.

I turned away, not wanting to intrude, and nearly stumbled over Lively behind me. I hadn't seen her since our arrival two nights ago.

"What's going on?" she whispered.

"Lev has died."

Her eyes grew wide. "He was nice to me."

I supposed not many of us were. "I'm going to make some tea," I announced, not knowing what else to do.

"I'll go with you."

I shrugged. Unless I wanted to make a scene, there was no way to prevent her. Love came after us silently.

There was no "making" anything in Sarael's kitchen. Servants appeared as if from the woodwork whenever any of us expressed a need. We sat about the breakfast table while a full tea service was brought to us. I tried to protest as the servant set down a tray laden with tiny mince pies and biscuits with iceberry preserves and clotted cream, but Lively reached for it eagerly.

Love stared into her cup. "Kirill is in there trying to pray Lev's soul to Heaven. I tried to tell him Lev's already here, but he wouldn't listen. He said Lev told him he liked to go to church. Can a demon go to church?"

"I suppose anyone can." I took a bite of mince pie. "Belphagor told me there have been fugitive demons in the clergy for centuries, since churches and monasteries are off limits to Seraphim." I hadn't thought of the Seraphim since we'd left Gehenna. I wondered what Aeval intended to do that would keep them forever in the Empyrean as she'd promised.

I remembered then what the syla had said to me: that I would make the Seraphim stop their slaughter by spilling the blood of a fallen angel close to my heart. But I hadn't done anything. It was Kae's actions that had depleted their radiance, and I hadn't spilled the blood of a fallen angel at all.

Lively was having trouble untying the string binding on the cheese, so I took my knife from my pocket to cut it for her. She stared as I unfolded the blade, as if she thought I intended to run her through with it.

Love leaned over to look at it, curious. "Where did you get that?"

"From Knud." I smiled sadly. "It was his knife."

"May I?" she asked, and I passed it to her. She turned it in her hand. "This is a *navaja*. A Gitano fighting knife. A very nice one." She paused and looked closely at the inscription on the handle, which I hadn't been able to read. "And a very powerful one. It's been charmed by a *vedma*."

"*Vedma*?"

Love hesitated over the translation and Lively answered for her with her mouth full. "A witch."

I'd read fairy tales about witches as a child, but like the fairies themselves, I'd never supposed they were real. But the syla existed.

Something else occurred to me. "Then this knife, it's magical."

"In a manner of speaking." Love handed it back to me. "It's more like it's been charmed against magic—a protection spell."

This was the knife I'd used to stab Aeval when I'd escaped from the Winter Palace. It had weakened her, and I hadn't been certain she would live. It was also the knife I'd used to stab Kae.

Perhaps the knife itself had freed him—and perhaps it was because of the knife that the aether had healed the wound. It was small comfort, now that Lev was dead, to know there might have been a reason Kae's wound had healed and his had not.

I hadn't been back to face my cousin, letting Sarael's staff provide for him, but I'd have to do it soon. Lying awake in bed last night, contemplating what could be done about him, contemplating what his place was now that he was no longer Aeval's slave, I had come to a decision. I had come to a great many decisions, in fact, though all amounted to one thing: I was the rightful heir to the throne of Heaven, and though it was a burden I didn't want, it was a responsibility from which I could no longer run.

Lively was watching me as I put the knife away. "I can tell you anything you want to know about witchcraft." She popped a sugared sultana into her mouth.

Love let out a sharp, humorless laugh. "Oh, I'll just bet you could."

"Actually, that might be useful." I met Lively's eyes, my face hard. "Do you intend to be useful? Or are you still loyal to Helga and the Party?"

Lively dropped her cup into her saucer with a loud clatter. "Well, let me see. Because of my aunt, I'm pregnant by a man who hates me, and I'm stuck in the ice tits of Heaven after fleeing an army of angels with a woman who has every right to hate me as well. In fact, I'm surrounded by people who hate me, and my labor will probably be attended by people who wish me dead. And in thanks for it all, Auntie Helga left me in Gehenna to be beheaded by a madman. After I'd done everything she asked!" Her eyes welled up with tears and she blinked them back angrily. "And I'm getting fat and I'm hungry all the time and I have to pee every five minutes. So, yes, I would like to be useful, and Helga can go to hell."

I sipped my tea to hide my smile, remembering how volatile my emotions had been when I was carrying Ola. "All right, then. I intend to put you to work. And if you're half as useful as I think you may be, you might even be able to make up for what you've done."

Love shook her head as if I'd lost my mind.

The decision was made to have Lev cremated so Dmitri could at least take his ashes home and scatter them in the world Lev had loved—the only world he'd known until, as Dmitri put it, he'd dragged Lev here to die for nothing. I couldn't help but feel he was blaming me, and he confirmed my suspicion after the ceremony, informing us that we could no longer count on the assistance of the Exiles.

"Vashti was right about one thing," he said as we sat glumly about the atrium. "When Vasily first came to me asking for help to rescue Belphagor, she thought we should draw the line at sticking our necks out for one of the Host. This isn't our fight, and it never has been. Now, I'm sorry about Ola, I truly am, but we're not Host, and I can guarantee you that whatever sacrifices the Fallen make for the Host, no matter how much we think we know them, the favor will never be returned."

Belphagor spoke quietly. "Need I remind you, Vasily is Host."

Vasily looked startled and turned red, as if he hadn't told Belphagor what he'd learned about his parentage.

Dmitri dismissed this. "I'm pureblooded, Belphagor. Being Fallen isn't about who gave birth to you. Vasily grew up in Raqia fighting for his food, as you've told me many times. But Anazakia grew up in a palace, living off the blood and sweat of people like you."

He spoke as if I weren't even in the room, but there was little I could argue with. I had lived a very privileged, sheltered life until the age of seventeen, and I had taken the luck of my birth for granted.

Vasily took my hand protectively. "Nazkia's done nothing to deserve what's happened to her. Nor has Ola."

"Nor did Lev," Dmitri snapped. "He died for somebody else's revolution. Who rules Heaven is no concern of ours, and it won't matter a damned bit."

Belphagor regarded him. "So it's celestials in general you have no use for."

Dmitri jumped to his feet with a look of anguish. "Bel, I can't do this anymore!"

"I know." Belphagor rose and put his arms around him. "I know. I'm sorry."

Dmitri hugged him tightly. "You know how fond I am of you.

And Lev—Lev adored you. But I'm done. The Grigori are done. The Nephilim are done. I'm taking Lev, and Margarita and I are going home."

"I know," Belphagor said sadly as they separated.

She'd been quiet through all of this, but Margarita stepped forward from behind Dmitri's bench as he sat down again. "With all due respect, sir—and my deepest condolences for your loss—I'd like to stay."

Dmitri looked troubled. "You won't be here with the backing of the Grigori. You'll be on your own."

"I understand, sir. But I think I can be useful here." She gave me an encouraging smile. I'd spoken to her already about what I had in mind, and I was grateful she hadn't reconsidered in light of Dmitri's decision.

I figured now was as good a time as any to make my announcement.

First, I went to Dmitri's side and knelt down beside the bench. "Dmitri, you and Lev, and everyone, have done so much for me, have suffered so much for me. I just want you to know I will never forget it, and I'll never forget Lev. I'm truly sorry for your loss."

He shrugged, unable or unwilling to speak, but it was all right.

"It will be difficult without any terrestrial help." I stood and addressed the others. "But I've discussed it with Sar Sarael, who speaks on behalf of the Elohim. I have agreed to accept their intent to declare me the rightful heir to the throne of Heaven. And that means that Ola, as my heir, is to be considered held by her captor as an act of treason against all the Heavens."

Vasily was staring at me as if he didn't quite recognize me. "Nazkia…what?"

"Aeval's claim to the throne was only ever as consort to the last remaining Arkhangel'sk. But my cousin was never a legitimate heir. And never will be. Not while I live. Not while Ola lives. Even you have greater claim to the throne of Heaven, Vasily."

He breathed in so sharply he choked on his own spittle. Belphagor patted him roughly on the back, and a perfect circle of steam came out of his shocked open mouth.

"You are the father to the last scion, and a grand duke of the House of Arcadia. If I were to die before Ola reached the age of seventeen, you would be Regent of All the Heavens."

"I'm—illegitimate," Vasily sputtered. "As is our daughter."

"Not under celestial law. The Elohim have studied the rules of succession very carefully, and blood supersedes any question of wedlock." I sat down, smoothing the voluminous skirts on the black funeral gown Sarael's staff had provided for me. "The Virtuous Court of the Elohim and the Princedom of Aravoth itself have officially declared themselves supporters of the true queen of Heaven and are prepared to make war on the armies of so-called Queen Aeval."

Everyone was staring at me as if I'd sprouted a second head.

I went on, feeling strangely at ease in this new role, feeling for the first time in control of my destiny. "The Elohim have also declared themselves at odds with the revolutionary faction represented by the Social Liberation Party, whose sole intent is to abolish the monarchy in favor of mob rule. Between the Party's civilian forces and Aeval's command of the armies of most of the other princedoms, we are not at an advantage, but our aims can be won."

They were still staring at me, and I was grateful when Vasily was the first to break the stunned silence. "You're serious about all this."

"I am. I've shirked the responsibilities of my birthright for too long, and it is costing lives." I searched his eyes, trying to judge how he was taking this. "I hope you're with me."

"I think you're mad," he said, but he smiled at me. "I'm with you to the end of the last glimmer of Heaven."

I let go of the breath I'd been unconsciously holding and resisted the urge to throw myself into his arms and kiss him until our light engulfed us both. It would have spoiled the air of authority I had to maintain.

"And Belphagor." I nodded to him. "I won't accept Vasily's commitment to my cause without your blessing. If you want Vasily out of it, he will be out of it. But I hope to have the support of you both."

Vasily glared at me indignantly, but I could see by his blush he was secretly pleased.

Belphagor's pleasure at the respect I'd given him was obvious. "Thank you, Nazkia." He stood and bowed to me. "And we would both be honored to serve the rightful queen of Heaven."

I smiled at him gratefully and turned to Love, sitting quietly beside me, and took her hands in mine. "Love, dearest, you've sacrificed a great deal for us." I kissed her cheek. "You are the most loyal, brave, and kindhearted person I've ever known. Nothing can adequately express how grateful I am to you. Nothing can make up for what you've lost because of us."

She looked down at our hands, tears dripping onto them, too emotional to speak.

"But I want you and Kirill to go home with Dmitri."

Love's head shot up in astonishment. "No! No, I won't!"

"You don't belong in this mess. I want you to be safe, away from here, to forget about this. Go home to the dacha and take care of Kirill. This has been too hard on you both."

She pulled her hands away from mine, her tears now hurt and angry. "You'll keep that horrid Lively with you after what she did. But you won't have me?"

"That isn't it, Love. You know it." I reached out for her, but she wouldn't have it. "You're like a sister to me." I tried to keep my own voice steady. "And I can't bear to see you hurt any more than you already have been. I've lost all my sisters."

"How have I failed you?"

"You haven't failed me. Never."

"I am Ola's nanny." She lifted her chin, though it was trembling. "I won't leave my charge. If you insist on sending me away, then you tell me to my face you're firing me. You tell me that it's because I've let you down by allowing that wicked Cherub to take her away, and you fire me. That's the only way I'm going."

I could see the fear in her eyes that I'd do as she said, that I truly blamed her. I was at a loss.

"I have made vow before God." Kirill spoke suddenly in broken angelic, his voice soft. "I stay with Sister Love, and I stay with angel child. God charges me to protect and I will protect." He laid his hand on Love's shoulder. "I do much wrong before God, but this I will not do wrong. This I make right, as God is witness."

His pale eyes were solemn and resolute and I knew there would be no dissuading either of them. And I could also see in his eyes that if I ever hurt Love, he would take me apart with his bare hands and pray over the pieces while doing it.

"I see. Then I guess that's settled." I stood up. "I'll let Sarael know you'll be departing alone, Dmitri. He's arranged an escort to Raqia with some loyal Archangels in his employ who won't draw the suspicion of the queen's forces. They're ready to leave as soon as you like. I'll miss you," I added. "I'll miss you and Lev both."

"Where are you going?" Vasily called after me as I headed for the vestibule.

"I have to deal with my cousin."

He came after me as one of Sarael's servants stepped forward to offer my coat. I braced myself, expecting Vasily to curse me for giving Kae any consideration at all.

"Nazkia, I think you ought to know something," he said instead.

I looked at him quizzically.

"I may have…beaten him up."

"*May* have?" I frowned as I buttoned the long, full coat.

"All right, did," he admitted, and his apologetic look turned to one of anger and defiance. "But you don't understand. You can't just let him go unpunished. I don't care if he was enchanted. What he did to Belphagor—"

"I don't understand?" I cut him off sharply. "I was there. I listened to him gloat about what he'd done in grotesque detail every night when he brought Ola to me. That was my price for being allowed to feed our daughter."

Vasily swallowed, looking grey.

I pulled on my gloves and looked him in the eye. "Have you forgotten I was also there when he cut his own child out of my sister's womb? Have you forgotten he put his sword through me? Because I haven't. I will never forget."

"I'm sorry." He lowered his eyes, chastened.

"He will not go unpunished, Vasily." I put my gloved hand on his cheek and kissed him, and he stared at me as if seeing me for the first time.

Perhaps it *was* the first time. I'd not been this certain of who I was, this determined that my fate lay in my hands—and perhaps all our fates, the fate of Heaven itself—since before he'd met me. That evening nearly three years ago in Belphagor's room at The Brimstone, terrified and heartsick as they shaved my head and dressed me as a boy to spirit me out of Heaven, I had ceased to be the Grand Duchess Anazakia Helisonovna of the House of Arkhangel'sk. I had been on the run ever since, even from myself. I wasn't running anymore.

I went out by the front entrance instead of taking the tunnel to the stables. The sky was clear at last and I needed the fresh air. Though we were high in the north, at the edge of populated Heaven on the cusp of the Empyrean, there was a breeze in the air after the bitter storm that promised the coming spring.

The sun was bright in the way it could only be on a perfect winter day, turning the glaze of ice that covered everything into a diorama of delicate crystal figurines. Branches encased in the sparkling winter glass tinkled together in the breeze like dainty bells. It was easy to believe all was well in this magical world. I half expected the *snegurochki* syla to materialize from the lacy chains of ice strung throughout the trees of Pyr Amaravati's dormant cherry orchards.

The path to the stables was like an ice rink. I crossed it gingerly, remembering the last time I'd skated with my sisters on Lake Superna east of the Summer Palace—Maia twirling and gliding expertly around me, teasing me for my graceless gait, while Ola and Tatia skated arm in arm ahead of us. Such a bright winter sun as this had shone on the rich curls beneath Ola's fur cap, and on the lighter cinnamon waves beneath Tatia's, the two shades of honey mingling as they bent their heads together and talked eagerly of futures they would never have. In just a few days, we would have been in Elysium, preparing for my coming out at the Equinox Gala. Already, though it was still her secret even from Tatia, Ola was carrying in her womb the heir to the House of Arkhangel'sk who would never be born.

I skidded on the ice and slid into the main doors of the stable, still hearing Maia's laughter in my head. I'd almost forgotten why I'd come. It was time for a reckoning with their murderer. As Aeval herself had said, even in Heaven there were claims in need of judging.

I opened the doors and felt for my *navaja* in the pocket of my skirt. Like a talisman against Kae's influence, the carved handle in my gloved palm, inscribed with the charms of a Romani witch, gave me courage.

The stall where I'd left Kae was around the corner of the central row. I stopped to pet the noses of a few horses as I walked the length of it, postponing the moment I would have to face him. At last I smoothed my coat over my gown, taking as deep a breath as the garment permitted, and rounded the corner.

The sight that met me was wholly unexpected, though in retrospect, it ought not to have been. Kae had hanged himself.

With one of the blankets I'd brought for him, he'd devised a noose and tied it around the top post of the stall door, suspending himself from the inside. He was still thrashing, and without pausing to think, I clambered up onto the closed bottom door and opened the *navaja*. I struggled with the knot, too tight to work the knife into with my hand still sore from the sprain I'd received at Gehenna. Instead, I cut loose the blanket where it stretched above him.

My dress caught and tore on a protruding nail as we both fell to the ground inside the stall. The knot was still compressing his throat. I tore at it frantically and loosened it at last, and he breathed in with a high-pitched stridor, turning away from me with a violent cough. He lay still for a moment and then struck out at me in a blind rage and knocked me against the stall door.

"Leave me alone!" His harsh gasp was barely audible as he crawled away from me. "Why can't you let me be?"

"I will not allow you to kill yourself."

"Why?" he croaked. "I was giving us what we both want most!" He curled onto his side, coughing, with a hand to his throat.

"You're a coward." I stood angrily and brushed myself off. "And you will face what you've done." From my coat pocket, I took the irons Sarael had provided and locked the bands onto his wrists behind his back with a small padlock. "On your knees."

Kae struggled to sit up before me. "Then why shouldn't I die a coward's death?" he whispered hoarsely. "What do you want from me, Nenny?"

My face hot with shock, I struck his bare cheek. "Do you think you can call me that? After all you've done?"

"No," he wheezed. "You're right, Your Supernal Highness. I am not family."

"You were my family." The words came through tears. "I loved you as much as any of my sisters or my brother. But you took them from me."

I wiped my eyes with the heel of my hand and composed myself, drawing on the strength of my resolution before I went on. "I didn't want to be reminded of any of it when you presented yourself here, but I cannot pretend it didn't happen, no matter what force drove you to it. I've given it a great deal of thought, and I've concluded that you're right: you must be held accountable for your treasonous crimes against Heaven—if not to bring satisfaction to me, which you can never do, to at least bring satisfaction to the people."

Kae looked relieved at last, but I was about to snatch that relief from his grasp.

"Right now, however, I need you alive."

He looked up at me in desperation. "Why?"

"Because you were the queen's field marshal. And before that, her consort. Aeval must have entrusted you with knowledge no one else has—the inner workings of her court, as well as her mind. And you know everything about her army. It was yours."

He started to shake his head, but I wasn't going to listen to excuses.

"This is war," I said darkly. "And you are going to win it for me. You are *my* field marshal now."

I regarded him more calmly once I'd said my piece. His scarred face was dark with bruises and crusted with blood, and his eye was so swollen I was amazed he could even see me. Vasily had indeed beaten him. I warred within myself between a dark satisfaction and detached pity. Pity won out. He was a ruined man.

"We should clean up those cuts before they get infected." I went out to the frozen lawn to get a bucket of snow, and when I returned, I tore off a piece of my ripped petticoat and soaked it in the bucket. Kae submitted mutely as I pressed the icy cloth to his face. "Was it Aeval who burned you?"

He merely shrugged. I didn't know what bruising there might be beneath the mask, nor did I know how badly he might be disfigured, but he probably hadn't removed it for some time.

"I'm going to take off your mask. I want to make sure everything's clean."

"Do what you like," he rasped. "If you think you can stand to see it."

The mask was fastened by a thin leather strap around his head, and a piece of leather hooked behind his left ear to hold the lower half in place. I unbuckled the strap, which seemed nearly rusted in place, and then pulled it carefully forward over his ear, not wanting to injure him if any infection were underneath. I gasped as I pulled it away.

"I warned you."

"Kae." I shook my head. "Why are you wearing this?" Except for some bruising around his mouth that was clearly from Vasily's abuse of him, his face was untouched beneath the mask. The eye that had been covered, which I'd feared must have been burned away, was pristine and whole. The only part of his face that was damaged was the small part he'd shown.

"Because it's hideous."

"Kae…there isn't a mark on it." I touched the rough beard that could only be a few weeks' growth. He had to have seen each time he shaved that there was nothing wrong with him.

"What are you talking about?" He wheezed as he tried to raise his voice beyond a whisper. "It was burned beyond recognition. I'm in constant pain from the scars."

"There aren't any scars." I found a polished metal feed pan and held it in front of him. "See for yourself."

Kae grimaced and turned his head. "That isn't funny. I almost believed you." He couldn't see what was right before him.

"Cover your right eye and look again with your left."

"There's no need to taunt me, Nazkia. I have no left eye." He blinked the perfectly intact grey orb at me. "Just put the mask back on." He coughed and swallowed painfully. "It hurts." He was as lost in his dark imaginary world as he'd ever been, but now there was no Aeval directing his delusion.

I replaced the mask and fastened the strap behind his head. "Get some rest while you can. We have much to do."

I walked back to the manor through rows of ice-glazed evergreens that caught the winter light like diamonds dancing in the wind. There was indeed much to do. Kae would have to take an army of peaceful, refined Virtues and turn them into a brutally efficient machine capable of taking down the Armies of Heaven, and he would have to do it without the help of the thousands of exiled demons I'd hoped to have on our side. At least I had Margarita, who promised to train me in the Russian *Systema* and to teach me how to use a sword.

I also had a strain of Seraph's blood within my veins. For many nights since Kae's deliverance, I'd pondered what Vasily had said to the queen, that he'd tainted Kae's blood and mine by touching it with his fire. But he was wrong. Something was different. Vasily had been able to heal me in the world of Man, and I had later healed him, but our shared radiance had never affected anyone else. My own element had never shown at all in Heaven—nor had any waterspirit's—before the day I'd knelt in the snow and held my hand to my cousin's wound. It hadn't healed him alone, but the blue glow had manifested, and it had nothing to do with Vasily.

There was one thing different about me since we'd arrived in Gehenna. I had taken a drop of my daughter's blood to restore my true appearance—and my daughter's blood was dominated by an element no one had ever seen in Heaven before. It was only a drop, but it was there. With Lively's help, I hoped to find a way to tap into its potential.

The syla had told me in the Midnight Court that I would spill the blood of a fallen angel within a circle of ice and fire. The circle could only have been the frozen Empyrean itself, surrounded by the Pyriphlegethon, and the fallen angel, I realized now, was Kae. No angel had ever fallen so low. It was the direct result of his spilled blood that had given me the ability to conjure the quintessence with my cousin; he wasn't tainted at all. My own tainted blood reacting with the pure elemental water in his was what had done it. And with the quintessence, we had sapped the Seraphim of their strength. With that same power, I might stand against the flower of the fern.

I pulled up the collar of my wool coat against the chill and sat for a moment on the ice-glazed surface of a stone bench to think. The empty beauty of Aravoth as it stretched into the Empyrean reminded me of Arkhangel'sk. It was unlikely I would ever see our earthly home again. If I succeeded in my bid for the throne of Heaven, I wouldn't have the luxury of traipsing off to Raqia to fall as I pleased.

Something Belphagor had said struck me then, something he'd told me the first time I'd stretched my wings in the world of Man: *Terrestrial magic*, he'd said. *It's why we fall.* I hadn't understood him then, but I understood it now. If I succeeded, I would never again know the power of elemental radiance as it existed in the terrestrial world, including the intense dance of aether on my skin when Vasily touched me. What existed of radiance in Heaven was a poor copy of its earthly counterpart. I would never again be touched by the Unseen World of the syla—I could only hope they were safe now from the Seraphim.

I wouldn't see the little dacha with its white wooden gate or sit in my garden of roses and wildflowers. I felt like weeping as I realized I would never see the intoxicating light of the *Belye Nochi*, or watch the mysterious glow of the aurora borealis.

Heaven held its own beauties, as this stark afternoon with its unearthly varnish of ice attested, but its beauty was so often wrought of a kind of desolate perfection. I'd fallen in love with the unpredictable, imperfect beauty of the world of Man without even knowing it. Perhaps, as Belphagor had also said once, we only saw beauty when juxtaposed with decay. Perhaps it was the entropy of earthly matter, the fleeting quality of terrestrial time, which lent that world its poignancy. It all seemed as if it might be gone in an instant.

But the time I'd spent there had changed me forever, and I believed for the better. It had taught me what no celestial education could have given me: that Host and Fallen were one and the same. Without falling, I would never have known the love of Vasily or the beauty we could create together, which Ola so perfectly encapsulated. I had thought once it would have been better never to have known Ola than to have known the pain of losing her, but I wouldn't trade a moment of my time with her to assuage that now.

And I would have her back. With the peasant magic of two worlds, I would find a way to extinguish the fire of the flower of the fern. Helga would be very sorry she'd taken my child.

I was *Padshaya Koroleva*. And the Fallen Queen was about to rise.

Epilogue

The boy had long since learned to make his way in the dark. He'd lived most of his three brief years in darkness. But lately, strange pictures had played in his head of places he'd never been and things he hadn't done, though it seemed as if he saw his own hands doing them. But they were the hands of a much older boy. They couldn't be his own. The more the pictures crowded into his head, the more agitated he became.

Though he didn't have the words to express what frightened him, his mother, when she visited him, assured him he had nothing to fear. In the pictures in his head, she was a younger, kinder mother who had nursed him through sickness and attended to his every need with toys and sweets, and fancy, warm clothes. He'd tasted a chocolate drink once in his head that his mother had brought him, frothy with foam, and stirred with a sharply sweet candy stick. He knew his mother had given him no such treat, but there it was in his head, an undeniable, happy memory.

He dreamed also of horses, though he'd only ever seen them at the front of the wooden cart that brought him to his home where the snow was. But how he longed to have a horse of his own. He would race it across the stone bridge over the red river and down through the mountains to the green valleys below. Except he'd never seen the mountains and the green valleys. But he remembered them just the same.

Now they'd left the snow and the red river once more and gone to the sea, but the sea also was something he hadn't seen. Arriving in the dark of night, he'd only smelled the sharp, savory air of it and heard the gentle rush of the warm waves upon the sand and their spray against the rocks—and yet he remembered its salty feel against his skin.

He waited in the dark room for suppertime, his stomach growling, dreaming of the trays of cakes and pies and puddings he'd never eaten but couldn't get out of his head. The light from above announced his mother's entrance, and he squinted as she descended the stairs with the bright glow behind her. She came with the two hard pieces of bread and two bowls of gruel she'd been bringing lately, but he knew better than to eat them both. Mother no longer stayed with him at suppertime, but she patted him kindly on the head, smoothing her locket against her breast, and left him to his job, which he was not to begin until she'd closed the heavy door above.

The boy put his finger in the second bowl of gruel, stealing an extra dollop of it, before setting the piece of bread in it and putting it in the wooden bucket. He dragged aside the thick plank on the ground and lowered the bucket on its rope through the hole to the bottom far below. Waiting until he felt the weight of the full bowl being replaced by the empty one from yesterday, he drew it back up. He put the plank back in place and sat down to eat his supper, glad she'd stopped crying. She had done it for days and days.

Azel thought she must be a very naughty child to behave so badly. He never cried at all.

Acknowledgments

Many thanks are in order—to my editor, Stacy Cantor Abrams, for indulging my naughty demons even when they raise her eyebrows a bit; to my agent, Sara Megibow, for her endless enthusiasm and her appreciation of tattooed, pierced bad boys; to my publicist, Dani Barclay, for juggling a plethora of blog appearances and for making sure I didn't run away to hide in the bathroom at my first signing; and to everyone in the Entangled Publishing family for just being awesome.

I'd also like to add a special thank-you to LK Gardner-Griffie for her tireless support and for always being there to listen to my rants on my bad days and celebrate my successes on my good ones; to my sisters, A and J, for believing in my writing all those years ago; and to Hillary Seidl for making a debut author feel like a superstar.